RAGAMUFFIN

TOR BOOKS BY TOBIAS S. BUCKELL

Crystal Rain
Ragamuffin

RAGAMUFFIN

TOBIAS S. BUCKELL

A Tom Doherty Associates Book New York

RAGAMUFFIN

Copyright © 2007 by Tobias S. Buckell

This book is printed on acid-free paper.

A Tor Book
Published by Tom Doherty Associates, LLC
175 Fifth Avenue
New York, NY 10010

www.tor.com

Tor® is a registered trademark of Tom Doherty Associates, LLC.

Library of Congress Cataloging-in-Publication Data

Buckell, Tobias S.
  Ragamuffin / Tobias S. Buckell.—1st ed.
    p. cm.
  "A Tom Doherty Associates Book."
  ISBN-13: 978-0-7653-1507-6
  ISBN-10: 0-7653-1507-6
  1. Life on other planets—Fiction. 2. Human-alien encounters—Fiction. I. Title.
  PS3602.U2635R34 2007
  813'.54—dc22

                            2007007314

First Edition: June 2007

Printed in the United States of America

0 9 8 7 6 5 4 3 2 1

For Emily

THE WORLDS OF THE BENEVOLENT SATRAPY

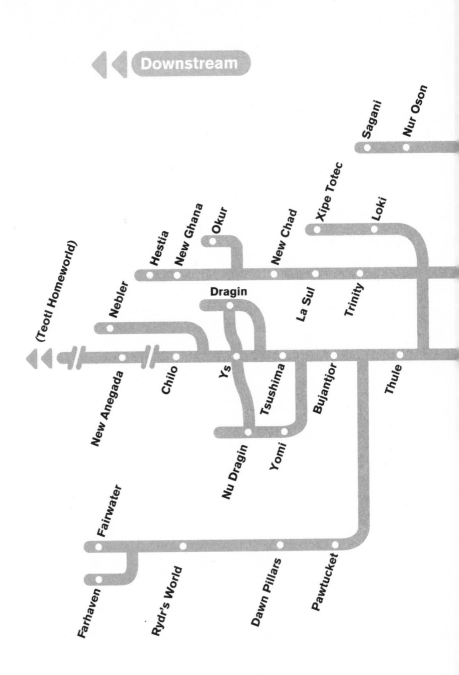

Downstream

Sagani

Nur Oson

Xipe Totec

Loki

Okur

Hestia

New Ghana

New Chad

(Teotl Homeworld)

Nebler

Dragin

La Sul

Trinity

New Anegada

Chilo

Ys

Tsushima

Bujantjor

Thule

Nu Dragin

Yomi

Fairwater

Dawn Pillars

Pawtucket

Farhaven

Rydr's World

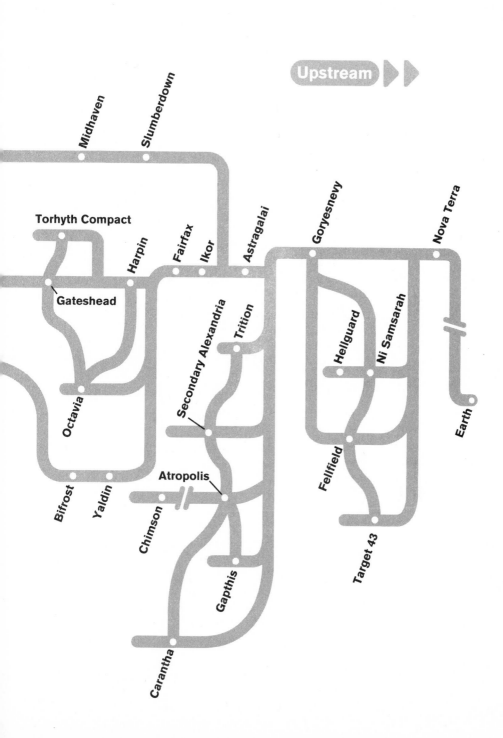

Upstream ▶▶

Midhaven
Slumberdown
Torhyth Compact
Harpin
Fairfax
Ikor
Astragalai
Goryesnevy
Nova Terra
Gateshead
Secondary Alexandria
Trition
Hellguard
Ni Samsarah
Octavia
Earth
Bifrost
Yaldin
Atropolis
Chimson
Fellfield
Carantha
Gapthis
Target 43

PART ONE

The Benevolent Satrapy

CHAPTER ONE

It had been three hundred and fifty-seven years, three months, and four days since the emancipation of humanity. And for most, it did them little good.

Nashara walked down the dusty road of Pitt's Cross reservation, her scaly leather boots biting into her ankle. Log houses and refugee tents dripped acid water from a recent rain, and the ground steamed. It was a desperate assemblage of buildings that dared call itself a city, and all that did was remind Nashara of what a city should really look like.

People could be more than this. She flagged down a van bouncing through the wet street.

The mud-coated van, yellow paint flaking off its sides, stopped by the bench outside a community center where a long line of ragged and desperate faces lined up for the soup kitchen. Nashara could smell whiffs of fresh bread and body odor.

A few eyes darted her way, seeing the functional but new clothing and no doubt wondering what she was doing here. And whether she was carrying money. It was just as likely surprise at her skin, as dark as the shadows these people seemed to try to sink into. Her hair, tight and curly, but shorn military short. Old habit. Pitt's Cross consisted mainly of the light-skinned. Or maybe, just maybe, someone was already tracking her, ready to shoot her and drag her body to the edge of the reservation for a bounty.

She turned her back to it all and got in the van. What was done was done, and now it was time to keep moving.

"Could rain again," the old man driving the van commented as Nashara threw a stamped metal coin into the small bucket by his seat. "I get more passengers if I wait around for the rain, charge more when they're desperate not to get stung by it."

Nashara sat down on the cushioned bench behind him and threw several more coins in. "Let's go."

"Where to?"

"Security gate."

The old man cleared his throat, leaned closer to the window, and looked up at the sky. Nashara tapped his back. He turned around annoyed, then flinched when she stared directly into his slightly clouded eyes. "I shit you not," Nashara said, "I'll break your neck if you don't start driving."

He swallowed. "Right." The van quietly lurched forward down the street, then turned an easy left. They edged past a large cart pulled by fifteen men, all yoked to it by wooden harnesses.

How far humanity could still fall. Nashara folded her arms.

Two years mucking about in Pitt's Cross, building contacts, until she'd found a job that would make her enough to leave. She watched a landscape of ruined housing and people slide by the dingy windows of the van. The buildings petered out until nothing but bare, scorched ground surrounded her.

The reservation's wall crept into view over the horizon. The black and smooth, two-hundred-foot edifice spread for as far as she could see in either direction. Spotlights stabbed at the ground and sky. It was scalable, she'd done that to get over last night, and back over in the morning.

Though not without trouble. Her left shoulder had a cauterized hole through it as a result of getting back over.

"You have a pass?" the old man asked, incredulous. "Or will I be waiting at the wall for you?"

"Are we not emancipated? Can't we travel anywhere we want?"

"Don't spout that crap at me." They both knew they needed a "human safety pass" to be allowed out there, and passes were rare around the reservation. "Even if you get through, how far can you get on two feet when all you have is reservation coin?"

"You'd be surprised." Nashara looked out the window. One last look at the barren landscape.

"Waste of my time, all the way out here for one passenger." They slowed and then jerked to a stop. The driver leaned over and pointed a small gun at her. "Hand over your coin and get out."

Nashara looked down at it. And snapped it out of his hands before his next blink. She casually snapped his trigger finger, and to his credit he bit his lip and bore the pain as he looked around for the gun. Reservation-born and accustomed to the pain of it all.

"You should have shot before speaking," she said. He might have had a chance. He stared at her, realizing his underestimation would probably cost him his life.

"Come on, get out," Nashara said as she opened the door. She didn't blame him for trying. What did he have to lose? A lifetime behind the wall? A faint mist sprinkled down. It blew inside the cab and tasted acidic. It burned the tip of her tongue as she tasted the air. It would stain and then dissolve her outfit if she walked out there, so she'd take the vehicle. "I have a pass, and therefore a schedule to keep."

"How the hell did you get that?" the old man asked as he stepped out into the rain and turned to face in.

"Same way I got this," Nashara muttered. Someone had underestimated her.

She shut the door to the van and drove on without looking back. Several minutes later she threw the gun out of the window into the mud.

No sense in approaching a massive security perimeter like the wall around Pitt's Cross with a gun.

The gate groaned slowly open, responding to the presence of the pass hung around her neck.

Several snub-nosed pipes tracked her progress through the tunnel. If she so much as twitched wrong, they'd smear her against the wall.

The floor lit up just forward of each step, leading her onward to a set of doors that rolled aside for her. Several guards in khaki protective armor and reflective-visored helmets surrounded her.

"Pass?"

Nashara pulled the necklace off and handed it over. The nearest guard scanned her with a wand. Even if she were naked, it wouldn't detect anything under her skin. Her skin bounced back the wrong signals to his crude scanner. And neither guard would find the crude slivers of gold and silver stolen from the Gahe breeder's house. She'd cut slits in the skin of her thighs. The skin had congealed over the small bounty.

The other guard verified the data inside the small pendant at the end of the necklace. He looked back at her. "Nashara Aji. You have twenty hours outside the reservation. After that the pass will broadcast your violation and you will forfeit any rights to travel. You will be jailed and fined. You may give up your right to emancipation."

He handed the necklace back to her and leaned in close. "Visiting a breeding program, eh?"

That was what the pass indicated her business outside the wall was. Nashara ignored the guard.

An alien stood safe inside a bombproof glass enclosure behind the guards. A Gahe, one of the rulers of everything currently around Nashara. It stood five feet high on four legs. Its bullet-shaped head, so hard to reach around to snap, Nashara knew, swiveled like an owl's to track her. The rounded, silver eyes didn't blink.

The alien's massive mouth yawned open. From inside, gray, tentacle-like tongues wormed out and flicked at a clear panel in front of it.

"Human, stop," the translated voice in the air around her snapped.

Nashara froze.

"Pause for decontamination that your stink may not infect our honorable citizens."

Nashara knew the routine. She stripped with her back to the human guards behind her. A biting spray and explosion of UV light later she walked out of the checkpoint.

She was out. Out of the reservation and its starving, population-exploding sovereignty and freedom. And just ahead of the mess that would soon be after her.

The guards were the last humans she saw for the next hour as she walked down the paved road. No vehicles passed her. What reason did the aliens have to go to the reservation? They avoided it if at all possible.

The road led into a larger highway three hours later. Nashara's clothes dripped sweat from the heat. She had no water; no one was allowed to bring anything out of the reservation but the clothes on his or her back.

Still, she pressed on as the occasional vehicle trundled past. Each one looked completely different, from number of wheels to color to design. The Gahe prized individuality to a bizarre level.

Seven hours later she stopped in a small town and looked around. The Gahe built their houses like their cars, every one different to their own taste. It looked like something out of a nightmare, random curves and angles jutting out every which way, dripping walls.

Three Gahe loped toward her, tentacle tongues lolling. One of them held a gun aimed at her. Nashara held her necklace up, showed it to them, and inserted the pendant in her ear.

"I am legal," she said.

The large Gahe dropped the gun into the pocket of a biblike shirt over its chest. It thumped the ground with a hind leg and spat at the ground.

"What are you doing here?" The pendant translated the gestures into tinny words in her ear.

"I am waiting for the bus." Nashara remained still. They didn't seem like any kind of Gahe that were here to arrest or detain her.

The Gahe sat down in front of her. Nashara waited for a translation of that, but none came. She relaxed and pretended not to see them. She stared off into the distance and waited.

She could disappear here and no one would care, or notice. The Gahe around her knew it too. But they weren't aware of what she'd done last night. They were just trying to intimidate the free human. Nothing to worry about, and she'd kill them too if they tried anything funny.

Another human was on the pumpkin-shaped bus that showed up, a dark-haired, old lady in a glittering dress and complex, braided hairdo fixed around the top of her head like a crown. The Gahe clustered along the left side of the bus. They lounged in their round chairs and stared out the windows, ignoring her. Nashara thought she smelled mushrooms as she walked down the aisle and sat down.

The lady growled at her and drummed a syncopated rhythm on the ground. She smiled at Nashara.

"Nice clothes," the pendant in her ear translated the thumping and growling. The lady cleared her throat. "I am Growf." She slapped her hand on her wrist and growled. "You live behind the wall?"

"Recently, for a while, yes," Nashara said.

"You hate me."

"No." Nashara shook her head. "I'm sorry for you."

"I may be pet," the lady growled in Gahe. "But I eat. My great-grandfather pet. Good pet. Eat well. Not starve. Do tricks."

A Gahe stood up and barked at them both, too quickly for the pendant to translate. It walked over and its tongues reached out and grabbed the lady's crown. They were strong, strong enough to yank Growf up to her feet.

Growf whined and bowed, kissed the floor, and shuffled over to the back of the bus.

Nashara turned away from the scene and looked out of the window at yellow grass and squiggly trees.

It all depressed her. The whole damn planet depressed her. The Gahe ruled Astragalai firmly, and there were too few humans here to do much about it.

A few hundred thousand lived behind the wall in Pitt's Cross, most of the rest as professional bonded pets to Gahe.

She'd killed a high-ranking Gahe breeder late last night for some shadowy, idiot organization formed by offworld humans that wanted to free the human pets. The League of Human Affairs. They'd repaid her with a ticket that would take her off Astragalai and aboard a ship heading toward the planet New Anegada.

Five years, planet by planet, trying to get there, the last two a particular hell stuck here in Pitt's Cross.

Nashara couldn't wait to get the fuck off the planet. It had been a mistake to head into a nonhuman place. A two-year mistake.

She checked the pendant cover, squinting. Just a few hours left. Any Gahe would have the right to take her as property or kill her when that ran out. Gahe authorities would be moving to deport her right back into Pitt's Cross. Gahe breeders paid prime for wild pets.

The pickup zone was a clearing, bordered by well-maintained gardens, and a ticket booth. A round pod with windows sat in the middle of the grass. Nashara walked over the cut yellow grass, squishing her way to the ticket booth.

"You travel alone?" The Gahe behind the glass shook its squat head. Round eyes looked her up and down.

"My ticket is confirmed. I am here. I am a freedman." No damn pet. "Here is my pass." She waved the necklace at the window. She had no time for delays. The body of the Gahe breeder she'd killed would have been found by now. It wouldn't take long for its friends to figure out it wasn't one of its pets or human breeding pairs that had killed it. Enough checking and Nashara's DNA would be found somewhere on the pen she'd stabbed it in the large eyes with.

"I guess this is okay," the Gahe informed her. "Go to the pickup pod."

The pod stood twice her height with a massive reinforced hook at its tip. Fifteen Gahe seats ringed the inside. Reclining Gahe sat strapped in half of them.

Alarms sounded throughout the clearing as Nashara stepped in the pod. A Gahe attendant outside licked the pod with a tongue and the pod sealed shut.

Gahe stared at her, panting. One of them growled.

Nashara strapped herself in as best she could. It was clear they never expected human use of these seats.

Another timbre of alarm started. Nashara turned around and looked down the length of the clearing just in time to see a shadow and then the long line of the orbital skyhook coming straight toward them. The strong rope of carbon fiber led all the way back to orbit. It spun slowly, each end touching down to snag cargo several times per day.

The massive, rusted, industrial-looking hook on the end whipped toward them and struck the top of the pod.

Nashara's neck snapped back. She swore. Gahe pounded the floor with their front feet. "Laughter," the pendant noted as she pushed it back in her ear. The joke was on them. Right now word would be spreading that a human had killed a Gahe. If the League person who'd paid her to do it had told the truth, then the last time that had happened had been a hundred years ago. And that same small insurrection that had left a Gahe dead by human hands in Pitt's Cross had led the Gahe to isolate the free humans on the planet there.

The pod accelerated, hooked onto the almost indestructible cable. It swung up into the sky past the clouds in a long arc toward space.

CHAPTER TWO

The space habitat Villach orbited Astragalai. It hung in position to receive pod traffic and redirect it onward if necessary.

The two cupolas of Villach looked like perfect spheres split in half. They were connected by threadlike wires of the same material as the rotating tether that snagged Nashara's pod and whipped it into orbit. A material that the Gahe sold to humans but humanity was prohibited from making.

Villach's two separate half spheres spun around each other, connective wires singing a constant low hum in the background as Nashara took the elevator from the center of the configuration down through the clouds hovering at the open top of the space habitat.

Pets wandered around on leashes, their Gahe drumming or slapping their tongues at them. Beautiful hairpieces and costumes glittered everywhere Nashara looked.

Nashara pulled the pendant out of her ear, not interested in hearing alien tongues anymore. The pass beeped, indicating her time was up. But Villach wasn't a reservation. It wouldn't have dedicated hunt packs waiting to swoop in on her. By the time something came to investigate the violation, Nashara would be long gone. Besides, a human shouldn't have been able to afford the price of getting off planet. That would leave them confused for a while.

She broke the necklace off, crushed it to dust between her hands, and let it drift to the floor.

The human section of Villach, a long, pie-shaped area of the five-mile-wide cupola, reminded her of the reservation. But not as desperate. Tight streets, waterproof paper houses and greenhouses. She found a market packed with several hundred people. It was the first time in two years she'd seen that many people gathered together that weren't lined up for the food kitchens. As on the reservation, they spoke Anglic here, not human imitations of Gahe's thumps, growls, and whistles.

She pulled out the last of her coins and stopped at the nearest toy shop. Several kids behind the table of used equipment smiled at her. The tallest bowed and stepped forward with a flourish of his waxy red robe.

"Help you?"

"I need a lamina viewer," she said. "Got anything?"

They handed her an oversize, bright green wrist screen. Designed for clumsy kid fingers, it strapped on easily enough, and she tapped it on. A simple point-and-shoot viewer. She pointed a finger at the boy and information popped up for her.

His name was Peter the One Hundredth, fifteen years old, owner of the stall. Previous customers rated him "competent" on average, with some complaints about equipment breaking down.

"You like it?"

Some speculated that the goods were stolen.

Of course they were.

Nashara stopped pointing and tapped some more, accessing Villach's various streams of public information, and checked the habitat's outbound transportation schedule. She found what she was looking for. The *Stenapolaris*, due to leave in two hours.

Cutting it close. But she had a berth reserved, and *Stenapolaris* would be headed close to New Anegada. Once she was aboard it, the Gahe would be hard-pressed to ever find her.

"Lady?"

Nashara looked up. "Yes, I'll take it." She threw him the reservation coins from her pocket.

"We don't take this," Peter the One Hundredth protested. "It's devalued crap."

Nashara sighed. She propped her boot up on his table and dug her thumb into her thigh until she broke skin and peeled it back with a grunt. She slid a piece of silver out and wiped the blood off it. "Assay this."

She needed the lamina viewer. All around her in the habitat's information-rich data streams lay important information. Such as directions to get to the docks, or what elevators to take. Whom you were talking to. Layers of it tagged everything, a myriad of ways to view the entire world lay around them.

Kids ran around the stall seeing virtual monsters they chased and shot with their friends. Merchants quietly passed information among themselves. The station's public lamina carpeted the sky with up-to-date general information, or provided tags about everything one saw.

To be unable to view lamina meant being illiterate among those who read to survive.

Nashara had to use lamina indirectly or the technology built into her head would get out of control. She bit her lip and focused on the transaction in front of her.

Peter passed the piece of metal to the kid behind him, who walked back into the tent for a moment. Peter's head snapped up as he heard something inside his own head. "Silver?"

"Good enough?"

All three nodded. Nashara turned and walked into a bulky man dressed in trousers and a yellow utility jacket.

"Nashara Cascabel?" She liked her first name, but always kept the second one changing.

She looked him over. "Who's asking?"

"Steven." He looked around, dropped his voice. "We've been trying to contact you."

Nashara held up her wrist and looked at the tag that popped up when she pointed at him. It identified him as Gruther. "I just got access."

"Shitsticks," the man swore. "That explains that."

People up here in orbit had the technology implanted behind their eyeballs from late childhood on. Only four-year-olds or the impaired couldn't wrap their minds around constantly seeing things that weren't really there.

"I have my reasons for not plugging directly in," Nashara said softly. "Your organization and me, we're done. I'm getting ready to leave. What the hell are you doing bothering me?" She didn't like this. She glanced around, looking for eyes staring back. This screamed wrong to her.

"The package you delivered has been discovered," Steven said, meaning that the Gahe had found the breeder she'd killed. "The recipients are not happy, and they're looking for the postmaster. They'd like to make an example of you." Too many people around, Nashara thought, to really deal with Steven.

"They thinking to look up here yet to express their gratitude?" Nashara stepped back from him and jostled an old man in a ragged suit who swore at her.

"I'm told they'll finish their sweep of house's garden"—that would be Pitt's Cross—"within the hour."

"Steven, or whatever the hell your name is, why is this your problem again? You paid me, I did it. I'm leaving. You're making yourself traceable. You're holding me up."

Steven swallowed. Nervous, Nashara thought, but about what? "We're impressed with what you did. They want to help you more. Do you want to see full freedom, do you think humans should be able to exercise all the same rights as the Gahe? Or any other damn alien?"

"All bullshit aside"—Nashara folded her arms—"what are you trying to offer here? I have a berth to go to. I need to leave."

Steven took a deep breath. "You don't actually have a berth."

Nashara stared at him. His neck would break a lot easier that some Gahe's. "What do you mean by that?"

"Do you really think that . . . that package delivery was worth the price of a ticket to another world?"

Nashara shook her head. This wasn't about the assassination. They'd underestimated her again. "You didn't think I would make it back out of there." It wasn't a question. Just a statement.

"No one down there has the ability to deliver packages. But we're working on it, and we'd hoped that what you did would encourage others to try. And if that happened, we would assist them. We've been secretly building a network of couriers, and not just here, Nashara," Steven brimmed with excitement, "all throughout the worlds. We've been preparing for *decades*. We have ships, secret couriers, and lots and lots of packages we want delivered soon."

They'd expected a martyr. The League needed someone to strike against the Gahe and die, and then they would help Pitt's Cross rise against the Gahe. But she had no desire to join. She had a mission of her own.

Nashara unfolded her arms and tapped his chest. "I'm going to kill you. It's going to be very slow, very painful, and you're not going to care about packages," or any other simple code words.

"We're willing to help," Steven belted out quickly. "Truly. We really need someone with your talent."

"That was a onetime thing, Steven. I was a desperate girl in a bad situation." The toy she'd purchased from the stall couldn't even be purchased with Pitt's Cross coin, let alone a trip into orbit. She'd had to do something.

There. She spotted a simple table knife on a stall table.

She was so close to getting away from it all. So close.

"For a onetime thing, you were very good at it." Steven sensed her weariness. "We'd like to hire you."

The eagle-eyed vendor didn't spot the snatch, and now Nashara had a weapon. "I have a pressing mission of my own that doesn't fit in with being a League 'package deliverer.' I'm sorry. I need to get to it, Steven, and you're telling me I'm not going. That's a problem. And of all people you should understand that when I say I am not for sale, I really mean it."

She whipped around him. He jumped, but before he could do anything more, she'd draped one hand around his shoulder and pressed the knife against the small of his back with the other. Bystanders didn't notice the move, and by keeping herself pressed close to Steven, no one would notice the knife. They just looked overly chummy.

The kid behind the stall twitched. He reached under the table, and Nashara raised an eyebrow at him. With a smile the kid stepped back and watched.

"What are you doing?" Steven asked.

He tried to pull away, but she yanked him right back and whispered into his ear, "Steven, this is just a table knife, but I'm strong enough that I will begin by puncturing a lung of yours with it. Do you know how much that hurts? After letting you writhe about for a while, I'll slam this knife into your heart. Of course, you can stop this by giving me what I was promised for doing a very dangerous and dirty job."

"We have someone sympathetic to the League," he said quickly. "The owner of the *Daystar*. It's docked here at Villach. We'll spirit you aboard."

Nashara watched as three men in long, green robes picked some items over at a nearby stall while watching the two of them.

"Headed for?" A pair of grubby women with baskets waited to look at the toys on the table. She was in their way. They looked somewhat impatient.

"A Freeman colony in orbit around the world Yomi," he hissed out of the side of his mouth.

One of the ladies snapped her fingers. "You gonna stand there all day, you two?"

Yomi lay over fifty wormhole transits downstream and in the right fork, the Thule branch. But it was still fifteen upstream from the dead end of New Anegada. Nashara shook her head. "That's not as close to the planet I was promised."

One of the green-robed men glanced over at the increasingly irate ladies, then at Steven and Nashara.

"No, but it's not here, where you're certain to be taken down by a Gahe hunting pack. We need to leave now. We'll help you find your way to where you need to be once you're at the Freeman colony. There's something we need to tell you about New Anegada anyway."

He was being too nice. She was half tempted to snap his arm. And Steven specifically avoided looking in the direction of the men in green.

"Any Ragamuffin ships at dock?" she asked.

"They don't make it this far upstream. You might find one at Yomi though."

Nashara leaned closer. "Tell those three men to back way off."

"What three men?" Steven looked around.

She dug the point of her improvised knife into his skin, enough to make her point. "Steven, back them off before things go bad."

He looked over at them. They moved back.

Nashara dug out several bloody pieces of silver and tossed them at Peter. They bounced in a trough of chips and wires. A teenage girl with blond hair and sunburn joined Peter, and the two women in front of Nashara stared at the silver.

"I have a favor to ask you all," Nashara said to them.

"What are you doing?" Steven twisted, shoving his shoulders against her.

"I'm going to pay a handful of these nice people to walk to the *Daystar* with us with any friends they can round up, board with me, and then leave once I'm nicely ensconced aboard the ship."

He tensed. She'd figured that out as well. With a crowd around them the Villach security programs would keep a close eye on a mob. And for all the rhetoric the League of Human Affairs deployed, she'd bet her life it still preferred to skulk about in the shadows.

"Now let's go before Gahe start showing up," Nashara hissed. Time was running out and things were getting complicated.

Peter pocketed the silver and tapped the air, and as Nashara stepped forward, kids flowed in toward them, jostling closer as the word spread throughout the lamina that some crazy lady was paying Peter in silver to help walk her over to a ship.

The *Daystar*'s cramped quarters made her feel cornered. The grimy passengers bored her. Three indentured workers escaping to the free-zone still dressed in grimy coveralls and casting relieved and yet still suspicious looks around. A human pet with his hair styled in a tall ringed cone and shaved eyebrows, glitter on his cheeks and lips. He didn't have a name, but he showed her the bar code on his inner thigh. A handful of rich tourists in blue leather. All human. Aliens wouldn't deign to ride dirty human transports.

The tourists relaxed, eyes closed, immersed in environments that only they could see. The walls were gray and bare, there was nothing else to do but immerse deep into some personal entertainment lamina. The better part of a day accelerating out from the habitat Villach had already passed. Nashara camped out in the cockpit of the *Daystar*, a gimballed sphere deep inside the very center of the long, cylindrical ship.

The portly captain, Danielle, danced from one edge of the cockpit to the other. Her crisp, new emergency gear made Nashara wonder if she was safe aboard the leaky, old tramp ship.

Danielle admired Nashara, she said. Ever since the moment Nashara had marched aboard her ship surrounded by thirty scruffy stall kids and Steven at knifepoint, waiting with all of them in the cockpit until she could verify that every last League agent had walked off the *Daystar*. And now Nashara remained in the cockpit with her.

No doubt the moment Nashara left, the captain could track where Nashara walked, vent a corridor, and leave her exposed to the vacuum. She could survive some of that, but eventually, the captain would win. And if Nashara killed the captain, she could take control of the ship, yes, Nashara had those skills. But once she inserted herself into the ship's lamina, she would die.

So Nashara remained in the cockpit, watching the captain, the captain watching her.

The captain smiled, her belly wobbling in the lack of gravity as they fell away from Villach. "This story I will tell to all my passengers from now on."

"That exciting? I thought you were a League sympathizer."

Danielle spread her arms. "Whoever my masters will be, I want them all to know that I am loyal to them."

Nashara grinned. "Cynical."

"Honest." Danielle tapped the air to give commands. "You are a glorious human being, Nashara. You will die in the most amazing way, someday, and people like me will talk about it for years. Do you believe in the great-person theory?"

"The what?"

"There are some people who always sit in the middle of big things. They live large lives. Like you. It is not enough for you to settle into a life in Astragalai and give up, no, you have panache. And I get to sit here in my ship and sail from star to star and watch people like you pass through lives. You'll make my best dinner anecdote, I think."

"It's hardly great." Wires snaked all around the cockpit. That couldn't be safe, could it? "All I want to do is get to my destination in one piece. I'm tired. This is all temporary."

At the front of the cockpit Danielle waved her hands, and the cockpit walls faded into screens that showed perspectives of space. Lots of inky darkness. Nothing that really stirred Nashara's soul. She preferred worlds, not the empty vacuum.

"The League wanted me to stop and turn you over, you know. I told them you'd kill me. I like my life too much, and they know it. You're okay aboard my ship." Danielle chuckled, a bit too high-pitched, as if nervous. "Where are you going?"

"As close to New Anegada as I can get."

"New Anegada?" Danielle shook her head. "Honey, you aren't going all the way to New Anegada, you know. It's not only way downstream of here, but it doesn't exist anymore."

"Yes, I know." Nashara sat on the curved floor.

"The wormhole leading there got cut off. Hundreds of years ago."

Nashara turned on Danielle, the sinking, tired feeling in her stomach having nothing to do with the thump and shudder of the ship's engines. "I'm well aware of it. I just need to get close."

Danielle looked at her as if seeing her for the first time. "Why?"

"It's none of your damn business."

"You're out of your mind." Danielle shook her head. "Clean out. Near New Anegada is where the Ragamuffin ships prowl. They're liable to board and shoot up any ship you take out there. Only good thing I see the Hong-guo do is patrol against them."

Nashara rubbed the side of her temple. "The Ragamuffins, you sure they're pirates, or do you just hear that they're pirates?"

"Seen video of their attacks." Danielle folded her arms.

"Sure you have. Ever seen an attack in person, Danielle?"

"No," the *Daystar* captain conceded.

"Probably because they're silently docked next to you at habitats, keeping as low a profile as possible. Just a bunch of merchant ships left on the wrong side of the wormhole when Chimson, and then New Anegada, got cut off." The Black Starliner Corporation had settled both Chimson and New Anegada with islanders and other refugees from Earth, and the Ragamuffins had formed out of necessity. When alien aggression started up, they needed a more militant arm for protection. Humans cheered the Ragamuffins on, until they lost. Then suddenly they were "pirates."

"You know a lot about them?"

Nashara shifted. "Known a few. They used to route between Chimson, Earth, and New Anegada until the Satrapy declared that human ships weren't allowed to use the wormhole routes or fuel up without licenses. Licenses they refused to grant to New Anegada or Chimson."

"You sound annoyed."

The Gahe and Nesaru had found humanity through the wormholes and used them. The Satraps dragged the Gahe and Nesaru off their homeworlds into space hundreds of years ago. Humanity was only the latest addition to the benevolent Satrapy. "The aliens don't know how to make wormholes. But they get to say who uses the wormholes and who doesn't?"

"You think the Satrapy doesn't know how the wormholes work?" Danielle looked sharp and interested, with a half smile.

"If the Satrapy were that powerful, would they be that scared of human beings running around without supervision?" They could shut down the wormholes to human-occupied worlds that scared them, such as Earth, in agreement for Emancipation. They could do it to stop the nuclear suicide bombers, or to Chimson for trying to gain independence. And Nashara bet that they had also shut down New Anegada for some reason. But Nashara, and many back on Chimson, believed that all the Satrapy could do was shut the wormholes down.

Danielle shrugged. "Who knows? Look, Nashara, how long are you going to remain in my cockpit? We're approaching the first wormhole on our little journey downstream towards Yomi. We have a lot of wormholes and miles to cross before we get there. You going to camp out in here for three weeks?"

"If need be."

Danielle laughed. "Nashara, if I'm going to kill you, or dump you out the air lock, or whatever you think I'm going to do, there isn't much you can do about it unless you plan on having all your meals in here."

Nashara did not laugh. She had found a spare set of acceleration webbing and pulled the retractable ribbons from their recessed spots. She wove the fabric around herself. "That offer sounds good. You have a jump seat here. I'm happy to ride with you. Where's the catheter?"

"My best dinner story . . . ," Danielle muttered. She turned and got into the soft chair hanging dead center in the cockpit and strapped herself in. "The League will be waiting for you on Yomi. They'll kill you there."

"Of course."

Danielle raised a finger and closed her eyes. She settled into her chair, and

the thump of the engines changed. By now the *Daystar* had climbed high out
of Astragalai's gravity well, almost enough to break free of the planet. The
Gahe choose to keep their wormholes far out from the clustered near-planet
orbits.

On the screens Danielle provided, Nashara saw a cloud of communications buoys as large as their own ship. They pulsed a riot of laser light at the
blank piece of inky dark in front of them. Buoys on the other side would
snag the light, parse it, then pass it on. Forty-eight worlds ruled by the se-
cretive alien Satraps, connected through thousands of wormholes strung
throughout almost random parts of the galaxy, held together by threads of
light. It sounded tenuous, but the Satrapy ruled strongly enough through its
surrogates.

It took attention to thread this needle. Anything less than true center and
the ship risked tearing itself into debris against the sides of the wormhole.
Meanwhile, Nashara was sure Danielle had to listen to the chatter of traffic
control, contending with other ships in line to transit.

Nashara stared into the round plate of nothingness on the screens until it
swallowed them and the lines of flickering laser light all along their sides.
A tunnel of light illuminated by stellar dust. Her stomach flip-flopped, her
brain trying to process something that it couldn't understand.

Now the screens showed more buoys and the remains of a half-processed
chunk of rock. Girders and docking tubes thrust out from the side.

"Transit number one," Danielle said, and reopened her eyes. "Of many
more to go."

The *Daystar* coasted toward the debris. No planets existed out here. A
light-year away from Astragalai, the planet's sun just a pinprick from here.
The next wormhole lay on the other side of the rock, a few thousand miles
away. A smart captain such as Danielle wouldn't waste much fuel speeding
up to it but coast toward it with a few adjustments.

Nashara's wrist screen chirped. She looked down. A simple text message
from Steven: "You are now a wanted criminal in all forty-eight worlds of the
Satrapy for the detonation of a nuclear bomb in the Gahe section of Villach.
Happy travels."

Nashara deleted it.

"Congratulations," Danielle said, revealing that she'd gotten a copy of the
message. "My best story yet. And a wonderful move on their part, pointing
the finger your way."

"They're insane," Nashara said, and Danielle frowned. "A nuke?" They probably killed more humans at Villach than aliens.

"They said the Hongguo will be hunting you," Danielle said. "Your name and DNA profile will be on every ship of theirs. Now you've made enemies of both the League and the Hongguo. Dangerous."

Nashara sighed. "Every move I dig myself in deeper."

"You hungry?" Danielle asked. "I can have one of my guys bring something over before the next transit here. It's squeezy stuff, right, but I'm hungry, for one."

Nashara stared at her. "And then when I use the bathroom in a couple hours, you have the ship lock me in, suck the air out, turn me into a mummy?"

"You're paranoid." Danielle shook her head.

"Everyone has been out to get me of late," Nashara snorted. "I feel it's justified."

Danielle laughed. "If you have to use the shitter, I'll come with you, I swear."

Nashara wanted to like her. Wondered if she'd have to kill her eventually. It would be a waste to get cornered into a losing situation like that.

Besides, the *Daystar* would stand no chance of outrunning any Hongguo ship if they decided she was worth the trouble of looking for. And now that the League assholes had sicced them on her, she only had to worry about them. The League would stand clear and just watch.

Just as long as the League hadn't told the Hongguo to find her aboard the *Daystar*, she'd be okay. Hopefully they needed their sympathetic captain Danielle's goodwill more than they wanted Nashara dead.

Hopefully.

CHAPTER THREE

Six days and eleven wormhole transits later Nashara lowered her guard and took the luxury of a quick sponge bath as the *Daystar* passed between a trio of wormholes spaced a thousand miles apart. They trailed each other in geostationary orbit around a massive gas giant. Several massive storms near the equator stared down on the speck of a ship as it slowly drifted from one wormhole to the next over several hours.

They were downstream of Astragalai and getting close to Harpin now. Certainly moving in the right direction, Nashara thought, although Harpin was a habitable world with a Satrap living in a habitat in orbit over it. And maybe a Hongguo ship or two. Not somewhere to loiter.

Danielle hung just outside, keeping a hand on the top of the opaque curtain so that Nashara knew where she was.

"What would you do if I just kicked off for the cockpit right now?" she asked.

"I'd kill you." Nashara pulled her leathers back on. She'd added an assortment of blades fashioned from parts found loose in the cockpit. She'd had a lot of time floating around to make shivs.

The rest of the *Daystar* didn't really exist for her. Only the nearby bathroom and the cockpit's sphere. And Danielle. Two more weeks to Yomi. So far no Hongguo ships had caught up with them and demanded a boarding.

She played for time now. But then she'd been doing that for five years now. Keeping her head low, trying to meander her way toward New Anegada.

Danielle looked Nashara over. "So what's your whole story?"

"You really want that dinner-story prize, don't you?" Nashara stared back. "Or maybe you just want to sell the information to your League friends. Your new masters."

"Would the League of Human Affairs be any worse than having the Satraps, and the Hongguo doing their dirty work? Who cares who's in charge?"

Nashara shrugged. A point. But anyone crazy enough to set off a nuclear bomb in a habitat wasn't fit to be in charge of anything.

"Seriously, where the hell did you come from?"

Tired of evasions, Nashara looked at Danielle. "If I tell you, will you level with me on something?"

Danielle shrugged. "If I can."

"You got a copy of that message from Steven. You're a lot more than just a League sympathizer, aren't you?" She was probably Steven's superior.

"Somewhat, yes." Danielle smiled. "It's a very loose organization, and I have things that the League needs. They pay close attention. But trust me when I say I'm no threat to you. If anything, I can be an ally. I'm already diverting my ship somewhat to help you out, because I would like to help rebuild your relationship with the League. Besides, you're interesting."

An ally. Nashara hadn't had an ally in a long time. "I'm from Chimson," she said.

"That's old history," Danielle said. Chimson had been cut out of the wormhole network hundreds of years ago. Just after Earth and before New Anegada.

"I'm very old," Nashara said. "You have some closely regulated antiaging technologies around. Chimson excelled at them and I'm a product of that. One of the reasons the Satrapy had the Chimson wormhole shut down was that fear that we would make it cheap and spread it."

"Hundreds of years old?" Danielle fidgeted in the middle of the bathroom doorway.

"Hundreds, yes. I was there, for the final battle at the wormhole, trying to keep the Hongguo back." The Ragamuffins were not just New Anegada's mercenary protection, Chimson had its own as well. Nashara smiled. "I was with the Ragamuffins when we killed the Satrap in orbit around our planet."

"I've heard that rumor," Danielle said.

"We took Chimson from them with our bare hands," Nashara said. "And even though they shut us away from the rest of humanity, it was still a glorious thing." Here in the Satrapy communication was monitored, and there were only millions of humans scattered around among the aliens. Monitored. Tagged. Herded. They put up with delayed messages being passed through the buoys for no reason. But on Chimson . . . "You should see what ideas and people flourished as we all jammed together. It must have been like Earth before the pacification, with all those billions of minds so close together." She stopped.

Danielle just hung there, listening. "And?"

"It didn't stop, after we were cut off. We grew. And we decided to give something back to everyone out here. I volunteered to come back. I was packed away with nine others in a vehicle flung out to the nearest working wormhole, almost a light-year away. Took many decades to get back into the wormhole system, get back into the forty-eight worlds."

"But why in hell's name would you do that?"

"You've seen me in action. There were ten cloned and rebuilt like me, my sisters. We were sent back here." But not as mere soldiers. Their bodies were just containers, a delivery mechanism. But she wasn't going to be talking to Danielle about that. She crossed her arms. "A Hongguo ship captured us and we woke up in interrogation cells. My nine sisters wreaked a particular hell on them before they died, and only I got out. Five years ago. We were supposed to offer our services to New Anegada, but it didn't take long to find out they didn't exist." And hearing that a free human society lived in Pitt's Cross had led to a two-year mistake. Pitt's Cross didn't have the tools to even begin to wrap their minds around her particular talent.

"And now?"

"Now I'm just looking for a quiet place, run by humans. That's all. I need a home, Danielle. I just want to stop and be home."

Another wormhole approached. The conversation ended as Danielle moved them into the cockpit.

Three more transits. Danielle smiled and turned to look at Nashara.

"What?" Nashara heard something skitter through a tray of hoses and wires wrapped around the equator of the cockpit.

"They're waiting for you on Yomi."

"Hongguo? Or your buddies?"

"Hongguo. The last buoy forwarded a warning."

Nashara took a deep breath. She would have to roam around the *Daystar* and see if she could cobble together what she needed for a showdown. Anything explosive, anything sharp. And of course, at Yomi she'd be near a powerful and massive lamina.

She'd probably die at Yomi. But the havoc she would wreak would never be forgotten by the Hongguo.

Nashara's mind was the real weapon. The moment she made a direct nueral connection, it would rip free through lamina, spawning copies of itself and infiltrating every corner of the environment.

Chimson scientists had told her she needed monitors and machines to help her infiltrate and infect the lamina properly. At Yomi she would have none of that help. Just as her sisters had had none of that help when they'd awoken in the Hongguo interrogation cells. Like them, she'd burn her own mind out in the process.

"Do you think others could do the same?" Danielle asked. She slipped out a sharp knife from the belt of tools around her waist and looked over at the mess of conduit.

"What do you mean?"

"Govern themselves like you described. Without Hongguo, or Satraps, or League freedom fighters? Could we spread out?" Lightning-quick Danielle stabbed at a pile of wires that sparked. She pulled out a six-inch-long cockroach. Its feelers twitched as it squirmed to get free of the needlelike knife spearing its thorax.

"I've been in it," Nashara said. "It's messy, but it's all ours."

"I'd like to see that someday." Danielle looked away from the dying insect and reached in the pocket of her flight suit. She tossed a piece of plastic at Nashara.

"What's this?"

"We're making a quick stop to drop off some cargo. An original painting from Earth, the *Moaning Lisa* I think. Another priceless trinket that only the aliens get to own. The habitat orbits a rock called Bujantjor, two habitable worlds upstream of Yomi. I have a cousin there. I assume you have some more precious metals on you?"

Nashara nodded. "Yes."

"That's your pass in."

"Why are you doing this?" Nashara frowned.

"You tell a good tale. Besides, this won't be free. I want all those pieces of silver or gold you stole off that alien you killed on Astragalai. You can find a job on Bujantjor, we'll give you a fake identity."

Nashara didn't budge. Danielle had tipped her hand. "How did you know where the silver and gold came from?"

Danielle smiled. "It was my idea to kill that Gahe breeder. The League needs a spark for their revolution; we have so much ready and waiting to strike against the Satrapy. They wanted to use the nuke, but I suggested the martyr approach. It seems to work for us humans so well. But you lived, the nuke got used, and here we are."

"And yet you claim you're not really League. You could be handing me off to anything or anyone out there."

"Look, have I done anything to endanger you? No. I'll walk with you into Bujantjor."

"Right by my side?" Nashara laughed.

"Just like you and that League page boy you dragged aboard. If I'm lying, you get to slit my throat. And we'll call it even."

Nashara thought about it. She brushed her hand over the tiny healed scars all over her thighs. "Give me a sharp knife, a proper knife."

Danielle tossed Nashara the knife with the dead insect on the end. She pointed at it. "Do you believe we're just roaches swarming around in the edifices of greater beings than ourselves? Hitchhiking our way around?"

Nashara looked down at the massive cockroach. "Obviously not. I've seen different."

"Then consider that I want to see that for all of us, which is why I help the League, and why I'll help you."

Nashara reached down and tapped the gold leaf taped to her inner thighs. "You make yourself out to be an altruist, but you're going to gain a lot here."

Danielle laughed. "Of course. I know that."

Nashara would miss her. She slid the dead roach off the knife. "Without that gold and silver I'm dead in the water."

"You still don't trust me?" Danielle asked.

Nashara decided to see how far she could push. "I think you're an opportunist. You talk about wanting self-determination, but like all others, you'll keep doing what you do in comfort, siding with the winners as you see fit."

"Oh." Danielle raised her eyebrows. "Come with me."

"Where?"

"Cargo hold." Danielle spun. Nashara paused a moment, then followed her through the ship past the passengers and their sections and out to the edges of the ship via corridors and air locks where the cold made their breath hang in the air.

Nashara could feel the vacuum leaking through shoddy joints and bad seals. One failure and they could be blown out into space with failed equipment. She could live through that. Danielle couldn't.

Danielle opened a door leading into one of the containers along the hull of her ship. Frost rimmed the metal. Too much longer in here and Danielle would damage herself. Nashara could see that the captain's fingers shook. She hadn't dressed warmly enough to be out here.

"This is a sealed storage unit." Danielle grinned, her teeth chattering. "If anyone official checks, I can't access it. I have no idea what I'm carrying."

"But you can open it nonetheless."

Danielle nodded. She walked over and tapped one of the boxes. It heaved open and lit up. "Small-yield nuclear warheads, and other such arms for ships like mine." She closed it. Then waved her hand at another part of the hold. "Cloaked comms buoys. We've been setting up our own alternative communications array to link the League together when the time is right. We laid some of the first ones nine years ago. The League has the will, Nashara. When the time comes, it'll wipe out every last one of them."

Nashara actually felt the tug of a smile starting. She stopped it. "And you contribute to this, or just ferry it?"

"I contribute damnit. I'm rich, extraordinarily rich, Nashara. I worked for the Satrapy. Spent years exploring the wormhole network. From upstream Nova Terra all the way downstream to Farhaven, and a lot of the forks along the main routes. And now I'm atoning for my sin, for working for them. Their rewards to me will fund their own destruction."

"You're bitter," Nashara said.

"Why shouldn't I be?" Danielle snapped.

Nashara floated closer, reading the heat in Danielle's face and looking at her body language. "Who did they kill that you loved so much to turn on them?"

"It's none of your fucking business. We'll kill them for what they've done to all of us. That was the problem with the Emancipation, the Earth fighters, they wouldn't go all the way. Backed off for the promise of a closed wormhole and being left alone. They left the rest of us to twist out here. We won't make the same mistakes."

"Was it someone you loved? Or a family member?"

Danielle looked at Nashara. "Someone I loved. Dearly. In one of their antitechnology shutdowns. And they didn't kill them. Just wiped their mind clean, put them to work for the Hongguo."

And that's why she wouldn't hand Nashara over to the Hongguo.

"Fair enough," Nashara said. "I'll take your help."

Danielle looked at her. "You're still paying. Consider it a donation to the upcoming fight. I'm buried in deep with the League, but I'm no idiot. Handing you off to the Hongguo is how they work often enough, and that irks me, but who else is there but the League? We'll need everyone to stand up after the Satrapy is hit, and the League will lead them. I'll give you my help now, because I know we'll need your help later. We'll need people like you who've actually fought back."

Danielle shut the storage container. Now they understood each other. Good enough. And Nashara knew where to find the nukes if the ship was boarded. That made her feel a little bit better.

CHAPTER FOUR

Four weeks later Nashara stood in the corner of a clear plastic observation bubble and stared at the panorama of glints from free-floating dockyards and shipping lanes. The industrious hive-ishness of civilization in orbit.

The pearl orb of the planet Bujantjor hid behind girders, half-assembled ships, docking ports, and whatever else floated in between those structures. The distant star it orbited glittered blue from behind a series of oval mirrors floating in orbits nearby.

Nashara jerked out of the trance, looked at the time. Had she spent two hours staring out at that? With her Nefertiti-like face reflected back at her from behind the plastic's scratches, she lit a cigarette and allowed her eyes to film over. Her heart sped up to clear out toxins.

A few people passing by scrunched their faces up in disgust.

"What's she doing?"

She ignored them. Looked down at a hologram ghosting over the inside of her forearm on the screen.

Three hundred cubic feet of oxygen debt and accumulating. Danielle had cost her everything, and now Nashara was broke. At five hundred cubic feet of debt they would toss her into an ecocell and boost her toward the location of her choice. In perfect equilibrium she'd eat single-cell proteins and recycle her own wastes for years, floating out in space as her own unique ecosphere.

It beat being simply pushed out an air lock. Small habitats were brutal. You pulled your own weight. No one had time for dilettantes. Still, this all beat the hell out of Pitt's Cross. And League people playing games with her.

"Be careful," Danielle had told her, before shutting the lock door to leave. "The Hongguo will come across you if you slow down and sit still."

"I'll be looking for work aboard a ship. I need to get to New Anegada."

"Right." Danielle grabbed her shoulder. "Listen, if you really want a place in the League, contact me. It may take a week more, you know how throttled buoy traffic is, but I'll help you. They need your skills, your experience. Just contact me when you simmer down, okay?"

"I thought you weren't League?" Nashara raised an eyebrow.

"I'm not." Danielle smiled. "Not at all." And then she'd shut the air lock.

Nashara took another drag from the cigarette, watching the tiny numbers at the far right of the display tick up. It flicked over. New dockings.

Takara Bune. On its way into dock. What was that? Some freighter, run by Buddhists out of Avak Samarah. They had docked a long way from home, but were headed downstream toward Ys. That could put her closer to New Anegada.

Heart of India, a Nova Terra–bound ship. There was a long journey upstream for you. All the way up to the spot where a wormhole used to lead to Earth. Nashara took a final long drag from the cigarette and rubbed it out between her fingers.

Shengfen Hao. Hongguo. Her heart skipped a beat. The Hongguo were here. But hopefully not for her. They would have shut down the station and issued warrants already. It would have been loud by now. So far they'd only shut down the outgoing buoys so that no message traffic came in or out, standard Hongguo protocol before docking at a station, though it made everyone here nervous and on edge. Rumors had been percolating about a full communications lockdown throughout dozens of worlds. Just jittery rumors.

And the *Queen Mohmbasa*. Just docked within the last several hours. That old name that triggered a flicker of memory. Ragamuffin ship? Maybe. If her memory wasn't tricking her. It was worth a shot. She would have to talk to them and see if they were what she suspected before they left port tomorrow.

But for now she already an appointment with the *Takara Bune* she meant to keep. Even if *Takara Bune* worked out and she didn't check with the *Queen*, she could flit from system to system and take her time on the other, figure out what to do next without pressure. It sounded appealing.

Nashara flicked the images away and looked over to see a teenager in greasy paper overalls. Pale face. She could almost see the veins under his skin.

"Hey, station boy." He quit staring, eyes flicking aside, embarrassed at being caught. "What you looking at?"

"That a cigarette?" he asked.

Nashara held up the brown cylinder, end stumped off. "If it isn't, someone ripped me off."

He cracked a smile and his posture eased. "A sinful decadence in these closed quarters."

Nashara looked up at the metal bulkheads slowly curving away overhead. Corroded metal merged into stroid dirt and then turned over to large, distant patches of sustainable greenery.

Mankind came into space to become farmers, she thought.

"I think the ecosphere can handle me," she said.

"Maybe the ecosphere can," he said. "But I don't know about the citizenry. They may be freedmen, but they're awful uptight."

Nashara laughed and threw him the cigarette.

He caught it. Looked at her in surprise.

"Not many indulgences in a place like this," she said.

He pocketed it, and Nashara smiled and walked past him, reached out and ran a finger down his cheek. He pivoted with it, his eyes fixed down her hand to her neck.

"What's your name?" he asked.

"Out of your league, deckboy."

She took an access tunnel out of the Commons and down toward the docks. But the quick flirt had put a nice spin on the day cycle. The corners of her lips lifted.

Now all she had to do was get moving again.

On the *Takara Bune* the ship's captain introduced himself as Etsudo. He treated Nashara to pot noodles and some tiny sugar cookies with decorations of smiling animals traced out in the glaze. It was evening on ship, lights dimmed and slowly fading as she made her way through.

They met in his cabin, looked down on by pictures of his family in formal mounted frames.

He chattered with her about their ship, his face flickeringly lit by a pair of candles in ceramic bowls. A nuclear engine ran down the center of the ship, and a small pebble bed reactor gave it power. Cargo bays ran along the interior of the ship's short but cyclindrical body, and the *Takara Bune* usually spun up to one-third a standard gravity. More if the cargo demanded it. They ran on a standard twenty-four-hour cycle with the usual four-hour crew shifts, alpha, gamma, and zeta, though Nashara saw no crew out anywhere. Just Etsudo in a plain, gray jumper.

Nashara settled in for interview, but once she put down her pair of chopsticks, he clasped his wiry hands together and leaned forward.

"While I always enjoy the pleasure of an interesting guest, I will be honest and tell you we have no positions for a person of the, um, skills that you forwarded to me." He held out his hands, showing her rough calluses. "We work hard and are just a small crew. A ship's bodyguard, or security force, as you call yourself, is unnecessary to us." He smiled. "You must realize the *Takara Bune* is not in the habit of making enemies. That is not our way."

Nashara also leaned forward, placing her hands on her folded legs.

"Etsudo, we do not always choose to make enemies. Sometimes they come whether we create them or not."

Etsudo rocked back slightly. "I won't argue that. However, it is simply not the desire of me, or the crew, to do this. We are comfortable in our practices and will take the chance of ill will against the desire to follow certain peaceful precepts."

Nashara folded her arms. "Then why am I here, Etsudo?" Her voice dropped an octave.

Etsudo spread his arms. "Reading the information you forwarded, and looking at you, I'm sure you have a skill we need. Our secondary pilot left. We are short someone with the ability to pilot a ship, access our lamina."

"No." Nashara said. "I don't do that."

"But you *are* built for this? My ship's scanners show an amazing buildup of machinery in your cortex and spine for interfacing with advanced lamina."

Nashara breathed deeply. He shouldn't have been able to see past her skin so easily. Something wasn't quite right with this.

"I don't access lamina via straight neural interfaces anymore."

"If you have had past experiences that trouble you, we can teach coping mechanisms. I am a teacher. I am good with people's minds."

"Etsudo, I have my reasons." Nashara unfolded her legs and stood up. "I would say, if you are truly a wise man, you would find ways to also lessen your dependence on such things like that."

Etsudo stood up with her. He groaned and held the side of his chest as he did so. "I could hardly call myself a teacher if I did not offer such cautions myself," he said. "Can you really live here while you wait for another ship out?"

Nashara shrugged. "I've managed."

He smiled. "So far. Yes." He helped her back through the ship to the air lock, guiding her by an elbow, and paused at the entry back out onto the docks.

Nashara blinked as the door opened into full light. A blazing station high noon with full-spectrum lights glowed all up and down the curved corridor.

"Well, good luck," Etsudo said. "If you change your mind in the next eight hours, please contact me."

"You leave that quick?"

"There is nothing in the warrens of this small habitat for us. In the quiet of space we have the time to meditate, studies to attend to. Goods to deliver."

Nashara smiled. She liked Etsudo. He was straightforward enough. "Thank you for your time, Etsudo. I wish you the best."

"I'm truly very sorry this didn't work. The best to you as well." Etsudo smiled sadly and the air lock hissed shut.

Damn.

Double damn, she thought, walking past an empty air lock between the *Takara Bune* and the Hongguo ship not too far down from it.

She paused outside the ship, shaking an odd feeling of dislocation. Something that kept evading her, like a blind spot, the more she thought about it. Several feng walked out into the dock bays. Smooth-moving, like oiled machines, human warriors bred back for far too many generations, then trained in the martial algorithmic arts of the Hongguo. Nashara watched them melt out into the crowd dressed in khaki overcoats. Overcoats: an oddity on a weather- and temperature-regulated station.

What weaponry were they packing? It made her nervous. She needed off this habitat. Soon. She must have spotted them out of the corner of her eye and gotten the jitters.

She turned back the other way, putting distance between the Hongguo's trained killers and herself. Next she needed to talk to the *Queen Mohmbasa*.

"You what?"

Her roommate, Len, sputtered the words. Danielle's cousin had balked at splitting a room, but Nashara had come with a message from Danielle and some fresh Villach produce from the *Daystar* to guarantee a place and some time to get things in order.

He raised his hands in frustration.

"Turned them down," Nashara said. She tossed him a plastic pack of body sponges. He reeked of the shitfarm. The whole room did. He hardly noticed it. And sponging off didn't cut it for him, he needed disinfected and run through a sterilizing chamber.

He'd come in the door several hours earlier than she'd expected. First thing, he'd asked her about her visit aboard *Takara Bune*, and she'd just laughed and asked him if he paid the dock gossips for their chatter.

No smile. He asked her if she'd gotten anything.

And Nashara told him.

Len looked down at the packet, kneaded it, then looked back up at her.

His baby-face looks, earnest brown eyes, curly hair, strong arms, all of that melted away. Just anger now.

"I can't fucking believe you." He threw the body sponges down. "You're ruining me. I put you up for three weeks since you ran out of money, and you've been lurking around the docks, smoking up your debt, and you finally get an offer and you turn it down. I agreed to help Danielle out, but that's bullshit."

"Look," Nashara said.

"No. I have no debt to you. I have been nice. Now I know you're just taking advantage of me." He quivered as he shouted at her.

Nashara bit her lip. She owed him, but this was getting annoying. He'd been nice enough before, thinking he had an attractive roommate. No doubt some sliver of hope about *that* had let her get three weeks of rooming off him. "They wanted me to interface with their ship, pilot it."

Len squatted and picked up the packet. "You know, there are some who could only dream of being given an offer like that."

Nashara looked down at him. Stained boots, dirty fingernails, waterproof waders.

"I can't do that . . ." Her existence in this room rubbed his face in his status. Len worked deep in the almost literal bowels of the station in recycling, monitoring the bacteria levels in giant pools of sludge percolating around the waste-disposal points.

In his view, she had some psychological hang-up not to make more in a few months than he would ever see in his life. She could go anywhere, do almost anything.

He would spend his life here.

Nashara *was* doing anything she could to get out of this as-yet-unnamed, still-under-construction orbiting pit of a tin can.

She just couldn't allow a direct neural access with the lamina. She couldn't afford to unleash herself on it. Chimson had created her as a weapon. She'd watched her nine sisters let loose on lamina, out there in the cold space. Watched them rip apart an entire ship as they took it over.

It was her secret. Her burden.

"Len. You know I owe you. Big."

That was all that kept her here. He knew that she had more opportunities than he did, that she could repay him. Big. And damnit, she would.

"Yeah." He didn't look too excited about it.

The door chimed.

Len looked even less excited about that.

Nashara nodded at it. "Who's that?"

"No one."

He walked around her to it, pulled it open, and revealed four Honggua. Their black-and-white leather uniforms identified them as zhen cha: station scouts for the Hongguo. Had it been Hongguo feng, she wouldn't have had time to worry about uniform design.

All across the habitat alarms sounded, doors locked. The Hongguo had shut the place down. They'd just been waiting, cautious, biding their time.

"They paid you," Nashara said.

Len looked down at his dirty boots. Avoiding her eyes.

Three zhen cha remained guarding the door, one of them covering the corridor with his eyes, hand near his belt. The first one, a pair of gold pips on his tight collar indicating he led the group, stepped in front of Nashara.

He pulled out a Geiger counter with a flourish, ran it over Nashara's chest, arms, then stomach. It blipped, gave a reading, and satisfied, the man snapped it back onto his belt.

"You are under arrest for technological progress violations under the Benevolent Satrapy. Do you have anything to say?"

Nashara shook her head.

They cuffed her while she stood there glaring at Len. Moron. He had no idea what he was turning her over to. And for all his hatred of antihuman Hongguo, Len had rolled over quick for a large reward.

Stupid, she chided herself. But then she knew almost nothing about lying low or settling down.

She did know, however, that she did not want to end up as a brainwashed foot soldier for the Hongguo.

"Len." He looked up at her, face uncertain. No doubt hovering somewhere between happiness at finally seeing a drain to his financial security gone, and guilt at turning over a family member's friend. "You know what the Hongguo do, right?"

"You'll be given a fair chance to explain yourself," the zhen cha cuffing her said.

Nashara shook her head. "Did you and Danielle set this up when she dropped me off? A little extra profit off the whole experience?"

Len shook his head. "No. It's just me."

"You lousy shitfarmer—" One of the zhen cha put a patch over her mouth to shut her up.

"If you've done nothing wrong," Len said, "then it should not be a problem. They'll get your DNA sample, give you your documentation back. They'll prove you didn't set off a nuclear bomb on Villach. I gave them the records from Danielle's ship proving you were aboard and couldn't have done it. You can open a formal line of credit. It'll be okay. Everything will be fine." He still stared at the ground miserably.

Nashara's eyes narrowed.

He was hunting for ways to sleep at night now.

Full of shit.

She walked past him, looking straight ahead.

Best of luck to you, Len, she thought. He'd need it if she ever ran into him again. She should have roomed with one of the human pets that got off the *Daystar*, she could have kept him intimidated and quiet.

Enough remorse. She focused on figuring out how to get out of this, wondered how she'd make him pay for this.

Of course, the way things really worked, there was a good chance she'd be brain-wiped before he saw her again and all hell would have broken loose.

She hoped he'd at least lose some sleep over it all.

CHAPTER FIVE

Random passersby stared, then cleared out of the way, as the zhen cha marched Nashara down the corridor. Fear fluttered through the air. *The Hungguo bagged someone, check it out.*

Glad it isn't me.

Nashara didn't see a chance to break free of the zhen cha just yet. And then she spotted several feng dressed in dockside paper overalls, mixing with the crowd, eyeing her.

Run now and they wouldn't give her the courtesy of living.

Head down, shoulders slumped in defeat, Nashara shuffled along, watching, waiting. It took fifteen minutes to get to the docking locks. They passed the berth to *Takara Bune,* and Nashara looked over at the locked air lock with a wistful gaze. She continued to shuffle on.

The berth for *Shengfen Hao* came into view around the curve of docksides. Black-and-white leather uniforms mingled outside the open maw leading into the ship.

One lock to go before they had her in their vise.

One empty lock.

Forget lying low. Forget being nice. Time to move. Time to be herself again.

Nashara tried to smile underneath the patch, but couldn't. She snorted with annoyance. Using the slightest of movements, brushing too close to the zhen cha on her right, she started subtly herding the whole group closer to the empty lock.

Closer.

Maybe fifteen feet.

The zhen cha pushing her along frowned and started to move them back away, adjusting the direction of his gait.

Nashara stepped forward and head-butted the zhen cha next to her, spun around him, kicked the next one in the chin while she dislocated her shoulders with a popping shrug.

The zhen cha holding her turned. Good. Nashara stepped backward over her bound hands, holding them up in front of her, and shook her shoulders back into place. She kicked the stun prod out of the man's hands and into her own.

She grabbed him by the hair, holding the prod at his skull and raising her eyebrows at the remaining zhen cha.

He stayed frozen, not sure what to do next.

Three feng moved out of the crowd, disguises dropped and their guns raised. They ran at her, cutting off escape vectors.

Goddamn, they moved fast: half the docking bay in three easy loping strides.

But they weren't thinking *quite* like her yet.

Nashara kept dragging the struggling zhen cha with her until she backed up against the massive docking lock. She cracked the prod against the control panel, listened to it short out.

She grabbed the emergency handle and yanked as the zhen cha pounded uselessly against her. He made a good temporary human shield in case anyone started shooting.

The internal motors whined loudly as the inner air-lock door, five inches thick, ten feet tall, began to split open with a puff of stale, grease-smelling air. One, two, three seconds, the feng stopped and frowned.

Yeah, watch this. Nashara hit the zhen cha over the head with her cuffed hands and slid sideways through the opening as he slumped. She stood inside a massive chamber facing the outer set of air-lock doors. There was no attached ship beyond them.

The inner doors continued their slow crawl open. The feng would wait until they'd opened farther before exploding in after her.

She waited behind the door to jump them anyway, standing right next to the emergency ship-release lever. First though, she flexed her arms using clasped hands as a lever point. She watched as the cuffs bit into her skin until they hit the stratum basale and stopped against something infinitely harder than skin.

Then she pushed harder, watching the metal warp until it snapped. She threw the cuffs aside and took another step backward to compensate for the still-opening lock doors.

Okay.

She looked down at her inner forearm, tapped a few menus, made a call.

"I am Nashara Cascabel." She was pretty sure she'd used that last name before with New Anegadans before both Chimson and New Anegada were cut off from the Satrapic worlds. "I think, I think I remember your ship. You are Raga. I am Raga also, from Chimson. I will be at your air lock in five minutes and I need shelter and protection."

The only kind of gambles left were the big ones. Time to suck it up. She was going to have to hurt someone, fight to make it out.

She hyperventilated, supercharging and oxygenating her blood until spots danced in front of her eyes. Orifices clamped closed with triggered muscle, clear dark membranes shuttered her eyes.

She yanked the emergency ship-release lever.

The docking clamps on either side of the bay rolled open into release mode and the outer air-lock doors blew open. Klaxons blared, so loud they buzzed through her despite the closed ears.

With another series of shudders the inner lock doors reversed their direction to stop the massive gale of air rushing out of the station. Another few seconds and it would just be Nashara in an airless air lock.

The first feng somersaulted in high, paper overalls crinkling and giving her a split-second warning. Nashara plucked him out of the air and grabbed his chin to snap his neck. Like a cat falling out of a tree he twisted around and grabbed her forearm.

It didn't snap.

His eyes only registered a moment's dismay. He punched her neck as he landed on his two feet.

His fingertips splintered.

Nashara kicked him in the stomach. Threw him against the lock doors. Grabbed his head and slammed it against the five-inch-thick metal and felt it give in. Instant lobotomy; crushed frontal lobe.

One feng down.

She unlocked her nostrils and started hyperventilating again. The doors had five inches to go.

Another feng slipped through. He took her rib-shattering kick, sprang up, and ran to the other side of the lock. He looked back at the lock doors as they sealed.

The outer doors, what felt like the gravity-determined "floor" of the lock, opened in an explosion of escaping air.

Nashara ran toward the crack and jumped through.

The feng, insanely quick for his packed muscular frame, jumped with her. He exhaled all his breath in fog of crystals. Smart, his lungs wouldn't explode. He had a slight chance. Nashara ignored his grip. She caught the lip of the lock and jerked to a jarring stop.

He wrapped his legs around her waist and squeezed. Nashara twisted, trying to hold on to the door and dislodge him. If she let go, they would both be spun clear of the station.

They wriggled around each other like a pair of greased eels, trying to gain a hold on one another, until the feng began to bloat. Ice formed around his eyes.

An inhumanly skilled fighter, true, but just a human in a vacuum.

He began to forget his training, his centered warrior calm. He scratched at her skin, ripping lengths of it off in his fingernails.

Nashara turned and faced him. He froze. A midnight-black face with whole midnight-black eyes was what Nashara knew he would see. A demoness.

Convulsions began.

She kicked him free. Watched him drop down away from her, pitched out into space.

The wrestling left her heart rate up. Nashara forced it down in the sixties, a third of what it had been. The adjustment dizzied her.

Then she moved along the outer docks. Hanging from ladders where she could, using crevices, cracks, and anything else she could hang on in other places. The station's rotation made this feel as if she were hanging above a very, very long fall into an abyss.

She kept in the camouflage of the constantly moving shadows of spinning station's curved outer wall, eyes searching for a particular dock number. Outer skin flaked off in the vacuum. Her hair broke off and fell away from her.

Fifteen minutes later. She almost doubted she could make it. But here it was. The *Queen Mohmbasa*. Ragamuffin. Maybe. She prayed for it.

Nashara struggled along the hull of the long, cylindrical ship to find a small service air lock. She hit open, banged on it, and kept banging and banging until it opened and she swung in.

By the time the air cycled in and pressurized, she was on her hands and knees, barely able to see from oxygen deprivation.

The first breath, when she ripped the patch off her mouth and sucked it in, was insanely sweet and cloyingly fresh.

"I'm Raga," she croaked when two fuzzy, but seemingly armed, forms appeared at the door. The membrane over her eyes refused to open, frozen shut. She couldn't focus.

A pair of hands grabbed her, pulled her out of the lock, and laid her on a cold metal grating. "Grab some tissue for a look at her DNA. Run it, get that back to me as soon as possible."

The nearest shape reached down, pricked her arm.

"Broke the syringe." The shape rustled around, then Nashara felt a swab scraping the inside of her cheek. "She modified to survive vacuum."

"You think?"

"Get ready to burn out the dock if the Hongguo twitch. Throw her in one of the empty rooms."

Nashara remained limp, regathering strength as she was picked up onto someone's shoulder. They walked her down through a corridor, hitting her head against a bulkhead, and then into a room.

Nashara leaned against the wall, shivering from heat loss and burned-off energy reserves. She stood there, unable to pass out thanks to her combat-enabled body, experiencing every wave of pain, every severed, screaming nerve.

"Don't know the hell you is," one of the two blobs said. "But you gone and pick the wrong ship to get aboard. The moment we try to blow out this station, the Hongguo go come hard for we tail. Blow us out the sky, you too. We dead, and now you is too."

The door shut. Locks clicked. Nashara slumped to the floor facedown.

Triple damn it, she was alive. Fuck if the pain wasn't somewhat sweet because of that.

CHAPTER SIX

Four days before his ship had arrived at Bujantjor and before meeting Nashara, Etsudo Hajiwara had watched the destruction of an entire habitat once home to tens of thousands inside its protective shell. His stomach churned slightly as fifteen low-yield nuclear charges detonated three hundred kilometers away, each a tiny blinding flash of light. The windows before him darkened as the flash grew. The habitat Dragin-Above ceased to exist.

"Magnify that," Etsudo ordered. A bald acolyte near the periphery of the semicircular room, his crimson robes hanging in the air around him, spun dials until the window in front of Etsudo visibly flexed. Its width and curvature changed, and the great globes of the destroyed habitat jumped into focus. Etsudo watched as they split apart in a fiery mass of debris.

The men beside him watched from the curved windows and safety of the five-mile-long Hongguo flagship *Gulong*. They shook their heads.

"A waste," one whispered. "They were warned."

A thousand had refused to hand themselves over to the Hongguo for reconditioning. Just a handful, really, of the millions scattered throughout habitats and some of the forty-eight worlds of the Benevolent Satrapy. But still . . . Etsudo swallowed. He'd come to this habitat once three years ago. They talked freely to him about building artificial intelligences, and Etsudo had done his best to buy their patents to do nothing with. He'd even used shell companies to hire their best neuroprogrammers away. It hadn't been enough to stop this.

A losing battle. So often, despite his best efforts.

One of the Jiang shifted closer to him. Deng. Always following behind Etsudo to suppress that which Etsudo failed to keep in check. Like today.

"They knew their options." Jiang Deng folded his arms.

"Memory wipes and servitude to us, or death." Etsudo shook his head.

"Artificial intelligence is an illegal technological path. You sympathize with them?" Deng's eyes narrowed in on Etsudo. The other Jiang, the generals of the Hongguo, looked over.

"It's my job," Etsudo said, looking at the debris. He used nondestructive means to control illegal technologies. Deng used destructive ones.

"You are passing some sort of judgment on me?"

"No." Etsudo looked back at the eleven Jiang who hung in the air around him. They wore tightly fitted ceramic body armor, many of them with the long-tailed-dragon sigil originally used by the Hongguo founders. "The Satrapy doesn't stand certain technology. We keep emancipation alive. We're all free as long as Hongguo are around to keep research carefully directed." The words were rote and etched in his memory. And too true.

"Indeed," Jiang Deng said. Etsudo, looking to avoid conflict, stared back out toward the destroyed habitat. Behind the debris the orange orb of the planet Dragin stared back at Etsudo, reproaching him, he imagined. The windows closed. Five-inch-thick blast doors slid down as the debris field from what had once been the habitat Dragin-Above, home to five thousand families, pattered against the thick hull of the *Gulong*.

Maybe humans would orbit the planet Dragin again in a few decades, Etsudo thought as he turned away from the control center and followed the Jiang out toward the docking bays to return to their respective ships.

"We have someone new for your crew," Jiang Deng told him as everyone coasted along one of the corridors of the *Gulong*. "We're beginning something new. The Satrapy needs us, Etsudo. Do you understand?"

Etsudo did. They didn't trust him any longer. Now they would be appointing a second captain to ride along with Etsudo. He'd been expecting this for several years now. "This new crew, he'll split the captainship with me, won't he?"

"Yes," Deng said. "The Satrapy is sending us out with new tasks, new missions. Brandon will be there to help you during this transition. We'll be stepping up our enforcement activity."

They would say handling a whole ship on his own for so long was too much. It would be for Etsudo's own benefit to share the burden. It would be a polite farce.

Etsudo knew there used to be more Hongguo ships with the same charter as his. Trading ships. All disguised suppressors of advanced technology. All endowed with massive budgets, seeking to keep things in check.

Now he was one of a handful. Transition indeed. He was being phased out.

He didn't dare question it. Some tradition, a momentum, that kept him in his place as the captain and ruler of the *Takara Bune*. Etsudo did not want to lose that.

"This is Brandon Saxwere." Jiang Deng introduced him to a tall man with a shaved scalp, green eyes, and pinched face. Brandon waited politely by a crux in one of the corridors, obviously expecting them. He wore a simple gray robe, the fringe clipped to his ankles for zero gravity.

"Good to meet you." Brandon smiled a warm, honest smile and Etsudo hated him.

Etsudo snagged the railing to come to a stop and bowed his head. "And you."

This was the beginning of the end of his life. He should have felt more anger about it. Etsudo turned to one of the windows along the corridor and looked into a vast cavern. The walls teemed with an orderly nest of people. All with shaved heads, blank eyes, and wearing crimson paper robes carefully clipped to their ankles as well. They sat at rows of plastic desks, strapped in with acceleration webbing.

Each one worked on a small calculation using an abacus on the desk in front of them. The result was passed on to a station in the next concentric ring, or if the instructions on the card passed to them dictated, to one of their sides. Waves of human-computed math rolled up and down the sides of the massive ball of humanity. And Etsudo could see through spokes into smaller and smaller spheres of humanity, all the way to the center of the sphere where the central controllers sat, staring outward at their machine.

No computer virus would ever take this ship. Only slide rules and abacus could compute orbits, or calculate the speed of the *Gulong*, or position the slender needle of the ship's nose into the heart of a wormhole to destroy it. A gift from the Satrapy after it was used to cut Earth away from the wormhole network, to keep the rest of the race in check.

When Etsudo looked back from the human computers, Jiang Deng excused himself. "I must head to the Stage Two briefing."

"Stage Two?" Etsudo had heard nothing of a briefing, or of a second component to the shutdown of Dragin-Above.

"It's a military operation." Deng smiled. "Destruction-oriented, not of interest to you."

He left. Brandon hovered in the air and looked in at the chamber of human calculators.

"It's a test chamber for the Dragin-Above refugees." Brandon said. "The main processing chamber for the *Gulong* is closer to the heart of the ship. They're just checking here to make sure the reconditioning is holding and that the new training is working."

"We're not tools," Etsudo muttered. "We're not just things to be used.

We're unique creatures, thinkers, inventors, believers. When we stop remembering *that*, we are no longer human, are we?"

"Better than death." Brandon bowed his head as he said this.

"Are you sure about that? What is *your* last memory?"

"I'm as mentally pure as you." Brandon folded his arms. "And what is your critique? The crew of the *Takara Bune* are reconditioned, aren't they? Don't they serve you well enough?"

They served Etsudo well. But not because he allowed Hongguo to recondition their minds. Etsudo changed the topic. "Why are you really coming aboard my ship?"

"You've held your own ship together long enough. I'm your second-shift captain, your night captain." Brandon raised his hands. "I don't know how you've managed alone with just a reconditioned crew for so long."

Maybe Brandon was really coming to help, and not to take over Etsudo's ship. But Etsudo doubted it.

On the shuttle ride back to the *Takara Bune* Etsudo leaned over to Brandon. "You question my ability to run my ship, which I have done smoothly for years. There are nine crew aboard my ship and one captain. How exactly do you fit into this?"

Brandon did not reply. He stared straight ahead.

Etsudo knew about men who didn't need to prove themselves. They were dangerous. As the long seconds dragged on he watched the foot straps, lost in thought, until the shuttle jerked to a stop.

Once it shuddered rudely into place by docking collar, Etsudo pulled his feet free. Brandon floated first through the air lock and Etsudo closed his eyes. Through the *Takara Bune*'s lamina he accessed the scanning equipment built into the walls of the air lock.

As the air pressure equalized, they both hung in place. And Etsudo scanned Brandon inch by inch. He found the man laced with machinery, no doubt to broadcast back to Jiang Deng everything they said. Brandon was feng, ready to be unleashed on Etsudo the moment Jiang Deng had an excuse.

Etsudo looked up as the door into the *Takara Bune* rolled open. No one waited for them. The alpha crew remained on shift in the cockpit, magnetic and physical locks in place to slow down any forced entry as Etsudo had ordered before leaving the ship. Gamma and zeta crew remained locked in their quarters, waiting for the all clear.

"I apologize. You know I'm related to the founders of the Hongguo." Etsudo rolled his sleeve up and showed Brandon the dragon tattooed on his bicep. Much like the sigil the Jiang wore on their ceramic armor. "When you get settled in, come find me in the captain's room. I want to show you something. A piece of their legacy. Maybe then you'll understand my reluctance to give up all the years of history my family has within ships like the *Takara Bune*, and why I'm so testy right now."

Brandon nodded. Etsudo left him by the dull metal doors of the air lock. He needed to prepare for what came next. Burning through people's minds, re-creating them into a new image, it took time, calibration, and special equipment.

All of which Etsudo had in his cabin. All of which was completely illegal by decree of the Satrapy.

But first, a hard burn out away from the ruins of this habitat and upstream toward more heavily populated systems. Up away from Deng and his heavily armed ship, the *Shengfen Hao*. Back to his own devices. Etsudo relaxed and accessed the ship's lamina, sliding into the world of data sitting all around him. "Sabir?"

"Listening," the alpha crew's pilot responded.

"Upstream to Thule via Tsushima. Get updated traffic maps for Pawtucket, Gateshead, and Trinity." At Thule he'd have the option to go to one of three forks. All three had enough human population density for him to justify a search for illegal technology.

"Crew change is coming up in fifteen minutes," Sabir's voice whispered in Etsudo's ear. "Should we remain in the cockpit?"

"Yes. Stay put until Brandon enters my room. Then change shift. But remain locked down after shift change. This man could be dangerous. Now, get the ship moving." The longer he remained near the elite of the Hongguo, the more nervous he got.

"Of course."

Warning lights flipped on, turning the interior of the ship dark red. The *Takara Bune* accelerated as Etsudo fled his fellow Hongguo.

The door to Etsudo's cabin rolled aside. Etsudo brushed past a pair of tortured bamboo plants running along the room's midrail, his fingers brushing green shoots as he pulled himself over to Brandon. The *Takara Bune* coasted now, not too far from Tsushima with the better part of a day already gone.

"Come." Etsudo waved the man in.

Brandon took in the red-cushioned room, looking briefly at the comfortable half sphere of Etsudo's couch, the tatami stapled to the walls, and several sparse paintings of Earth landscapes. Waterfalls, ponds.

"You really want to talk about your family, or something else?"

"My will won't stand long against all the Jiang of the Hongguo. I have no choice but to let you into the ship, and to give your reports back, and to do what is asked of me. But, look, come closer and you'll understand my own pridefulness." Etsudo pointed out a small printed picture, framed by a brassy-looking wood. "Read the plaque."

Brandon floated two feet away from the picture. The fathers of the Hongguo: Hajiwara, Nakamoto, and Singh.

"That was my great-grandfather." Etsudo hung by Brandon's elbow. As he continued, he closed his eyes, accessed his ship's lamina, and gave a simple command to the machinery behind the picture's façade. "The only reason Jiang like Deng haven't made me disappear yet. There are those who would notice one of the sole family members of the founding fathers gone missing."

Brandon didn't reply; he hung motionless in the air. A short pulse of energy had scrambled his synapses and knocked him out.

"They're such proud, fine men," Etsudo said. "It's a shame I was adopted and couldn't really care less about blood." He spun Brandon around. The man's face hung slack.

The Jiang would disapprove of this piece of illegal technology housed behind that frame. As well as all the other equipment Etsudo kept throughout the walls of his cabin. He was a good candidate for reconditioning, or execution.

But this was *his* ship. The Jiang could go to hell. Etsudo moved Brandon to the couch and strapped him in. Then he folded his legs and hung before Brandon as he waited for the man to wake up.

When he did, he struggled to free himself. Etsudo shook his head. "Don't do that, I'd hate to see physical harm come into this equation."

Brandon's green eyes pinned Etsudo in the air. "What do you think you're doing? Deng will flay you for insubordination."

"That's interesting. Because he's technically not my superior, is he? The trade arm of the Hongguo is charged to eradicate illegal technologies through nonlethal methods. We're a separate and equal arm."

"If your means are nonlethal, what is this about?"

"Have I hurt you yet?" Etsudo asked. "Are you in pain?"

"You threatened me with physical harm." Brandon twisted, but there had been stronger, faster, more dangerous men in that chair before.

"The silky cords wrapped around your arms have a monofilament wire in their center. Break the silk and you'll slice your hands off. If you continue to struggle or get more agitated, you will be responsible for your own self-amputation."

Brandon stopped straining. He stared at Etsudo, who experienced a brief rush. The power of direct force. A heady drug, and addictive. "What do you want?"

Etsudo leaned forward. "What are you doing aboard my ship, Brandon?"

"Nothing. You're entirely misguided. This is beyond inappropriate."

"Okay." Etsudo held up his arm and clenched his fist. Brandon blinked and looked around, frowning. "Every time I do that, the machine around you, which I've disguised as a simple acceleration couch, will rip something of your mind free. A memory, a skill, a part of your personality. I will not harm you, Brandon, but you will cease to be a functioning person when I'm done if you aren't forthcoming."

Brandon stared at him. "You can't recondition my mind. Your ship doesn't have the permission to keep that equipment. Only the *Gulong* has it."

"A special Satrapic allowance, that. Everyone aboard the *Takara Bune* has had a trip to this room, Brandon. Trust me, this is all very much real. I do really have these machines in this room." Etsudo made a fist, sending the command through lamina to strip another memory out from the surface of Brandon's mind.

"What did you just do?"

"Do you remember how you got aboard this ship?"

Brandon blinked several times. He didn't. It would be a hole in his mind, an odd interruption that eluded him as he tried to reach for it. "Oh, shit. Oh, shit."

"Yes, this is very real, Brandon. It's happening. Again, why are you on my ship?"

"Deng's going to kill you, not just retire you."

"Stop worrying about things outside of your control, Brandon, and tell me what I want to know or I'll turn you into a drooling idiot. Why are you on *my ship?*"

"Giving them an excuse to get rid of you." Brandon looked directly at him. "You're the last of the pacifist arm. Your 'balance' and 'yin/yang' concepts aren't policy anymore."

"They never were." Etsudo shook his head. "The Hongguo began life as a company. Profit was king, Brandon, the trading arm wasn't pacifist, just mercantile and nonlethal. And good at what it did."

"It's not needed anymore, it's been recalled."

Etsudo nodded. "Yes, but why?"

Brandon looked up toward one of the paintings. The waterfall. Tears leaked out of his eyes and hung in front of him. "Deng told you, you'll be supporting antipirate activity in the area."

"That's such a shame you won't tell me the real reason." Etsudo didn't want to rip Brandon's mind down to almost nothing. Etsudo was an artist. He wanted a functioning human being. Destruction was for amateurs. And after watching thousands die earlier, he had no desire to see more death. But threats did not seem to work with Brandon, so Etsudo would try another use for his machine. "But I can help. In just a few hours, Brandon, you and I are going to be best friends, and you won't even think twice about telling me everything I need to know."

Brandon groaned as Etsudo clenched his fist. Etsudo guided the machine as it probed the man's mind with magnetic feelers, sifting through Brandon's synapses and recording them, building up a ghostly image of Brandon's mind that Etsudo could access, then model. And using that model as a guide, he could begin altering Brandon's mind.

It took the better of ten hours, even with all the heavy computing power at Etsudo's disposal in the *Takara Bune*.

When Etsudo was done, the reconditioning over, Brandon looked up. "I'm so sorry, Etsudo, I'm so sorry."

Etsudo nodded, grabbed Brandon's shoulder, and stared the man eye to eye. Brandon's mind had already been tampered with by Deng, he'd found traces of that. But had he gotten deep enough into Brandon's head to undo that? Or would Brandon turn on him suddenly, subject to triggers buried deeper in the back of his cortex. "The things Deng has done to your mind are horrible. But I helped you. Everything is back the way it was, Brandon. You're back to normal. And I'm glad you were able to get a transfer to my ship, where I can protect you."

"Thank you," Brandon whispered. "Thank you."

"It's been a few years, friend. But you're okay now. You're okay."

Brandon shook with tears as Etsudo unstrapped and pulled him free. "Come on. I'll take you to your cabin. You'll rest. We'll have tea next shift. And then you'll tell me everything."

And as conditioned to do, Brandon nodded. "Etsudo, we have to be careful. Very careful. Things are changing, we're all in a lot of danger."

"You'll tell me all about it." Etsudo guided the dangerous man through the air.

It was always dangerous to tackle gods in their own territories, Etsudo thought. And here aboard the *Takara Bune* that's exactly what he was.

What else could he be? If he ran away with his ship, the Satrapy would revoke his docking and fueling rights. If he left his ship and ran into hiding, his fellow Hongguo would hunt him down and wipe his mind down to blank, leaving him as another calculating machine for the *Gulong*.

He had been doomed to this ever since being born among the Hongguo.

CHAPTER SEVEN

The machine had been a gift. An inheritance from Kenji Hajiwara, the man Etsudo thought of as father, a father whose bloodline included the original Hajiwara of the Hongguo.

Etsudo grew up aboard the *Takara Bune*. It never bothered him that there weren't any other children. Not even into his teens as Kenji taught him how to thread the *Takara Bune* through a wormhole. Not even into adulthood, when the Hongguo began to assist the Satrapy and its alien subjects control human technologies.

"Do you remember your mother?" Kenji had asked him once.

Etsudo remembered standing in the observation gallery by her casket, crying, watching it slide out from the habitat until it dwindled away on its long, decaying orbit toward the blue-tinged sun in the distance.

"Of course I do. Always," Etsudo replied.

"Do you remember your mother?" Kenji had asked him again, just before Kenji died, riddled with an artificial form of infectious cancer.

"Of course," Etsudo had told him.

But then an hour later a message came, a recording Kenji had left with a date stamp on it that was over ten years old. Kenji, younger but more tired, faced Etsudo one last time.

"Do you remember your mother?" the recording asked. Kenji looked more incredibly sad than Etsudo had ever seen him. "Because I have a confession to make, my son. A hard one to make, which is why I'm recording this, and locking it to be released when I die. Though I guess that is easier than telling you this myself."

Kenji had always wanted a child, so he'd taken one from a small orbital research habitat. A five-year-old, whose parents where about to be reconditioned. Kenji created a new mother in his mind, and a new father.

Did Etsudo remember his mother? He didn't know. That face that had kissed him in the mornings, sung to him, that might have been the same face. Or one that Kenji stole from a database somewhere. Etsudo never bothered to find out. He destroyed the message and walked back to Kenji's room in the hospital.

Looking in at the body of the man, Etsudo crumpled to the floor to cry for the last time in his life. His father had died and his mother had never existed, and neither did he.

And here was this loyalty to the Hongguo built into him by his father, and yet the knowledge that he was one of their victims. The love of his mother, who didn't exist. The love of a father who did, and had betrayed him.

A ship to run that was his. Kenji had worked hard to make sure Etsudo had full captainship of the *Takara Bune*.

Etsudo heated a bulb of tea over the hot pad at the center of the round table in the cramped galley. Brandon gripped the edges of the table as if he would fall away from it if he let go. Vertigo was a small side effect from reconditioning. Etsudo had a sick bag in his back pocket. He handed the bulb to Brandon, who cradled the handcrafted glass in his two callused hands. The etched silver swans on the sides caught the glint of the cabin lighting as he rolled the bulb between his fingers.

Brandon looked up from the tea, a brown drop of liquid hovering above the tiny lip. "Etsudo, I've been wired to send everything I see and hear back to Deng."

"You're okay." Etsudo shook his head. "Nothing leaks out of this ship unless I want it to. But Deng will be contacting us soon when you don't report back to him."

Brandon shuddered.

"I know." Etsudo nodded. "But we will be okay."

"I'll fall apart facing him right now."

A message pinged for Etsudo's attention. He relaxed and settled into the lamina. The image of Jiang Deng appeared before him, standing on the table. "Etsudo," Deng snapped. "Check in." Then the Jiang folded his arms and disappeared.

Etsudo subvocalized his response while looking at a tired Brandon sip tea. The man did not look up or even realize Etsudo was multitasking. "Brandon has yet to finish his tour of the *Takara Bune*. If you've been worried about him not checking in, it's because the ship is shielded. His personal communications have to route through the *Takara Bune*'s lamina first. We keep a low profile."

The message would get bounced out to the nearest buoy, shot through the wormhole back downstream. Even with Hongguo priority codes on it, Etsudo had maybe ten minutes before Deng received it, though he wasn't sure where Deng was. Then the message had a ten-minute return. Could be a long twenty minutes.

Brandon looked up. "Our Jiang's strategies have changed."

"How?"

"Four days ago the three Consuls were asked to make a trip to a habitat with a Satrap in it. When they came out, everything was different. New orders, new thoughts. Like the new initiative against the pirates."

"The pirates? That was for real?" Etsudo asked. And Jiang Deng appeared again. Etsudo frowned and held up his hand, and Brandon waited. That had been, what, a minute? Two at the most. That mean only a handful of wormholes lay between him and the *Shengfen Hao*. Deng's ship was a lot faster than Etsudo's unless the *Takara Bune* ditched all its cargo. So much for running away. Deng was catching up to him.

Deng waved a hand. "I don't care about Brandon. I need your direct assistance. "We have a problem."

Again, Etsudo wondered if he'd overreacted with Brandon. Maybe they'd genuinely thought he needed assistance running his ship. Maybe they were actually trying to eliminate the Ragamuffins.

Maybe.

Deng continued, "Jiang Wu and Jiang Li suffered damage to their ships while attacking pirates. They managed to destroy four ships, but a fifth escaped. I'm in pursuit, but I need your help."

Etsudo stared at the tiny figure of Deng. Attacks in space? In a hundred years maybe a few Hongguo ships had actually attacked others. Brandon was right, the Jiang's strategies had changed.

"What's wrong?" Brandon had realized Etsudo was staring off into space. "Is it Jiang Deng?"

"Don't worry," Etsudo whispered. "Just give me a second."

Jiang Deng's message went on, "We didn't get the identity of the fifth ship, but it leaves a recognizable gamma radiation trail our drones are following. Your message ping time indicates you are just upstream of us and close by. We're jamming the ship to stop it from calling for help, but they may get ahead of us. We're shutting communication buoys down. It begins at Thule and goes downstream from there. This whole downstream branch is being put under a blackout as we work to squeeze any pirate ships down towards their home base. We did not brief you because your ship isn't involved." And because Deng didn't trust him. "But now I need you to run support for our mission. When the pirate ship overtakes you, blow your cargo and keep up with them, you have a faster ship than I do. Send confirmation you received this and are acting."

Etsudo gripped the table as hard as Brandon. Why attack them now?

Spaceships cost immense sums, and the Hongguo had a lot invested in their fleet strung across the Satrapy. Some of the ships creaked along at almost a hundred years old, like the *Takara Bune*. Risking them in direct confrontation with other ships didn't fly well with the captains. Better to hunt the pirates once they docked at a station somewhere.

"Has it begun?" Brandon asked.

Etsudo regarded the man. "What?"

"Removing the Ragmuffins." Brandon swallowed. "The Satraps ordered the destruction of the pirates. We've been keeping records and collating activity of all the ships coming out from where New Anegada used to be. We start upstream, begin working our way downstream. If they don't allow boarding, we destroy them."

"That's a whole-scale war," Etsudo said. "Since when have we been the Satrapy's direct enforcers?" The Maatan could do this. They'd dropped asteroids on Earth during the pacification and destroyed Earth attempts to strike back. Why the Hongguo?

"But look at what it means." Brandon had an eager smile. "For all these years we tried to prove to the Satraps that humans were trustworthy. We kept technology in check, surgically killed off the worst elements. We're proved our worth, we're standing at their right hand now, and since we have access to all those technologies anyway, we'll be like monks after a dark age. We'll be able to slowly introduce things again. The Hongguo will stand at the front of humanity."

"I don't know," Etsudo muttered. "We were doing well at our job before."

"Let me tell you something personal though, old friend." Brandon leaned over. "You want to know why we should really help Deng any way we can? There are damaged ships out there, big ships whose captains have screwed up, Etsudo. Do well now, you and I could get a bigger ship, more crew. You could get off this small trading ship and into bigger things."

Etsudo stared down at the smooth table. He missed the days Kenji had told him about. The days when the Hongguo was just a company paid to explore the wormholes and map out all the forks and streams connecting the various worlds, just a trading company.

And what of his ship when this was all done? Etsudo looked around. What would become of him, and all his memories as the Hongguo changed into something else at the Satrapy's bidding?

Etsudo folded his arms around himself, feeling alone in the heart of his ship. He stared at Brandon as he sipped his tea. He wasn't sure what was going to come next. For all his loyalty, and the loyalty his father had instilled in him to the Hongguo, Etsudo would hardly give up his ship and his own mind without a fight.

To Thule then. Alarms sounded as his ship prepared to transit another wormhole on its path upstream.

And now it was also time to introduce Brandon to the rest of the crew. The murderers, rapists, and criminals that Etsudo's life depended on. Brandon now the latest in his set of odd acquisitions.

CHAPTER EIGHT

Do you believe in redemption?" Etsudo asked Brandon as he entered the cockpit.

"Redemption?"

"Yes, redemption." The cockpit sat nestled deep in the heart of the ship. Acceleration chairs dotted the tight confines of the smooth blue cocoon. The cockpit door sealed itself behind them. In emergencies the cockpit would re-filter its own air and use its own tiny nuclear reactor to run everything on the *Takara Bune* except its antimatter engines.

"I'm not religious," Brandon said.

"You don't have to believe in religion to believe in redemption." Etsudo looked around at the gamma crew. "Bahul, the pilot for this shift, he fired a nuclear bomb into the heart of a habitat from a shuttle. He did that for the League of Human Affairs."

Brandon looked over at Bahul, who nodded back at him from the pilot's couch. Strapped in, brown eyes glazed, he stared back at Brandon.

Etsudo turned and pointed at the sallow-skinned man with green eyes and emaciated face. "And this is Fabiyan, our mechanic. He cut three men's heads off. Kept them as trophies."

Fabiyan nodded and smiled.

One more for the gamma crew. "Michiko." Etsudo nodded his head. "Gamma's deckhand."

"What did she do?"

"A very bad bar fight." All three of gamma crew's shaved heads gleamed in the cockpit light.

"Welcome aboard, Brandon." Michiko smiled.

"Redemption." Etsudo grabbed Brandon's shoulder. "They all remember their crimes. Michiko remembers stabbing her best friend in the heart, Fabiyan remembers cutting the heads of three innocent victims off, and Bahul lives with knowledge that he killed thousands. The alpha and zeta crew are the same. This is my crew, I cull them. These are my friends."

Nine crew, three on each shift, and him the captain. Ten made for a nice number. Brandon upset that nice symmetry.

Brandon wiped his face with a sleeve. "Usually we recondition all memories, don't we? This is unorthodox."

Etsudo chuckled. "Welcome to my world, Brandon. Are you ready to be in charge of them all?"

Brandon looked at Michiko, Fabiyan, and then Bahul. "Did I . . . do something? Is that why I'm here?"

"Jiang Deng and you conspired against me. But only because he altered your mind. I've liberated you from those changes Deng made."

"We're friends?"

"Oh, yes," Etsudo lied. He squeezed Brandon's shoulder and let go. "We're longtime friends." And for now Brandon had no ability to access anything outside the ship's lamina. For Brandon, anything Etsudo said became reality.

Brandon wouldn't be leaving the ship either, not until he'd earned his redemption. Not until Etsudo knew exactly what was going on out there with the Hongguo.

"Fabiyan, Jiang Deng just sent orders. We're speeding up and getting ready to keep pace with the pirate coming upstream towards us. They're thinking it's going to dock at Bujantjor. That's where they'll try and stage a raid to get into it. They want the ship in one piece, and the pirates as well."

"Pirates?" Fabiyan raised an eyebrow. "Ragamuffins?"

"Yes, them." Etsudo showed Brandon a spare acceleration chair. "We may have to drop our cargo."

"Do you think we'll need acceleration chairs?" Brandon asked.

Michiko twisted in her restraints. "It's never hurt. But if you're not willing to strap in, please leave the cockpit. I'd rather not get my neck snapped by your flying body if we have to accelerate in a hurry. Captain."

Brandon sat and let the chair's fingers reach up around him.

"Pinging buoys up the stream," Bahul reported. "They've been shutting down. People will be flying blind through wormholes, they'll be jumpy."

Etsudo let his chair wrap itself around him. "But we still have access to the buoys. We know what's on the other side, we can dodge." The price of drones would be going up from Thule on downstream. Trade wouldn't stop because of a buoy outage. They might serve as both repeaters and traffic advisers, but commerce went on. Ships would just be more cautious, using drones to poke ahead and make sure they wouldn't hit anything on the other side after transit.

Speaking of which. His stomach flipped as they passed through the next wormhole. The ship shook as Bahul let the ship drift several feet clear of exact center. Waves of gravity tore at the sides of the *Takara Bune*, unbalancing the ship.

Etsudo opened a window in the lamina before him, using the ship's cameras to create a vision of where they coasted now. They moved between a pair of wormholes that hung in the black emptiness, far from life-nourishing suns.

"I imagine our Ragamuffin friends will be here soon." Etsudo looked over at the gamma-shift pilot. "Get us out of the way." Etsudo used the lamina to drop three of *Takara Bune*'s drones behind. From their viewpoints he could see the lines of light beamed into the wormholes all flicker out.

Bahul accelerated the creaking *Takara Bune* farther away from the flight path between the two wormholes. There were no planets to worry about, no orbital wells. These wormholes just drifted in the dark of a heavy cloud of dust.

"There," Michiko said, piggybacking on one of the drones. "Drones."

A trio of yellow-and-green drones flew through the downstream wormhole. Chemical rockets flared as they adjusted their course. The downstream wormhole dumped ships out a few degrees off course. An arrangement the Satrapy liked as it kept any one ship from being able to move through the forty-eight worlds in short notice. Coming out of each wormhole usually required wasting fuel to adjust course.

The drones hit the upstream wormhole and disappeared.

"Incoming," Bahul said, breaking the quiet in the cockpit as everyone watched along. "No identifying marks on it."

The cylindrical ship adjusted its course, following the drones at fifteen thousand kilometers an hour. The entire ship rotated sideways and fired its engines. A long, fiery plume of chemical boosters jerked the Ragamuffin ship for a fast course-correction change. Then it twisted back around to plunge through the upstream wormhole headfirst.

Bahul shook his head. "Don't know if I'd have the steel to take a ship in at a wormhole at that speed."

Etsudo silently agreed. Bahul wobbled too much. That was why Etsudo remained the best on the ship. And alpha's pilot, Sabir, got nervous with every transit, while zeta's Anjelica never transited above five thousand kilometers an hour.

But they were a good crew. They were his crew. He had made them that way.

"Power up!" Etsudo snapped. "But don't ditch the cargo just yet, let's see if we can keep up."

"There's a five-thousand-kilometer-per-hour deficit," Brandon noted. "We'll never catch them."

"We don't have to," Etsudo said. "They're not getting past Thule. Deng will catch up and block their rear escape, we're just making sure they don't escape the net."

But since the Emancipation the Satrapy only worried about technological violations. Why all this? The pirates mainly purchased antimatter fuel off the black market.

Change bugged Etsudo.

"Where do you think they'll end up?" Brandon asked.

"Bujantjor," Etsudo said. "There are Freeman colonies in orbit there, they'll be sympathetic, they'll let them dock and try and fuel them."

"If we catch them, the Jiang will reward us well. Your name is well-known, your father was a good man among the Hongguo. We'll rise far."

Etsudo didn't say anything. The Satrapy would win this battle against the Ragamuffins. A handful of armed trade ships against the money sunk into Hongguo ships and weapons by the Satrapy. No contest.

He was going to have to adapt. The Satrapy had entered a new stage of its existence with humans. If Etsudo could gain a ship like Deng's, then he could hardly be at the mercy of one like the Jiang. He leaned forward. "Catch up to that ship, Bahul. Drop cargo as you need."

Would it be worth trying to please his masters for a bigger ship? He wasn't sure. Brandon had been imprinted with it before he boarded the *Takara Bune*, no doubt to pass that on to Etsudo. The Jiang thought this was what Etsudo wanted, they were trying to co-opt him. But what did Etsudo want?

Etsudo bit his lip. Another message from Deng arrived, only five minutes ping time behind them. What was that? Five wormholes?

"I've got another task for you, Etsudo. This ship is likely to dock at Bujantjor." Deng waved his left hand and a grainy image appeared of a woman standing in a busy market area.

"Who's that?" Etsudo wondered out loud, even as Deng continued on with his recording.

"This is a very dangerous woman, Etsudo. She uses the first name Nashara, but the last one changes. We know for sure that she killed a Gahe breeder on Astragalai. She may have also set off a nuclear bomb inside Villach. There may be some League of Human Affairs connection, we're not sure. She was last seen heading downstream towards us. Keep close to that pirate for now, but if they head past Bujantjor to Thule, let them go, we'll continue the chase. You stay in Bujantjor. Someone turned her in for reward money, a Len

Smith. See if you can get her aboard your ship. You claim to be good at this. We want her for questioning and reconditioning if you can. If not, we'll assist."

Etsudo looked at the picture.

"A nuclear bomb?" he whispered, impressed. Right in the heart of Gahe territory. She made Bahul look like a kitten.

He wanted her for his crew. Oh, yes. She'd make a pilot. Maybe even another captain, to balance Brandon. That would bring symmetry back. Three captains, three pilots, and so on. Twelve crew.

Etsudo rubbed the back of his hand. A bit of order could be dragged back into his chaotic world. That appealed to him.

CHAPTER NINE

The pirates bled speed coming out of the wormhole into Bujantjor, Etsudo shadowing them and reporting back on their movements. They did not move on to Thule, they docked at the new Freeman habitat. A mess of girder and metal, primitive by Satrapic standards, and one of the handfuls of human-only habitats starting to spring up throughout the forty-eight worlds.

"Lock down?" Anjelica asked, once they had docked. She hadn't shaved her head in a few days; the stubble covered her head roughly. She hadn't been sleeping.

"You know the routine. We can't risk the ship being compromised." Only Etsudo walked off or on. Redemption. One day they'd be allowed off, when they'd worked off their debt to humanity. Etsudo would see to that. But for now, they remained in their rooms.

They didn't complain.

They already had a request from Nashara to interview before even getting connected to the habitat. She offered her security services. Etsudo granted the interview.

"She'll be aboard soon," Etsudo said. "Is my cabin ready?"

"It is set for tea," Lee said. He bobbed his head down. "I laid out mats and a proper kettle."

Etsudo nodded back at him. "Thank you."

Excitement strummed through Etsudo. He almost hopped his way up through the ship to the docking air lock to wait. Deng might know him too well, giving this to him.

Was it a trap?

That made him pause. Maybe Brandon hadn't accomplished what Deng had hoped for, and this woman was here to finish the job.

Too far-fetched, he thought. But when she arrived and he opened the outer door, he still held his breath as she crossed through the air lock. He almost didn't let her in.

Underneath the epidermis the woman was more machine than man. Far from legal, and into theoretical-research territory. Did he detect a whiff of radiation? She had a tiny reactor buried somewhere deep in her body.

Etsudo couldn't help himself, he opened the air lock and stood there.

"Etsudo Hajiwara?"

He nodded. "Nashara." He didn't use the fake last name she'd supplied. He shook her hand. She had a dry, firm grip.

Those hands could break him in half, he realized with a smile.

"Would you care to have tea with me?" he asked. "And we will talk about your offer."

She nodded, dark eyes studying him. "Tea. Sure."

"Come." Etsudo led her toward the cabin. "It's just this way." His hands shook when he entered the room.

She followed him in. "Are you okay Etsudo? You don't seem together."

Of course, she was trained to spot lies. Trained to spot odd responses. "I don't let many people into my cabin, and I'm just a peaceful trader. You offer us your skills as a mercenary, but you make me nervous."

She cocked her head and frowned. No doubt something seemed off to her. So many dangerous people had walked into this room. Some of them were knocked out in the air lock, but Etsudo preferred the unmonitored cabin. The sooner the criminal was in the chair and bound, the safer he felt.

Etsudo waved her over. "I want to show you a picture of my father. The man who basically gave me this ship."

Nashara walked over. "Hajiwara? That's a Hongguo family name."

Etsudo gave the command via lamina to scramble her mind, and Nashara slumped forward. He tried to catch her, but pitched forward. She weighed two or three times as much as he expected. All the machinery laced throughout her.

Gods. Etsudo dragged her to the chair and wrapped her wrists and legs to the chair using the monofilament scarves.

She started to wake up as he did it. She head-butted his chest, knocking the air out of his lungs as he fell back. He gave the mental command to disrupt her neural activity before he even hit the mat behind him and she slumped back into the chair.

Etsudo sat back with a groan of triumph, holding his bruised chest and feeling a broken rib, and looked at the greatest mass murderer he'd trapped yet.

She was beautiful.

"Nashara, wake up." Etsudo kept his distance, pacing in front of her. Sweat beaded his forehead, and he'd ignored Deng's requests to talk about how he was going to capture her. He didn't want to share this. Deng might want her handed over. But if he did that, Etsudo would lose her when the Satraps used whatever tools they used to wipe minds to mold Nashara into another simple foot soldier. That would be a waste.

This was an interesting dilemma. He could talk Deng into letting him take her to a reconditioning facility. He could forge her reconditioning certificates. This was a risk, but a good one.

First he had to find out if she was another weapon Deng had sent against him like Brandon.

"Wake up," Etsudo repeated.

The dark eyes snapped open. "What did you do to me, Etsudo?"

"Do you trust me, Nashara?" Etsudo asked, his face honest, open. "Implicitly, fully? You'll answer just about anything I ask?" Of course she would. She was like any of his crew now.

"Yes." She looked annoyed and thoughtful. "But why?"

"Do you believe in redemption, Nashara?"

"I don't have much use for theology." She looked around the room, then down at the silk bonds. "Filament?"

"Yes. Don't move about." Etsudo crossed his legs on the floor before her. "Did Deng send you?"

"I don't know who the fuck Deng is."

"Are you sure?"

She looked at him with contempt. "Yes, I'm quite sure. What is going on?"

"I have a machine in this room that reprograms you. It's like what we do to get the zhen cha, I know that is no secret. But me and my machine are more subtle. I want you to stay you, with all your memories. I just change . . . some things. Make a better you. One that wants you to pay for your crimes, Nashara. Like the deaths of all those people on Villach."

Nashara nodded, pulling slightly at the scarves. "Only one problem, buddy. I have no crimes to confess."

"We know for sure you killed the Gahe breeder."

"Yes. I did that."

Etsudo cradled his chest. "You don't think that was a crime?"

"I'm under orders. It wasn't a crime, it was a mission." Nashara rested back into the chair. "I'm not a criminal, I'm a damn POW."

A mission? "Who are you on a mission for?" Etsudo asked.

"Chimson mongoose-men. Nashara Capsicum is the name I used there. Do you knock out all the girls you bring back here? Will I end up being your willing sex slave?" Her eyes glittered, and Etsudo wondered at what point even his artistic tweaks would fall apart. There was a coiled, snakelike danger here.

"I would never do that. What's a mongoose-man?"

"Think feng, but more deadly. We work for the Ragamuffins. They used to protect Chimson and New Anegada, before you took them off-line." Nashara twisted. Scoping out the room.

"What is your mission?"

"Deliver myself to the New Anegada Ragamuffins, if they are still working for the benefit of humanity. If they're not still worthy, then I'm to cause as much trouble as I can by myself. I'm a virus, for the Satrapic lamina." She smiled.

Etsudo's mouth dried up. "A virus."

"What were you going to do with me, Etsudo?"

He crumpled a bit. "I was going to try and keep you. You'd be my prize on this ship. The most dangerous yet. Now I think I'll leave you to Deng."

Unleash her to Deng.

"You want to destroy the Hongguo then? Is that it?" Nashara raised an eyebrow.

"Destroy?" Everything fell apart again, but instead of the instigator being Deng, it was this woman.

"Chimson knows about Honggou mindwipes. After a mindwipe I will reboot and slip into the lamina, just bereft of all my recent memories since I left Chimson. I eat lamina processing resources up and reproduce my mind over and over again until there is nothing left. Then the real fun starts."

Gods. What had he gotten into? Etsudo looked down at his feet. "My whole crew is like this."

"Like what?"

"I believe what my father put in my mind, what he believed, which is that the Hongguo help humanity keep its balance with the Satrapy. That we will lead our race to stand shoulder to shoulder with the other client races."

"You really believe it?"

Etsudo looked up and sighed. "I would have loved to have known you as a crewmember."

"Are you going to kill me?" Nashara looked at him, a steady gaze. "Look at me, Etsudo, don't even try to lie."

"No." And he wasn't. If he lied now or entertained the thought, she would see it. It would break that loyalty. She'd find a way right now to rip clear and kill him. He knew that with a certainty that shook him.

"Okay." Nashara relaxed. "I trust you. You're going to patch me up so I don't remember this and send me back out. Détente?"

Etsudo nodded, still staring directly at her. He snapped his fingers, and Nashara slumped.

When he woke her up, several hours later, he did it by walking through the door to the cabin with a full tea set.

"Sorry I forget the pot noodles in the galley," he said. Nashara nodded, looking around the cabin. He'd pulled her to the floor and left her cross-legged, sitting with her back against the wall. She'd gotten up and moved to the center of the room.

He let her eat, and when she put the chopsticks down, leaned across. "While I always enjoy the pleasure of an interesting guest, I will be honest and tell you we have no positions for a person of the, um, skills that you forwarded to me." He held out his hands, showing her rough calluses. "We work hard and are just a small crew. A ship's bodyguard, or security force, as you call yourself, is unnecessary to us." He smiled. "You must realize the *Takara Bune* is not in the habit of making enemies. That is not our way."

It was a peace offering, one that if she was ever somehow able to reaccess these memories he'd buried, she'd maybe understand.

She leaned forward. "Etsudo, we do not always choose to make enemies. Sometimes they come whether we create them or not."

He couldn't argue with that. He barely remembered what else they discussed. He grabbed his chest as they stood with a tiny gasp, then escorted her out.

Let Deng take her. Let her escape. He just wanted the danger she represented off his ship. She wasn't the order he wanted. She was chaos.

Etsudo all but limped back to his cabin. Once a place of refuge, it seemed a little more bare, a little more empty. He took several painkillers and checked with the cockpit.

"Sabir here," the pilot said.

"I'm taking a nap," Etsudo said. "Stall Deng, tell him the woman was too dangerous to try and knock out. We'll try later, under better conditions. Tell him to stay well clear of her." The last thing they needed was Deng setting her off.

If Deng tracked her, found when she was next taking a shuttle off the habitat, it would be worth lives to take her out.

Maybe. But how would Etsudo explain that?

If he gave her time, maybe she would escape Deng. Or maybe he wanted the Hongguo to deal with her unawares and fail. Had he let her go because of that?

Etsudo washed his face and hung his head under the flowing tap while he tried to wrap his mind around what had just happened. Running water, always an intermittent luxury for spacers.

He curled up by the vacuum sink. The painkillers kicked in. Etsudo pressed the back of his head against the wall and started to drift toward sleep as he turned things over in his mind. Where did his loyalty lie? The Hongguo, or humanity, or himself? What trumped what? How could he tell what to do? His father had buried the Hongguo oath into him: service to mankind. But then he'd buried loyalty to the Hongguo into him as well. It felt as if he could rip himself in two. And always, always was the knowledge that he needed fuel. The Satraps controlled the fuel, and without that, he was nothing.

It was Sabir who woke him up, an insistent whisper in his right ear from the cockpit.

"Captain! Deng wants to talk to you, right now! Etsudo!"

Waking up felt like climbing out of a pit. "What? What does he want?"

"The woman, Deng tried to capture her."

Etsudo pulled himself up. "What happened?"

"They tried to capture her and she escaped. There are dead zhen cha and feng all over the place."

Etsudo rubbed his face, clearing the artificial sleep away. "I'm on my way. Unconnect us from the habitat. Get ready to leave." If Deng was going to take it out on him, they'd have to run. He wasn't sure, but the more time went by, the more the idea of running appealed. If there were people like Nashara out there, then maybe there could be room for him.

Maybe.

So many maybes.

Etsudo let Deng's request for a live session trickle through. He braced himself.

"She escaped," Deng said. A simple statement. "Did your sensors detect that she was equipped to handle exposure to vacuum."

Yes, they had. "My sensors picked up nothing like that. She seemed well trained and dangerous, too dangerous for me to pick up."

Deng nodded. "A wise move. I'm sorry to have doubted your analysis. I had thought it would be an easy pickup while we covered the area to get ready for the pirates."

"And?"

"She fled to them. There seems to be a connection of some sort. The Ragamuffin ship just blew its dock seals and is clear of the habitat, they have the drop on us."

"Why didn't you destroy it?"

"Near a habitat? Etsudo, I'm not putting lives at risk. These people haven't disobeyed any Satrapic edicts we know of. If the ship flees in open space, we'll fight it. At dock, we'll use feng. We won't fire on it at dock."

"Okay, but where can they go?" Etsudo heard the hissing and clanging of his ship disconnecting from the lifelines of the habitat. They were on their own power and air again.

"Not upstream," Deng said. "Fifty ships are coming down from Thule towards us. Nowhere to run upstream. With the buoys out they'll probably guess this. I think they will try and turn back downstream, avoiding the handful of ships around, and get warnings to the others at their home base, but they didn't get a chance to fuel up here."

"So?" The *Takara Bune* shivered as the habitat's clamps released her. Several sirens squawked, letting him know that the antimatter heart of the ship had come online.

"You're going to have to keep up with them again, Etsudo. Help us close this net, help us end the pirates and gain the good grace of the Satrapy. Do that and we promote you to Jiang. Do that and we know where your loyalties lie."

"So they are in doubt?" Etsudo asked.

"You ply upstream, downstream, wherever you feel. You are part of an older generation that is obsolete within the current Hongguo. But you are good, Etsudo. Very good. And we need you. You are right, I can't order you to do anything. But your actions will mean a lot."

Jiang Etsudo. Etsudo rolled the idea around in his head. "Sabir, where do we stand?"

"Free and clear."

Etsudo looked back at Deng. "We'll pursue. You follow." Nashara would be less a threat dead out in the cold vacuum. Whether he chose to run or not, that would be the truth. If she really was a virus, she could destroy the communications systems between the forty-eight worlds. Even if the Hongguo and Satrapy controlled them, they were a lifeline to civilization.

Jiang Etsudo . . .

Deng flickered away. Etsudo reached the cockpit, floating now. Inside it, Sabir, Todd, and Raul looked at him as he entered. "Where's Brandon?"

"He's in his cabin, he wasn't sure how to break shifts with you," Sabir said.

"Get him in here," Etsudo said. "We'll both be in the cockpit for this. Sound acceleration alarms, everyone needs to be strapped in and secure."

"The ship is the same one we saw earlier," Sabir said. "The pirate ship. It used the name *Queen Mohmbasa* when it docked."

"We'll use that to identify her." Etsudo added the tag. The cockpit dripped with lamina, screens, trajectories, notes from the Port Authority demanding to know why they were leaving dock without formal permission.

Etsudo swept it all away.

Time to focus on one thing for now, keeping up with the *Queen Mohmbasa*. Because the Hongguo would not mindwipe a helpful ally in its new war, nor deny him fuel for his ship.

They might even promote him.

CHAPTER TEN

Kara and her brother watched the slow sunset. The inside of Agathonosis curved up on either side of them. The patchy green farmlands rose until they met far up above them. Agathonosis was shaped like a can, with the brilliant fusion-powered thread of the sunline running right through the weightless center to provide the light the crops so desperately needed.

Night began slowly at the far end of the cylinder, a dark bead that appeared on the line as it came out of the haze and then began to grow. The line slowly turned off, a half-mile section at a time slowly dimming, until flickering out. It had started at the far end cap of Agathonosis, almost ten miles away from them. It would continue until it reached the other end, ten more miles farther behind them.

On the walls of Agathonosis you could walk and feel heavy, but near the sunline at the center of Agathonosis, you could fly. As long as you didn't get close enough to the sunline to burn. The sunline mainly provided light and the right kind of it, not heat. Heat came from the ground in vents or warm pools of water.

Then came the sound, carrying in the approaching twilight. Mortar fire?

Kara stopped and turned, trying to locate where the sound had come from. A puff of smoke drifted over a muddy hill. She grabbed her brother, Jared, and pulled him down to the ground, then used the zoom function in her eyes to peek out from behind a false decorative rock that shifted as she pushed against it.

Several hundred yards down the drying trickle of the Parvati River, fifteen self-styled "hopolites" broke cover. Green strips of ripped cloth hung from their skeletal bodies.

Kara thought she recognized a few faces in the group. Maybe one of them had sold her an ice cream cone once or bumped into her on a public trail somewhere. Maybe it was a cousin of hers, or an uncle, running down to the edge of the muddy water.

They carried their weapon with them, slipping and sliding in the mud as they crossed over to the opposite bank. The mortar looked homemade: several pieces of scrap welded to the bottom of a tube to create a makeshift tripod. Maybe it had been someone's potato gun at one time, or a teenager's launch tube for a model gyroplane. Now it was a weapon of desperation.

The hopolites settled behind the ruins of what had once been a boat dock near the bank of the Parvati. Jared sat up slightly and Kara put her arm on his shoulder. "No," she whispered.

She remained focused and zoomed on the muddy river.

A series of footprints appeared near the far edge, as if by magic, slowly tracking toward the hopolites as they loaded their homemade mortar. A long-haired man in nothing but trousers sighted and gave the thumbs-up.

The mortar thunked. The projectile arced upward leaving a slight trail of smoke. Up, up, Kara and her brother craned their necks looking straight above them to watch until it dwindled into a small dot against the great brown patches that curved far over their heads. The other side of their world right above their heads. It made Kara shiver, thinking of explosions and weaponry being fired all throughout the habitat. Already the air seemed hard to breathe. She wondered if that was due to the great machinery in the depths of Agathonosis failing, or if war had broken the world's skin. She'd never seen the Outside of Agathonosis nor been inside the world's skin, but she could imagine the cruel midnight of vacuum shoving its airless emptiness through the cracks of the world, curling into the sky to snatch the air away from them all.

One of the hopolites carried a telescope, she saw. He looked through it intently, then shouted. Kara thought she saw a small flash, a tiny orange ball of flame, on the land far over her head.

A hushed cheer erupted. Yet there was nothing happy in the sound. It was a vindictive-sounding group whoop, cut short by several small spitting sounds. A second pair of invisible feet splashed through the mud.

Kara dug her fingers into Jared's bony shoulders and stared past him at the chaos behind him. "Oww . . ."

"Quiet, it's the stratatoi," she hissed.

The hopolites scattered and ran. Four of them fell to the ground, one of them writhing and screaming. Bright red splotches of blood dripped from his forehead.

Oh, no. One of them zigzagged, running straight toward her. She unzoomed her lenses, looked around.

"Come on." She pulled Jared along, slowly, very slowly, backing into the dried-up remains of an oak tree that had toppled over. This had once been a gravity-defying copse of oaks. It was now a tortured, surreal nightmare of dead trunks and burned stumps gathered around a failing river. Stomach acid burned at Kara as fear and hunger ate its way up out of her.

"In here again?" Jared complained. They sat underneath the bleached, twisted branches and looked out. Jared hugged their knapsack to his chest, though his bony arms offered it little protection.

The hopolite staggered on, coated in mud. He panted, arms flailing to keep balance. Jared squirmed, but Kara pushed him down and kept him from looking out.

Branches slapped them in the face as something jumped and ran down the length of the trunk. Jared whimpered, and Kara covered his mouth as a mud-covered ghost grabbed the hopolite, threw him to the ground.

Kara strained the lenses over her eyes at the ghost. Despite the Catastrophe, despite the famine, the world of Agathonosis itself still responded to her. The air sang information. Kara could still choose to augment anything she saw with her actual, organic eyes with information overlaid onto them with her implants. The standard public lamina appeared to her: a small triangular tag popped into her vision every time she looked at the tree. Information scrolled at her.

Oak tree 23. Planted the third year of the Evthria's [the "eastern" side of Agathonosis, click for more] founding by the first human president under the benevolent Satrapy. Commemoration . . . It would have scrolled more information, but Kara killed the blather with a mental wave of the hand.

Any moron youngster in Agathonosis with a pair of data contacts or a wrist screen could see that particular lamina.

She had something else in mind: her own augmented reality. It would let her tap into a private lamina. It was something darker, more useful, encrypted and never spoken about because it was forbidden, as was any human addition or tinkering with the Satrapic Information Systems.

"Remember," her mother had said before the stratatoi came for her and Dad. She'd crouched by Kara and run her fingers through Kara's hair. "Things might get better. This might be temporary. So you only use this if it is an emergency!"

Kara had nodded. "I understand."

"Take Jared with you if that happens, and don't talk to anyone. You know the drill, we've gone over it enough. We'll be back. We'll see what the Satrap says about this. We have to try to petition it. We can't let this go on."

Her parents had been archaeologists. They'd studied the lamina, sometimes illegally, digging back down into the tiniest bits that talked and made it work. They were the most known lamina explorers in Agathonosis, well re-

spected. They'd hoped their position would help influence the Satrap to fix
the world and stop the stratatoi.

But they'd never come back.

And things had gotten worse. And worse.

So now Kara triggered the filter her mom and dad had created. When *that*
filter came down over the world, the artificial rods and cones in her eyes
painted very different things.

The ghost, the invisible man, appeared to her outlined in reds and oranges.
She watched the man raise a large weapon, point the barrel at the hopolite's
forehead, and pull the trigger. The hopolite's head exploded, fragments dripping to the ground. Kara looked down at the mud.

Jared squirmed. She grabbed his hand and squeezed as hard as she could.
He understood and froze. Kara's fingers waved a quick mantra to execute the
code the whole family had worked on in secret when the troubles had begun.
The invisible man turned, looked right at them. His face twisted, a rictus of
heat lines.

Now you know, thought Kara. Now you know if it works. There's always
info around. Like air, but more pervasive even. Info gathered by nearby sensors under the ground, in the remains of the tree, built into the very fabric of
Agathonosis on a molecular scale. Infodust hanging in the air, testing the
ecology of the habitat. Information gathered, reformatted, and presented to
her when she asked for it.

She'd accessed lamina all around her since she was a kid, seeing things that
weren't really there with her contacts on, playing games with other children
that other people weren't a part of. The world was always more mysterious,
more layered, deeper, than it would have been without the various lamina
they all used.

And the invisible killer staring right at her would see *nothing* of her because
he used the lamina too. Like all stratatoi he got orders, maps, plans of attack,
and info from his fellow murderers through *his* augmented reality. Kara's private lamina had been developed slowly over three hundred years, exploiting
small bugs in the meshes of realities the Satrapy had created inside Agathonosis. Kara's parents were descended from a long line of tweakers who had carved
out some small freedoms for themselves from the ever present and powerful eye
of the Satrapy. Such as invisibility to allow them to gather and hold meetings.

They'd thought that one special, but it looked as if the stratatoi had it as
well.

She let out a deep breath as the invisible man turned around and ran back toward the homemade mortar.

"Go," she ordered Jared.

He obeyed her, slowly crawling out and skirting the oak tree with her.

They left the river. Kara didn't think it was safe anymore. More stratatoi had appeared. They were securing the water, she guessed. Turning off the river's pumps. That hadn't been in short supply yet, and the Parvati was muddy, but apparently they wanted control of that too.

Like everything else inside Agathonosis.

Kara returned her vision to normal unaugmented reality as they walked out of the brown wastes of the public park and into a series of alleyways. The park reeked of urine, and it was worse here. Perfectly recyclable sewage oozed out of the gutters, piss stains splattered the paper walls of houses. Many maiche walls drooped, ripped off in the first rounds of riots. The houses revealed the insides of rooms and apartments. Frames poked through like skeletons.

A dead neighborhood. Flayed.

They passed houses with roofs that sagged from recent rain. *Rain.* In what had been a perfectly controlled ecosphere. It had all gone so wrong so quickly. Agathonosis had been a paradise. Lakes near great forests that had trees reaching up, unhindered, and less and less constrained by gravity as they grew taller. Sure they were somewhat crooked from Coriolis forces, but at those heights, you couldn't tell if it they were bent or just *tall*.

Now Agathonosis was a festering disaster.

An occasional face peeked out from a hole in the walls, then disappeared.

"Can we stop and eat?" Jared asked. Too loud. Idiot ten-year-old kid. And all she had left. She hadn't talked to any of her peers or seen her parents in weeks.

"Shhh. We're not far from where we need to be," she whispered. Don't mention food, Brother. Damnit.

The air-lock door lay just around the next small alley, down underneath a manhole cover. Air locks would lead them into the skin of Agathonosis, into the heart of the Satrap's traditional domain, but also to freedom.

She hoped.

Kara double-checked a heads-up map display in her personal lamina, looking around at markers and tags. She looked back down the street, at the good soil running down the gutters washing off into the storm grates, and heard something rustle.

"Open the manhole cover," she ordered Jared.

He looked piteously at her. "You make me do everything. Carry the—"

"Do it," she hissed at him. "The sooner we get there, the sooner you can eat."

Her temple hurt as she concentrated. I am a shadow, she thought. Just a shadow. She backed up against the plastic frame of an alley wall, tiptoed, and waited as Jared grunted and yanked at the manhole cover.

She slit the paper with a pocketknife and stepped through. She sealed it back up with several tiny pins fished out from her pocket and looked around. A few weeks ago this was someone's apartment. A dead woman lay on the bed, the back of her head staved in. Spoiled cans of fish lay underneath the bed.

The manhole cover rustled outside. Jared grunted, then paused. "Kara? Are you sure we're allowed to do this? This goes *in*."

Someone had tried to eat the cans of fish, then thrown up.

"Kara? Where are you? Please don't leave me. I'm sorry. I won't complain again."

Kara cut two small eyehole slits and watched the street as Jared turned around in a slow circle, looking for her. She could hear muffled sobs. Kara swallowed the lump in her throat, squeezed her wet eyes.

Sorry, Brother, she thought.

After another moment of crying Jared stopped, looked with a few sniffles, then unslung the knapsack and unzipped it. Kara looked down the street and saw what she'd been fearing: a wiry man with a bat walked down along the torn paper wall toward Jared.

She waited, waited until the man's shadow crossed the paper in front of her, then burst out with the penknife. She stabbed him in the back with the four-inch-long blade as hard as she could, thrusting at his shadow through long, ragged strips of paper wall. The blade sunk in with a sickening puncturing sound and her victim screamed. He backhanded her, reaching up for the knife.

Jared sat and stared as Kara sprang off the ground. The man got hold of the knife and screamed again as he pulled it out.

"Get in the manhole, quickly." Kara grabbed the backpack and zipped it. Jared looked up at her in something approaching awe. And fear.

They clambered down the ladder into the skin of their world, aiming for the hull.

"Faster," she ordered her little brother. Neither of them had the strength to replace the manhole cover from inside. Soon someone would come after them. Either the man she'd stabbed, or someone else noticing the racket.

It was quiet down here. And sterile, like the inside of a house, but on and on and on. No natural sounds, just a steady thrum. Biolights ran along a track on the floor and a strip over their heads. The smoothly bored rock walls with metallic vacuumseal sprayed on were physically painted blue with red or green numerals indicating where they were, just as Kara had hoped.

Stratatoi would soon realize they had intruders in the heart of their domain, inside the warrens and corridors honeycombing the great hull of the world. She had mumbled the words to shut down the telltales inside her that would report where she was, but she wasn't sure she had done such a good job on Jared. Thankfully they couldn't see through his eyes; she'd taken his contacts out the day the Catastrophe had fully realized itself.

Kara kept Jared moving with expert shoves and a kick or two. He stumbled a lot. Eventually he sat down, refusing to go farther.

"We're lost," he cried.

"No, we're not," Kara snapped. Then, softer: "I know where we are. Trust me."

"We're lost and *they're* going to find us." Jared clutched the sack.

If they stayed here, giving up, then, yes. Kara grabbed his arm and squeezed it. "You get back up or that man will come after us and kill us for sure. I can leave you here for him." Jared got back up. "Keep going straight," Kara said, her voice cracking.

Somehow he'd forgive her. For know, she just wanted to make sure he lived. Her little brother was all she had left.

They went deeper in, following mental maps. Twice she used her invisibility trick to avoid stratatoi walking the corridors. She would hold a hand over Jared's mouth, lean against the cold wall, and freeze. The stratatoi were looking for something. She hoped it wasn't them.

Jared's stomach growled loudly enough for her to hear several times. She wondered if that would give them away at some crucial point.

They finally got to it: a small access door leading to what looked like a utility room. Kara stood and stared at it for a second, looking at a tag that told her the door was more than it seemed. She walked forward and kissed the cold metal.

Did the stratatoi know about this place? Her parents had found the location when digging around ancient hand-drawn pictures from the original colonists, the pireties. History was frowned on but protected by the general Emancipation. People like her mom and dad pieced together what they could from records hidden deep in human-made lamina. And they'd found this alternate control room. The primary control room had been destroyed in a suicidal fight between the hopolites and the stratatoi two weeks ago when the hopolite insurrection against the habitat's Satrap began. The hopolites had slowly been exterminated ever since. The Satrap was rumored to have moved into the secondary control center and reinforced it with hordes of stratatoi.

But the great engineers who had designed Agathonosis did so in triplicate.

When Kara convinced the first door to open, her breath caught. The doors were several feet thick, not the standard utility inch that they seemed to be. They groaned loudly, echoing through the corridors as they opened, one after the other.

"In, in, now!"

They ran in, sideways, squeezing themselves into a twenty-by-twenty-foot room. Dusty control panels ringed the entire room, and several chairs with illegal neural jacks sat in a corner.

"Jackpot," Kara whispered, even as she spoke the riddles and poems to close the two sets of doors behind them. She started crying. "Jackpot."

She'd been a zombie until now, just focused on getting here, hoping to make it, doing anything to make it.

The doors sealed behind them. She walked over and started waving panels into life. Jared looked at a display that showed the outside corridor.

"When they come for us, we won't be able to get back out," he said, furrowing his brow. "There's only one way out."

"I know."

"How long can we stay in here?"

Kara unsealed the knapsack and helped Jared lay out the contents. "A few days," she said. "That's long enough. Long enough for someone to reach us."

The can of beans made her salivate just looking at the picture. She also took out several dried, salted small fish, and some crackers in packets.

And a dirty cloth doll, with red, clumpy hair. Jared snatched it away.

"Can I eat?" Jared stared at the can of beans and licked his lips. His hands trembled.

"The fish."

Kara handed them to him and packed the crackers and beans away. Jared needed protein right now. But more than anything they were both going to need fruit soon enough. She was pretty sure he was getting scurvy. Or maybe a half dozen other types of malnutrition problems.

Jared took the fish off to a corner and began eating, smacking his lips noisily in a way that, several months ago, she would have hit him for. And the doll, that Raggedy Andy doll, she would have snatched it from him.

But that was all *he* had now, and he clutched the doll protectively under an arm.

She turned to the panel by the door, put her thumb to it, and the corners of her mouth tugged up. When the stratatoi came to the doors, trying to shoot or hack their way in, they'd find she'd locked them shut with some old security codes. Ones that would only allow the doors to open from an inside command.

Then the smile disappeared under a huge mental load of weariness. Oral human history maintained that Agathonosis was a cylindrical, man-made world that flew in circles around several giant holes in the Outside, holes that led to other worlds like Agathonosis, and some vastly larger. So large that they were inside out, with the air lying on the outside of the world. Kara started trying to figure out how to send a message out at the "wormhole" and to someone who could maybe save them.

Several hours later a series of relays around Kara's small world caught her audio message. The message used hundred-year-old protocols, but the relays still recognized them. They'd been stolen from someone who'd once worked communications for the Satrapy, and the thief had made sure to bury them into the lamina as deeply as he could, in case they were ever needed again.

The relays dutifully started spreading the message forward, until it hit a communications buoy near the wormhole. The message started out spoken in Greek, the language of Agathonosis, and ended in stumbling Anglic:

This is Kara, from Agathonosis.

We're starving. They're killing each other inside.

Please send help, whoever hears this. We only have days left.

Oh, shit. Stratatoi have found us. Can they really stop me from . . .

The beacon followed its instructions and kept repeating the message to anything that would listen.

CHAPTER ELEVEN

Kara pressed her fingers against the knapsack's seal and it puckered open. A single can of beans and half a pack of protein-fortified crackers. She stared at them for a minute, then chose the crackers.

She resealed the sack before Jared could turn around and see how little food was left and slung the knapsack over her back so he couldn't try to open it. They'd filled several bottles with water from the tap in the small bathroom, but the water had been turned off now, and the stench of the unflushed toilet was getting worse.

Jared still had his back to her. He sat facing the inner door, shivering at the constant high-pitched whine coming through. He jumped slightly every time something clanged against the outer door.

"I hate you," he said.

He knew they were trapped. He probably suspected they were almost out of food and that the water wouldn't last that much longer.

Kara sighed, but not loud enough to let him hear. She walked over to a flat console and waved it on. It glowed alive and became a window to the area just outside the door. Fifteen stratatoi in black uniforms struggled to control the massive bulk of a diamond-tipped drillcar. Dusty, corroded, and old, the insectlike machine hailed from the earliest days of Agathonosis's creation when the habitat was still just a rock in the Outside. The hundreds of counterrotating bits chewed at the door, spitting and sparking metal shavings aside.

Dark gouges ran back along the corridor behind them where they had shoved the drill through, spinning and spitting all the way.

"See," Jared said. "You were wrong. They'll get in here soon. We should give up now."

Kara reached out a hand, then put it back down at her side. "I don't think they would let us give up."

Jared bit his lip. "It smells really bad in here. I want to get out."

There is no out, she wanted to scream at him. Even if we leave, the whole world is like this, another room, just bigger, and everything is broken there too. But she nodded. "I know. Just trust me and be patient, please."

"I want my eyepieces back. I'm bored just waiting. At least let me play some games."

Kara shook her head. Jared clenched his fists, opened his mouth, then stopped. The room had fallen silent.

They both looked at the console. The drillcar had been rolled back off to the side and a new entourage of black-uniformed stratatoi walked toward Kara's screen. Kara could hear the tiny fans and pumps deep inside the vents now that the drilling stopped. The comfortable universal hum of Agathonosis hung around her once more.

A single stratatoi walked all the way forward until he stood just beneath the camera. He filled the entire view, standing up on some platform Kara hadn't noticed. His eyes gleamed in the reflected light around him.

The man held up a blank white pad. Kara had turned off all outside feeds but this one visual to the outside. When his lips moved no sound came through. But the pad he held up blurred and words formed. The man held the pad up to the camera so Kara could read the words.

Whatever I speak will be written on this pad. I am both this man Nikos and I am the Satrap himself at this moment, as I have taken personal interest in this situation.

Kara shivered. She'd only heard about such a thing happening in the days of Thrall, when the Satraps used the power of the world to break men's minds to their will. Men had worked ceaselessly for the Satrapy for generations before they were emancipated, though the Satrap of Agathonosis still carefully ruled its world. Had the days of Thrall returned?

The puppet man's mouth moved again and the pad shifted to display new words:

Your time is limited. I can cut the air supply to an entire section of this world, the section that includes the line this room taps. But if you open the lock and surrender, you will be treated with mercy. If you wish to negotiate, speak to me within the next thirty seconds.

The Satrap could use audio to send commands to the inside of the room. Kara knew it could; after all, it was said that the Satraps had created the lamina all around them. They'd created everything that *was* Agathonosis, even if the physical things had been made by the stratatoi in the days of Thrall. Talking to it would be dangerous.

Jared read the note and shouted at her, "They can't turn off the air, can they? Can they?"

"I don't know." Kara listened to the mechanical hum of air being delivered. It had never been held from the people before. Even in the days of

Thrall. But then maybe what she knew of the past was wrong. She leaned against the panel and stared down at the ruler of her entire world and trembled. "It's the Satrap, and the Satrap can do almost anything, can't he?"

"Then we need to give up now, we really need to give up."

Kara sniffed, just as frightened as he was. But she couldn't show it. "Be quiet, Jared. Let me think." She bit her lip so hard she tasted salty blood. Then she stabbed at the console. "If you are the Satrap, then why did it all go bad?" she demanded, her voice cracking and wavering. "Why are so many dead, and the world not working? The world is under your command, why isn't it working?"

The man's mouth worked some more in silence. Kara tapped the console. "The sound only works one way, from me to you. You'll still need to use the pad."

It looked down, then raised the pad toward them again.

The world does not work because I wish it not to. Humans have been warned to keep their population in check, but have failed. Humans have been warned to not meddle with the systems of the Satrapy, but cannot refrain from tinkering. Humans want more freedom to self-organize, travel, and consume, and the resources of all the Satrapic worlds cannot sustain these abuses. The Satrapy has come to the decision that there is to be a population reduction. Humans are incapable of managing this themselves. Only thralls will be left to do our work. The Emancipation of humanity has been revoked.

Words did not come. Kara's mouth was dry, her heart sped. *They were no longer free?*

"We may no longer be free in the Satrapy, but we can still flee," she said. There were others out there. Kara's people had little contact with outsiders, trapped in the other Satrapic worlds. But she knew there were other Satraps in other worlds, and that the Satraps ruled all worlds. Humans had been taken from *somewhere*, and there had to be more . . . there had to be somewhere safe.

But now Kara understood why people had been rounded up by the stratatoi, and why the starving few adults left fought to the death. Those who didn't fight were no longer human, but now extensions to the Satrap's mind. Including her parents.

She imagined other Satrapic worlds, far away outside in a vacuum of their own, where this same battle was being fought.

The pad's words shifted again. *Fleeing is pointless. Humanity's status as a protected race has been revoked throughout the Benevolent Satrapy. But I have a deal for you if you surrender the control room now. You are obviously intelligent and quick to have done this. I would offer you a prime position among the strata-toi, a position of leadership, free cognition, and very little Thrall. Very few will get this status.*

Why was the Satrap bothering to confront her? Kara leaned in closer to the image, trying to see if the body of the man was blocking something, and looked deeper into the Satrap's eyes. They were blinking. The reflected light in them wavered somehow.

No. They transmitted light.

Kara slapped the console off. She spun around the room, threw open links to check everything around her, desperately hoping she hadn't given it enough time. Stupid, stupid, stupid.

"What's going on?" Jared asked.

Most of the status glyphs hanging in the air came back green. Even after probing several levels deep, she couldn't discern anything.

"Kara? Why'd you shut him off?"

"He tried to hack in. Some kind of light code, using his eyes." The Satrap wanted them dead quicker than he could starve them of oxygen. Why?

The only thing Kara could think of was communications. She'd sent a general message out into the Void. Was that what had spooked the Satrap about her?

It felt right.

She created another link to the system she'd used before. But instead of making a link that would skip outward beyond them, it bounced back from a point several hundred miles outside the world.

Repeater buoy closed to all outgoing traffic, the denial read.

But she could still call out to anything near the world. Maybe that worried the Satrap, that someone would check out her previous message, and that she could still talk to them.

Kara was still mulling it over when she noticed a lack of noise. Jared walked with her over to a vent.

"How long can we last without fresh air?" he asked.

"Two days." A wild guess at best.

"Are we going to give up now?"

"Do you want become thrall to the Satrap, just one of his many mental hands? A thing?" The Satrap's offer didn't give her hope. It had to be a lie. And if it wasn't . . . she couldn't imagine living to see the next age of Thrall.

Jared looked down at the floor, eyes watering. "No, but I don't want to die either."

"I know, Jared. I know." Neither did she.

When she next checked the outside, the screen showed only an empty corridor.

Empty of air as well, no doubt.

CHAPTER TWELVE

The bulkhead doors throughout *Queen Mohmbasa* all thudded shut simultaneously.

"Commence departure prep," a toneless warning protocol advised the entire ship.

Nashara stirred. The orientation of the walls shifted, the floor ceased being, and all sense of up and down floated away. She twisted around and put a foot to the blue wall on her left.

The ship's engine groaned. The walls vibrated, the air around her hummed, and the inside of Nashara's head pounded. Gently the blue wall became the new floor as the ship accelerated.

She stood and looked around, still a bit wobbly.

The door hissed open.

"You up?" the man at the door said. He stood five feet eight, with lithe musculature under well-fitting industrial-templated paper coveralls. Graying dreads hung around his head and the tangle of his beard. Two polished sticks hung from either side of a brown belt.

"Barely." Nashara blinked as the shivering stopped. The man adjusted himself so that he hung in the air before her.

Another automatic warning filled the cabin: "Lane approach. Acceleration in five minutes." The world shifted, orientation and gravity falling away from her.

"The captain want see you." The sound of the New Anegadan dialect relaxed her. At least one thing about Ragamuffins hadn't changed.

Nashara pushed off toward him. "Okay."

The dreadlocked man slapped the doorframe and floated clear. He held a palm-sized gun aimed at her. And he kept at least ten feet clear of her.

Tension. Even in friendly territory.

He directed her downshaft. Or at least Nashara assumed so. Even, vertical shafts; odd, horizontal. Assuming the cylindrical body of the ship accelerated along a lengthwise axis.

Nashara held up her wrist screen, but nothing appeared. She'd been shut of the ship's lamina. Odd.

"What's your name?" Nashara kept the comfortable double body-length between them for his comfort. She looked back at her toes. "I can't access any ship information."

He flipped a lone dreadlock out of the way and kept the pistol aimed dead at her. His hazel-brown eyes waited for any sudden movement. "Ijjy."

"Ijjy?"

"Ian Johnson if you looking up official records. Ijjy to me friend them."

"Okay, Ijjy."

"Lady, you ain't no friend." Nothing in those eyes for her. Not annoyance, hatred, friendliness.

Nashara turned back around to face the direction they coasted in. "Okay, Ian."

They passed on in silence. The *Mohmbasa's* corridors here screamed age. Warped bulkheads with airtight doors that didn't even shut properly. Bits of corroded metal flaked off and floated in the air near faded lettering. Access panels with hastily patched fiber optics and conductives remained open, exposing the ship's guts.

But the next section's damage wasn't age. Fresh emergency sealant. Corridor after corridor saw great gobs of the gooey, gray stuff that had hardened just after being pulled this way and that by gloved hands of some emergency crew. They had attempted to get the ship airtight again as the expanding goop solidified. The ship had suffered a major disaster to have sealant patching almost every hullside wall for the past several hundred feet.

She realized why the silence bothered her.

"Where is everyone?" A ship like the *Mohmbasa* had several hundred living aboard it. If it was Raga, whole families lived aboard.

Ijjy looked over at the hasty repairs. "That the least of what all happen. The other side the ship even worse. Only ten percent of the *Queen* airtight. The rest . . ." He shrugged.

"Survivors?"

The tired brown eyes again. Not patient, or waiting for her to move. Something far more hollow. "Gone. Just three now."

Nashara looked back at the tortured goop. "What in the hell have I got myself into?"

"A whole lot more shit than what you running from."

The *Queen Mohmbasa's* captain was cyborged out and looked as if he hadn't slept in days. Or maybe longer. Extra head-casing gleamed in the dull light of the cockpit, high-bandwidth optical jacks ran up the side of his left arm. No doubt he was as much a mechanical human as an organic human. The type of captain that only a ship could slowly create over the decades, influencing him to keep adding more and more features to himself to become more a part of what he controlled.

He looked her over with one dilated eye; the other remained half-closed and reflecting tiny images bounced off the back of the retina. Nashara would bet that this man never left the confines of the ship's immediate lamina. Getting cut off from the cloud of data that filled and brimmed out of the ship would be like losing half his mind.

But the rest of him was mahogany, and if not for the head casing, he would have had beautiful curled hair.

"Hello, Nashara," he said. Just in those words she could hear a strong upper-Anglic accent, smooth, but still with traces of the standard Raga dialect. "You say you are Raga?"

"You took a DNA sample off me, you tell me." They faced each other in the spherical cockpit of the *Mohmbasa*, deep within the center of the ship. The captain's chair hung from the top of the cockpit. "So you know who I am. Who are you?"

Nashara hung off one of the rails crisscrossing through the cockpit chamber. Wood trim decorated several of the four stations arranged equidistantly from the captain. An incredible luxury if real, and Nashara suspected that it was. The Ragamuffins remembered the islands on Earth that they came from.

The captain smiled. He palmed a small vial from the pocket of his black overalls and nudged it through the air at her. "I am the Captain Jamar Sinjin Smith of *Queen Mohmbasa*."

"Pleased." Nashara snagged the vial out of the air and pocketed it. "Thanks for giving me my DNA back."

Jamar held out his hand and twisted it to let the light catch the optical jacks. Green flesh rotted between implant and skin. "Aboard ship one doesn't get much exposure to infectious environments, particularly if you're born into it. The ship's pharma was destroyed, and we're out of vitamin supplements, plasma, super antibiotics, and antifungals. Half an hour more and we would have had those aboard thanks to sympathizers in that habitat. But more importantly," and each of his words became a calm whipcrack, "and I hope you understand this, your intrusion represents an even more fundamental problem for us in that we were never able to refuel." He crossed his arms and regarded her.

Nashara returned the gaze just as calmly. "I'm sorry for the inconvenience."

"Why are they after you? What have you done?" Jamar twisted and leaned in closer to her. "And what do you want out of us?"

Nashara nodded. "No dancing around with you. Yes, I am Blood. I could order you around. I could take your ship. But I don't want your ship. I'd rather not cause any trouble with you, but I had to make some kind of choice. I'm dodging the Hongguo. If we outrun them, drop me at the next station. I'll melt right back into the crowd. If we can't outrun them, you can toss me out the air lock and make a getaway."

He sat and thought about the latter, she could tell. She sped her heart up and felt the fizzing rush of oxygen burst through her again. She sucked in a deep breath of air and calmed herself down. "If we dock again, I can even get you some of the medicines you need again."

"It isn't that simple." Jamar shook his head. "They're after us too. More than likely if we shove you out the air lock, they'll still come after the ship first, then go back for you. Or they'd split up."

"Split up?" Nashara looked back at him with newfound respect. "More than one Hongguo ship's chasing you?"

Jamar nodded. "Four or five midsized ships downstream. I'd feel accurate in guessing that more are coming down our way from Thule. It's a logical choke point, but we can't be sure since the blackout. We gave the others a black eye. They didn't expect our maneuverability. The *Shengfen Hao*, the fellows you got to deal with, is more savvy. That ship's still with us."

"What have you done?" Petty smuggling got Port Authority or individual habitat security forces after you. Maybe even bounty hunters. Hongguo only got involved in development issues. "Passing on very illegal technology outside the Satrap's control?"

"Your DNA indicates that you are not just Raga, but Blood, Nashara." Upper-class Raga, descended from the great founder of the Black Starliner Corporation, yes, Nashara thought. And a bit more than just descendant. Direct clone of the founder as well, with all the baggage that came with that. More baggage she didn't want from the men who had single-handedly created Chimson and New Anegada. But it got their attention, which was just what Nashara's creators wanted.

Jamar waved his hand, and her wrist screen lit up. She'd been let into the ship's world. "This is just a higgler ship. Traders and sellers. We have no weapons. Since Chimson and New Anegada's wormholes got cut off, we've just been scraping by out in space. No base of operations, really. Ragamuffins?

All we are is a habitat and some ships. Mostly we are left alone if we stay quiet. So understand the importance of this: the Hongguo hunt my ship because they're hunting all Ragamuffins now. I'm pretty sure the Satrapy wants us wiped out."

Ragamuffin ships smuggled anything black market, as well as a shitload of illegal tech. Nothing new there.

The Hongguo had kept tabs on the creaky old merchanters of the Black Starliner Corporation ever since it had been founded, back when it helped ship islanders out from Earth by the hundreds of thousands. Enough that the company disbanded, each ship claiming now to be an independent owner and operator.

Even closer attention had been paid when the corporation started to defend its newly settled worlds. The mercenary arm called itself Ragamuffins. A ragtag group of ships armed to fight against outside threats to New Anegada and Chimson.

So now the Black Starliner Corporation didn't exist. The Ragamuffins and the Hongguo now played tag, and finder's keepers. But since Chimson and New Anegada had collapsed, only three ships had been destroyed in the deep dark between habitats.

Usually the Hongguo put up a stink just outside legal lane areas, boarded a ship, and combed it thoroughly. Punishment involved heavy fines, loss of visa privileges to a given system, or even occasional "recruitment" of crew to the zhen cha.

Ragamuffin ships conceded the boarding if maneuvered into an awkward hole—or ran like hell.

No one got hurt. A spaceship was an investment in the billions. Neither Hongguo nor Ragamuffin wanted ship damage.

But Jamar Sinjin Smith's story played out different. A convoy of five Raga ships set out for Dragin, just plain higglers looking to trade for bottled antimatter at a friendly habitat.

"They were waiting," Jamar said. His voice repeated what he had just said from the speakers in the cockpit around Nashara. "The *Windseeker* kept thinking they detected something out in the dust three wormholes downstream of Dragin. We got pretty jittery, decided to keep close.

"They hit us the moment we transited. Two ships, destroyed, in four minutes."

"Two whole ships?"

"They boosted right in after us and we scattered. We were terrified, not thinking straight. No one ever saw anything like this. Not since New Anegada. And that was the wrong move. They blocked the downstream wormhole we'd just come through, and they had the upstream one blocked as well. And for Dragin, that's it. No more choices. They'd trapped us.

"They hunted the *Windseeker* down first. Aliyah X kept calling out over every single frequency, pleading. She said she would let them board. She said she hadn't done anything illegal. And then, just static." Jamar's reflective eyes drilled into Nashara's as he continued, his sentences clipped short, his tone breathless. "Instead of running and being rounded up, I headed like hell right at the upstream wormhole, taking missile hits and energy beams the whole way, damage crew working constantly to keep us up and running. Everyone suited up against vacuum."

"That's insane." Nashara leaned forward. "You had families aboard."

"They would have hunted us down." Jamar folded his legs into a lotus position and rotated forward toward her. "That was their plan. We threw drones, wastewater, garbage, spare parts, anything we could think of, ahead of the ship. Rotated on our tail to fire the engines right at them before transit. And that's when the cockpit crew noticed Dragin's habitat was gone."

"Gone?"

"Dragin-Above, when we swept the area, all we got pings back on was debris."

"They destroyed a habitat." And all the thousands aboard it. Nashara swallowed. Something was going horribly wrong out there. "It's like living back in the days when Chimson declared independence and the Satrapy ordered it put down."

"In more ways than you think," Jamar said. "We saw the Gulong there, before we transited upstream."

"I've seen the *Gulong* before," Nashara whispered. A five-mile-long, slender, mirrored needle of a machine. It was not just the Hongguo flagship. The mile-long needled spike at the front had a function. "When it shut the wormhole down to Chimson."

Jamar looked through her and sighed. "I've seen it once now. I hope to never see it again. Nashara, why are you here?"

"Hospitality. Help. Place to run to." Until the Hongguo caught up with them.

"Nashara, we actually need your help," Jamar said. "Scanning you when you came aboard, we can tell you can meld with the ship. You have the neural prosthetics. I need you to captain the *Queen* with me. I haven't slept in two weeks." He was close to collapse. Probably been cycling different sides of his brain's hemispheres eight hours each.

Damn. They'd been seeing their captain dog-tired, nerves frayed. Then they'd see him left-brained and creative, totally disorganized and touchy-feely, and then anal and orderly and constrained. Cycling over and over every day as he struggled to remain one with his ship and bring them all through in one piece. With no sleep as he tried to remain alert at every second.

He was a hero, and she was turning him down. "I can't."

Jamar folded in on himself and cradled his head. "I only have two crew left," he murmured through his fingers. "Hanging by a thread. All I want to do is sleep. Sleep forever and just stop this all, goddamnit."

"I can't do that, Jamar."

"I order you."

She stared him back. Predatory, muscles tensed, every minute cell calculating the distance and time involved. "No." A calm, single word.

He was dead already, he just didn't know it. He wouldn't push her that far, and if she had to take the ship, he'd never get it back. She'd never get *herself* back. She wasn't sure if that was worse than dying, but they weren't in enough danger for her to risk plugging directly into the ship.

Maybe as the Hongguo got closer. In a day or two. If it really remained her only chance of survival. Yes. But until then: "I swear to you. If there's anything else I can do, I'll do it."

He must have seen something in her eyes. She willed him to understand it, and he shivered as she stared at him. He backed off the subject.

"Fuel." Jamar's shoulders shook. "We can run if we have fuel. Every off-angled wormhole transit we have to adjust for costs, every maneuver when the Hongguo ships get close costs. We can keep running. We're that much faster than them. But we don't have the fuel."

He was crying. Nashara stared at a spot of wood trim behind the captain's shoulder, trying to pretend it wasn't happening. For both of them. "Swear, they were all so beautiful. Each tiny life, gone. Fireflies in the night, snuffed out by a foul wind of those sick creatures that dare call themselves human beings. Hongguo." He spit the name out.

Then the tears stopped. Jamar straightened up. Ramrod. His eyes glittered again. He was cycling hemispheres, right there. Not on eight-hour runs, but randomly, as his brain gave out in sheer exhaustion.

"Captain Sinjin Smith?"

"Fuel," he grated the word out. "Find me fuel. Antimatter. You have access to the whole ship; we use the Ragalamina aboard here, not the Satrapy standard. So adjust your little wrist trinket accordingly if you won't access directly. At one standard g we have exactly one hundred minutes and forty seconds of acceleration left. Without the fuel we were to get we are unable to escape the Hongguo, and they've been jamming our attempts to forward messages. We have to get away, head downstream, and pass the message on to the other Ragamuffin ships before the Hongguo attack them as well. You understand?"

Nashara nodded carefully.

"Welcome aboard the *Queen Mohmbasa*, then."

"Thank you."

She had jumped out of the pan and into the fire.

CHAPTER THIRTEEN

Free to float through the ship, Nashara shot her way back to the room she'd come from. Ijjy still kept his distance from her, but he showed her back through the corridors.

As they coasted, Nashara tapped the wrist screen. She got it synced in with the ship's network. The Ragalamina probably creaked through a neural interface, but it worked well on a wrist screen. Very two-dimensional, used to taps and menus. It had been developed out of a several-hundred-year-old set of cobbled-together human software systems. Legacy of a time when humans tried to make everything themselves. It was nice to be back in familiar environs.

The *Queen Mohmbasa's* lights flickered off and everything fell into pitch black. Emergency luminescent strips ran along parts of the corridor, but emergency sealant over the damaged sections left huge swathes of the area a dark pit. Nashara slammed into a hard lump of the stuff and grabbed hold.

"Should I be worried?" Nashara asked the dark as she tried to access her wrist display. Nothing. Must have been an electromagnetic-pulse weapon that hit them.

"Only if the backup system don't come on." Ijjy's voice came from farther down the corridor. "Feel the engine still running?"

Nashara closed her eyes and focused on her fingertips. "Yes." It thrummed through the sealant, the vibration reaching everywhere.

"Got no need to panic just yet, then."

A set of emergency lights flickered back on. The wrist screen lit up and error-checked itself.

"Come. The room you in for visitors," Ijjy said. "Whole lot of the other room free closer by the cockpit. Captain say you could take one of them."

"Thanks, but no." She knew if she took a former crewmember's room Ijjy would be annoyed. And she was probably not welcome in the cockpit until she had helped find a solution for the fuel problem.

Nashara paused outside the door. "I've met you, and the captain of the ship. You said three survivors. Who's left?"

"Sean. Out working on fixing things."

"The captain wants me to help find a way to get fuel. Are there any other Raga-friendly habitats downstream of here?"

"Dragin-Above," Ijjy said.

"But they don't exist anymore."

"Seen." Ijjy brushed a dreadlock aside.

"You given up?"

He straightened in the air. "You ain't seen half the shit we seen, I tired, not whipped, hear?"

Good. Nashara turned back into the room without further comment.

The guest room's walls turned to screens. Nashara used them to display information coming from the *Queen*'s tactical updates. Sensor maps of the area, trajectory projections, colored the walls with long, curving lines with dots moving along them.

The *Queen Mohmbasa* pushed the legal lane speed from the habitat and climbed into a higher and higher orbit, racking up fines and complaints from a distant Port Authority. Camera shots of the hull drove home the tattered condition of the ship. It was blind dumb luck that Nashara had pulled herself aboard in an untouched area of the ship. These areas she roamed through now featured gaping rips and tears in the hull that hardened, shapeless foam pushed out of. Black streaks and craters everywhere. She shook her head.

Jamar edged them just a little bit higher and ahead every second. The Hongguo were holding back on attacking them in such a public space.

The two wormholes here orbited high above Bujantjor and followed each other closely. The leading one led upstream to Thule via several more wormholes. The trailing wormhole led downstream to a nexus, giving one the choice of Tsushima or forking over to Yomi. Either way eventually lead to Ys, and from there downstream was the dead wormhole to New Anegada.

Though most of the parties around Bujantjor chose to keep their distance from the wormholes, a few small structures cluttered nearby to offer ship repair or depot services.

A few security drones fired thrusters to lower their orbits and move to intercept. Satellites and other ships cluttered the map.

Nashara strapped herself into the acceleration chair as warnings kicked on. Jamar broke all lane-speed limits, three gravities of acceleration pushing Nashara hard against her restraints as alarms still blared.

"We'll never be welcome here again," Ijjy muttered over the ship's open channel.

A third voice, Sean's, chuckled back. "If we get home, I ain't coming here."

Oscillations shook the ship. Jamar added another half g to the acceleration and dumped what looked like a cloud of chaff in a carefully plotted arc right by the mouthes of the wormholes. Wastewater and garbage, Jamar had told her.

Radar stabbed out from the Hongguo behind them.

The *Queen* rose too quickly as they caught up to the wormholes, they were going to overshoot. Garbage filled the display, washing out everything. Then the *Queen Mohmbasa* spun itself around and the drives fired. Three, four, then five g's of acceleration.

The ship dived for the wormhole, covered by a jettisoned cloud of confusion. Any mistake now while accelerating, adjusting, not putting them dead center through the wormhole would see them coming out the other side of the wormhole in pieces.

Jamar would be one with his ship, a hivemind of shipwide calculations ripping through his head as they hit the wormhole at the blink of an eye.

Nashara smiled just before she felt her stomach flip, the world turn inside out and then back, and a chime sounded.

"Wormhole transition complete."

Bull's-eye. Jamar appeared on her wrist screen. "We beat them here, so they'll come through slow and cautious, drones first, looking for surprises." They had the jump, just not the fuel to continue. Jamar drew the new figure into the air. They'd eaten up a fifth of their stored fuel in that little activity. "We need to find fuel. Ijjy's hunting down leads as well."

"I'll find your fuel." Ys lay downstream, the last of the tightly controlled Satrapic worlds. If she got them fuel, she might also find a way to get off this hunted ship. Get into one of the shipping depots and find a way to get out of this mess.

Nashara started querying the *Queen Mohmbasa*'s databases for what resources lay out there.

Possibilities. The buoys around the wormholes held the latest info about fuel prices, maps, and passed on information of interest to ships like this. The blackout froze them, but Nashara had all the previous pieces of information to sift through from before it fell.

Several minutes of searching turned up only dispiriting findings. Fuel ran expensive right now. Several waves of price shocks and inflationary pressures putting the quantities they'd need for running and fighting out of the ship's reach. The *Queen Mohmbasa* had no formal credit accounts. What gold or silver they had aboard was not going to be enough.

They could, Nashara thought, just take it. Everyone labeled the Raga-muffins pirates anyway.

She perked up and reset her filters and found something odd enough to catch her attention. A distress call from the carefully controlled confines of Ys. From the habitat the Satrap there inhabited.

This far downstream, Ys was a distant frontier for a Satrap. Most Satraps dwelled past Thule, except this notoriously silent and withdrawn one.

The Hongguo wouldn't expect the *Queen* to run straight into the arms of a Satrap, now would they?

Nashara leaned back and let her breath out. Her duty was to hand herself over to the Ragamuffins. But to this doomed ship? Would it make it all the way back so she could hand herself over to the Ragamuffin council leaders? And what were the Raga now but a sorry group of tattered merchant ships huddling on the other end of a burnt-out wormhole, harried and harassed by the rest of the worlds. How would she help them?

There was no Earth, no Chimson, no New Anegada for her to go to. Just humanity scuttling around underfoot of their alien superiors. She had no home. Any future would involve running.

Nashara leaned forward, tired. If Jamar was right that the Hongguo were out to destroy the Ragamuffins, then hiding out wouldn't help them any. She needed to help any way she could right now.

And it was better to run while well fueled, she thought.

Three hours later Nashara met Sean outside the cockpit. Covered in grease, cut up, and his eyes wary, he sized her up. She returned the critical gaze: a built man, but not natural muscle, she could tell just by the way he held him-self. She spotted one pistol holstered by the ankle, another under his left shoulder, and a two-foot-long, varnished stick hung from his belt. Well armed. She liked that in a man.

"Nashara." He shook her hand.

"You're Sean?"

A nod. Nashara squeezed past him into the cockpit and looked back. "Nice wood."

He blinked and looked down at his hip. "Thanks. It's from Earth." He pulled the stick free and handed it to her. Confident.

"Kalinda?" It was a stick-fighting martial art common among the Raga-muffins.

"Yeah. You fight?"

"Capoeira," Nashara said. "Usually with machetes. You?" She rolled up the sleeve of her shirt.

"You a mongoose?" That broke the ice. Sean rolled up his sleeve to reveal the same tattoo Nashara had. Among the Ragamuffins the mongoose-men were an elite set of fighting specialists, the wickedest tools in the Ragamuffin arsenal.

Ijjy appeared and Nashara noticed the two sticks in his belt again. Kalinda as well? Ijjy wobbled through the air at them and tossed her a covered cup and a pouch. "Real food." He grinned.

Nashara caught them and looked at them. Ginger beer, and some stew in the pouch. Homemade. "What is it?"

"Peas and dumplings," Sean said. "Need to use it up before it go bad. Made it back when we could still cook."

Nashara twisted the top and squirted. The ginger beer triggered memories of sitting around with friends before armoring up and heading out to fly wormhole patrols.

The back of her head prickled. Didn't need those memories. She pocketed the ginger beer and stew. "Thanks, I'll eat these later." She floated into the cockpit, over to a screen, and tapped her wrist to bring up what she needed.

"You have something for us?" Jamar opened a single eye.

"Yes." Nashara faced them and tapped the screen.

"This is Kara, from Agathonosis," the screen vibrated. *"We're starving. They're killing each other inside.*

"Please send help, whoever hears this. We only have days left. Oh, shit. Stratatoi have found us."

"What the hell a stratatoi?" Ijjy asked.

Nashara shrugged. "Maybe station security? Don't know, not important. What is important is that this was passed on by a ship called *Toucan Too* that was going to swing by the habitat to see what was going on. The habitat this little girl is caling from seems to be in crisis, and it's just hanging in empty space near the upstream wormhole at Ys. The habitat Agathonosis will be the last place anyone expects us, and I will bet has fuel."

Ijjy was already shaking his head. "No way, man."

"This is a Satrap's habitat," Jamar said softly. The Satraps hunkered in their forty-eight habitats ruling from deep inside the massive structures they had built around them. The Satrapy may have emancipated humans, but in a Satrap's own habitat no one had much in the way of freedom.

"True." Nashara tugged at her collar. "But the Satraps rely on the Hongguo to police humans, and similar organizations for the other aliens. They don't do their own dirty work, making Agathonosis a safe place for us because the Hongguo wouldn't think to look for us there. It's close to the downstream wormhole out of Ys."

Jamar looked at his two remaining crewmembers. "What do you think?"

"Idiocy," Sean growled. "I say we need keep running."

"We simply don't have the fuel." Jamar closed his eye.

Ijjy looked at Nashara. "No one else closer?"

"Not with fuel you can afford."

"People in them habitats with the Satraps," Ijjy snapped, "they hardly more than slaves. We never get involve with that."

"I know." Nashara felt tired. "But as it is, if the Hongguo start catching up, we'll barely make to Ys ahead of them, right, Jamar?"

"Yes."

Nashara pushed off into the center of the cockpit. "Agathonosis is our only hope to warn the rest of the Ragamuffins that the Hongguo are after you," and herself. "It's risky, but so is getting destroyed in the dead of space. I say we see if we can buy or steal the fuel."

They still looked dubious.

"Hey." Nashara looked at them all. "I'm good at that sort of thing. If there's fuel to get, one way or another, I'm your gal."

Jamar sighed. "Prepare for acceleration. Fifteen-minute count. Secure the ship."

"Damnit, Jamar, this go be a huge mistake." Ijjy spun around and leapt out of the cockpit, bouncing off toward the rooms.

Sean turned to follow, but Jamar raised a hand. "I haven't committed to anything yet, understand? Just giving us the option to stop at Agathonosis."

"Don't spend too much time listening to what all she say," Sean said. "Don't forget, she ain't seen half what we already gone through."

He left with a single angry push.

"Looks like I'm not so popular," Nashara observed.

Jamar opened his bloodshot eyes. "You go easy on them," he warned.

"We're all edgy. It's almost a suicide mission, right?"

He unstrapped himself. Nashara bumped over to his chair as the gentle rumble of engines started up. She sank slowly toward one of the curved walls. He grabbed her hands. "Come, I want to show you something."

She hesitated. There was a lot of prep to be done. But she could see he needed something, badly, and she couldn't turn him down.

He hobbled slowly with her for a long time, past the galley, past crew rooms and niches. And finally he stopped, much farther forward.

"See that?" He pointed out a small brass plaque mounted behind glass into the side of the corridor. "My great-grandfather put that on the *Queen* himself, the day the Black Starliner Corporation first met. All four broken-down ships were there, leaking air, barely able to make a few wormholes before breaking down."

The plaque, green with age, declared the *Queen Mohmbasa* a BSC founding ship.

"You should be Blood," Nashara said. She hadn't realized the ship was hundreds of years old; no doubt hardly an original part existed on it anymore. "Your family was there when it all started." The exodus from Earth, trying to find worlds to call their own and finding them all occupied. The terraforming, the attacks by aliens opposed to seeing free humans docking at their habitats.

Jamar shrugged. "Grandpa Jamal was never a leading type. Just wanted to deliver people to a promised land. He lived on Earth, before they cut themselves off. He told me how things were like back then, our nations still struggling, still ceding to the other larger nations. He believed just one planet of our own and we could break all that to start anew."

"Sad, if you think about it," Nashara said.

Jamar turned. "Sad?"

"Sad. Sad that they agreed to do the old superpowers a favor and keep working on illegal technologies while hunkering down in their little planetary reservations," Nashara spat. "We were fall guys."

Jamar looked startled. "That's harsh."

Nashara snorted. "Sure they'd give us a planet, while they kept orbitals overhead and control of the wormholes. We were their goddamned little experiments, Jamar, and they all should have guessed that from the beginning. And if it all went wrong, well, no need for the Hongguo to come, they'd start the job from up on high so that they didn't get discovered."

Jamar pulled himself closer to her. "You come from New Anegada or Chimson?"

"Chimson." She missed it. Missed beaches and swimming and the skies and the dark red forests.

"My grandparents were in Chimson," Jamar said.

Nashara looked at the aged plaque. Jamar deserved to know her little secret. "After the Hongguo destroyed the wormhole, Chimson built a starship. A true starship, not one of these little things that pops around using the wormholes. They loaded it with ten of us who could live long enough to reach the nearest wormhole, and each of us had a weapon we were to bring to New Anegada, to help them."

"Does this have something to do with why you won't help me pilot my ship?" His breath brushed her cheek. It smelled of protein bars and juice.

"Yes," she whispered.

Jamar sighed and let go of her. Nashara stepped back. "All ten of us were women, Jamar. We gave up our wombs and in return were fitted with quantum computers running intrusion devices that can overpower lamina and make it extensions of our minds. It would be like being one with your ship, but anywhere. Your mind replicates, copying itself endlessly until you have control of all it is in contact with."

He looked at her, face pained. "Your wombs?"

"I saw what happened to the other nine when they attacked the Hongguo who intercepted our ship. They destroyed the Hongguo ship, but their bodies died as they took over the Hongguo ship's lamina. It's a bomb. You can't unexplode it, and when it happens, you *are* that lamina. You're no longer human."

"Ragalamina isn't Satrapic lamina."

"Which could make it worse."

"Or better."

"There's only one way to find out, Jamar, and I'm not willing to do that right now. I want to deliver this thing inside me to someone who can study it. I don't want to pull a trigger on something that's wired right into my head. So I'm going to have to stick with you and help you survive so I can do that."

"You know, even with your weapon, you couldn't help New Anegada. I was there in the closing moments." Jamar tapped the plaque.

"And?"

"The battles were all but lost, the planet being bombarded. The aliens had cloned human assassins and soldiers as ground troops. We kept a lot of this stuff quiet; many wouldn't know that the Hongguo didn't shut the wormhole leading to New Anegada down. We did. And the wave of electromagnetic energy that hit everything left the *Queen*, even on the other side of the wormhole, dead until we got towed. Whoever is left on New Anegada is probably living in the Stone Age. The Teotl no doubt suffered the same fate."

"Teotl? Is that what they called themselves?" Nashara asked.

"No, that was us. The first time we saw a Teotl warrior with a flayed human skin as a cape . . . it's the Azteca name for god, and it was a comment that stuck."

"You think we're destined to drift between the wormholes, dodging about underfoot everything else?"

Jamar looked at her. "We seem to have a better success rate when doing that, yes. Come with me."

He found a downshaft, turned them around several times, and led her to a series of air locks.

Nashara looked in through the windows. "Shuttles?"

"Shuttles." Jamar looked up at her, thoughtful. "When it really gets bad, I want you to promise me you'll save the crew."

"Promise? I can't make that promise."

He grabbed her hand. "Promise. Nashara, they're not going to stop coming, and if what you told me is true, you will be their only help if the Hongguo catch us."

"Jamar, I'll die if I unleash this, just like my colleagues did."

"You'll die anyway if the Hongguo catch you," he hissed. "But at least you'll die saving someone. You understand? You weren't sent out here by your superiors to squander this, but to use it to help people. So do so."

"And what, get shot out of the sky in a *shuttle*?" Nashara turned away from the bay windows.

"If I cover you in enough cast-off garbage to hide your run past a wormhole out in the system and lead them on a chase, you can hide out until this all finishes."

"No offense, Captain, that's just as crazy as my idea. We have Agathonosis, and some time to hunt for fuel. Let me go in there. I'm good at this sort of thing."

"Maybe. I think someone is following," Jamar said. "I'm getting backscatter and echoes every time I sweep the area behind us. Besides, we have no credit here, no sympathizers, not enough to barter for fuel with."

"When I said I was good at this sort of thing, I didn't mean bargaining over price." Nashara scratched her itchy scalp. Her hair had started growing back in since her vacuum-jumping stunt. The ability to quickly heal applied to that as well. "I'm not just a pretty face here. If there is some sort of insurrection happening in Agathonosis, it makes for a nice cover. Drop me off via shuttle, give me ten hours. If I can't make it happen, leave me."

"You going to skip out on us?"

"That's bullshit," Nashara said. "Don't try and jerk me around. I owe you nothing, but I'm going to stick my neck out for you."

"Did it really need to take you years to get to us? And almost too late now? If you really have a superweapon buried in you, it could have been useful before all this."

Nashara grabbed him. "I got delayed in Pitt's Cross. I couldn't get the fuck off that shithole without killing people and almost getting caught. I wouldn't have done much good as a Hongguo test subject, or captured by a Gahe hunting pack, would I?"

"I'm just saying." Jamar grabbed her wrists. "You're still a bit fuzzy around the edges, you're still complicating our lives, not making them simpler."

Nashara let him go. "I'm sorry to have disturbed your routine, but you were deep in it when I arrived, I only hastened the conclusion. Don't blame me for your problems, I'm trying to help."

"By talking us into storming a Satrap's habitat?"

"I'm the one offering to do the storming. And if you can pull a better idea out of your ass, I'm happy to go along. You have, however, a limited amount of time to come to a decision because Agathonosis is just a day away."

Jamar nodded. "I'm only angry because I can't come up with a better solution."

"You're in?"

"Until something better comes up. What will you need?"

"I know your ship is armed only with an engine and garbage for chaff, but please tell me you have some small arms aboard."

"I'll have Sean and Ijjy bring everything to you."

"It'll be okay, Jamar."

He ignored her and drifted off.

But she wasn't so sure, though. Messing around with aliens never ended well. Never had.

Sean and Ijjy came to the guest room several hours later towing a large duffel bag behind them.

Ijjy unzipped it and let the contents float out. Pistols, machetes, a few machine guns, dynamite—all hung in the air in front of her.

Nashara snagged a machete out of the air and tested the edge with a finger. "Thanks."

"You going in alone?" Ijjy asked.

"An antimatter cell weighs, what, a few hundred pounds in habitat gravity?"

"Yeah." Ijjy looked her over. "You got that. But we still think we coming with you."

Nashara looked at Sean. "You're a mongoose-man, I can use your help. Ijjy, I don't want you to risk your life."

Ijjy looked at the nearest pistol. "Oh, see, a whole lot history don't exist between you and me, I can handle myself, thank you. I coming anyway, you need all the help you can get, and I want make sure we get that damn fuel, seen?"

They didn't trust her to get the fuel alone, didn't trust her not to disappear into the habitat. "Seen. But I run the show."

Sean raised an eyebrow. "I know you come from a group of Ragamuffin with all the stuff of legend. Like vacuum protection, bulletproof skin—"

"Dearie," Nashara interrupted. She handed the machete. "Don't. Tell you, if you want to be in charge, draw blood."

He stared at her. "Blood?"

"Just a drop. I do have bulletproof skin."

He struck, and Nashara rippled out of the way with a shrug. He slashed again, but she grabbed the back end of the blade and flung behind her hard enough to propel her into Sean.

She casually bent both his arms back behind him. "If I'm going to risk my life for you, the moment I step off this ship I'm your captain, understand?"

Ijjy started laughing at them both. Nashara let Sean go, and he pushed out of the room.

"Do I need to prove something to you too?" Nashara asked Ijjy.

"Lady Nashara I knew you was a sackful of danger the moment I drag you in through the air lock." He saluted her. "You just bust he ego down a bit, Captain, nothing wrong with it, he go survive."

"Good." Nashara looked at the duffel bag. "Help me repack all this?"

Ijjy nodded. "Yeah, we go need it all."

CHAPTER FOURTEEN

Nashara's stomach flip-flopped. Prefight jitters.

"Approaching Agathonosis," Jamar announced. His eyes remained closed, his skeletal frame strapped and webbed into the captain's command chair. "No navigation buoys, no Port Authority. Oddly quiet around here."

It was odd for a habitat to be so silent at the arrival of a ship. They usually had particular preferences about how to be approached, who docked where, and who was allowed to approach. Particularly ones with Satraps living in them.

The habitat floated high in orbit around Ys, an uninhabitable terrestrial world due to a series of nuclear wars on its surface hundreds of years before humanity ever took its first step into space. A large mirror hung between the habitat and any view of the planet, though, to help light up the interior in addition to the usual sunline.

"What you thinking?" Ijjy asked.

"Jamar, any ships docked? Anything floating nearby? It would be easier if we could raid them for fuel."

Agathonosis was starting to feel like a graveyard.

"I'm not seeing anything. This is interesting." Jamar opened his eyes. The front of the cockpit lit up to display a section of the habitat: a great expanse of gleaming glass down the central curve. Air steamed out of cracks, becoming crystalline as it froze and spewed out into space.

"The glass is covered in sediment," Nashara observed.

"Sludge," Sean said. "Like the entire ecosphere in there fell apart."

"Some kind of attack had to have caused this. The Satrapy would never allow anything like that. They're control freaks," Nashara said.

"Even more reason to be alert," Jamar said. "This is very strange. We already saw Dragin-Above destroyed by the Hongguo. Could they have done this as well?"

"Turn on the Satraps? Nah." Ijjy shook his head. "They loyal to them."

"I agree," said Nashara. "Could be the humans in this habitat revolted, like at Chimson."

"But they would at least hail us," Jamar said.

"Are you getting anyone?" Nashara asked. "Even the girl?"

Jamar shook his head. "Nothing. Static and more static. I want to dock us, not a shuttle. We'll be harder to spot, someone would have to visually check the habitat with drones, and since this habitat is all silent, it won't pass out a docking list to the Hongguo when they come."

"I'm game," Nashara said.

Jamar cocked his head. "Yes, a docking would be good after tossing out some garbage to confuse things."

"Still think we're being followed?"

"Maybe. It isn't a large Hongguo ship if it is, not a warship, something smaller. Just odd reflective scatter." Jamar sounded annoyed.

"Forty minutes," Sean muttered.

"Let's saddle up," Nashara said.

Fifteen minutes to dock.

Nashara, Sean, and Ijjy stood outside the main air lock, with Nashara leaning comfortably against the round seal. Jamar had been angling them around the entire cylindrical mass of Agathonosis toward the far end-cap docks. Occasionally the ship vibrated and shook them around slightly as Jamar changed course.

"You hear from that child?" Ijjy asked.

"Not happening," Jamar said.

This close to a habitat, space should have been singing with information and communication.

"You bringing everything?" Sean asked, pointing at the duffel bag.

"No sense in wasting options." Nashara tapped the duffel with her foot.

"The Satrap got you running scared."

"You know what a Satrap looks like?" Nashara asked.

He shook his head. "No."

"When we hit the habitat in Chimson to hunt down the Satrap, I helped out. They look like giant trilobites." Nashara held out her hand, palm out toward Sean. She wiggled her fingers. "Creepy crawlies. They found it deep at the center of its habitat in a giant pool, big fucker, several hundred feet long."

"And they control minds," Ijjy added.

"Rumors," Nashara snorted. "Chimson's Satrap didn't control shit. It's mounted and shellacked in a museum. Kids visit it on school trips."

"Still . . ." Ijjy shrugged. "How you think the Hongguo get the ability to wipe minds?"

The *Queen* shook again, then something outside clanged. Pumps thrummed and air hissed, motors whined as locks engaged.

"Contact," Jamar said throughout the ship.

The air lock opened with a hiss. Nashara patted the small machine gun slung by a strap on her hip and the extra ammo clips in her vest pockets. She could feel the two knives with ankle holsters. Good.

She looked over at Sean. "What's with the rope?"

Sean looked down at his waist and the coiled rope hanging from it. "In case we need to tie anything up."

"Fair enough."

"Always useful," he muttered. "You coming or what?"

Ijjy and Sean stepped in and Nashara followed. They stood and waited as the air lock sealed behind them. All three faced the metal door leading out.

Sean adjusted his belt, moving a pair of cutlasses with polished wooden hilts to a more comfortable place on either side, and rested his left hand on the hilt of a barker gun strapped above his crotch. His baggy pants and shirt covered the armor that could seal up in case of vacuum or handle small-arms fire. Protective plastic gave his face, neck, and hair a reflective sheen. It would give him half an hour's protection from vacuum, but gave him dark circles under his eyes. Nashara laughed.

"What now?" He turned, annoyed. He tapped the plastic coating. "It save my life the first time the *Queen* got hit."

Ijjy had applied the same stuff.

"You look like fucking pirates," Nashara said as the air-lock door groaned open.

From the claustrophobic corridors of the ship into the claustrophic corridors of a habitat's outer skin.

The habitat had been a twenty-mile-long, potato-shaped asteroid once. Then the Satrap had it baked by solar mirrors, or high-powered lasers, while spinning slowly to create a cylindrical shape. Miners would have bored into it with drills while the center was baked out. And that gave them an immense, livable cylinder that could remain spinning to provide gravity. In several places massive clear diamond patches had been installed so that the habitat's denizens could look out into space and see the stars when the habitat shut down the sunline to create night.

How many human lives building the habitat had cost, Nashara didn't want to think about.

Inside, the docking area looked like more of the same. Gun-gray metal.

She tapped the small earpiece as Jamar whispered to her, trying to seat it properly. "I got the girl," Jamar told them all.

"Good for you." Nashara dashed across the mouth of an open corridor to cover and waited for her vision to catch up so she could analyze what she'd seen.

A brief flash of black. A uniform? "Ask her where we might find some fuel and she could be useful," Nashara said.

"You're cold," Ijjy jumped in behind her.

"Don't mind her." Sean looked around at the signs on the wall. "Habitat customs is down this corridor. Let's see what we can find."

"I saw something at the end." Nashara looked at the two of them. "Black uniform."

"Could be security," Sean said. If standard Satrapic design held true, this tunnel out from the air lock led down to another set of reinforced doors that usually housed a booth with a customs agent.

"Mmmm." Nashara ducked her head and looked down the tunnel. Nothing now. Clear, she nodded to Sean.

"From what I remember passing through a few times, Agathonosis is a real insular place." Sean checked the corridor also, then walked out into it. "The Satrap keep the habitat locked down something serious."

"Not a fan of Emancipation?"

Sean shrugged. "Different places interpret it differently, right?"

They turned toward the customs booth. A short man in black, utilitarian pants and a similarly colored shirt stood near the wall watching them. He held no weapon. He stood rigid, shaved head beading sweat, staring at them.

Nashara almost hailed the man, then realized neither Sean nor Ijjy saw him.

Jamar's voice crackled in her earpiece. "The girl says she can guide us to fuel. Says she knows a lot about Agathonosis. But she says she's in a lot of danger, barricaded up in a room that's running out of air in this end cap. It's depressurized around her as well. She's not all that far away. She's got a location and maps for us. I can send them."

"Okay, hook me up with that," Ijjy replied, tapping his temple. "We can get by she place, see if we can help. Sean and I both got vacuum-protection plastic sprayed on, should be good for a quick exposure."

Nashara couldn't care less. "You guys, uh, see anything strange?" Her hand lay on the machine gun, ready to pull it free. The man in black stared even more intently at the three of them.

"Nothing," Sean said, looking around the corridor. "Where the hell *is* everyone? Inside the habitat itself, not in the skin?" He walked up and looked into the empty customs booth. He tapped the glass a few times.

Ijjy tapped the control pad of the door leading out of the corridor. The door shuddered open, rolling aside, and the two men stepped forward.

Nashara swallowed. They'd stepped out into a larger hallway. Black-uniformed men lined the walls for several hundred feet.

They weren't all unarmed. The first had been a test.

Ijjy and Sean walked forward out of her reach before she could say anything. Nashara caught up and whispered, "Jamar, this discussion encrypted?"

"Yeah," Jamar replied, even as she heard feet behind her. Cutting them off.

She didn't dare turn and look. She did her damn best to ignore the slack faces alongside the walls. All of them not even ten feet away from her on either side.

Shit. Shit.

"You all have artificial retinas, don't you, to access lamina?" she whispered.

Jamar's answer disappeared under a wash of static.

The door behind them shuddered back shut on its own. Ijjy turned around. "It should stay open."

"Fail-safes," Sean said. "Dangerously close to an air lock just to remain constantly open."

He could have been right, except that Nashara could see the man in black standing by the door controls, and the handful of other men with him blocking their way back to the ship.

"Sean, send that map to my wrist screen," Nashara said. She held it up as the lines faded in and looked at it, then back up at the men around them.

As long as these eerie people believed them blind, they might let Nashara's group walk just a little bit farther. And whatever was in control was clearly interested in determining who they were, what they were, maybe even interested in capturing them alive.

"Okay," Nashara said to Ijjy as she looked down at the map. "You were right."

Fuel was the least of their worries now.

He turned back to look at her, confused. "Right about what?"

"We need to see this girl right away." She walked past the two of them and glanced at the sides of the corridor. Fifty people on each side before the corridor jagged, all with out-of-control beards, long, raggedy hair, and dirty faces.

Goddamn creepy.

"Why the change of heart?"

"I've seen the light," she lied through clenched teeth. "That poor girl, all alone in a room, scared, hoping we'll help."

Although, how the hell had the girl survived alone in here? Nashara and her new friends were already trapped, just a few minutes into this.

"Right . . ." Ijjy frowned and looked at her, and Nashara stared back.

Sean grinned. "Maybe she's human after all."

"Shut up and lead us to her, Ijjy."

Nashara held up her wrist, blanked the flexible screen embedded in it, and used it as a mirror to see the crowd forming behind them.

They had handguns, although three carried a massive minigun on a bipod between them.

Ijjy dogged them out into a new direction, and suddenly they were just in empty corridors again, out of the gauntlet.

Nashara realized she hadn't been breathing, her pores had shut down, and that she'd quadrupled her heart rate. She reset her internal fight responses and took a deep breath.

"Will you trust me on something, Ijjy?" she whispered. He turned back to look at her.

"What?"

"Don't fucking look back at me," she hissed. He turned away.

"What?" he called over his shoulder.

"When I say run, both of you run like hell."

"Why?" Sean asked. Too loud.

"Because I think we're going to die if you don't. Trust me. I see something."

Nashara used her wrist screen as a mirror again. The crowd behind them edging after them at a safe distance, but looking somewhat tense. They moved as one in a creepy, duplicated fashion, every step mirrored by the others.

Ijjy turned a corner.

"Run!" Nashara sprinted. They broke into a run with her.

The next corridor in front of them stretched four hundred feet long. The door at the end rolled shut.

Nashara spun back to the edge of the corner behind her and whipped a knife free from its ankle strap. She held it in her left hand and allowed the machine gun to drop to her side.

"What going on?" Ijjy turned to look at her.

Choices. Kill first, or see whether they were really friendly, though she doubted that. No one carried a damn minigun to a meeting unless they expected to use it.

But they hadn't attacked. Nashara's hand quivered slightly. All instincts screamed to start picking them off sooner, but something else held her back.

She took a deep breath, remembering cramped corridors in ships and firefights she'd scraped through. Thought of blood-slicked floors and shook her head. Now was not the time for doubts.

The first man around the corner didn't spot her at first. He just skidded across the floor and fired at Sean.

That answered the dilemna, it was kill or be killed. Nashara shot him between the eyes and dove around the corner. The group didn't expect to see her come screaming straight at them.

Arms grabbed her, several shots were fired, but the screams as bullets thudded and burst into flesh weren't hers.

The three men around the minigun she aimed for didn't have time to react. Nashara killed the first with the knife, the second with a kick to the head, and the third she flung clear.

She yanked the massive fifty-pound gun up, flicked the safety, and pulled the trigger down to within a hair of firing. "Drop your damn weapons." She dragged the large ammunition box with her. A chain of bullets led back into it with more carefully coiled inside. A good thirty seconds of high-rate firing, she estimated.

As if one organism, they pulled back from her, boots all thudding to the ground at once. Guns hit the floor and Nashara backed away from them.

The entire group spoke to her, every single mouth opening at once. "If you pull the trigger, the recoil will knock you over," they choroused.

Chills ran down Nashara's back. "Maybe. Or maybe you're really underestimating me."

She kept stepping back, and the crowd melted away from around her. She faced them all and kept thinking about Ijjy and mind-controlling Satraps. If she was smart, she'd pull the trigger and obliterate this faceless mass of mindless people.

Her arm shook as Ijjy and Sean ran around the corner to her.

"I think I owe you an apology," Nashara hissed at Sean. But he wasn't looking at the crowd in front of them, just at all the blood on her hands.

"Nashara, what the hell is going on?"

"What do you see?" she demanded.

"A lot of blood."

She felt faint now, dizzy. An afteraffect of the animal fight-or-flight response and some neurological changes happening as her body came out of combat readiness and into postaction relief. She rode a wave of endorphins.

"You're going to have to turn off your eyes and your lamina. They've been hacked into so you can't see things. Now come on, I'll cover us, but we need to get to that girl, and quickly."

"But then I can't navigate without lamina."

"I've got the map on my wrist screen. Kill your damn eyes. Do it!" Nashara said. "Do it now!"

Ijjy gasped. "Where the hell did you get that gun?" He'd shut down lamina, then. Then he looked down the corridor for the first time and jerked.

Sean looked over as well.

"They're more back there," Nashara said.

"They could be herding us." Sean pulled out a pistol.

"True that," Ijjy agreed.

Ijjy looked nervous. "We should get back to the *Queen*."

"Then we still have no fuel," Nashara snapped. "We go to the kid. You two want to try and turn back, be my guest. I'm going on."

"She got a good point," Sean said.

Nashara looked behind her. "Can you force the manual locks on that door, Ijjy?"

"Yeah."

"Then do it."

She kept the minigun trained on the black-uniformed crowd. But just barely. Even for her, amped up and designed for combat, the fifty pounds refused to be held steadily unless she let it rest against her hip.

CHAPTER FIFTEEN

Kara jumped up as the face of the man who'd talked to her earlier appeared. His eyes glowed as he looked at her, but behind that, he looked like a tired, old man.

"I am sorry about that, our earlier connection got cut." He spoke in Anglic, just as some of Kara's oldest family had. Even Kara's parents had once insisted she learn it; it was, they'd said, a fairly common tongue among the rest of humanity.

She'd practiced it enough that her grammar was proper, but she was sure she had a horrible accent just listening to the way the man pronounced his words.

"Will you still help us though? And what is your name?" She looked over at Jared, sleeping by the door, his arm curled around the cloth doll. She felt slightly dizzy.

"I'm Jamar Sinjin Smith, captain of the *Queen Mohmbasa*." He sighed. "I'm sorry about the signal quality, there is a lot of jamming going on."

"The Satrap does not want anyone hearing anything," Kara said. "It said Emancipation was revoked."

Jamar frowned. "Humans are still mostly Emancipated out there."

He didn't understand. "The Satrap says all humans are no longer free, all Satraps will be doing this."

"That can't be true," Jamar said calmly.

The universe suddenly seemed better. An outside human, talking calmly to her. Things weren't like that elsewhere. Kara dried her watering eyes. "I think we only have hours of air left."

Jamar grimaced. "Three people went in looking for fuel, and to get to you, but I've lost contact with them. I think they're still trying to get to you, though."

Kara hugged herself and crumpled down to the floor. "The three men, do you think they can fight well?" She looked up at the face.

"At least one of them can." The distant man faded for a second, then solidified. "I wouldn't give up yet, Kara. Let's give them some time and see what they come up with."

Jared shifted, opened his eyes. "Are we being rescued?" He sat up and rubbed his eyes.

"Okay," Kara told Jamar, then turned to Jared. "This is Jamar. He's on a ship outside of the world. He says someone might be able to come to us."

A big smile broke out, and it was slightly infectious, despite the complete flips in hope and despair she'd just been run through. Kara stood up. "I'll monitor the outside for them," she said. "Jared, try going back to sleep. Sleeping conserves air."

Jared nodded, wide-eyed, and shut his eyes and hugged the doll tight to himself. He took a deep breath and coughed. The stench was unbearable now that they'd been forced to use the bathroom's floor. Her lungs hurt.

But she remained standing, waving a virtual window into existence that looked down at the outside of their prison.

Please, please make it, Kara silently appealed to the empty window. Jared shouldn't have to choke to death because she'd made a mistake. It wasn't his fault. He was just a kid brother.

"Listen," Jamar said. "Make sure to tell the people who show up that I'm pretty sure a fully fuelled ship called the *Toucan Too* on the other end cap's docking bay. It's a small transport, I didn't see it when I swept the habitat coming in, but I think I have a read on it. I'm getting more jamming, I'll try to deploy—" Jamar Sinjin Smith winked out of existence in a haze of fuzz.

Kara touched the space where he'd just hung, then turned away to wait.

She'd almost fallen asleep standing and watching video of the outside when she noticed the movement. Two helmeted figures standing by the outer door.

Then a third, a woman walking backward, carrying the largest gun Kara had ever seen.

Jamar Sinjin Smith hadn't returned to talk to her yet. But who else could these people be? Kara triggered the outer door to open.

The nearest man looked around, then ducked in. He waved the rest of them on. The woman with the gun backed in.

Kara sealed them in. Jared stirred.

Then she opened a window into the area between the two doors. There would still be no air in there, but she saw the woman slump against the wall and leave smears of blood on it.

Kara looked back at the space where Jamar's head had appeared. He had said three. This couldn't be a coincidence. Still, she remained cautious and cracked the inner door just slightly. Her ears popped and she could feel the air shift as it filled in the empty area. Jared jerked awake.

"If you are from the ship on the outside," Kara yelled at the half-inch crack she'd allowed, "then what is your captain's name?" The man with the long, bunchy hair turned and walked to the crack.

"Jamar Sinjin Smith, you talk to him?"

"Yes." Kara released the door. It rolled halfway open. "But then we lost each other."

There were now five of them sucking up the air, the three adults using more than Jared or her. Where they stuck in here too now?

The very black woman stepped forward. "We'll want to wait here as long as we can to see if we can reconnect with him before making a try to get back out." She turned to look down at Kara. "You understand it's bad out there? Dangerous?"

Kara nodded again. She'd known that for a long time. "Your captain, he said I had to tell you there was a fueled ship at the other end cap. What's your name?"

"Nashara. Ijjy has the long hair. The other is Sean." She sat down with her back against a wall. "I could really use a nap."

"We don't have much air," Kara protested. "We should leave as quickly as possible."

The woman, Nashara, waved at Sean. "See if she can help you talk to Jamar. If not, we'll move out to that ship."

Jared darted between the two men to Kara's side and stared back at them, not sure what to make of them. "She's scary," he whispered too loudly, and pointed at Nashara.

"Not now, Jared." Kara turned to the one with the short hair and tight curls. "Let me help you with it, I know a lot about them."

"Thanks, you never find me turning down extra help." Sean walked over to her side.

Kara watched out of the corner of her eye as Nashara pulled Ijjy aside and whispered to him. She couldn't hear it all, just the word *kids* and a nod toward Jared, then her.

"We'll make do," Ijjy told her, breaking out of the whispering, catching Kara's glances at them.

"I just don't think it's a good idea to bring them into a firefight."

"We've been caught in enough of them already," Kara said, turning her back to Nashara. "He won't cause *you* any problems."

Sean tapped her shoulder. "It's okay, don't worry about her."

Nashara snorted from behind them both as Kara focused on trying to find a signal from the outside.

Jamar reappeared, though the video kept dropping until Sean froze the image of his captain's head over the panel, and Jamar's voice filtered out from un-moving lips.

"I'm glad to hear you all," Jamar said. Everyone crowded near. Both the men were sweaty from running, and Kara found herself edged out behind them. "I was worried about you all."

"We okay. How you doing?"

"I'm undocked. I have a small surprise for you," Jamar said. "I found the *Toucan Too*. It's fueled. They aren't responding to me, but the ship responds to me, and diagnostics report to me that she's got fuel. All we need to do is get there."

"The girl told us."

"We go meet you there?" Ijjy asked.

"That's completely on the other side of the habitat," Nashara said. "Twenty miles of hostiles?"

"It's what you're going to have to do. I'm sorry. I'll try to meet you there," Jamar said.

"Try?"

"I think there is a Hongguo ship in the area for sure, I'm going to try and draw it off."

"Be careful, Jamar." Ijjy walked closer to the frozen image of the *Queen*'s captain. He looked a bit shaken.

"I'll be canny like Anansi," Jamar said. "We'll take that ship, but if we don't, Nashara, remember—" The link died.

"Heavier jamming," Kara said. She looked at them and shrugged. The three adults didn't say anything, but looked at each other. Nashara stared at the floor.

"How we going get there from this side the habitat," Ijjy finally asked.

Both men looked at the big gun by Nashara and she frowned. "Not like that. I won't have that much blood on my hands. I'm not psychotic."

"You the soldier."

Nashara looked down at a screen on her wrist. "I will fight if I have to, but I'm not going to slaughter those people just because the Satrap has their minds." But Kara saw her continue to stare at the gun. The woman was thinking about something.

"So what we doing?" Ijjy asked.

"Get the vacuum bags out." Nashara looked angry, her eyes blank. "I'm sick of breathing this shit anyway." She looked very, very angry.

"But what are we doing?" Sean asked.

"How's that plastic coating?" Nashara walked over and poked Sean's neck. "You safe to go back out?"

"We both good," Ijjy said. "Couple minutes exposure."

Nashara looked around. "They'll be waiting for us just past the decompressed area." She was obviously talking about the stratatoi.

"You got a big gun," Ijjy said. "We armed."

"To face tens, maybe." Nashara looked down at the massive gun and rubbed her temple, then glanced over at Sean's waist. She stopped rubbing her temple, stared at the loops of rope he carried. "Hundreds? No. You really want to walk over twenty miles of hostile terrain to get to the other end cap?"

"The Satrap will be watching," Kara agreed.

Kara flinched as Nashara spun and walked over to her. "The center. The sunline. Is there a shaft that will take us up to the sunline? We're deep on the cap on this end, we should be able to get to it, right?"

"Yes. There's an elevator." Kara closed her eyes, mapped out a location, and tried to pass it to Nashara, but nothing happened. "Um, you have access to lamina?"

Nashara shook her head and held out her wrist. "On here."

How quaint. Kara sent it, and Nashara looked it over. "We're going to seal you up for a few minutes in bags to protect you from the lack of air. We'll carry you out. Once we're in a safe area, we'll open it. Okay?"

Kara nodded.

"Good." Nashara caught a small, folded-up pack the size of her hand that Sean tossed at her. She unpuckered the top and shook it out into a four-foot-wide bag, then looked over at Jared. "Crawl on in, then."

Jared looked at Kara. "Go ahead," Kara said. "It's our only way out."

He stepped forward, still carrying the doll, and sat in the bag. Nashara pulled the edges back together, except for a last little bit for him to keep breathing.

Sean tossed another package at Nashara and she opened the vacuum bag. "You're next."

Kara looked at the filmy plastic and took a deep breath to steady herself. It was out of her control now. She had to relax and let these adults help the both of them.

She stepped forward into the bag, sat down, and drew the top over her head.

"Can you give the command to open the outer door from in there?" Nashara asked. Kara nodded. "Good." Nashara looked around. "Then let's roll. Open the door. Ijjy, Sean, keep back, don't shoot unless shot at. Let me pick the fights, all right?"

They nodded.

Nashara sealed both bags, then stepped forward to pick up the massive gun. Ijjy awkwardly picked Kara up and slung her over his shoulder, holding onto the back of her legs with one arm while he held a pistol in his other hand.

The outer door rumbled open at Kara's command, and she heard a brief rustle against the plastic as all the air escaped. Ijjy's shoulder slammed against her stomach and the world lurched as they began to move, and quickly.

CHAPTER SIXTEEN

The *Takara Bune* timidly approached Agathonosis, dropping drones and scattering them along its path. Only a few hundred thousand miles lay between the two wormholes here, both at the same orbital altitude above the planet Ys.

"They're here," Bahul said. "I can see the *Queen Mohmbasa*."

"Good." Etsudo closed his eyes as they approached. "Brandon?"

"Yes." The other man's voice sounded as hushed as Etsudo's. The habitat looked wrecked. Old and wrecked.

"Are those holes in the skylights?" Etsudo asked.

"I think so."

A ping alerted him to the presence of the *Shengfen Hao*, now just transiting the wormhole. Etsudo continued looking at visual updates of the habitat's exterior, hardly able to believe what he was seeing. Neglect.

"Have you ever seen anything like this?" Brandon asked.

"No," Etsudo said. "Not ever."

The *Shengfen Hao* hailed. Jiang Deng popped up. "Moving for the attack, good job tracking them, Etsudo."

Deng would certainly not try to capture them alive.

Disappointing. But safe. Nashara was probably aboard that ship; picking her up was too dangerous. He'd instilled some of the same loyalty into her when patching her mind back together that his crew had. Enough so that if he ever ran into her again, he had some sort of fighting chance. But he hoped not to meet her face-to-face again; the last encounter had shaken him.

The *Queen Mohmbasa* accelerated hard out, curving away from the habitat. Etsudo watched the *Shengfen Hao* match it, then fire a dozen missiles.

Even the nimble *Queen* couldn't outrun the sharp sparks racing toward a point ahead of her. The Ragamuffin ship jinked hard, several missiles miscalculated and passed above her, but debris rained off the ship.

"No one is on that ship," Brandon said. He glanced over.

"Why do you say that?"

"That maneuver. Too many g's for a human to suffer, particularly at a right angle like that."

Etsudo snapped himself in. "Scan for any broadcasting. We're looking for a pod, or a shuttle, something that they're hiding in to control the ship."

The *Queen* spiraled, elaborate dodges, avoiding more missiles, and Etsudo smiled. He would love to meet the man piloting that ship.

Was it worth risking a meeting with Nashara? Sadly, no.

One missile finally struck the *Queen*. A geyser of hot metal, air, and water spewed from the side of the ship. No more shaking the missiles, something had been damaged, the *Queen* accelerated along a straight line.

A long line of laser fire faintly visible in the interstellar dust stabbed out from the *Shengfen Hao*. It razed the side of the ship, and the *Queen* began to spin slowly. The ship vented air and more debris.

"Deng has her," Bahul noted. "Quick dancing, but she's done."

Etsudo waved aside the virtual window showing the destruction of the *Queen* and looked at Brandon. "Anything?"

"Yes." Brandon displayed a small spot of dark moving slowly toward the hull of the habitat.

"Well done, Brandon." Etsudo strained against the straps. "He's headed to the other side of the habitat. I wonder why?"

Brandon shrugged. Etsudo changed course to follow the small craft. "Bahul, forward this all to Deng."

Then he sat back and waited.

"Incoming," Brandon muttered.

Missiles. From the *Shengfen Hao*. If Deng doubted Etsudo's commitment, he'd have to change his mind now. Or maybe Etsudo needed to invite Jiang Deng aboard his ship for some tea.

The missiles shot past the *Takara Bune* and on toward the pod.

They found their target and lit up the space outside the habitat in a brilliant explosion. Etsudo flinched and zoomed in on the mess to see debris slap against the side of the habitat.

A ship and its crew, all dead. Did that make him no better than his crew had been?

Everything fell back into the dark again.

Etsudo shook his head and turned the ship's external cameras away from the wreckage. Such a waste. They would have made good Hongguo, he would have made sure of it.

CHAPTER SEVENTEEN

The elevator shot toward the center of the habitat, and Nashara could feel that the minigun now weighed a fraction of what it had when she'd picked it up. She bled from her arm, a chance shot when she'd turned a corner.

Several of Kara's stratatoi had done their best to slow them down, but it had been easy enough to disable them. The Satrap had not been expecting them to head this way but either back toward the docks or toward the inside of the habitat.

It had been expecting an all-out firefight as they tried to force their way through the habitat.

"You sure the Satrap can't shut this down?" Nashara asked. She stood face-to-face with Sean in the corner.

"Pretty sure," Kara said.

"Pretty?" Nashara twisted to look at her. How old was this girl? Late teens? Their lives rode on her ability to manipulate the lamina the way the Satrap had and she was *pretty* sure?

"It can cut the power, but then how does it send the stratatoi after us?" Kara said.

She was right. The elevator shuddered after several more minutes, slowing down, then gently slid to a stop. Nashara pushed everyone aside and braced her now weightless self in front of the doors. She aimed the minigun ahead, just in case, and flicked the box of ammunition free so that the long belt floated free in the air.

Nothing waited for them out there.

She coiled the ammunition feed into a large spiral and let it float off the forearm holding the gun.

They floated out onto a large half circle of a floor that hung out over this side's end cap. Ten-foot-tall windows curved around the edge, and a large set of oak doors with hand-carved images of triangular gliders flitting about in the air led out into the air above the sunline. The world of Agathonosis lay in dark night all around them. Shadows curving up on all sides and stretching off into the distance. A dark, menacing blackness broken only by random patches of lights and orange fires raging throughout the habitat's interior.

"People used to use the balconies to launch their flyers from, until a month ago they were banned." Kara twisted in the air, unused to weightlessness. Clumsy.

"Time till the sunline comes on?" Nashara asked.

"Not for another hour," Kara said. "The windows will turn dark and the doors will shut ten minutes before. You're not allowed to try and fly when the sun's on. You have to be out there and away from it already."

The elevator chimed. Another car coming their way. Filled with stratatoi, no doubt.

"Sean, your rope."

He tossed it to her, and Nashara began to create loops. They stared at her, still not catching on.

"We're going to cross to the other side." She threw the end at Sean. "Start strapping in."

They looked at her as if she were insane. "Nashara," Ijjy said, but she cut him off.

"We have a minigun and enough ammunition to fire it for maybe thirty seconds. It's not much use in an actual battle. We're outnumbered. This is no different than flying a ship. It's basic physics."

"Basic physics?" Sean yelled.

Nashara tapped the ammunition box. "Each bullet has mass. Every time you fire one off, there is recoil. How many bullets do you think are in this box, Sean?"

"Couple thousand," he whispered. Nine or ten grams each exiting the gun at a thousand meters per second. Nashara eyed the group and guessed they massed four hundred kilograms total.

"A thousand-shot burst from this gun would leave us going ninety kilometers per hour," Nashara said. "We get to the other side of this habitat in just under thirty minutes. Unless the gun jams. In which case . . ." She shrugged.

They were spacers who flew from world to world, but Sean looked out toward the darkness. "I am no ship. No gun my rocket."

"The only difference is the method of propulsion and the surroundings. We're in zero gravity just the same. Just don't look . . . anywhere."

Kara walked over to her brother. "Jared."

His face had gone white. "I can't."

Nashara continued roping herself up, then tightened the knot so that it zipped Sean right up to her hip. "Move yourself so you're sitting on my back," she told him. She wobbled as he did so, then spun in the air until Ijjy, his dreadlocks floating up around him like some wild Medusa, grabbed them and pulled them to a filigreed pillar.

"Ijjy, strap yourself to my back, but facing Sean," Nashara said, and then waved Kara and Jared over.

Sean and Ijjy lashed the rope over Nashara's midsection in a crosswise pattern, lashing their folded legs to her. "This go hurt," Ijjy said.

"Kara, Jared, sit with your legs wrapped around each other on their legs, but like you're in a circle. Hold Ijjy and Sean's shoulders while they lash you all in and each other around your waists and shoulders."

"Barely got enough rope," Sean reported from over her shoulder.

"Make it work."

Nashara held on to the pillar with one hand, the other holding the minigun, as the acrobatic structure of the five of them wobbled.

It *was* madness. She was faking her cool. The sunline still glowed with enough ambient heat from its fusion-powered light to scorch their skin if they bumped it, and controlling their flight would be a bitch.

"Elevator's almost here," Kara called out.

"Everyone strapped in?"

"Best we can," Ijjy said.

Nashara kicked off from the pillar toward the nearest window. They all wobbled and started to spin.

"This is *not* going to work." Sean shook the group as he shifted.

"Don't move," Nashara snapped as they gently struck the window. The minigun smacked the window hard enough to cause a crack. The ropes pulled at her stomach and, even more uncomfortably, rode right up under breasts and pulled at them.

She swore and kicked them toward the doors.

They struck those with more tumbling, and Nashara grabbed the handles of the doors and threw them open.

The motion pushed them back away from the opening doors, slowly. Nashara reached for the small machine gun with her free hand and fired three single shots to rotate herself to face the interior of the balcony.

Three shots to stop the rotation. The shots buried themselves in the floor nearby, kicking up plastic shavings.

Then she aimed the machine gun at the wall and fired for a full three seconds. The oak doors slowly slid past them on either side, and Sean swore.

"Don't look around," Kara said. "She told you that."

"Damn, that chafes," Ijjy said as the ropes shifted with another burst of machine-gun fire. Twenty feet lay between them and the lip of the balcony. Nashara glanced "up" to the slightly glowing sunline, then back at the balcony.

An excruciatingly slow departure. But controlled.

She let the machine gun drift on its strap and held the minigun against her stomach.

The elevator opened and ten stratatoi flew out in a star pattern. They spotted Nashara, and the star pattern shifted as they spread out for windows.

"Oh, fuck." Nashara tensed and pulled the trigger on the minigun. The barrel spun up, then the howling scream of the minigun deafened them.

Glass exploded from the stratatoi firing at them, but Nashara wiggled the minigun and the stratatoi bounced off each other to duck for cover. The entire space of the balcony became a flensing cloud of glass flechettes from exploding windows, and Nashara's stomach strained against the damaging recoil. Tracers lit the end cap up, exposing balconies and windows.

Bullets winged by, cracking the air. But none hit.

The balcony dropped away and a spin began. Nashara let go of the trigger, and the group tumbled on, ropes chafing and cutting skin. The sunline and the dark curves of the habitat spun around them in a dizzying whirl. For a second it felt as if they were falling away from the underside of a giant mountain. But then as Nashara was spun around, they hung at the bottom of a giant vortex of darkness. Tiny specks next to a spire reaching up through the eyewall of darkness into a foggy night, where it disappeared.

She'd felt like this in night parachute jumps, the look of the land as she broke out of the clouds and looked down at the patchwork of land and civilization. People as tiny specks on the landscape she looked down upon them like a god.

A raging forest fire lit up one side of the habitat in odd orange hues. Dried-up lakes looked like gouged-out craters. Empty rivers could be glimpsed at the center of the conflagration. And then hints of towns and cities lurking in the reflection of the fire cast from the undersides of dirty black smoke clouds that drifted up and out over the land, starting to spiral down the length of the habitat due to Coriolis forces.

"Just close your eyes, Jared, keep them closed," Kara whispered. "Just keep them closed."

Nashara closed her own as well for a second after sizing up the rate of rotation. She could see a cloud of spent casings slowly dispersing on her left, falling away from them.

Then she opened her eyes again and pulled out the small machine gun and began firing. Shots to her left, then down, then down again, right slightly, all timed to the sunline's flashing by her field of vision.

It all slowed down, each flip coming gently, until finally she righted them, then used another few shots to orient herself back down the sunline.

She estimated that she'd gotten them up to seventy kilometers an hour, but from their perspective it felt as if the group fell slowly down the giant spire toward an inky bottom.

Stratatoi followed them, a perfect circle of figures in the air, their backs to her, firing their machine guns to chase them.

"Think they go catch up?" Ijjy asked. They had pulled well away from the balcony in the last couple minutes; it dwindled into a morass of other smaller windows that clustered around the sunline. Farther out, as the apparent gravity increased, ruined gardens on careful slopes dotted the outer rims, along with walkways. Four minutes down, twenty or so to go, Nashara thought.

"I don't see any other miniguns, they're using light machine guns." Nashara slitted her eyes. "Carrying clips, so maybe five hundred rounds max. Lighter caliber, lighter bullet speed. I'd say they could get going just a little bit faster than fifty or sixty kilometers an hour if they save ammo to stop."

"The Satrap doesn't care about their lives," Kara said.

"If they use up all their ammo they could catch up, yes," Nashara said.

"So how you go solve that?"

"The kids facing forward?"

"Yeah," Sean said.

Nashara settled the minigun against her midsection again, wincing. The skin there had bruised. The stratatoi scrabbled in the air as the roar started. All five of them jerked around as Nashara swept the minigun around in a precise cone of fire. Red clouds of blood burst out from the stratatoi. Nashara made a face.

Again they spiraled out of control. The dim glow of the sunline got closer as they veered toward it.

"The sunline!"

"I see it, I see it," Nashara muttered. She pulled out the small machine gun and fired off in its direction.

It wasn't enough. She used the minigun again, and it howled. They changed course, and then Nashara pointed it back at the stratatoi and fired it again. The sunline blurred above them.

"Moving quick," Sean said. A bit faster than ninety kilometers an hour, yes. But the nearest stratatoi had been killed. Limp in a spreading cloud of their own blood, they fell behind.

Nashara relaxed in the crude harness and watched the end cap fade into the inky dark. She listened to the distant burst of gunfire from stratatoi working on catching up. It sounded like popcorn for several minutes, and she used the firefly sparks of the muzzle flashes to track how many and how fast. Several bursts from the light machine gun emptied her clip for another few kilometers per hour added, and she swapped it out.

Fifteen minutes to go.

At the balcony, now just a tiny, toy like piece of the end cap, a section of the sunline vented steam and fire, then lit up. The whole end cap reappeared five miles behind them.

"Kara, is it morning yet?" Nashara shouted. "Because the sunline is turning on."

"No, it shouldn't be doing that yet."

Crap. Nashara handed the minigun to Ijjy as another section of the sunline lit up. It silhouetted a new cloud of stratatoi with its brilliance.

"The Satrap is going to try and burn us out of the sky," Nashara said. If they moved far enough away from the sunline, the pressure of the moving air inside the habitat would act just like gravity, speeding them up to match the spin and dashing them to the ground.

And six of the stratatoi were catching up, the dots of black growing in size compared to the general cloud. They had a machine gun in each hand and clips of ammo hanging like necklaces around them.

Nashara waited for a minute as another section of the sunline vented steam and lit up, then fired a burst with the machine gun. One down, another limp body tumbling through the air. Nashara fired to correct the motion started from that.

A second burst as they grew in size.

The four now still alive spun around to face her.

"How we doing?" Sean asked.

"They're getting close."

Gunfire cracked past them. Nashara fired again. Three. Again. Two and one. The lone man whipped past them as he replaced the clip in his gun.

"Ijjy, Sean!"

Both men fired pistols at the same time as the man fired the machine gun. Kara screamed. "Jared!"

"Get him?" Nashara asked.

"Yes," Sean said. "But he got the little boy." Kara kept screaming.

"Easy, easy," Ijjy whispered. A stream of blood trickled by Nashara's left. She heard him rip fabric, and the blood stopped trickling by.

Kara sobbed and both Ijjy and Sean shifted.

"How bad?" Nashara whispered.

"Bad enough," Sean whispered back. "Got it stopped, wrapping it up, but we got to get to that ship quick now."

Nashara still looked back at the sunline, lighting up section by section, another cloud of stratatoi popping their way toward them. "Ten minutes."

Another section of the sunline vented and lit up. It was going to catch them at the same time as the stratatoi. Tinny, distant screams from stragglers reached them. A third of the habitat was lit up, shadows cast from tall buildings.

Nashara fired the minigun and felt one of her ribs crack. She ignored the pain and let the gun continue, just another few seconds, then stopped. "That's as fast as we dare go." In fact, slightly more.

"Half the ammo gone?"

"Yes." She opened the ammo box floating in the air by her. It had been reduced by half. Smoke from the minigun streamed back as they flew on. The air around the barrels rippled from heat.

Nashara watched another section of the sunline come on and licked her lips.

"You gonna slow down soon?"

"Sunline's coming for us. Have to wait until the last possible second." Nashara watched the sunline snort again. Dawn had come to them.

The next batch of stratatoi would hit them as they came in to the end cap. There might even be stratatoi waiting there.

"The boy, how is he?"

Tense, she waited and watched the stratatoi and sunline race each other toward them. Kara twisted and cried, and Jared remained quiet. Sean kept shifting around, no doubt checking the boy. "He got a pulse, still. He got a pulse."

The sunline made it hard to see now.

"We're coming in fast, Nashara," Sean said.

Bullets cracked by them. This time going the opposite way. "I can see the other balcony, a bunch of them men up in there."

The Satrap had gotten stratatoi there in time.

"Give Kara a gun," Nashara said. "Everyone get ready. This'll hurt. When the minigun runs out of ammo, Ijjy, cut us loose. If we spread out we're harder to shoot. Use your guns to slow down the rest of the way. Sean, take Jared with you. Ijjy, show the girl how to fire."

Nashara fired a shot to slowly spin them around. The balcony on the other end cap of Agathonosis grew, until she began to make out the windows. More rounds slapped through the air as the stratatoi bettered their aim.

It didn't feel as if they were moving through the sky, but that they were falling through a vortex of land and clouds toward the ground of the balcony, Nashara first, with the mass of strapped-on people behind her.

She shook her head roughly and bit her lip as she aimed the minigun down, psyching herself into pulling the trigger.

The minigun howled, the pain shot through her whole body. Blood leaked out from around the bruises, then stopped as the gun chewed its way through the skin and hit the armored underlayer of her body.

Still it howled. Then Nashara let go of the trigger.

The barrel whirred loudly.

They still flew toward balcony, only it was a disastrous mess of glass shards and the doors were barely hanging on. They rushed toward it all.

"Cutting," Ijjy yelled.

Nashara burst free of the rope and kicked clear. She had two hundred rounds left. They yanked free of the ammunition box with her.

Bullets cracked past. Ijjy and Sean returned fire.

A figure whipped past them, badly burned, but still trying to aim and fire at them. It disappeared ahead of them into the balcony.

Nashara aimed the minigun at the now rapidly moving cloud of men chasing them and fired the last two hundred rounds in a last three-second scream.

Without the mass of the others it kicked her back up to fifty kilometers an hour toward the balcony. But judging by the puffs of red, she'd done a lot of damage.

Nashara tossed the minigun free as she flew toward the balcony, switching to the machine gun to fire at any movement. She struck the entry door and shattered it. Wood splinters pierced Nashara and a bolt struck her in the head.

Dazed by the impact, she flailed and spun wildly, striking pillars, and the inside wall of the balcony. For a second she hung in the air, assessing damage, then the rest of her group burst in.

Ijjy was swearing, but sounded alive. She heard crying.

One of the stratatoi waiting for them survived, somewhat. A moaning echoed around the room.

"Everyone, get behind a pillar!" Nashara yelled.

A patter of spent casings began to ping against the inside walls, and then it turned to hail. A loud, wet smack of a body moving over a hundred kilometers an hour hitting something solid made Nashara wince. And then came another.

Then burned, shot, or screaming stratatoi rained down for the next two minutes as Nashara huddled in safety with the others. Glass flew, viscera floated by, and Nashara kept counting the impacts as she flashed back to estimates on how many had jumped out after them. The blaze of the sunline filled the room now that the autotinting windows had been destroyed.

The sound of bodies slowed, the occasional pinging of spent cartridges died off.

"Okay, let's get moving."

She pushed over to Ijjy, who held Sean by the legs. Ijjy looked up, tears pooling around his eyes and breaking off into the air. Nashara shook her head, but Ijjy nodded. A giant slab of glass protruded from Sean's chest.

"He's bleeding again," Kara screamed.

Jared lay still in the air, a bullet hole in his chest still pumping a faint fountain of blood into the air above him.

CHAPTER EIGHTEEN

Kara had her face buried in Jared's chest, her hand pressed against the hole in him, begging the blood to stop spurting. But it kept coming and she kept screaming as it trickled out between her fingers.

He looked at her. He kept mumbling something to her, but she couldn't hear him, couldn't stop screaming, until suddenly strong hands ripped her clear and flung her aside.

Kara grabbed at empty air and Ijjy caught her.

Nashara hung over Jared, ripping up a piece of her shirt to use as a bandage. Kara saw Sean and gasped, horrified at the jagged slab of glass that had impaled him.

A hundred feet away one of the stratatoi kept screaming.

"Is he going to live?" Kara sobbed.

"Maybe." Nashara packed the shirt on. "Ijjy, hold that on him tight."

Kara trembled and raised the gun they'd given her to slow herself down. It was still armed, and large in her hands.

Kara kicked off the pillar hard toward the sound of the moaning man. She bounced against the wall and slid until she found a handhold near him.

"Kara!" Nashara shouted.

Kara sighted down the notch above the handle, and the burned face of the man on the wall turned to her.

She screamed, pulled the trigger, and moved back from the man. She'd missed.

Nashara slapped into her. "What the hell?"

"They deserve to die," Kara yelled. "All of them. They killed Jared."

She got spun around by Nashara, who was covered in blood. "That's a dangerous path you're aiming for. You sure you want to go down it?"

Kara grimaced. "The Satrap took their minds. They're not human."

Nashara turned away. "Once you start this, you never really get to go back to the way you were. No matter how hard you try. There's a lot you can do. You can still help your brother. Understand. Help your brother. Talk to him, keep something on the bleeding, and help Ijjy with him. You don't have to do this. Let me."

She shoved Kara back toward them, taking the gun from her as she did so. Kara watched, then, as Nashara moved over to the mewling stratatoi and fired. She jerked back from a sudden cloud of red and gray matter. The body jerked off the wall and floated away, slowly spinning as it trailed blood.

Kara threw up.

CHAPTER NINETEEN

The *Toucan Too* had been moved out to the rim of the end cap, ready to get flung clear of the habitat. After hanging in the air so long, it felt good to be able to walk around. But Nashara could hardly appreciate that. She almost tore the *Toucan Too* apart, looking for a medpod, near frustration, tired, bleeding from another damn shot that had winged her on the way down the claustrophobic corridors to the outer-rim docks.

"Damnit don't just stand there!"

Ijjy held the limp boy in one arm, held his chest in another, and the kid would probably die from all the running. Internal bleeding. Clots.

The *Toucan Too* was a bullet-shaped capsule mounted on a slender anti-matter drive, a long tube with a nozzle. A central shaft with rungs and rails led from the cockpit to the end, rooms radiating out from the core shaft. And Nashara broke into every one of them.

"They'd be fucking insane if they didn't have one," Nashara snapped. Crossing the long distances between wormholes and planets without a medpod was . . . well, she'd already voiced her opinion.

Kara's sniffling echoed off the gray metal all around them.

She forced a door open. There they were, five medical pods, crudely bolted onto the room's walls.

Nashara snatched Jared away, pulled the bloody cloth off, and placed him underneath the nearest bright yellow hood. She slapped the thing in place and put her palm to the contact pad.

They all watched as wires and hoses wriggled into place, seeking out veins, slithering up Jared's nose with a trickle of blood.

Three arms snapped into place, dropping an egglike mechanical heart dripping with placement fibers onto his chest. Kara jumped when it latched onto the boy's chest and his back arced up as the machine whined.

Defib. Once, twice, three times, four times, and then the beat. A heartbeat.

"He's stable," Nashara said.

"What does that mean?" Kara looked through her, so sharp.

"Get him to a Ragamuffin doctor within a week," Ijjy said. "He go be okay."

"Right." Nashara let go of the panel.

"So we have to go, we have to find him a doctor." Kara leaned over the panel. "Please."

Nashara looked back down the central shaft. "Ijjy, raise the captain."

Ijjy looked up. "I been hailing since we got aboard."

They looked at each other.

"We need to find a doctor," Kara said again. "We need to get moving."

"We'll get going soon, but we're waiting for someone right now." Nashara backed out of the room with Ijjy and shut the door.

"We could cast off," Ijjy said. "Jamar said you could fly these things."

"We aren't going anywhere anytime soon," Nashara said.

"Why not?"

"Because Jamar lied to you, I *can't* fly this thing."

She walked into the cockpit and left Ijjy standing in the shaft. Alone, she sat on the floor facing the captain's chair, hanging from the current top of the cockpit. She folded her arms in front of herself and closed her eyes.

"Captain Sinjin Smith, where the hell are you?" she asked the empty cockpit, then she closed her eyes and rocked slightly.

He couldn't die. It wouldn't be fair. These people's lives were not her responsibility. Sean had died. The kid was almost dead. It was all a total fuckup. Jamar was off leading the Hongguo on a chase, but he was probably dead.

The sound of something smacking against the air lock finally penetrated.

"I think they trying to get in," Ijjy said. He held the sides of the round doorway and looked at her.

"Think he's coming?" Nashara asked, staring at the floor.

"Don't know," Ijjy said, folding his arms now. "We could end up a sitting duck."

Nashara tapped the wrist screen and the *Toucan Too* shuddered. The air lock groaned and seals hissed.

"Ditched the umbilical, should be harder for them to try anything in vacuum," Nashara said. "Gives us ten minutes before they break out the suits to come for us."

"Okay. But you think ten minutes enough?"

Nashara rested her head in the palms of her hands. "I got us fuel," she said.

"You did good."

"Not good enough, Ijjy. Not near good enough."

"We went up direct against a Satrap," Ijjy said. "What more you want?"

Nashara folded her arms. "He's dead, isn't he?"

Ijjy didn't reply.

"You have a smoke?" Nashara asked. "I just need a few minutes."

Ijjy shook his head.

"Talk to me about the Raga. If we are able to get this ship to them, talk to them, what can they do against the Hongguo?" She didn't want to waste her own life for nothing.

"You head downstream. This the last of the forty-eight worlds, so we got another fifteen wormholes to go. Got a hot-clouded world you pass through call Chilo, and then three down from there you got the end of the line. We got Morant, a small habitat, maybe ten thousand people in it. Twenty ships left with us." Ijjy frowned, then corrected himself. "Sixteen since Dragin-Above. Six for defense, ten higgler ships if the *Queen* alive. Don't know know how many of the higgler ships go be around, they out trading."

"You have family there, don't you?"

Ijjy nodded, but didn't go into details. She silently thanked him for that.

That was the might of the Raga now, a bunch of refugees huddled around a failed wormhole.

But with the Satrapy and Hongguo bearing down on them, who else would step forward? It was going to be the closest thing to a home she would find out here. It was worth defending.

Nashara started strapping herself into the captain's chair and looked around the ship. It had been a long time since sitting in the center chair.

"Things could get weird, Ijjy. I'm going to die, but not really."

He raised an eyebrow. "How?"

"I'm not just built to be quick, or to survive vacuum. I have a device in me that will scan my brain, slowly, and as it does that, it will upload into this ship's lamina. But in order to scan my mind it will destroy the synapses."

Ijjy stared at her. "Uploads go insane. Ground-up-built artificial intelligence don't make no sense, too alien. We been playing in the labs in Morant."

"Uploads go insane because your physical body is as much a part of your being as your mind. You can't divorce the mind from the organism and the environment. But lamina is computer power and a layer matching the environment. If you accept physical tags, your mind will cope."

"You seen it done."

"Seen it done by my sisters, before they destroyed the ship they were aboard to save my skin." Nashara pulled out an optical jack and slid it under her skin, felt it connect. Much higher bandwidth connection.

"Nashara." Ijjy grabbed her shoulder. "We should wait."

She looked back at him. "If Jamar hasn't responded yet, you know he's dead or unable to help us. Prepare for acceleration."

Nashara initiated a link to the ship's lamina. The backs of her eyes filled with information as she accessed everything directly. The machines inside her sensed the connection and leapt into action.

She felt dizzy, then tired. Sedatives flooded her system. She closed her eyes.

Nashara felt swept out on a brief tide of information, then opened her eyes again. She could see herself slumped in the cockpit chair through a handful of sensors. Classic out-of-body. Disorienting, not safe.

She reached in and restarted her heart, checked her vitals. Everything still worked. She wasn't *in* her body, but she could use it the way she'd use a drone.

Nashara opened her eyes again.

"You alive," Ijjy said. A single second had passed.

"In a manner of speaking." Nashara struggled to maintain the old point of view. This was her body, this was where her mind resided.

That hadn't been too hard, she thought.

"Hey, little lady."

Nashara jerked up and faced a mirror. "What?"

A perfect copy of her stood in front of the captain's chair. "There's enough processing power in the ship's lamina for the both of us," the second Nashara said. "Been trying to wrap my head around it, took a microsecond longer than you, so I missed getting my body back."

Nashara stared at herself. "Oh, shit."

"What did you expect? We're supposed to spread out." The mirror image held out her hands. "Freaky, huh?"

"You have no idea . . ." Nashara paused. "Well, you know."

She smiled at herself. "We have immediate problems."

"Which are?"

"Who's in charge and who's called what? Do we time-share our body? And what do we do next with our new ship, here?"

Both of them pondered that for a few microseconds. Nashara twisted her fingers and reached out through her new twin, just to make sure. "I know you feel like the real copy, just like I do. But since I snagged the body first, I'm going to take dibs on Nashara and the body."

A brief stare-down as the other Nashara thought about it. "Ah, fuck it, I'm not going to fight myself over it. But I don't like the idea of changing my damn name."

"Is a rose by any other name as sweet?" Nashara asked herself.

"Oh, that's so cute of you, yes, funny." Her other self snorted. "I should just take on the name of the ship for convenience, but some people just have bad taste. What the fuck is a *Toucan Too?*"

"Just take one of the last names we use," Nashara suggested.

"Cascabel."

"Done."

"Everyone, gear prepare for acceleration," Cascabel announced throughout the entire ship.

"You're flying?" Nashara asked.

"Hell, yeah." Cascabel grinned. "You're staying with the body, we might need that, the Hongguo are still out there sniffing around. You know the scientists say the more you pretend to be a body and interact with the physical, the more human you'll remain in this little experiment."

"Yeah, but that's what the eggheads think."

"Nash, please. I get the flying." Cascabel looked insistent. It was something to hang on to that was familiar. Nashara understood.

"Fair enough."

The *Toucan Too* let go of the habitat. Thrown toward the downstream wormhole, Cascabel adjusted their course with a few slight bumps of acceleration. Debris chattered against the hull.

"Escape-pod debris," Nashara said.

The two stared at each other. "We'll be all right," Cascabel said.

Nashara didn't need reassurance from herself. She could use the same instruments. A ship had died here, and another ship hovered near the downstream wormhole.

Poor Jamar.

"Something's covering the downstream wormhole."

"And more somethings are covering the upstream," Cascabel said.

Nashara looked. A cloud of reflections signifying seven or eight ships. And something very long.

"We've seen something like that before," Cascabel muttered.

"The *Gulong*," Nashara said.

"They're planning to cut the Ragamuffins off. Kill the wormhole leading there."

"Or it's being used as a flagship for the Hongguo. Either way, it's downstream for us."

Nashara nodded. "Can we dodge it?"

"You and I can survive some high acceleration. The rest can't."

Nashara folded her arms. "We'll do what we can. Get them into the medical pods. Even if they black out hard, we can revive them."

"Be hard on the boy."

"Could be hard on the Raga to face an unexpected visit by the horde coming from upstream."

"True. If we're lucky, maybe they'll try and contact us." Cascabel smiled. "Give us some bandwidth and you know we'll spread."

Nashara smiled back. "Do it."

The *Toucan Too* dove for the downstream wormhole.

CHAPTER TWENTY

Kara stood up as Nashara walked into the room. "We're moving? Have we left the station?" Kara had never been aboard a ship before, the noises and sounds were alien, scary. No one had told her what was going on, she'd remained near Jared's pod, hoping all would turn out okay.

But even these adults seemed nervous.

"We need you to get in the medical pod next to your brother," Nashara said.

"Why? What's going on? Am I sick?"

"No, but you'll be safer in there. We need to do some dangerous things."

Ijjy walked in. He looked nervous. "Why can't I just join you in the cockpit for the acceleration?"

"It's going to be crushing." Nashara walked over to the pod, then right through it. "Fuck."

Kara and Ijjy stared at her.

"How'd you do that?" Kara asked. "Are you projecting yourself through lamina?" Kara tested the air around her, searching for lamina, searching for any information she could find. The air felt closed off by something large, dark, and slightly angry.

"Don't do that," Nashara said. "You're pushing at my mind."

"Oh."

"Please, now, get into your pods."

Ijjy closed himself in, shaking his head. "I don't like this," he said as the pod sealed.

Kara crawled in, the fabric closing softly in on her and holding her secure as she lay down in the pod. It smelled like oranges.

"Nashara?"

The woman leaned over. "I'm Cascabel, not Nashara."

"I don't understand."

"I'm in the lamina, it's where my mind is now." Cascabel waved her hand over the pod, and it sealed itself shut. "And I'm a second copy, there is another in the lamina. She's keeping the name Nashara."

Kara looked through the filmy cover at Cascabel. She knew she couldn't be heard, but said, "I'm scared."

Cascabel leaned over. "It'll be okay, don't be scared."

"You can hear me?"

"I'm in the lamina." Cascabel disappeared and her voice continued, "I'm all around you, in the ship. I just projected myself to your eyes. If you couldn't see lamina overlays, you wouldn't be able to see me."

"Wow." Kara had never heard of anything like it. What amazing things these outsiders could do.

"Yeah, that's been my take on it too," Cascabel snorted. "Don't worry, I'll stick with you here while we boost out, okay?"

"Okay." Kara closed her eyes as she felt weight slowly press against her. "What's it like out there, out past Agathonosis?"

"It's ugly out there," Cascabel said. "Not a whole lot of love for humans."

"But why?" Kara fought to breathe. "What did we ever do to them to make them hate us?"

"Not hate. Hate implies emotional attachment." There was a sigh. "It's about control."

"The Satrap said we couldn't control ourselves. That we had too much population." A massive groaning sound shivered through everything. Something snapped. "What was that?"

"Just another boost in speed. What the Satrapy fears is what we create. Before the Satrapy came to us, we flew our own craft, built our own computer programs."

"Lamina?"

"An ancient form of it," Cascabel said. "The Satraps believe that if technology accelerates and becomes uncontrollable, it will destroy everything. They seek to leash development, to leash our minds."

"So no humans are free?" Kara asked.

"Freedmen mainly skulk around the edges of the Satrapy." Cascabel cleared her throat. "There are habitats run by us, I think fifteen scattered all throughout. New Anegada and Chimson used to be human worlds. We terraformed them."

"So few?" Kara felt crushed.

"About thirty million free humans." The ship jumped left, slamming Kara against the pod and leaving bruises. "The other fifteen billion are 'free' but aboard habitats run by aliens, or Satraps, or on surface in reservations."

Kara closed her eyes. "Nowhere to run to." Another brutal slam, to the right. "We're being chased, aren't we?"

"The Raga can help. At the least they can help your brother."

It could be adult noise to reassure her. Kara looked at the scuffed, clear pod to her left. Would her brother make it through all of this? Would she?

"Take a deep breath," Cascabel said, breaking her thoughts.

"Why is that?"

"It's time to sleep, things are about to get a bit ugly."

Something hissed behind her, the smell of roses filled the pod, and Kara drifted off as she began to feel so heavy it hurt to even try to move.

CHAPTER TWENTY-ONE

Just before Deng took the *Shengfen Hao* through the downstream wormhole after the Ragamuffins, Etsudo hailed him.

"Thank you for your assistance," Deng said, curt and to the point. "We don't need your speedier vehicle. Your assistance was helpful, appreciated, and noted. We have other ships giving chase that should be able to catch up shortly."

Etsudo nodded. The *Toucan Too* had initiated a killing acceleration burn ahead of Deng's very nose and missiles, but they would still eventually catch up. There was nowhere for them to go.

Only Nashara could live through that. If anyone else was aboard that ship, they would be suffering cardiac arrest. He wanted to warn Deng about Nashara's ability. But to do that would uncover his dark little secrets.

No, let Deng find that out himself, if ever. Chances were more likely that the new, fast attack ships crossing toward the downstream wormhole right now would fire missiles into the *Toucan Too* and take care of that.

"Be careful," Etsudo said. "We don't know the full extent of the Ragamuffin defenses. Keep your ship moving slow and your communications low-bandwidth."

That would have to do.

Deng plunged through the wormhole, and the new might of the Hongguo continued to close in.

"Bahul." Etsudo looked over at the gamma-shift captain. "Keep us near the habitat. Just in case anything else comes out."

"Will do." Bahul looked bored as he kept them floating nearby.

Brandon floated through the cockpit door. "Afternoon."

Etsudo glanced up. "Afternoon. Change of shift?"

"Yes."

"I'll stay on," Etsudo waved. "Grab an extra chair."

Brandon hung for a second, something flitting through his face. Anger?

"Some of our ships are slowing down," Bahul said. "Moving in towards the habitat."

"Really?" Etsudo verified that and frowned.

"Oh," Bahul said. "Etsudo?"

And Etsudo saw what Bahul was looking at. Explosions ripped down the sides of the habitat. Pinprick after pinprick of light, but with a zoom of the cameras Etsudo could see water and air jetting out from the breached areas.

"What is going on?" Etsudo breathed.

Larger explosions almost blinded him. The center of the habitat slowly cracked open, vomiting dirt, trees, air, water, chunks of the layered hull.

"Are there people aboard that?" Etsudo asked. "Or was it evacuated yet? What the hell is happening?"

With only a few thousand miles between the habitat and his ship, Etsudo considered trying to move closer. If someone survived, maybe he could save them.

More explosions rippled down the end of the habitat, splitting off one of the end caps from the rest of the dying structure. It looked like a giant metal cup losing its top, disgorging debris.

"How many people lived in there?" Etsudo asked, horrified.

"The last registry says a couple hundred thousand," Brandon said.

Hongguo ships moved closer, five tiny chips of reflected light. But instead of moving to search for survivors, the five ships passed around the debris for the separated end cap.

"What are they doing?" Bahul asked.

Etsudo knew. He zoomed in on the end cap to where the ships cast out nets. Three of them were smaller merchant ships, like the *Takara Bune*. The other two Etsudo recognized. Large, heavily weaponed sister ships to the *Shengfen Hao*: *Datang Hao* and *Wuxing Hao*. Even closer. He froze the image for his crew to see. "They're recovering the Satrap."

"Is it dead?"

"No, they're perfectly fine in the vacuum," Etsudo said. His father had talked about once helping build a new upstream habitat for a Satrap.

"So that is a Satrap," Brandon breathed. A lump of chitinous flesh almost a hundred feet long being pulled into the belly of the *Datang Hao*.

"Behold our masters," Etsudo whispered to himself.

"Does it disturb you we aren't included in any of this? We didn't even know it was about to happen." Brandon looked wounded.

"We proved our worth," Etsudo said.

But Brandon didn't look quite convinced. It'd be time to take him back to the room soon, Etsudo thought. Too much restlessness bubbled up from inside the man, restlessness that threatened Etsudo.

Etsudo looked over at Bahul. "Get us moving, head downstream."

"We have business upstream," Brandon said.

"I want to observe what comes next," Etsudo said. Something important was happening. Something big. And Etsudo wanted the pieces to the puzzle, because he had a feeling it would be important to his future.

If the Satrapy had big changes in mind for humanity, Etsudo at least wanted enough warning to figure out what he wanted to do next.

And with a small chance that Nashara still lived, he needed to be sure his deceit didn't get uncovered.

In the off chance she was captured alive or without unleashing her talent, Etsudo had been spending all his spare moments in his captain's room, working hard to prepare his equipment in case it ever happened again.

CHAPTER TWENTY-TWO

The *Toucan Too* whipped around Chilo, a choking-hot and heavily clouded planet offering no traffic except a series of science satellites jostling between the two orbiting wormholes. Moving from the upstream wormhole to the downstream took a morning, and at noon Nashara faced herself. "You holding on?"

"Somewhat overwhelmed." Cascabel rubbed her eyes and leaned back through a chair. "We have the lead. We're almost there."

"At a cost." The pods had dragged everyone back to life after the last set of transits. Fast in, bump down the momentum, correct course, slam downstream. But the pods estimated they would fail the next time Cascabel pushed the *Toucan Too* that hard, and Cascabel bet the ship would shake itself apart at those speeds as well. Ijjy, Kara, and Jared slept under sedation, blissfully unaware of it all.

"They're alive, right? We're just a few wormholes upstream. We'll try to take it easy now," Cascabel said. "But better we save the thousands than the three."

Nashara closed her eyes and agreed. "We should see a ship soon, though." They were ever so close to old Ragamuffin haunts.

Though what the handful of aging ships Ijjy described out in the end of this run could do for her she wasn't sure.

They continued on, each withdrawing into her own private space. Hours bled into each other as the *Toucan Too* drifted from wormhole to wormhole, each transit dangerously close to ripping the ship apart.

But under Cascabel's quick guidance, they always pulled through. The hours bled into a day, then a second day, and on the third Cascabel appeared with a smile.

"Contact." They had just two more transits to go; it made sense that they encountered a Ragamuffin ship.

"I'll get Ijjy up."

The *Toucan Too* shuddered as it slowed and the other ship paced them.

Nashara kicked her way down the central shaft to the medical room, giving the command for Ijjy's pod to open as she opened the door.

He coughed, spitting up a tiny bit of blood. "My chest hurt something evil," he complained.

"You've had three cardiac failures," Nashara said, helping him wobble out of the pod. "But a Raga ship's pacing us. We're two transits upstream."

"That go be the *Starfunk Ayatollah,* I bet you anything," Ijjy said. "I know the captain."

"Let's get you strapped into the cockpit."

They coasted back, and Nashara helped Ijjy secure himself. "Cascabel, let's talk to the ship."

Her other self appeared. "Is that a good idea?"

"What do you mean?"

"Do we want to be taking over Ragamuffin ships?" Cascabel asked.

"There are controls built in regarding Ragalamina," Nashara muttered.

"But if they're using Satrapic technology . . ."

Ijjy shook his head. "Nah, all homegrown, all the time. Just open the channel and make sure I visible."

Cascabel shrugged. "Okay. And in one, two, three: the *Starfunk Ayatollah*'s on."

A leathery-faced man with grayed dreadlocks appeared before them all. "I Don Samuel Andery, captain of *Starfunk Ayatollah.* Who you is?"

"Mr. Andery, my name is Nashara. This is Ian Johnson, of the *Queen Mohmbasa.* We need to talk, and quick."

"Ijjy?" Andery frowned. "Where the *Queen?*"

Ijjy swallowed. "Gone. The Hongguo attacked."

"The Hongguo? For real?"

"They also had attack the other higglers we was with," Ijjy said. And then he launched into a recap, answering Andery's questions as the conversation grew heated.

"I find all that hard to believe. Hongguo enforce the rule of the Satrap, but this?"

"Believe it," Nashara said. "Why else do you have armed ships? Why else do you cluster around a dead wormhole instead of trying to integrate with the rest of the worlds? The Satrapy doesn't have our best interests at heart."

Andery looked at her. "That true, sister, true, but we can't just take you word for it. You go have to come in, call a grounation with the Dread Council to talk. Then they can send out some ship to check all this."

"You think you have the time for that?" Nashara waved in the air to display an image of the upstream wormhole. A Hongguo ship breached the wormhole, cautious, tasting the air ahead of itself with a score of drones that swarmed out tossing chaff and bleeping random static across frequencies. Nashara shook her head. No way back through, Hongguo would be piling up on the other side of the hole any moment now.

Another ship followed it. Then a second. Then a third.

"Taking us a bit more seriously now?" Nashara asked. It surprised her the Ragamuffins only had one ship out patrolling.

Andery looked serious. "Get you self moving, we right behind." He looked away from them, then nodded. "The *Magadog* coming in."

A new face appeared, scarred with short-cropped hair. "*Toucan Too*, this *Magadog*, Ras Christopher Malik here. Been listening to what all you saying. Don Andery got the right of it, head downstream, we sending back explanation, mobilizing."

"You have preparations for such an event?" Cascabel asked. A Ras ranked higher than a Don; this captain would know more about Ragamuffin emergency plans.

Ras Malik nodded. "Morant being towed out system, deep space. Worse come to worse we keep going, head out into them Oort cloud, hide out deep, forget the wormhole them, hunker down. We already an hour into it, you'll find out what happen when you get in system. Just be careful, we all jumpy, seen?"

Nashara saw a blip moving out from beside the downstream wormhole now. The *Magadog*. The two ships played chicken for a few brief minutes, until *Magadog* curved out of the way.

"Good luck," Nashara said.

"You too," Ras Malik said. "Thanks for the heads-up. Make sure to drop all you speed coming out the wormhole, it mined."

Magadog whipped past them, mere thousands of miles apart. Cascabel upped acceleration, and the *Toucan Too* hit the downstream wormhole toward the Ragamuffin home territory.

Sweeps of the area around lit up their displays. Ships, shuttles, drones, chaff.

"Shit, Malik wasn't kidding." Cascabel dumped velocity, spinning them on end to fire the main engines and bleed tens of thousands of kilometers per hour.

The two wormholes orbited a rocky world, and that in turn hung out near a brown dwarf. Nothing of interest to the Satrapy here.

"*Toucan Too*, this the *Xamayca Pride*." An audio-only connection of a woman's voice. A cautious choice. Nashara respected that. "Ras Monifa Kaalid here, we sending you a path through the mines hanging all around you."

Cascabel nodded. "It's here." The *Toucan Too* puffed, adjusting orbit to sink down into the cloud of mines.

The round face of Ras Kaalid appeared, her dreadlocks floating loose around her face. "Sorry about that," she said. "Things really getting hectic here and everything on a full stand-up. We already getting Morant towed out."

"You knew about the Hongguo?" Nashara asked.

Ras Kaalid shook her head. "The downstream wormhole to New Anegada reopened. Everything upside down."

Nashara and Cascabel stared at each other, and Ijjy leaned forward. "That even possible?" Ijjy asked.

"Apparently," Ras Kaalid said. "Now we have to find out what coming up through from there, and what coming down on all of we with the Hongguo."

Nashara looked at Cascabel. "We have to get there. We have to find out what has happened."

"Maybe, but it ain't big enough. We waiting to see what coming through."

"Make sure we're there too," Nashara told Cascabel. She had to see what lay on the other side of the wormhole, what had happened to New Anegada.

Her long quest might almost be over.

And they might have a new ally in the coming fight against the Hongguo.

PART TWO

THE RETURN OF THE GODS

CHAPTER TWENTY-THREE

Pepper wrapped his oilskin duster around himself tighter as the wind kicked up through the trees and water cascaded down on his dreadlocks and behind his collar. He shivered.

He needed a new duster. He'd bulked out too much over the last few years. Good food, a free schedule. It sounded good. Nice planet, New Anegada. Or Nanagada, as the Caribbean descendants here had taken to calling it sometime in the last few hundred years. Only, somewhat annoyingly, the locals called their land on the other side of the mountains Nanagada, just like the planet.

He still wanted to get off the damn planet and see if it was possible to get back to the rest of the worlds. The destructive dying spams of the war against the Teotl the Black Starliner Corporation had raged in space had left the planet with no wormholes out anywhere and with the destruction of technology. It was hard to step back from centuries of progress and not miss it, and Pepper found each year grated harder at him.

A branch snapped.

Someone sniffed.

Pepper's gray eyes flashed back a bit of moonlight, like a cat's. He flipped back an edge of his coat and pulled out a long hunting knife.

Five days in this dirty, muddy, humid, sticky-leafed outskirts of the Azteca city Tenochtitlanome.

It was something to do.

The warrior-priest he'd been stalking stepped around the large banyan tree and Pepper picked him off the ground by his throat. He tossed the sniper's rifle the man carried off into the bush.

"Niltze," Pepper said. Hello. Pepper had been practicing his Nahautl.

He flashed the knife in front of the man, who whispered, "Pepper," and wet himself.

Word apparently got around.

Pepper shoved the man down onto his back. Mud exploded outward as the flat of the warrior-priest's back slapped against the sloppy ground.

"I die gladly for my gods," the priest choked.

"That's nice." Pepper leaned forward. "I have a question. Which one of your gods is giving you the orders to try and kill delegates from Nanagada?"

The Azteca's gods, the Teotl, couldn't leave well enough alone since their defeat and the overthrow of their priests. They still tried to manipulate things here in Tenochtitlanome from the shadows.

"I'll die a thousand lives before giving you any information," the priest spat.

"I can do that," Pepper growled. A twig snapped nearby. "But you're lucky today."

"Pepper?"

"You're late, Xippilli." Pepper looked over at the Azteca nobleman who stepped off the muddy path toward them. "Told you I'd catch one skulking around here."

Several Jaguar warriors in yellow-and-red capes stepped forward, rifles aimed at the warrior-priest on the ground.

"Take him for interrogation," Xippilli ordered. The Jaguar scouts ran forward and bound the warrior-priest's hands with leather thongs and carried him away.

Xippilli stood with Pepper in the rain, looking through the foliage toward the pyramids rising over the top of the jungle. Tenochtitlanome, the capital of Aztlan, was home to tens of thousands of Azteca. And home to a small delegation of Nanagadans, their housing not too far away from the copse they stood in.

"It's a good thing I'm here," Pepper said. "Or some of them would be dead by now."

"The old priesthood despise the moderates and preach against the new leadership," Xippilli said. "They can't accept the outcome of the Great War. They think if we had fought harder, a little bit longer, that we would be the masters of Nanagada. It's not surprising they're still out trying to affect things."

"I should have come out earlier, cracked some heads, sent a message." Pepper pulled his collar up and shook his head.

"Does the boy mean that much to you?" Xippilli asked.

Pepper looked over. "I asked John deBrun for a favor. In return, he wants me to keep an eye on his son right now. Yeah, it's babysitting, but who better?" He didn't agree with the delegation. Opening the Wicked High Mountains, such a perfect barrier to the Azteca, seemed stupid.

But he wasn't in charge, and no one had asked him. Instead John had come to ask him to keep a close eye on Jerome, as many Azteca would welcome striking back against one of the main people who'd helped end the Great War.

"Indeed," Xippilli said. "Who better?" Both men stood in the rain for a moment, then Xippilli walked over to the road.

A few moments later a steam-powered car slowly chuffed down toward them. Red-and-yellow-caped Azteca hung from the sides, watching the road. Pepper moved back into the brush and watched it go by.

"How are things going with the delegation?"

Xippilli shrugged. "They're still touring the city, seeing the sights. The cocoa plantations today were the main event."

Pepper watched the steam car creak off into the city. "I think I feel worse for the boy in there."

"Politics do drag on," Xippilli said. "But they run the world."

"Flapping mouths."

"They might bring our two cultures together." But of course, Xippilli had a strong interest in all this. Since leaving Capitol City politics, Xipilli had turned to trade. His knowledge of Azteca and Capitol City customs and people let him build airships and trade routes over the Wicked High Mountains. And he wanted the two connected more permanently. More profit lay there. "That's worth all this, don't you think?"

"I'm just fulfilling my side of a bargain." Pepper brushed past leaves to step up onto the road. The rain paused, a break in the dark clouds showing the light blue sky.

"What was this favor you asked of John?"

"Checking to see if that damn spaceship of his is healed up yet."

"Eager to leave us?" Xippilli asked.

"You have no idea." Pepper looked up into the sky at a small, bulging twinkle. The Spindle. Legend said that it would one day disgorge the Azteca's gods in vast numbers.

Unlike most legends, Pepper knew this one was true. At some point the energies that leaked out to create the always visible Spindle would force the wormhole back open. When the alien Teotl returned in force, all hell would break lose. Been there, done that, Pepper thought. And he didn't want to be around for it the second time.

CHAPTER TWENTY-FOUR

A gaudy airship with a bloated gasbag and peeling red paint floated high over the walls of Capitol City, propellers churning as it fought the sea-breeze headwinds that kicked up in the evening.

An Azteca airship.

Once it would have made John deBrun nervous. Today it was just another trader. A lot had changed in the last decade, particularly in the last seven years since the fall of the old Azteca leadership to more moderate rulers. Airships moved back and forth over the almost impassable mountains that separated the Azteca from the Nanagadans. Trade boomed in Capitol City and the land recovered from the Great War. The Teotl had led the Azteca to the city walls, but had been dealt a blow in that war that toppled the old leadership and sent them back over the mountains.

Nanagada's masterful specialist fighters, the mongoose-men, had built up their numbers along the Wicked Highs to prevent a repeat anyway. It was a secure, stable, and prosperous time for Nanagada.

The airship slowly dropped into the heart of the city, disappearing behind the massive walls perched on the peninsula's tip.

John watched the spray drift up from waves constantly smacking into the rocks at the city's seawall base. It would be a salty day if one stood on the wall walkway.

A larger steamer churned by John's small fishing skiff, giant nets hanging from long metal arms off either side. The men on the deck waved.

The fishing fleet steamed farther and farther out these days. Water currents changed, the ocean had slightly cooled.

It would keep cooling as Nanagada failed to get enough sun. The orbital mirrors keeping the planet warm had fallen two hundred years ago. Ice had crept over the northern continent, and fishermen reported icebergs hindering the fishing grounds.

The technological proficiency needed to keep a terraformed planet going had been lost in the war with the Teotl. Electromagnetic pulses from nuclear weapons and the destroyed wormhole leading back to the Teotl had left the whole planet shattered, only just now reacquiring the tools it needed. But, John knew, not soon enough to countereffect the cooling of the planet.

Before Pepper got to use the *Ma Wi Jung* to try to bridge the depths of the stars to the next wormhole, a centuries-long journey, John needed the still-working spaceship to help Nanagada. That would be an interesting conflict when the time came.

John sailed on, letting Capitol City dwindle until it felt as if he were all that sat at sea. A tiny speck of a boat bobbing out in the ocean.

He knew exactly where he was. John could close his eyes and see a map of the area, complete with his exact location, the city, and the spaceship he looked for.

He dropped the sails and threw the anchor over. He walked back to the bench by the mast and sat down.

Beneath his boat John could feel the presence of the spaceship *Ma Wi Jung*. Deep beneath the waves, sucking nutrients and metals out of the water, it slowly repaired itself. One day it would fly again, lift itself into the air and spring for space.

Maybe.

John queried the ship, feeling his mind connect with it like a snake burrowing down into a hole. Images floated over his eyes as he accessed the ship's datasphere.

Status?

The answer impressed itself somewhere deep in the back of his head. Another fifteen years. The starship's self-repair mechanisms were working at double the speed they'd been designed for, a little hack thanks to John.

He glanced overhead. The Spindle hung in the sky. Its geosynchronous orbit kept it at the same spot, day or night. An omen for many, a worry for the few who knew what it really was.

John sighed. The Spindle was the remains of a wormhole, and when that wormhole reopened, something he hadn't known was even possible when he'd helped try to destroy it, there was going to be a world of hurt. Nanagada's old enemies would come through.

And the other wormhole in orbit around Nanagada, the one that had once led out to allies and that John had come through to get to Nanagada, that one didn't seem to be reopening. It was invisible.

They were alone.

He pulled a lure out of the tackle box beneath him, rigged a pole, and cast over the side of the boat.

As the sun slipped beneath the horizon, John ran a light up the mast. He'd stay the night; he enjoyed the fishing.

He didn't have any obligations, and he had no worries as Pepper was keeping an eye on Jerome off in Tenochtitlanome. He missed the sea, salt drifting over him, night sky packed with stars. He'd stay. He'd nap. It would be refreshing.

The old wooden boat rocked an easy rhythm, mast swaying, as John leaned back, closed his eyes, and smiled. Almost four hundred years old, and fishing still hadn't lost its appeal.

But he kept glancing back up at the sky.

As the sun rose, John tied the small fishing boat to one of the low wooden piers in Capitol City's harbor. Capitol City jutted up out of the peninsula's tip, a great amphitheater with one edge slouched in the water.

Several hundred years ago the entire city had been grown from scratch, using an experimental and highly illegal form of nanotechnology powered by microwave radiation focused down on the spot from orbit.

Well before humans had come down to settle Nanagada. Well before the Ancient Wars hundreds of years ago, when they were reduced to no technology, scrabbling around on the surface trying to get by.

"Good catch?" someone in a long fishing skiff asked.

John stretched out the several fish whose gills he'd run wire through and held by a foot-long wooden stick. "Not bad." His accent sounded flat, as even after all his years among the Caribbean descendants of Nanagada he had never picked up the dialect as fully as he would have liked.

"You catch them good, John."

He smiled. A good catch, but only because the *Ma Wi Jung* heated up the water below, attracting fish and activity. He'd fry this batch up and enjoy a good breakfast.

John shifted the catch to his right hand and climbed the steps up to the stone cobble of the main waterfront. He waved at a few fishermen scaling fish on stone tables.

The apartment he lived in lay half a mile through the tight alleys and shortcuts John had internalized easily enough. A ghostly series of compasses and lines hung in the air before him that only he could see. It was a talent wired into his brain hundreds of years ago to allow him to plunge ships through wormholes in haste.

John closed his eyes and relied on the internal map still visible to him. He took thirty-seven steps forward, stopped, turned right, and started walking.

A dumb trick. He opened his eyes to avoid tripping on alley trash.

A Toltecan walked toward John, one of the moderate Azteca who spurned human sacrifice and lived in Capitol City. Many had returned and reformed the city of Tenochtitlanome when the government had fallen apart, bankrupt due to the costs of its invasion of Nanagada. Quite a few remained in the city, though. The Toltecan's fringed hair was brushed down almost over his eyes.

"Morning." John nodded as they approached one another. With barely room for each to pass, John turned aside to let the man through.

The man, a true Azteca, drew a knife and struck John's shoulder. It hit bone, and the pain drifted down John's arm. "Your time is over," the man hissed, pushing the knife farther in. Waves of dizziness grabbed John. "You now pay for defying the gods."

John dropped to his knees. A second man grabbed him from behind. John twisted just far enough so that the knife bit into his left lung instead of a kidney.

He tried to scream, despite one punctured lung, and despite the fingers jammed down his mouth as they pushed him down to the ground. The first man yanked the knife free from his shoulder, slick with blood, and John grabbed the next stab with his left hand. The knife impaled the meat of his hand.

All three of them struggled on the dirty, wet alleyway ground.

Deep inside, old technology struggled to maintain his consciousness, suppress pain, and keep him standing. John hadn't been in combat shape in a long while, though, and only his body's natural shock prevented him from passing out.

More footsteps. John kicked a kneecap in and struggled to get free, but he just couldn't draw a breath.

"Hey!" Someone yelled into the alley. "Somebody get help, is a mugging going on!"

John pulled the knife out of his left hand as his attackers looked up. He stabbed it deep into the belly of the man who sat on his chest. The man screamed and stumbled back.

The remaining assassin spun and took off running. John pushed himself onto his hands and knees and looked over at the corner of the alleyway. Something glinted back at him.

A homemade bomb.

John struggled forward out of the alley.

The world roared, shifted, and John flew forward. His back exploded in pain from shards of rock and metal embedded in it.

Face, shoulders, and back streaming blood, nose broken, eyes too blood-shot to see, his head ringing, John crawled out. He felt the larger cobblestones of the road under his hands.

He collapsed into the dirty water of a gutter. Strong arms grabbed him to pull him up. "We need get you to a hospital." The faces of several Raga-muffins, the city's policemen, looked down at him.

"No," John croaked. "Boat." The men who'd tried to kill him, Azteca spies posing as Tolteca, had done a good job. He was as good as dead unless he got back to the ship.

He pushed them away and dropped to his knees.

"He hit he head too hard," someone offered.

John turned toward the sound of the voice. He focused down into himself to try to manage the pain. "I'm perfectly clear of mind. If I don't get out to where I need to go, I'll die, there's nothing any doctor here can do for me."

"But . . ."

He coughed blood. "Do not argue with me."

They argued about it, each taking a minute too long, but someone had recognized him and commandeered a small boat with a steam engine still hot. John could smell fish everywhere as they gently moved him into a hammock.

"This ain't no good," the captain of the small vessel protested. "You go die if you don't get help."

"Will you just trust that I know what I'm doing?" John asked him.

With his eyes closed he could see exactly where they had moved. Each step remained in his mind since they had left the edge of the alley to walk down the docks.

Now at sea he gave them orders, moving them out toward the *Ma Wi Jung.*

His heart rate dropped, close to failure. "Hurry," John told them. "Hurry." The small boiler next to the hammock radiated heat, which made him drowsy. The door clanged as someone fed it wood.

By steamboat it took only a couple hours, though by then John's eyes started to glaze.

"Stop!" John whispered, and the captain coasted to a stop.

The waves tossed them back and forth, rocking steadily.

John fumbled out of the hammock and felt his way to the rail. His legs protested, but he used every last ounce of strength to walk over and grab hold.

"What you doing?"

Before they could stop him John pitched forward into the cold water. The world fell silent, the distant crash of waves against the hull of the boat nearby becoming the entire world.

He sank, expelling air to speed up.

Ma Wi Jung?

The ship lay hundreds of feet below him. It had the medicinal technology to heal him.

The ship responded as John queried it, asking it to rise and meet him. He swallowed hard as the reply came to him. The ship did not have the ability to rise from the seabed. The water had grown cold.

Far beneath John an air lock slide open and belched massive bubbles.

Already he had fallen a hundred feet, his ears popping as he equalized them. If he could see, the ocean would be inky blackness.

He hadn't taken in enough air with a collapsed lung to do this.

The pockets of air released from the air lock buffeted him.

He fell faster now, arrowing down, long seconds passing, the water getting even colder. John started shivering as his body's core temperature dropped.

Behind his eyelids he could see the last fifty feet through the ship's data-sphere. The ship had spotted him. It lit the area up, and what it saw, John also saw. He could see himself, trailing blood, shivering, falling down toward the ship.

Just a little left, and John struck the hull headfirst. He dragged himself the last few feet into the air lock.

The lock shut. It slowly drained away the water until John floated faceup in air he could breathe. The pumps failed at that point, unused to the strain of pumping in enough air to force the water out.

John burst inside the ship along with hundreds of gallons of water as the inner lock opened.

He lay on the floor as it absorbed the water.

The medical pod lay inside a room ten feet away, and for John, gasping like a fish, it may have been twenty miles away.

He closed his eyes and curled up in a ball of pain on the floor, then straightened out. Foot by foot he crawled until he could pull himself into the medical pod and close it.

CHAPTER TWENTY-FIVE

John woke up with a pounding headache, aches, and scars all over. A meal sounded good, but there was nothing on the ship but the nutrient drip the medical pod had retracted from his arm several hours ago. He checked the time. Three days. Three days ensconced in here. The boat above had left, no doubt assuming he was dead.

The inside of the ship looked a lot better since the last time he'd visited, when it still bore smoke and fire damage.

An alert pinged patiently from the cockpit, as well as in the back of his head. The *Ma Wi Jung* needed him to take care of something.

John sat down and tapped a panel, looked down at the series of readouts that appeared in the air.

Radio signals.

They'd started while he was in the medical pod, coming from the vicinity of the Spindle, and moving their way from the geosynchronous orbit of that wormhole into a low orbit.

John felt as if he'd been punched in the stomach. The wormhole had reopened. Which meant that the energies pouring through what had once been a tiny hole in the sky to create the always visible Spindle and force the hole back open would soon fade away, and the whole world would know it.

Teotl would be coming through. Tenochtitlanome was going to become the most dangerous place to be on the whole planet.

John checked the ship's inventory, looking for an escape raft. None, and it would take too long for the ship to create one for him. But it did have an inflatable vest and a flare gun.

That would have to do.

That evening, as the fishing steamers were returning toward Capitol City, John burst out of the air lock toward the surface.

After his first deep breath of salty, cold air, he fired a flare. Three flares later a bewildered fishing crew hauled John up onto their deck.

"You dead," they said.

John ignored them as they wrapped him up with blankets and took him into the engine room near the giant boiler to keep him warm. He lay in the warmth thinking of his son in the heart of Azteca land unaware that everything was on the cusp of changing for the worse.

Before he left the fishing boat, he borrowed some heavy-weather gear, flipping the hood up to obscure his face.

He fought his way back through the crowds of Capitol City. Everything seemed normal in the fading light and inside the great walls of the city. Crowds of people, from dark to light brown and even a few white, filled the streets. All manner of accents filled the air. It was a bit packed for this late. Although the city's electric lights would be on, most people in the city had candles. They left for home at sunset. But now vendors shouted at each other as John got on one of the street buses running down the center of the city. Several people stood over large bundles.

The whip antenna sparked and slapped the metal grid overhead. The bus accelerated toward the next stop.

John had been happy to move out from Brungstun, the town he'd lived in almost thirty years and raised his son in. Too many memories there, most of them of Shanta, his wife.

Capitol City felt safer than the small town right beside the Wicked High Mountains, the first place overrun during the Great War. He still had nightmares about waking up to find Azteca rooting through his house, binding his wrists, and dragging him off to be a sacrifice.

Better to remain in Capitol City, behind the solid walls, with hundreds of miles between the mountains and him.

The bus stopped near the red-painted stone building John lived in. He got out and jogged up the outer steps to his apartment, almost knocking himself out on a clothesline as he couldn't see much above eye level with the hood up.

The door was unlocked. It swung open and a pair of mongoose-men stepped out from the shadows to grab him and pull him in.

"Who you is?" they demanded. One yanked the hood down, and they both froze. "John deBrun?"

John nodded.

"Yes. What are you doing in here?" he demanded.

The two soldiers looked abashed. "We was sent to guard the place, see if anyone showed up. General Haidan hear you was dead."

"He angry," the other mongoose-man said.

"After all the years we've known each other, I'm glad to hear that." John walked over to a chest under the small table in his cramped kitchen. "Someone did try to kill me. Azteca spies here in the city."

He pulled out a handful of gold coins, a change of clothes, and a pistol.

"You in a hurry to leave, Mr. deBrun, but where you going, sir, Haidan go want to know."

"Tenochtitlanome."

"Is dangerous for you. The Azteca go want catch you and torture you, they want to know where to find you ship, how to get into it."

"I know, it doesn't matter now. Now look, time is short." John stood up and looked at the two mongoose-men in their beige uniforms. "You need to tell Haidan the Teotl have come from the Spindle, and that the wormhole is open again. He needs to make preparations. Tell him as soon as possible."

The two men glanced at each other. "We already know."

John stopped. "How?"

They threw open the wooden shutters on the north side of his apartment. "Look up, above the jungle."

John walked over. Above the clotheslines outside, the alleyway and bubble of conversation and street noise, above the great wall of Capitol City, was a band that stood over it all. And a large black dot hovered in place in the distance, visible just over the lip of the wall. Hood up, lost in his own worries, he hadn't looked up to see what everyone else in the city had already seen.

That was why so many people were out this late.

"A ship?" John asked.

"Just hanging there," they confirmed. "Although rumors is that one of them drop off Azteca near the center of the city, near the gardens. We ain't see it, but things getting crazy already."

There would be no outgoing airships, or probably even trains. John grabbed the peeling windowsill with both hands and hung his head.

In the distance a siren sounded. The city's air shelters would be filling up, civil defense officials moving out onto the street, and the whole population getting ready for a new war.

Only this one would feature attackers from above.

They could not win it, John knew.

Outside the door, when John walked out with the two mongoose-men, an old lady with her hair in a bun held up a hand.

They all paused. "Mother Elene?"

"No, I am Sister Agathy," the lady whispered. "But Mother Elene sent me. John deBrun, the Loa need to see you."

Capitol City's so-called gods were worried. The Teotl had struggled to wipe them out as well, now their more powerful brothers from space had arrived. The Loa had every reason to fear what would come next.

Their human delegates would be moving all throughout the city to prepare for this. And they'd sent a Vodun acolyte to get John.

"There is little time," Sister Agathy said, looking at John.

The prospect of speaking to the alien creatures in their dens made John sick to his stomach. Hundreds of years of death and manipulation lay at the feet of the Teotl and Loa. It never went away, except for the few brief decades when John had lived in Brungstun as a fisherman, his memories erased.

That felt like a second childhood.

He really missed fishing.

Sister Agathy took John's hand, and he sighed and followed her away from his apartment and deeper into the panicking city.

CHAPTER TWENTY-SIX

Jerome deBrun watched as the Azteca priest prepared his squealing sacrifice. The priest stank, his hair matted into long clumps of black, foul-smelling snarls due to the blood that remained on him. Two younger acolytes held the sacrifice down, its limbs tied with rope.

"Thank God it a pig," Thomas, from Grammalton, whispered to Jerome. Jerome nodded back.

The pig squealed loudly, the priest held up his stone knife, and Jerome looked down at the muddy floor. This would have been how they killed his mother ten years ago. He bit his lip until he tasted his own salty blood.

When he looked back up, the priest held a beating heart up toward the sun, blood streaming down his hands into his face.

"We give this gift," said the priest haltingly, unused to translating the words for his audience. "To the sun."

To make sure it came up again. Right. Jerome sighed.

Behind the priest a large pen with barbed wire held eighteen more pigs, rooting in the dirt, scuffling around. Jerome wondered if they heard their companion's squeals and could understand their fate.

"They going kill all eighteen?" Thomas asked.

"Yes." Thomas needed to quit asking questions he should already know the answer to.

The pen's wall stretched too high to hold in just pigs. Jerome's mother, as well as other people from Brungstun, must have been locked in a pen like that once.

But that was past. Jerome let out a deep breath.

"They having a reception for all the delegate them after all this." Thomas leaned in. "You go come, or lock youself in you room early again?"

Jerome took a deep breath and almost gagged on the scent of blood. "Maybe."

"They say we go meet the pipiltin there," Thomas said. "You know what they is?"

"Noblemen, businessmen, the people that run the place other than the priests."

Jerome stared past the priest at the city of Tenochtitlanome and the tips of all its buildings. The delegation, all twenty in stiff-starched black suits soaking up the heat, stood on the flattened-out apex of a pyramid five stories tall at the center of a plaza.

The city ran outward from the pyramid, city streets like spokes from a hub, layers of Tenochtitlanome radiating outward from the core. Thousands of Azteca milled about around the pyramid, staring up at the apex.

Smoke curled up from several marketplaces out near the rim, and from house yards. And people packed the streets everywhere, moving quickly about their business.

"Remind me of Capitol City," David said from Jerome's left. He hailed from a small settlement near Batalun.

Jerome shook his head. "Only pigs for eating get killed in Capitol City."

David shook his head. "At least it ain't us."

People kept repeating that. "As if that cancel out all that had go on before," Jerome spat. Probably a bit too loud; an acolyte looked at him.

"You know Tolteca good people," David said. "Lot of them never believe in human sacrifice, all this time. Lot of them had to get over the mountains to come to Capitol City to escape all that, and others could never escape, had to stay here. Now they in charge. Now they rule. It all good."

"Sure," Jerome said. "Sure."

He spat on the ground. The mongoose-men who had traveled with the delegates from Capitol City stood at rigid attention, their faces glistening with sweat and khaki uniforms sopping with it. Nanagada's best bush warriors, wasting their time in the heat.

A local chief of the new pipiltin held the reception in a tented platform on the edge of Tenochtitlanome. Here the roads petered out into jungle, and lower-class Azteca followed donkey carts into the city or carried large bales of wheat on their backs.

Newly acquired electric lamps swung from poles, lighting the interior now that the sunlight faded.

Chiefs stood around in traditional padded-cotton armor, their hair carefully combed forward and fringed, with feathers twined throughout.

"Hi-lo." An Azteca woman with lightly tanned skin and bangs over her eyes smiled at Jerome. He held a glass of fermented something, too strong for him, and considered her plain white cotton dress. She chewed something rubbery in her mouth. A prostitute for the delegates' pleasure.

Jerome looked down at the drink and walked back over to the bar. "You have any beer?"

The man stared at him, then held up another mug of the foul-smelling fermented stuff.

"Clot it." Jerome took a breath and drained it. He almost gagged, but it warmed him up. He grabbed another and downed it. And then another.

"Take it easy." Xippilli sat next to him and intercepted the next mug. "This goes straight to your head."

Jerome glared at him. Xippilli looked a bit fuzzy in the strong electric light. "What you all about?"

"This is a place to be seen, Jerome, not to get drunk." Xippilli pointed out a series of Azteca chiefs. "Those are very powerful, and rich, men."

"The worse kind." Jerome looked back at Xippilli. "You know how many of them rip through Brungstun?"

"Yes."

Jerome grabbed Xippilli's arm. "Which one of them over there was in Brungstun? Tell me."

"Let it rest." Xippilli shook his head. "You can't kill them, they're a part of all this." He raised his cup and waved it all around. "They're at least willing to help move us to moderation, they see the direction things go. Without their support we wouldn't even have this."

"We don't need it."

"You agreed to represent the town of Brungstun in these negotiations, Jerome."

"You know I can't say no. What they go say if I don't? John deBrun, look, he son refuse to stand for the town. No, I know what they all expect." Jerome grabbed another mug before Xippilli could intercept.

"If we open a road through Mafolie Pass in the Wicked Highs, trade will triple as we're able to easily cross from Aztlan to Nanagada, both civilizations will be able to know each other. You were given a great honor by your town, a tribute to what your father did."

"I ain't John!"

"On that"—Xippilli pulled away from Jerome—"we both strongly agree."

"I representing Brungstun, trust me." Jerome watched him leave. Xippilli, despite his protests, was really no different from the people he'd run from. He'd crossed the Wicked High Mountains and trekked all the way to Capitol

City for a new life. Yet here he stood, walking over to a nearby chief, and laughing. Talking to murderers.

Brungstun, first town on the other side of the Wicked High Mountains, had been the first overrun when the Teotl launched the invasion of Nanagada. They'd poured over the mountains into his town. Why should Jerome help make it easier for the Azteca to do it again?

He'd make sure any way over the Wicked Highs remained closed.

Jerome stood up and walked over to Thomas.

Thomas turned. "Yes?"

"I'm going to leave before it get too dark."

"Damn it Jerome, already?"

"Thomas . . ." I ain't you friend, he wanted to say. But stopped. They were both in their twenties. Jerome here because of his father's heroic status. Thomas because he was the oldest government man in Grammalton after the Azteca passed through. Neither of them would live up to the responsibilities put on them. John's father was an old-father, one of the original settlers of Nanagada hundreds of years ago, near immortal due to strange, tiny machines in him from before the wars that destroyed all such things and left them stranded on this planet.

And Jerome was just Jerome.

"Don't worry. I understand, you know. I understand." Thomas looked out across the crowd and jerked his head. Two mongoose-men in gray uniforms walked over. They carried holstered guns at their waists, but not their famed rifles.

"Bed already?" one of them chuckled.

Jerome nodded. They took their positions at either side and walked him up the road along the flickering torches that were just being started up by runners along the many roads. The torchlight flickered by their faces, and they stared at him as they ran by.

He didn't belong here.

Jerome tossed and turned in his bed, skimming just over the edge of a deeper sleep. He sat up finally, disturbed by some noise outside, and mopped sweat from his forehead with his sheet.

In the still air a steady thunder shook the windows.

The mongoose-man by his door came in. "Everything okay?"

"Yeah." Jerome walked forward and opened the heavy wooden windows.

"You need leave them shut, in case," the mongoose-man warned him.

Jerome looked out across the tiny flickering lights of lit torches at the sky, trying to see if there were any clouds.

None.

But the thundering increased. A trail of fire glowed white-hot in the sky as it crossed the far horizon and approached.

"What that?"

Jerome shook his head. "I don't know."

They watched it grow closer, the white-hot glow lighting up the night sky as it approached.

It couldn't be a sign of anything good.

Jerome snagged mongoose-men khaki from one of the men his own size, his movements hurried.

"We all know what things returning from the sky go mean to the Azteca," he said as he dressed. "Some of them go think Teotl returning to the earth from the sky."

"But is it true?"

"Who know?" Jerome looked around the small house they all had shared for the last week. Eight mongoose-men, four of them dressed and at guard, the other four he'd woken up. "But that no meteor, coming in too slow, burning too long."

"Clot," someone swore.

"I know." Jerome pointed at the dressed and armed men. "Get back to the party, bring all of everyone back, quick now. The rest of you, get ready and get you rifles ready."

They stood still. "We think—"

"How many you all know what come out the sky just then?" Jerome asked. "None of you? Okay then, until any of we all know better, you best had move!"

"Okay, Jerome." The four turned and took off.

"The rest of you all, get dress. Then we getting ready to board this place all up."

"With what wood?"

Jerome looked down at the floor. "This nice hardwood plank right under we feet."

The house was a small island in an ocean of danger. Jerome looked out of the windows into the flickering gas lamps of the Azteca city, then moved a bit until he could see the flattened top of the massive stone pyramid at the heart of the city.

Torches leapt to fire at the pyramid's top. An ordinary but still chilling omen. Jerome walked over to one of the chests the mongoose-men had dragged all the way from Capitol City. Several rifles lay nestled in a bed of straw.

He picked one up, checked the bolt, and grabbed a box of ammunition.

"Careful with that," a mongoose-man with a close-shaved head said, buttoning up his shirt and coming down the stairs.

"I know how to use this."

"You jumpy."

"I got reason. We go need to board up the window them, and then the door. If Teotl come from the sky, we go be ready."

The mongoose-man laughed. "That an old bush legend."

"You saw my father land from the sky in Capitol City in he flying machine, right?" Jerome spat. "You were in the city, right?"

The mongoose-man nodded. "Yeah."

"Then don't be no chucklehead. When the Teotl land, it go be in machine just like my father flew."

Footsteps outside. Jerome walked backward to the side of the door. He loaded the rifle and waved the mongoose-man to the kitchen.

A man burst in. Jerome swung the rifle up and almost shot him before recognizing Thomas.

"Clot! Man, I almost shoot you."

"Jerome." Thomas reached over and pushed the gun barrel away.

"What going on?" Jerome asked.

"The fire just hanging over the city. A whole lot of bright lights." Thomas wiped his forehead on his sleeve. "I ran all the way here, people saying the chariot of the gods landing in the city."

"The Teotl." Jerome looked around the house.

"They saying that." Thomas grabbed him. "Xippilli say to stay put, he go send help."

"Maybe, but even Xippilli go be in fight to save he own skin," Jerome said. "The old priests, they go come out the walls now."

After some thuds and the sound of ripping, the mongoose-man in the kitchen came back out holding several planks of wood. "Board it all up?"

"What you name?" Jerome asked him.

"Bruce Passey."

"Mr. Passey, get every way into this house nail shut." Jerome looked back at the tiny pricks of fire dancing over the rim of the sacrificial pyramid. He'd go down fighting rather than get dragged up those bloodied steps.

CHAPTER TWENTY-SEVEN

Xippilli had sat with the pipiltin and listened to the chatter of conversation flow around the table. The older pipiltin, such as the thin, scarred Ahexotl, had ignored the Nanagadans. Xippilli made a point by sitting near the man.

Since running for election in Capitol City and losing, Xippilli had turned to trade and business. His airships crossed the Wicked High Mountains to build a healthy flow of trade between Aztlan and Nanagada, but it was a trickle compared to the trade that *could* happen.

"That young *nopuluca*," Ahexotl said, leaning over and grabbing Xippilli's shoulder. Xippilli had mastered his distaste at the older pipiltin using derogatory terms for Nanagadans. "The one that left in such a hurry."

"Jerome deBrun, the son of the great hero John."

"Hero to Capitol City, not here." Ahexotl snorted. "Is he still opposed to opening Mafolie Pass?"

"I think so."

"He will take no bribes?" Ahexotl owned almost every chicle-producing plant in Tenochtilanome, and he kept his monopoly secret. But most knew about his wealth. And though Ahexotl did not hold a high opinion of Nanagadans, he held a much higher opinion of wealth.

"I doubt it."

"It would be shameful if he were to have an accident."

That was a bit much. Xippilli turned. "It would, because Capitol City would riot if the son of one of their greatest heroes died. We'd hardly make things easier."

Ahexotl had smiled at that. "It's a good thing that you're keeping a close eye on the boy then. He will not come to harm."

Exactly. That was why Jerome and the mongoose-men with him remained in a house that Xippilli owned, and few knew about. "Yes."

Ahexotl made Xippilli feel dirty every night he returned home. But Ahexotl and his friends had reformed most of Aztlan, outlawing human sacrifice and the continuous attacks on the Nanagadans. Almost bankrupted by the last war, Ahexotl wanted no more of massive wars. And most in the city felt as he did.

But he had no true love of Nanagada, not like Xippilli, who had been taken in by them and lived in Capitol City.

Xippilli ground his teeth. Jerome alone could cause a lot of trouble. He was young, young enough to be flighty. Young enough to still hate the Azteca so much he couldn't look beyond his past toward the great things that could be done.

Jerome might yet stop Mafolie Pass from being opened. Xippilli gritted his teeth. Jerome could stop the further liberalization of everything this side of the mountains, particularly if he traded on his father's status to make the Nanagadans refuse to open the one place in the Wicked Highs a road could be built.

But Xippilli hadn't wanted to think any further about that because the sky thundered and people outside the decorative tents craned their heads to stare up at the sky.

Now Xippilli got up with Ahexotl and they walked outside to look up as well.

Lights hung over the city, slowly descending to turn into a gleaming, fiery, bird-shaped machine. It dropped out of the gloom and toward one of the giant public squares near the main sacrificial pyramid.

"What is that thing?" Ahexotl asked.

"I think," Xippilli said in horror, "the gods have returned."

Ahexotl sniffed. "This is problematic."

Xippilli frowned. "For you?"

"The priests will come back out from the bushes. They'll refuse to keep using pigs and chickens. They'll want human blood on the temple grounds. We'll fight with the Nanagadans. My interests will suffer."

Xippilli closed his eyes. "Not if we act first, to keep the pipiltin that exist now in power. You have warriors under your control."

"As do you."

Both men looked back into the tent at the rest of the powerful men inside. "Then we must meet the new gods and find out what they need. And we need to control what comes next, even if it does include human sacrifice to placate the old priests and the Teotl that will come back in from the bush to meet their kin here."

In his life Xippilli had walked across the Wicked Highs on foot, almost dying of the cold, to reach the safety of Nanagada. There it had been free of the alien Teotl, who claimed they were gods and demanded blood on their account.

"I'll take a delegation of the pipiltin to the square," Ahexotl said. "You make sure our warehouses are well protected from the priesthood. We'll need to do a lot of bribing yet tonight."

Xippilli nodded. He'd fought Azteca from the walls of Capitol City to remain free, knowing that if they could hold them off, Nanagada could continue being a safe place. And he had come to Tenochtitlanome in Aztlan again to help reform his people, knowing that if it didn't work, he could return to Capitol City.

But now, there was nowhere to run. Not if the Teotl dropped in numbers from the sky.

CHAPTER TWENTY-EIGHT

Xippilli sat in the small stone office building he'd rented not too far from the airship warehouses on the edge of the city.

"Do *you* believe the sun needs blood in order to rise?" he asked Ahexotl. "Particularly since human sacrifice hasn't been fueling it for the past several years?"

"There have been ceremonies out in the bush," Ahexotl said. "The old priests would say it is hardly conclusive."

"But you?"

Ahexotl waved a hand. "I pay both sides gold and what they need to be satisfied. Maybe it's true, maybe not."

"The new gods haven't demanded human sacrifice," Xippilli said. "What happens if they do not approve?"

"They haven't not demanded it," Ahexotl said, brushing aside his bangs and straightening a gold necklace. "Our leaders fall back on old habits and tradition. They're making an offering. You'd do well to attend."

"It's hard," Xippilli said as Ahexotl pulled a formal cape around his shoulders. Outside the door a steam car waited, a driver picking his nails in the front seat.

"There is a machine that came from the sky sitting in the square, new Teotl walk the ground, and we are caught in the middle. If you would like control of your destiny, right now, Xippilli, you will come with me."

"Okay." Xippilli followed him out in the hot early-morning sun and shut the door behind him.

He sat in the back of the car, posture stiff, as it drove toward the center of Tenochtitlanome. A crowd milled around the central pyramid, and Xippilli followed Ahexotl as he pushed through the crowd to stand at the base of the pyramid. The tiny steps stretched up, hundreds of feet into the air.

The small figures at the apex of the pyramid moved around with deadly certainty, pulling roped victims forward to lay on the stone altar.

Xippilli looked down at the dark stone as the jade-hilted knife stabbed downward and someone screamed. He looked back up to see the priest, blood-soaked hair dark against his skin, hold the red heart up to the orange early-morning sun.

The priest's acolytes threw the body off the pyramid. As limp as a doll it rolled, limbs flailing, all the way down the steps to land before the crowd.

They erupted in cheers, and Xippilli looked at the body. A young girl.

Ahexotl grabbed his shoulder. "They're saying the sacrifice has been well received and that the gods are coming out of their machine. Come with me."

They cut their way around the pyramid toward the square where the alien flying machine sat. Xippilli walked, staring up at the upswept wings and curved lines that seemed to blend into the great hull of the machine, a seed-like pod with legs that splayed out on the cobblestones.

Pipiltin milled about near the shade of one of the wings. Sullen moderate and smug old-order priests ringed the edge of the square, but the pipiltin were the ones who approached the strange craft.

"The wonderful thing about all this," Ahexotl said as they moved past the ring of priests toward a collection of shaded divans, "is that you, me, and the pipiltin know that our gods are just creatures. More advanced, perhaps, as we once were before the cataclysm that left us in the ashes of our forefathers, but just creatures."

"You see good things in the oddest places," Xippilli said.

"The gods cannot read our minds, and we can bargain with them," Ahexotl said.

"What makes you think we can bargain with them?"

Ahexotl waved his hand at the great machine. "They're here in Tenochtit-lanome, are they not? They must need something from us, or they wouldn't be speaking with us."

"You have a point." Xippilli paused as a pair of Jaguar scouts stopped him.

"I'm sorry Xippilli. You must remain here. I will be using you in these days ahead, but the pipiltin, they only tolerate you." Ahexotl looked apologetic.

Xippilli nodded. Another pair of scouts set up a stool for him, gave him a cup of sweetened fruit juice, then stood on either side of him as Ahexotl continued on.

Their new masters stirred from inside the shadows of the divans, grublike skin visible from the distance. They were surrounded by the pipiltin. Ahexotl joined them, and Xippilli watched the crowd readjust to Ahexotl's presence.

The meeting lasted a mere fifteen minutes, then Ahexotl strode back out.

"I kept you on for this very reason," Ahexotl said, smiling, and Xippilli suddenly felt like a rodent under the gaze of a jungle cat. He had no illusions that Ahexotl would dispose of him if he did not serve some function in the man's calculations.

"And that is?"

"The gods want Capitol City next. They will use us as the front line in the occupation." Ahexotl brushed past the stool. Xippilli hopped off to follow him.

"We are their chaff?" Xippilli asked.

"They are searching for one thing: any ancients that might be alive still from the days when our world used to be connected to the other worlds. They were most insistent." Ahexotl had a spring in his step. "They have to be captured and brought to them alive."

"That seems to excite you." Xippilli struggled to keep up.

"They need something, they are not omnipotent, and they will be *giving* us Capitol City in exchange for what they want." Ahexotl, his eyes gleaming, looked at Xippilli. "And we have the first tool, a piece of leverage to use to gain all that, don't we? Jerome deBrun. You have him in a safe location, correct?"

Xippilli stopped with him at the steam car. The driver had spotted them and begun warming it up; the boiler hissed as Ahexotl opened the door. "Yes, I do."

"They want these people alive, Xippilli. That doesn't offend your sensibilities, does it?"

Xippilli stared at the dirt underneath the car. "No, no, it doesn't. But I view my promises as ironclad, and even in a situation like this, breaking a promise I made to protect the son of a close friend is hard to do."

Ahexotl grabbed his shoulder. "Your loyalty is why I trust you, Xippilli. Not many here struggle to remain true to their word. So I tell you this, deliver Jerome to me. Deliver his father to me. I'll make you the ruler of Capitol City, you know it best of all the people here, and I know what you promise me will stand, so I can trust you over in Capitol City more than any of the pipiltin back there."

"Capitol City?" Xippilli looked up. "In charge how?"

"Deliver me the men the gods want and I will not bother you there. Sacrifice thousands, or none, I don't care. Just keep my goods coming, keep the order, and you will rule that city for as long as you wish."

Xippilli held on to the door of the car. If this was indeed the age of the Teotl, they could do nothing against them, could they? What better way to protect Capitol City and the people he loved that lived there? As a powerful ruler for the rapidly rising Ahexotl, he could protect many who would otherwise have their hearts cut out.

"Don't delay your answer to this offer too long," Ahexotl said, "or I'll find someone else to do it."

Xippilli grabbed his arm. "The others would kill the very people the gods want," he growled. Then with a deep breath, he said, "I'll do it."

He had to.

Ahexotl grinned. "Where are they?"

Xippilli swalled the acid at the back of his throat and told Ahexotl where to find Jerome and the delegates who lived with him.

CHAPTER TWENTY-NINE

Jerome nailed the edge of plank across the window of his room. The morning light filtered through cracks between the wood. No one had returned for them. All night had passed in nervous silence.

Screaming and shouting came from down the street. Jerome peeked out through a tiny crack to see two priests pull a seven-year-old girl away from her mother. One of them clubbed a man down as he struggled to hold on to the girl.

Her foot slipped out of his fist. With one last kick the priests walked off down the street with the kicking girl.

Jerome dropped the hammer and ran down the stairs, across the foyer, toward the main door.

He grabbed the edge of the massive dresser they'd shoved up against the door, but Bruce held him back. "Ain't nothing you can do."

"That a child they taking," Jerome shouted, straining to get free. The bush warriors pushed him down into a chair.

"I know." Bruce let him go. "We all know. Now hush, we don't want them hearing no foreign voice out of here."

Jerome walked over and looked through the shutters. The mother held her husband's bloodied head in her lap.

"You think maybe we should run for jungle?" Jerome asked. He'd assumed Xippilli's men would already have arrived to take them away and that they had only needed to last the night with some caution.

"It light now. This place crawling with warrior-priest," Bruce said. "Got to wait until dark again."

"They got to know we sitting here," Jerome muttered.

"Mainly diplomat and Xippilli, and some people around this house. It go take a little while."

Jerome walked a circle. "We go tonight, make we way through the jungle and back over the Wicked Highs."

"The Wicked Highs going through storm season," one of the other men pointed out.

"Crossing the mountains never easy." Jerome had lived in their shadow most of his life. People died on the slopes more often than not. "Pack warm. Get all the food in this house pack up as well, we go need it."

A suicidal trek. Weeks of jungle, and they couldn't stop at villages or use the roads.

"Heard. Better moving than sitting still here."

Someone rapped at the door and shouted at them.

"What do they want?" Jerome asked. He didn't understand Nahuatl. "Who's out there?"

"For we open the door now." Bruce walked up and looked through the crack. "A whole bunch of Azteca with guns out there. A couple priest them. I don't see Xippilli anywhere. Open the door?"

Jerome shook his head. "I think we all know better."

Guns were taken out. Bruce took a hunting knife out and handed it to Jerome. He hefted it in his hand. "Think we should run for it?"

Bruce looked at him. "They like locusts out there."

"I don't want die in this house," Jerome said. "We run for it if they break in."

"We by your side."

Jerome shook his head. "Don't stick with me. Scatter." He raised his voice. "You ain't here for protecting me. We need get word back to Nanagada, hear? Scatter fast if they break in. Find a way to get the message back, somehow, anyhow."

Bruce stood still, saying nothing.

The Azteca on the other side kept shouting, then stopped. They'd given up on asking for what they wanted.

A bullet splintered the main door. Two mongoose-men walked to either side of the doorway.

"Come on." Bruce walked up the stairway to join the other mongoose-man perched along the railing, aiming down at the door and able to see throughout most of the house.

More commotion outside, then a thick chunk of log punched through the door. No one inside moved.

"Jerome," Bruce said. "Get up here, now."

Another hit from the heavy log and the door caved inward. Feathered Jaguar warriors clambered over the dresser. Jerome stood still and stared at them.

"Cut them down!" Bruce shouted, and the mongoose-men fired. Six Jaguar scouts lurched forward and screamed, their blood staining the wooden planks of the floor. One of them pulled himself forward, one hand holding his own guts in while bleeding out, the other hand reaching for a dropped rifle.

Jerome aimed his rifle at the man's head, hands shaking.

The Jaguar scout paused, looked back at him, and Jerome closed his eyes and pulled the trigger. The rifle bucked, the acrid smell of gunshot wafted up, and Jerome flicked up and looked at the mess of brains and blood and shivered.

He wanted to throw up, but Bruce ran down the stairs and pulled him up. "Don't make it so hard for we to protect you now."

More screaming Jaguar scouts tried to force through the door.

Jerome's heart pounded at triple speed as Bruce pushed him back into his own room. "Hey, I said we was going to run."

"Jerome, you done well, but we can't run. And we orders was to stay with you and protect you. We surrounded. Look out the window."

They grimly guarded the door. Jerome looked out at the street below. Azteca filled the street, fifty of them.

He was going to die here.

"They coming up." The mongoose-men downstairs had stopped firing. The stairs flexed as Jaguar scouts pounded up them, then the crack of rifles from the last two mongoose-men stopped them.

Jerome slowly reloaded his rifle and loosened the knife, each gun crack making him jump slightly.

"Hold the door," Bruce said, and stepped into the room with Jerome. He shut the door and flipped the wooden cradle of Jerome's bed up to shove it against the door's handle.

"Bruce—"

"Shut up and get ready."

Jerome stepped back and stood by the window.

The Azteca outside shouted in Nahuatl again, and Jerome looked at Bruce. "What they say?"

"They say they don't want kill you. If you surrender, you go live as a prisoner."

Jerome shook his head. "So they can sacrifice all of we later? No."

Bruce shouted back, and the downstairs door burst open, two Jaguar warriors pushing through. Jerome shot the first one in the head.

Gunsmoke filled the room. Jerome recocked the hammer and fired at the second man and missed.

Damn. He cocked and fired again, gun jerking, and hit the man in the shoulder, but he kept coming. Bruce stepped in front and knifed the warrior, but another Jaguar warrior pushing through fired. Bruce fell.

"Bruce!" Jerome shouted as. He pulled the gun up to aim at the warrior-priest that leapt into the air at him with a net, then stopped. His hair swayed, his mask slipped, and he gurgled. The priest hung in the air, a long speartip sticking through his chest.

The priest moved aside to reveal a tall man in a long trench coat and dreads. Jerome couldn't believe it.

"Pepper?"

Pepper tossed the priest aside. His coat dripped blood, as did his dreads. Dirt smeared his brown face, and he looked around the room. "A last stand, Jerome? I was expecting you to run for the forest."

"What you doing here?" Jerome walked forward to the door as Pepper moved over to the window to peer out at their surroundings.

"Saving your ass. I promised John I'd keep an eye on you. Bad timing to promise that, don't you think?"

Jerome could see a trail of bodies on the stairs. He hadn't even heard the slaughter Pepper had perpetrated. "What now?"

"Well, we're surrounded," Pepper said. "So let's move quickly." Pepper stepped backed to the doorframe, a shotgun poking out of the trench coat. He fired it, twice, then reloaded.

"Down the hall to the window." Pepper shoved Jerome toward it and covered him like a shield as he fired again down at the entryway to the building.

At the end Pepper smashed the wooden shutters out with a fist. Jerome looked down at the street. "What now?"

"Jump."

"That's cobblestone."

Pepper fired the shotgun again. "You want to wait for them to come back up the stairs?"

Jerome clambered out onto the sill and took a deep breath. He lowered himself by his hands awkwardly, then let go. He hit the stones with a jarring thump that knocked the breath out of him.

A stone-cracking thump behind him. Pepper landed on his feet, shotgun in each hand aimed down each side of the road. "Move."

They turned the corner, and Pepper stopped. Twenty Azteca with rifles clustered around a car. Pepper pushed Jerome behind him.

"Gentlemen," Pepper said in a calm voice.

"Hello," said the man in the car, standing up to look at them. He wore a feathered cape. His pronunciation sounded odd, not like Xippilli's but more halting and unused to the language. "My name is Ahexotl. Xippilli said you were here."

Jerome bit his lip. Xippilli. That traitor. They might have had a chance if he had kept their location secret just a little bit longer.

Pepper looked behind them as more Azteca moved into the streets, surrounding them. "What do you want?"

"Originally the boy, but now, just you will do. Drop your weapons. You can't get out of this."

Jerome felt Pepper twist, tense, then stop. "You've seen how many I can kill if I choose back there?"

Ahexotl nodded. "Maybe you could escape. But then the boy will die, and I think you don't want that. But to the reason I'm here: You are one of the Nanagadan immortals? Like this boy's father?"

"Maybe."

"I'll take that as a yes," Ahexotl said. "I'll let the boy live if you come with us and talk to the gods."

"The Teotl wish to speak to me? Why?"

Ahexotl made a face. "They have not deigned tell me yet. But they are most insistent that they talk to someone of your kind."

The two men stared at each other, two predators sizing each other up.

"I'll come," Pepper finally said. He dropped the pair of shotguns. "The boy comes with. Harm him and, Ahexotl, I will not just kill you, but kill you very, very slowly."

Ahexotl smiled. "May I offer you a ride?"

"You may." Pepper walked forward and pulled Jerome with him. He muttered, "Stay fresh, stay sharp."

"I've got a pistol," Jerome muttered.

Pepper laughed, and the two clambered into the steam car with their new enemy.

CHAPTER THIRTY

Mother Elene waited for John in the basement of an unassuming three-story house. From there she took over, leaving Sister Agathy behind and opening a door in the wall into a tiny, cramped room.

It was an elavator, which hissed and slowly sank down through the earth once Mother Elene shut the door.

She said nothing until the elevator finally shuddered to a halt. "This way."

John followed her into a large rocky chamber. They were deep beneath the city now. The walls dripped strips of bioluminescent slime that lit the chamber in a faint green glow, helped along by large flaming torches planted every few feet.

Large eggs sat at the far end.

"You welcome to a privileged sight," Mother Elene said. "The Metamorphosis."

John walked toward the eggs.

"Stay back," Mother Elene snapped. "Show some respect, man. Them the Loa."

"They are turning themselves into something different, a different physical form?" John asked.

Mother Elene nodded. "Yes, but it ain't for fighting, like you thinking."

"For what then?"

A hissing set of syllables from behind John startled him.

"The escaping," the Vodun priestess said, translating for him. She sat down in a wicker chair by the doors they'd just come in. On the other side of her lay a Loa, its body looking like a pearly seashell. Halfway to becoming an egg like the others. The head had become absorbed into the shell-like area, but the face remained. Large eyes, beaked nose, and a slit mouth etched onto the shell's surface.

In the last war the Loa had disappeared into the bowels of the city to ride out the invasion. They were not repeating that, but doing something else now. They also knew how dangerous things had become this time around.

"You know the Teotl are coming from orbit?" John asked it.

It wheezed back. "Yes. We hear them calling for all of we. But we don't respond," Mother Elene translated.

"So you're running from the fight," John said. "What do you want with me?"

The Loa spoke for itself. "Information, assistance."

"Your ulterior motives disturb me." John folded his arms. "You've caused us so much grief, and death, the Teotl and you."

For a few seconds the Loa hissed furiously, while Mother Elene looked down at the ground. Then it gathered itself. "You of all people know the damages your kind did as well. You yourself destroyed an entire lineage of my sisters in a nuclear attack. Do not presume yourself innocent of such vile things."

John blinked and then nodded. The creature was truthful, though he'd only had ten years to readjust to those memories and figure out who they meant he was.

Not always someone he liked.

"What am I here for?" he repeated.

"Well, once, a long time ago, I would have liked to have killed you," it said. "When you destroyed my sisters in a ship attack, I begged to come all the way out here and fight to wipe your kind out. We could not share a planet. Your DNA, right-handed, ours left. Our terraforming plans clashed, only one of us could live on a planet created by the other."

John looked over at Mother Helene. Had he been lured here to be killed? She gave no sign of what was about to come.

"I was sent away to study where your kind came from," the Loa continued, as if unaware of John's nervousness. "We were a young race, so proud and sure of ourselves. I have shared memories from this time, and, oh, how we sing with determination."

"Your DNA is left-handed?" John asked, trying to move the alien's attention well past memories of its dead siblings. "How have you survived all this time?"

"We were wrong to think only one of us could hold the planet. We both could, if we drastically changed ourselves physically, just as we are doing now. In the beginning this was to be a base, a new beginning, and the start of an exodus for us. Unfortunately, in the end, all of our assumptions were wrong. We found we could share a planet, if we suffered deep changes to ourselves. We also found out that we could not run from our problems."

"Why not?"

"We were supremely disappointed to find that the area beyond this planet was also infected. There was nowhere to really run to."

"Infected?" By what? John knew of no infections.

The Loa shifted painfully, rocking the shell of its lower body. "When we strode into space, there were . . . things waiting for us. Creatures that grew up in the dark of interstellar space. We were not the top of the natural order, there were predators and ecologies out in the greater expanse of space. Within a generation of spreading out beyond our world, we were found by creatures that took control of our bodies and used our minds as a resource. In short time we were their limbs, minds, and eyes.

"We fought back. We stored our memories chemically in backups, re-shaped ourselves, and tried to escape. That was why we came here and fought you so desperately. Only your kind was under the same yoke."

"I've never heard of any such thing," John said. "The Maatan and the Gahe occupied Earth, but they are their own races."

"Behind them lie another force," the Loa said. "But it does not matter now. We have come to believe that the truth is, intelligence puts us in competition directly with these, and other species. Our new metamorphosis will take us to the sea here in a new, safe form. Just as we adapted ourselves when we realized occupation of this world was pointless, that there were no clean stretches of space for us to live in. When we decided to try and help your kind against those of ours who dreamt in vain that holding this world, so far from ours, would be the right thing."

"What will you become?"

"Giant deep-sea fish," the Loa said. "Deep in the dark of the ocean."

"And if we can't keep this world from freezing, and the environment changes?" John asked.

"There are triggers programmed into us for such a thing. Listen, John, we have a gift for you."

Mother Elene leaned forward and handed John a small wooden flask. John made to open it, but she shook her head. "What is it?" he asked.

"We are masters of the biological," the Loa said. Its words were getting more strained, as if its mouth was hardening. "Now that we will be changed beyond recognition, we can leave you a dangerous gift. A plague. An infection that will destroy the Teotl. We have no need of this, we can move on. You are the ones stuck with this now, you are the young race. Do with it what you will, John, and we wish the city the best of luck."

And that was it. The Loa's eyes glazed over and it settled back into waiting to change into something different.

"Come." Mother Elene led John back toward the elevator.

As it headed up, John looked over. "How will they reach the sea?"

"We go help them."

"Even though it means they are leaving you," John said.

Mother Elene did not respond. When the elevator jerked to a stop, she pointed him at the basement. "Be safe with that thing and don't get kill. Is a powerful weapon."

John tucked it into a pocket, gingerly. "Good day, Mother Elene, and good luck."

She shut the door.

Outside, John blinked several times. Lines of Azteca soldiers marched down the street at the end of the block, making their way toward the walls of the city.

In the distance the sound of rifle fire popped and cracked, while several explosive booms echoed all across the city.

The occupation had begun. A large-bellied aircraft flew in over the walls and paused over the center of the city, then lowered itself into the large garden clearing by the Ministerial Mansion.

Fires burned, smoke columns reaching high into the sky.

"Hey, hey!" A woman peered through a crack in a nearby door and waved at John.

"What do you want?"

"Ain't no one allowed out on the street. You go get shot. Get in here before any of them notice you."

John ducked in, and they slammed the door shut behind him. Two women in long, gray dresses stood inside the small room, lit by a single candle. Chairs and tables lay scattered around; it had once been a restaurant. The smell of fried fish dripped out of the clammy inside air.

The woman who'd called John over wore a handkerchief over her mouth. "I'm Pam. This my sister, Violet. You know it dangerous out there. You John deBrun, right? I seen you once at the waterfront."

John nodded. "Thanks. Yes." So many in the city knew him it was useless to pretend otherwise.

"They looking for you, as well as any of the other councilmen who trying to hide."

"Any idea why?" John walked over to the window. They all shrank back from it as a pair of men in bright red capes and rifles at the ready walked down the street.

"Here. They had rain these down on the city not too long ago." Violet thrust a piece of paper in his hands.

It was a letter to anyone who had settled this planet several hundred years ago and still lived. The new Teotl needed their help and would pay well for it and guaranteed their safety.

John crumpled it and threw it on the concrete floor.

"You don't believe them?" Pam asked.

"Never had any reason to trust the Teotl yet," John said. "I'd rather not walk myself into my own death."

"What you go do next?"

"I don't know. What happened to the minister, was there any fighting back?"

"Not sure, but mongoose and ragamuffin fighting some. Mainly looking to get organize, it all happen so quick. Ship coming from the sky, Azteca pouring out," Pam said.

"Most of the shooting you hear is people like we shooting from the window at them," Violet said.

John patted his coat. Hide, or put himself in a position to strike back? Could he release a biological weapon against the Teotl? Would it be enough to turn the tide? "Can I get close to the Ministerial Mansion? That way I can watch who goes in, and maybe figure out what is happening in there?"

If they were really looking for people like him, they must need something. There were ways into the Mansion as well, and if he hooked up with mongoose-men, he could gain some help.

"We'll help you," Pam promised. "But for right now, we have to sit tight. Curfew is on for the next day, no one in the street. More feather-clot coming."

"Door by door," Violet said from the window. "They coming door by door to search we street."

"They're looking for us door by door?" John walked toward the window, but Pam grabbed his shirt.

"They looking for guns," she said.

"And?"

"That go be a problem if they look a bit too close in here." Pam pulled him toward the back of the room toward the kitchen. "Stacking plenty of rifle."

They turned the corner and she opened a heavy iron lid of a massive coal stove with a grunt. Rows of rifles gleamed underneath.

Pam pulled a pair out. "Head out through the kitchen to the back closet. That go take you to the basement, and from there you can get out through the window to the back street." She let the top of the stove drop. She took the lid off a large pot, pulled out a pistol, and handed it to John. "Get under the street using the grate, head north until you bump into someone. Let them know what happen. They'll help you get where you need."

Azteca started knocking at the door. "Just a minute," Violet shouted. Pam raised her dress to reveal a holster fashioned out of leather for the rifle. Another for the pistol on the left thigh.

She dropped the dress back down. "Hopefully they go be real polite."

"You think you can fight back against all this?" John asked. "They're dropping from the sky, better technology, better weapons, more people."

"This house been in my family since my granddad. I ain't go be running around in no sewer and giving all this over to them," Pam said.

"They looking like they go break the door in now," Voilet said.

"Chances is they won't spot nothing." Pam pushed back. "Now go quick."

John turned and followed her directions down into the basement. He barely fit out the window, looking around for the Azteca. Knowing there was no back door, they hadn't posted any guards.

As he scrabbled out, he heard pans and pots thrown to the floor and feet thudding around. Pam or Violet shouted angrily back at someone.

John tensed, waiting for the shooting. It didn't come.

Letting out a relieved breath, he moved toward the nearest grate and pulled it free. With one last breath of fresh air he dropped down under the streets, pulling the grate back over him.

CHAPTER THIRTY-ONE

Had Pepper taken any longer to reach Jerome, he might have been too late. That bugged him. Was he getting soft? Comfortable in his ways? Nanagada might look like a tropical vacation, but Pepper wondered if he'd grown accustomed to it.

The steam car stopped on the edge of a plaza dominated by Tenochtilanome's main sacrificial pyramid. Already today blood ran down the sides of it. A Teotl spacecraft had landed in the plaza.

"The boy stays," Ahexotl said.

Pepper looked over and considered killing him. "Why?"

"So you don't try anything strange, like attacking our gods."

"Fair enough." Pepper smiled. They had each other figured out all too well. He looked over at Jerome. "Remain calm. I'll be back shortly."

He stepped out of the car. Every muscle tensed, ready to spring at any second, Pepper walked forward with the several armed Azteca at either side. The wide-winged craft crouched above the stones, the pyramid rising up behind it.

Azteca warriors made a wall of bodies on either side of Pepper, feathered capes flapping slightly in the soft wind, rifles at the ready.

At the far end of the honor guard two Teotl stood. Warrior Teotl. Vaguely bipedal, they turned and faced Pepper. He noted the black, razorlike forearms, spiked fingers, and mirrored eyeplates. The creatures' thick, chitinous skin would be almost impervious to low-caliber gunfire and edged objects.

Hard nuts to crack.

And behind the warrior-grown Teotl sat the divans on which the Teotl leaders sat, watching him from the shadows with their beady eyes.

The Azteca guided him to the shaded pavilion under the protection of one of the swooping wings. Throngs of Azteca honor guards stood in the background, looking over the proceedings.

The Teotl had returned from the skies and adapted to the local conditions quite quickly.

"Proceed to within five paces. No more. No less." The voice came out of the air. The two warrior Teotl, polished and armored skins gleaming in the sun, moved to either side of him.

The three creatures in the couches stirred to stare at Pepper. Highly modified Teotl for thinking and planning, their bodies were crafted to support superfast brains. Radiator fans crested their skulls, the air above them rippling from dumped heat.

"Your body is laced with devices." The center Teotl spoke Anglic. "Your physical abilities are amplified. You are not a part of this fallow world here." A stubby, pale flipper flapped, as if it to indicate the city around them. "You come from beyond the outleading wormhole?"

"Yes." He saw no reason to lie to them. Yet. Pepper looked up at the smooth underbelly of the craft. It looked like metal from the distance, but up close he wasn't so sure.

"Did you come recently? The wormhole out to other worlds of your kind is closed."

"I came before it closed."

"And that was hundreds of years ago," they said in a chorus.

"Yes."

Three simultaneous sighs filled the air between the couches. They seemed disappointed. Or at least, were choosing to project it to him. A sigh was just as much a language marker as anything else.

Pepper regarded the mounds of flesh before him. "Why?"

A single measured tick of time passed as they conferred with each other with quick glances. "We have a deep need for emissaries." More shifting. "We can reopen the wormhole to the next system by shoring open the mouth with exotic matter. But our species has a history of antagonism with yours, and presumably a reputation out there. We need help and advice to cross over."

"Why?" Pepper folded his arms. Even though he didn't trust them, if they were really going back to the other worlds, it might be a way to get back out to civilization decades earlier than planned. The *Ma Wi Jung* still languished on the bottom somewhere near Capitol City, useless to him. And even if fixed, it would require hundreds of years to cross the space required to get to a working wormhole.

If the wormhole back could just be fired up again, that was appealing to him.

"Your kind manipulates." He spread his arms out. "We fell for your lies once."

"We are now refugees. We have no time for deceptions and deceit," the Teotl said.

Pepper stared at them. "Yes?"

"Our worlds have been destroyed for technological violations." The words dripped out of the air and continued. "We have been deemed dangerous, our lease on existence terminated. We orbit this planet because we flee those who would destroy us. The wormhole we came through is temporarily closed again, but we will eventually need help keeping it closed. We seek to open and travel through the other wormhole to the worlds you once knew, but we need ambassadors and assistance."

The beady eyes regarded him.

Pepper looked up at the craft. A working spaceship. Unlike the *Ma Wi Jung*. "I'm still listening," he said.

"There are others like you. Ahexotl and Xippilli will be working to find more of them in the other large city. We'll take you there to join up with these others, and there we will discuss terms and needs. Eventually we'll take you to our home."

"A whole other planet?"

"Our home orbits here right now."

Pepper looked around at the Azteca. The original Teotl had manipulated humanity enough. This new set of lies would probably mean even more danger. But a quick ride back to Capitol City to get Jerome reunited with his father, that was worth a quick flirt.

"Okay," Pepper said. "I'll take the shuttle ride to Capitol City."

The aliens hissed their satisfaction, and Pepper looked up at the giant wing overhead. Complex plots were not his thing, he preferred direct approaches.

But he would remain checked for now.

CHAPTER THIRTY-TWO

Xippilli followed Ahexotl toward the giant flying machine, looking at the Teotl with trepidation. He might know they were just creatures, as Ahexotl said, but somewhere deep inside he still retained the belief that these were gods.

He watched as a second flying machine climbed up into the air over the city. More than one had landed, and they had all filled their holds with Azteca warriors bound for Capitol City.

The strange creatures in their divans didn't so much as glance his way as he walked toward the machine and the crowd of twenty warriors standing around Jerome and Pepper.

"Pepper is what they seek," Ahexotl told him. "Eventually you can do what you want with the boy, but for now, I want him chained and guarded. Encouragement for Pepper. He's dangerous. I don't want him causing trouble."

Xippilli looked over. "Are you sure that's a good idea?"

"He needs controlled." Ahexotl looked over at the man. "He's dangerous. We know there are other immortal Nanagadans that have been here from the beginning, but these people are always hard to ferret out, and we already have what we need to please the gods. My thanks to you. Our task is already over, and we are in the gods' favor."

Xippilli nodded and continued to stare at the machine. Ahexotl waved at the warriors and they circled Jerome, cutting him off from Pepper.

"Hey," Pepper snapped. Xippilli flinched. "What are you doing?"

"We need to make sure you fulfill your end of the bargain." Ahexotl waved again, and the warriors clapped a collar on the boy's neck. "It is a prong collar. He'll be fine, as long as he doesn't struggle."

Nasty tips dug into Jerome's neck. Xippilli avoided both their eyes. No doubt they viewed him as the worst kind of traitor right now.

Maybe they were right.

"Please," Xippilli said. "Don't struggle against this."

He wanted to crawl into a hole and not come out as the warriors pulled Jerome with them, and they followed a spiked, gleaming Teotl into the great machine.

Ahexotl waited until Pepper followed, then spoke to Xippilli. "The attack will be over by the time you arrive to take control. You make sure to give the gods what they need and send me what I need, and all will be well."

"And the outlying areas?" Xippilli asked.

"We'll start with the city. I will decide what to do with the rest of Nanagada."

Xippilli nodded, then followed the warriors into the heart of the machine. Faint light glimmered and Xippilli waited for his eyes to adjust as the hull behind him sealed itself shut. The machine started to shake as it rose into the sky.

Xippilli swallowed.

The thundering pitched higher, and inside everything shook. Xippilli grabbed the wall.

Pepper balanced easily enough while crouched on the floor, staring at him. He was also poking at the wall, using a fingernail to probe at it.

Xippilli stared at the tiny crenellations all along the domelike chamber whose smooth floor they sat on. At the front, a tiny niche hooked off from the chamber. Fibrous strands draped from the walls of it to swaddle the yellowed, fat Teotl as he leaned back with eyes closed to control the ship.

A glass of some sort separated the niche from them, and on their side of it an inky black and spiked Teotl stared back at them. Xippilli had no doubt it would kill them if they tried anything. That and the packed crowd of warriors in here made this a very, very secure space.

Yet still he felt like frayed rope about to snap. Pepper *did things*, he did not sit around waiting unless it ended in something. But the Teotl didn't really know what Pepper was truly capable of or they wouldn't have let him aboard. Would they?

Pepper versus the spiked Teotl. Xippilli wasn't sure who would win.

"Relax," Pepper told Jerome, folding his arms and leaning back against the wall. He closed his eyes. "Now's the time you need to take a nap. Even in this thing it's going to take another hour."

Xippilli stared at the man, then at Jerome. Jerome leaned closer. "I will kill you one day, traitor," the young man hissed.

Xippilli turned his back and moved toward the warriors, who reverently whispered among each other in awe about being so close to the Teotl.

Pepper shifted just as Xippilli felt his ears start to hurt. The ship settled down, thudded, and the vibrating slowly wound down.

"And here we come," Pepper said, and stretched slowly, while keeping an eye on the twenty warriors packed in with them. "Xippilli, do me a favor? Step to your left two paces, and remain calm."

"Calm?" Xippilli frowned. But he stepped over. Teotl or not, he would not trifle with the man.

"You have a collar on Jerome, who I promised John nothing would happen to. I'm getting off, and I'm going my own way for a while."

"Your promise to assist the gods?"

"I might yet. But I disdain being told what to do." Pepper reached over to the nearest warrior and pulled his rifle away in a smooth, relaxed movement. Then kicked the man back into the tightly packed crowd.

The Teotl behind him leapt. Pepper rolled forward with the impact and threw it into the group. Its head bounced off to the side and clear fluid pooled quickly at the warriors' feet. Pepper raised the rifle and Xippilli grabbed the barrel.

"Wait." He had do *something* to avoid the bloodshed.

Pepper hesitated.

Xippilli pointed the barrel of Pepper's gun at the side of his own head and said in Nahautl, "You know who this man is and what he is capable of?"

They nodded.

"Then he's taking me prisoner for now," Xippilli said. "He does not want to currently go with us, and by fighting in here we endanger the god at the front." By offering himself as a temporary hostage he could calm Pepper and get the man out of the ship without causing more damage. And Pepper would owe him. That would be valuable in the future.

The warriors nodded in agreement, and Xippilli let out the tight knot of fear in his stomach. He faced forward to the Teotl at the front. "Great sir, please open the hull for us so that no one further is killed."

The hull cracked open and light spilled in. Judging by the carefully trimmed shrubs outside, Xippilli guessed they were in the gardens near the very center of Capitol City.

"I want that man's clothes." Pepper pointed at a jaguar-masked warrior with a long cape.

He handed the gun to Jerome once the items were handed over and changed, adjusting his dreadlocks. It was, Xippilli thought, convincing enough. Pepper as a Jaguar warrior.

Pepper looked forward at the Teotl in its niche, then walked over to where the hull had puckered, pushing Xippilli and Jerome in front of him. "You all wait for two minutes before following us out, or I'll kill Xippilli."

The hull opened further, more light stabbing into the dim interior. Xippilli walked out, and Pepper kept the rifle pointed at him. Ten Azteca waited outside in the bright sun, arrayed in a half circle.

Xippilli kept a cool expression as the Azteca stared at him. Pepper continued to push them forward.

"Where are our headquarters?" Xippilli asked the group, switching to Nahautl to talk to them. He looked around. The carefully kept grounds of the central gardens lay between the Ministerial Mansion and the docks. The mansion was behind them, and the closest Azteca in the welcoming reception pointed back at it.

Xippilli, Pepper, and Jerome moved toward it, and the Azteca fell in beside them.

"I am Atlahuah," the nearest man said. "I command the men for Ahexotl, and for the gods. *What is going here?*" They were obviously not sure whether they should be trying to shoot Pepper, but Xippilli seemed quite calm and okay.

"I'm temporarily being used as a hostage to get to that road." Xippilli handed Atlahuah a piece of parchment with Ahexhotl's instructions on it. "There is nothing we can do right now, so I'm going to walk with them, and then return. I know the mansion. Come find me in the lobby, but don't endanger your life by trying to rescue me right now, or shoot these two men. The gods want them for some reason."

Atlahuah looked slightly offended, but obeyed and left with his men for the mansion.

The three of them continued through the high shrubs and walkways until they came to the street, and Xippilli stopped.

Pepper leaned in. "You jumped quickly to becoming the Azteca ruler of the city."

"Better me than some warrior-priest, Pepper. What else can I do? It is either me or a far worse leader who will spill far more blood."

"He lying to save he life," Jerome said. "Kill him and let's run now."

Xippilli turned to face them both. "You move to anger too quickly. Both of you. Why was that necessary, why not talk to the gods?"

"You shackle his neck and expect calm?" Pepper said.

"That was Ahexotl's idea," Xippilli snapped. "Would you have killed everyone in there over his mistake?"

Pepper nodded. Xippilli fought frustration.

Xippilli looked over at Jerome. "Get to safety, or hiding. I'll find another ancient. And I'll bear Ahexotl's wrath. And I'll try to manage the city in this new time and save as many lives as I can."

"Be careful," Pepper said with a slight smile. "It's a slippery slope out there to becoming the dictator of the city."

"And what will you be doing?"

"Research," Pepper said.

"Research?"

"Yes." Pepper broke the ring off Jerome's neck with his bare hands and handed it to Xippilli. "The Teotl want to get through the other wormhole back to the rest of the worlds. But the question is, why?"

"They told you why."

"That may or may not be true," Pepper said. "And therefore, I'd like to do some research to figure out if they are telling the truth."

"How will you do that?" Xippilli asked.

"I'm sure there are Teotl that will be available to answer my questions, eventually," Pepper said. "For now, we're going to disappear."

He started to walk away with Jerome.

"Pepper, what were you going to do if I hadn't pointed that gun at myself?" Xippilli asked.

"Kill them all," Pepper said, and turned the corner.

CHAPTER THIRTY-THREE

Jerome hurried to keep up with Pepper. Capitol City was not the bustling world he remembered. The city remained clutched in dark, quiet, under some sort of curfew. Jerome thought he saw faces in windows, which retreated quickly into the shadows. Electric lights flickered as the power randomly failed throughout the once brightly lit inner walls of the city.

"You would have killed all those Azteca in there?" Jerome asked Pepper.

"Yes."

"And Xippilli too?" Jerome could hardly contain his anger just by mentioning the name.

"Maybe."

"If you didn't, I would." Xippilli had just turned him over. All those mongoose-men back in Tenochtitlanome had died because of him. They had died trying to protect Jerome, he wouldn't forget who had done the right thing anytime soon.

A few Azteca warriors patrolled the intersections, occasionally eyeing them. They challenged Pepper, who walked past them with a dismissive wave of the Jaguar warrior he was dressed up as and a snapped set of orders in Nahautl.

They let them walk on.

Jerome kept quiet until they turned a corner away from the Azteca. "What are we doing?"

He couldn't see past the mask Pepper wore, the stylized grinning jaguar face. Pepper paused, and Jerome froze. Something rustled, they were being followed.

Pepper reached under the cape he wore.

"Don't. Fucking. Move." The command was repeated in Nahautl. Five mongoose-men rounded a corner, rifles aimed at Pepper. "Let the boy go."

Jerome raised his hands, moving between them and Pepper. "Wait, don't shoot him, you don't understand."

"Get my son away from him now!" a familiar voice snapped. Jerome looked around and saw John push through the mongoose-men.

"Dad!" Relief vibrated through Jerome.

"Come over here, Jerome." John kept a rifle aimed at Pepper's head as he waved Jerome over. Jerome didn't move.

Pepper shook his masked head. "John, don't point that thing at me."

Jerome watched his father pause.

"Pepper?" John frowned.

"Who the hell else?" Pepper said, voice unhurried.

Jerome watched his father break into a grin and lower his rifle. John grabbed Pepper's shoulder. "You're alive as well!"

Pepper looked down at the arm. John stopped smiling and let go of him.

"Yes," Pepper said. He removed the Azteca mask and dropped it to the ground. His dreads fell down around his shoulders. "We made it back. I told you I would keep an eye on Jerome. I, for one, am good at promises."

"Let's get off the street," John said. "There'll be a patrol through soon."

The mongoose-men lead them down into the sewers. At this level it was stale runoff. Smelly, but nothing too bad. They sludged through the water.

"They're hunting for any of us who settled the planet, councilmen, me, maybe you," John said. "They're offering big rewards and promising no harm. You have any idea what that's about?"

Jerome and the mongoose-men around him struggled to keep up with Pepper and John. But having both men here made Jerome feel that things were happening.

"They approached me in Tenochtitlanome," Pepper said. "They seem to think they're also going to reopen the wormhole back out, and they need human help to deal with humans on the other side."

"And you said?"

Pepper paused at a junction. A pool of wastewater rimmed by railings. "Said I'd think about it. How's our starship doing, John?"

"The *Ma Wi Jung* is not going to fly us out of here."

Water trickled out of a storm drain. Jerome listened to his dad and Pepper and felt like half a man. Like all the other little people that gathered around those two and looked up. Here were the heroes of the last war with the Azteca.

And he'd been saved by Pepper back then as well.

John hadn't even looked back at him. Or touched his arm like Pepper's.

Pepper sniffed. "Here's the thing. They're still using the Azteca as pawns."

"They always have."

"The Teotl arrive in orbit, with advanced technology and superiority, and they're using Jaguar warriors with rifles to subdue the city? They're using a bunch of shuttles to ferry men with rifles around?" Pepper leaned back against the rail.

"They don't want to get their hands dirty."

"It's more than that." Pepper looked at the mongoose-men. "I think there are only a handful of them in orbit. They might actually be somewhat honest in needing our help."

"Help?" John looked disgusted.

"They claim they're refugees."

"But they're *Teotl*," Jerome hissed.

Pepper shrugged. "They want our help. I see advantages. I see me getting off this damn planet."

Damn planet? Jerome looked at Pepper. "So you go get off this 'damn planet' by joining them murderers!"

"They say something worse is coming through the wormhole after them."

"And you believe them?" Jerome replied. "*You* believe them?"

Pepper removed something from under the feathered cape. "I stole this from the Teotl that jumped me in the shuttle." Pepper held a fuzzy-looking, green necklace with a solid-silver section in the middle. In his other hand he held an oval. Jerome reached for it, but John grabbed his wrist.

"Don't. It's an aerogel necklace with a nanofilament, it'll slice your hand off it you tug on it wrong." John looked at Pepper. "It's a slave collar. And the oval is to trigger it?"

"Yes. Deceptions behind deceptions." Pepper gently tossed the necklace to John, who snagged it out of the air with a grunt. "I think they may need us. But they're not interested in being partners, ultimately. Things might be a little bit more one-sided once they have us where they need us."

"So what next?" John carefully pocketed the necklace.

"What are these mongoose-men up to?" Pepper asked.

"Heading on with explosives to cause the Azteca some trouble. They were helping me get near the mansion. They have to move on."

"Why?" Pepper frowned.

"Been watching to see if Jerome or you got captured." John turned to the mongoose-men. "Thanks."

They shook hands, glanced at Pepper one last time, then melted back off into the shadows.

"Can you remember how to get to the Crosswise bunker?" Pepper asked.

John nodded. "That memory is back, yes."

"Go there. You'll be safe. So will Jerome."

"What you doing?" Jerome asked Pepper.

"I need to go ask some questions." Pepper let go of the rail and walked off, brightly colored cape swaying until it was swallowed by the darkness.

"You been friend for a long, long time, right?" Jerome observed. "Know what he up to?"

"Whatever it is, someone's going to be unhappy tonight. I think Pepper's in a bit of a mood. Come on, we need to get to that sewer, it's dangerous here." Then John grabbed Jerome. "I'm glad to see you again, Son."

Despite feeling that he'd grown out of it years ago, Jerome hugged him. "It was bad there. It was really bad."

"I know."

The water continued gurgling, and the moment passed. The city wasn't theirs anymore, they had a lot more skulking around to do to get to this new bunker.

CHAPTER THIRTY-FOUR

Xippilli watched the lights of Capitol City flicker from his office's balcony on the Ministry building. The new, and quite hastily erected, wooden sacrificial pyramid flickered in the light of bonfires on the far edge of the gardens. It sat just past one of the strange flying machines.

He'd stood here, with dignitaries and leaders, coming to the office to seek their help. He'd done his best to try to get elected to the position, but had failed. Nanagadans weren't ready to elect someone from over the mountains just yet.

Now it was his at last. An ashen victory.

Someone behind cleared his throat. Xippilli turned. A warrior-priest stood by the curtains, and Xippilli's stomach flipped when the man walked forward. "There are thousands of people in our pens out there. Our gods blessed us. Shouldn't we return the honor?"

Xippilli walked past the man, brushing aside the diaphanous curtains. He sat behind his desk and tapped the document Ahexotl had given him. "There could be ancient humans in those pens, the 'old-fathers' they call them here. The gods are outspoken about needing these people. Disobeying that is unwise." He'd already met a Teotl by himself today. A strange-looking thing that was carried around, as it had tentacles.

It had been very upset.

It had reiterated how important it was that they capture, alive and well, any human beings who had lived three centuries ago when this planet had been settled. At that moment Xippilli had realized that he wasn't really in charge of anything in the city.

The warrior-priest stared at Xippilli. "You are right. But do remember, before long, our men will want blood. Is the holy thing to do. It is the right thing."

He left with a rustle, and Xippilli now sat alone in the office. That scared him more than anything else.

The burden of trying to save lives while maintaining his duties as the Azteca leader weighed heavily enough that he looked over at a heavily decorated pistol in a glass box on his desk.

But even suicide would be too horrible, as Xippilli knew that the lives of those in the pens would disappear along with his.

He sank into the chair and curled up in it.

CHAPTER THIRTY-FIVE

The night air stank of fear.

Pepper sat on the corner of a railing at the top of a four-story apartment complex and watched the city. A massive wooden pyramid now dominated the end of the large gardens at the center of the city. Nanagadans milled around in large pens covered in razor wire.

But they weren't being sacrificed.

He'd found himself a raincoat with big inner pockets to keep his gear in. The Azteca disguise made for better camouflage, but damn, he just wanted to be comfortable.

He sighed and walked over to a pipe and slid down to street level.

Two Hawk men standing by the corner of the street turned, slightly confused, and dropped to the cobblestones before even opening their mouths to shout a warning.

Pepper moved on.

In orbit the new Teotl were trying to stabilize and force open the wormhole that led back to humanity. He wanted that. Whatever he was going to do would encourage that. Pepper wanted to return home more than anything.

But after seeing the pens, he also wanted to make sure they paid a price for what they were doing here. If they helped destroy lives as they once had, Pepper would make them pay in kind.

But he had to wait, and it frustrated him. His plans had to be reset, on the fly, and that always led to mistakes.

Pepper sighed again, tired, and started zigzagging his way down the street, sniffing for something new, something a little sweeter, decayed, and familiar.

He found a Teotl half an hour later, ensconced deep in a basement room surrounded by warriors who had to be silently killed, one by one.

Pepper pulled out a knife in each hand and took several deep breaths, then kicked the solid-oak door in.

A handful of Azteca bodyguards turned around, grabbing weapons.

None of the mercifully brief struggles and choked silences drew much attention.

CHAPTER THIRTY-SIX

John turned to the thick stone door as it creaked open. No one but Pepper would know how to get here. Still, he reached into a small canvas bag one of the mongoose-men had given him and pulled a pistol out.

Jerome had fallen asleep against one of the walls. The few hours they'd had alone waiting for Pepper had been enough to catch him up on what had happened in Tenochtitlanome, as well as to snack on some fruit and dried meat John had found in the bag.

"Give me a hand." Pepper dragged a large wicker basket in with him. Three pale tentacles with gold tips dangled out of its side.

Jerome woke up, blinking, and jumped up to help pull it in. He shut the well-weighted door with a slow thud.

Pepper sat down, out of breath. "I almost got caught by the tide coming through." The Crosswise bunker lay deep under the city, hundreds of feet below Crosswise Street. Getting there took one through flooded storm drains and city tide-management sewers. It made it safe to hole up in.

A tentacle stirred. Pepper raised a hand. "Give me the collar."

"Here." John handed it over and Pepper snapped the ring of material on the creature in the basket.

Pepper leaned back, as if admiring his handiwork. "It was meant for whoever they talking into being an emissary. Now we put it on one of *them*."

The creature stirred and coughed up phlegm. Pepper grabbed the rim of the basket and flipped it to dump the Teotl out onto the ground. It tumbled and flailed until Pepper stopped it with a swift kick.

It looked like something that belonged underwater, John thought. More octopus than biped. Its skin shone in the low light of the ceiling's bioluminescent rock glow. Capitol City had been designed using some incredible tricks, most of them taught to the Nanagadans by aliens like this three hundred years ago.

Lidded eyes blinked, and it spat a series of syllables at them in a whistle.

"You can do better," Pepper said in a soft voice. "I know you understand, I know you speak Anglic."

It stared at them. Then from within the beaklike mouth it said, "You are insane."

"Excellent. It speaks." Pepper crouched in front of the creature and pulled a simple leather belt from inside the raincoat he now wore. "Come here, John."

John walked over.

"I'm thinking that collar is certainly evidence of bad faith." Pepper sniffed. "A sign that, even if they may speak the truth about needing our help, we'd be stupid to trust them."

"We have fifteen years to wait before our own ship could get us out there." John looked around at the green-stoned room. "We could lay low, wait for the *Ma Wi Jung* to heal. We don't have to get mixed up with all this."

"I'm not waiting fifteen years for anything." Pepper gave John the belt. It felt rough in his hands. The buckle made a *tink* sound. "They're Teotl. They can fix the *Ma Wi Jung* in exchange for our help. We just need to make sure we're not pushed around."

"The jungle would be almost impossible for even the Teotl to penetrate. We could hide well outside Capitol City." John looked at Jerome. His son had left his house a few years ago, but he couldn't help but want to choose the safest option for Jerome.

"We can't erase ourselves like that." Pepper pointed at the Teotl with a long knife that he pulled from his boots. "Besides, we already have this one now. I've committed us to a course."

"This Teotl, it's from orbit?" John asked. He felt weary.

Pepper turned and looked at it. "Oh, yes. This Teotl seems to be an important one. It had lots of guards."

This was Pepper's way. Direct. And John owed him for his son's life. He turned to Jerome. "Jerome, what we're going to do will be extremely dangerous."

"Yeah, I know."

"We could help you get out into the jungle. You could stay out there and stay low."

Jerome shook his head. "Anything you two doing, I want be there."

"It'll get ugly."

"Ugly like loosing people you had love to the Azteca? Like losing Mother?" Jerome snapped. "I seen ugly. I ready for ugly."

John nodded, reached over, and tied the belt around the middle of the Teotl's nearest tentacle. "I take it we're showing them we're quite serious? No messing around with us?"

He cinched it tight over the smooth, rubbery skin. It felt familiar to be falling into this pattern with Pepper.

"It'll be your turn to talk to the Teotl when this is done," Pepper said.

John nodded. "I figured."

"What are you doing?" the Teotl asked.

"Proving we have you captive." Pepper ran a thumb over the knife's edge. "And making a point about what I'm capable of doing when I suspect people might be lying to me."

John flinched as the Teotl screamed.

Over the night more Azteca had come into the city. They filled the streets, breaking down doors and rushing into houses.

"Please be calm. Please do as they say and you will not be hurt." A small man in beige pants and a red shirt stood with the Azteca, translating for them. "They want information about one of their own that is missing. A god. They say a god is missing."

John walked down the street, watching whole families forced out onto the street with their hands tied behind them by rope.

The Azteca were pissed.

"If you know anything, please tell us." The translator's voice quavered.

The translator was a man in a hard place, John thought as he shifted the canvas bag slung over his shoulder into a more comfortable position. The man had probably fled the Azteca years ago to settle in Capitol City. Fled the sacrifices and blood because he didn't believe in it. But he didn't fit in well in the city. He might have struggled to live and suffered some injustices based on who and what he was, except for when he was in Tolteca-town, where all the other Azteca refugees settled in the city. And now he faced his worst nightmare. The Azteca had caught back up to him.

A child burst into tears and his mother shushed him.

A Jaguar scout walked over to John. He pointed at the ground. John looked at the translator, who turned to see what the commotion was.

"Sir, please get to your knees," the translator said.

John reached into his bag. The scout shouted, then screamed when John dropped a whole foot-long piece of tentacle on the cobblestones between them.

"Tell him their missing god is not dead, and only I know where he is," John said to the translator.

The Toltecan shivered and did as John asked.

Silence fell across the entire street. Warriors walked away from their prisoners toward John. John looked up reflexively, for the rooftops. He caught the quick flutter of a raincoat and smiled. Pepper was waiting. He'd come down off the rooftops once John got the Teotl to agree to a meeting.

"Stay with me, translator," John said. "I'm scared too. But tell him I need to talk to the new gods. I have an offer for them."

The man nodded, then broke into a shy smile. "You're John deBrun, aren't you? You're back."

"It would seem so." John held up the bag. "Tell them I'd like to go now."

Behind him he could hear muttering as the word spread. For some reason it seemed to have changed the mood.

Not John's mood. It felt as if a great weight had been shackled to him again. He'd rescued them all once before from the hell of the Azteca; no doubt they found hope in seeing him again.

But some holes were deep enough there wasn't even a ray of light, and John felt as if he'd fallen farther into one than ever before.

Fifty Azteca warriors surrounded him, rifles and macuahuitl held ready, as Capitol City watched him be marched down the road toward the city's gardens.

CHAPTER THIRTY-SEVEN

Before Pepper left, he slipped a small oval disk into Jerome's hand. Jerome turned it over. A red button glowed in the center of it.

"Trigger the button, the noose tightens." Jerome looked over at the Teotl, which had grunted and flopped its way across the room to the far corner, dripping clear ichor all the way.

"The necklace?"

"It'll slice the alien's head from its trunk. So don't press it unless you really, really need to."

Then Pepper slipped out of the door after John.

Jerome sat holding his knees now, just watching the creature.

It remained in the corner, cradling the cut tentacle with its others, keening. Clear ichor still dribbled from the stump, a steady dripping that alarmed Jerome. Pepper had made it clear that they needed the Teotl alive as a bargaining chip. Would the slow-leaking wound kill it?

Pepper wouldn't have left it to die if that was the case.

Still.

"You understand me, right?" Jerome walked over. He kept the disk in his hand and his thumb ready to trigger the noose in case the living god attacked him.

It hissed. Jerome tightened his grip on the disk.

"Is there anything I can do to stop the bleeding?" His voice quavered, and he hated himself for being scared of it.

Just a brain on tentacles. His dad had explained it once. Highly developed and modified to plan, and think, a Teotl ruler.

Jerome stepped closer; a tentacle stirred. The creature backed away from him, scrunching itself into the corner.

It was scared.

"I'm not going to hurt you," Jerome said, slow and clear. "I promise."

The Teotl regarded him with its large eyes and blinked. "Bandage. Something to wrap . . ."

Jerome turned to the mess his dad had left behind when he'd dumped the canvas bag out and put the alien's tentacle in it. Jerome found several changes of clothes and food.

"Here." He walked back and tossed the shirt over. It puffed out, floated slowly down, and the Teotl caught it with a grunt. Jerome watched the Teotl carefully wrap the shirt around its stump.

"Thank you." It leaned against the wall again and looked up at the ceiling.

Jerome sat down and pulled an apple out of the pile. He used a penknife to cut it into sections and core out the seeds.

"What is your name?" the Teotl asked.

"Why?" Jerome bit into a quarter of an apple. It tasted sweet. He hadn't eaten all night.

"Every bit of civility in such situations is needed," it gasped.

The creature was, Jerome decided, too calm despite all this. It made him more suspicious. "I prefer you scared."

"My name is Metztli."

"I don't care." He cut another piece of apple, removed the skin with three careful jabs of the knife.

The Teotl continued, "You are called Jerome."

Jerome looked over at it. "So?"

"So now we know who we are." The Teotl had stopped bleeding. It looked down at its bandaged stump.

"You heal quick." Jerome pocketed the knife.

"One of our many gifts. And weaknesses." It sighed again.

Jerome cocked his head to the left. "Weakness?" Unusual that it would admit to anything like that.

"Maybe." Two sets of eyelids, the inner moist and transparent, flicked. "We specialize. Specialization offers many benefits, but during cataclysmic events renders a species vulnerable, and we are vulnerable, Jerome. Very vulnerable."

"You specialize in what?" Despite himself Jerome was curious.

The Teotl stirred. "Look at my current form. I'm useless, captured so easily, utterly unable to defend myself."

"If you had had a gun you could have shoot back."

"My only useful function is an ability to communicate."

"That it?"

The Teotl twisted the fat mass of its translucent head. Jerome saw small metal plugs glint. "That is all."

A life plugged into machines to feed itself, working only to learn languages and how they worked.

Then Jerome nodded. "You the most dangerous." This one in particular, talking to them. Its words were its weapons. Just because it could not physically attack him didn't mean it couldn't cause harm in other manners.

It cradled its arm and shrank. "What do you mean?"

"You manipulate me. Try to get me understanding you side of the story, get inside me head." Jerome held up the remote to the necklace on the creature's neck. "You go shut up now."

"But—"

Jerome threw the pocketknife at it. The Teotl flinched as the knife struck the side of the wall and clattered back toward Jerome.

"Shut up." Jerome stood up. "You poisoning me head with you 'communication.' Language you weapon. I see you now, Metztli, I see you now."

He paced the room. Working up that deep anger, thinking about his mother's bones lying in an anonymous Azteca mass grave somewhere outside Brungstun.

Here he was standing next to the very thing that had commanded the Azteca. "From now," he shouted, "I go ask the questions, you tell me the answer. That all."

Deep breaths, he told himself. Pepper needed him. Needed him to keep his calm and pull this all off. For Pepper.

"What you doing here?" Jerome asked the Metztli.

"You need the history if you are to understand," it complained. "You need grounded."

"Get on with it all," Jerome warned.

Metztli looked at him, eyelids flickering up, breathing heavily. "This was supposed to be where we gained our independence. Instead, your kind came as well."

"Why again?" Jerome crouched and stared across at it with fire in his eyes. "What you doing this time?"

"We run from our parasitic masters. We run from destruction of our entire race. We need your help. If we did strange things before, it was because we were arrogant enough to assume this planet would be ours. We no longer want it, we're refugees, running for our lives. If we do anything strange now, it is out of desperation."

They stared at each other.

CHAPTER THIRTY-EIGHT

John watched the fluid lines of the Teotls' shuttle with an outwardly disinterested eye. He'd been taken there almost straightaway.

The curves reminded him of the *Ma Wi Jung*, still lying under the water, resting easy on the rocky bottom several miles from the city's walls.

They shared a history. Somewhere, long ago, maybe even a line of design. The *Ma Wi Jung* had been a collaborative project between the Loa and the brightest minds in Nanagada's orbit so many hundreds of years past.

A chance, John had thought at that time, for humanity to leapfrog itself into a strong technological position.

A Teotl, bred for military prowess, cartilage-ribbed and edged razor sharp, stared him down. Fifty Azteca warriors with rifles casually cradled in their arms stood by, waiting for any trouble.

"We absolutely refuse." The pilot, plugged into a massive life-support sedan, ichor dripping around the edges of tubes that pulsed liquid life into its body, regarded him with milky eyecaps. It spit as it spoke. "You cannot expect a position of trust to be formed by kidnappers and terrorists like yourselves." The words, as usual, issued from somewhere deep in the Teotl's throat, but not from its mouth. A mechanical voice box.

Five warrior Teotl formed a guard between the pilot and John. All of them held long, large, deadly looking weapons aimed unerringly at him.

John held out one of the pamphlets from the Teotl that claimed they needed human emissaries. "You do not need us anymore?"

"We choose how this conversation flies on, not you," the pilot said after a long pause.

John would bet anything by the way it waited so long before each sentence that something, somewhere in orbit, was whispering translations into the pilot's head. He had someone else in on the conversation. And that suggested that translators were in short supply.

Pepper had chosen his prey well.

"That's true, but have you looked at the DNA of the specimen I carried with me?" John leaned forward. The hologram over the pilot's belly fluttered slightly. Loss of concentration on its part?

It hissed at him. John felt something flicker in the back of his mind. The Teotl was testing to see if his personal implants could be hacked. His navigation senses tapped directly into the cortex. They could have themselves a zombie to play with.

If they were good enough. John's ability to tie into lamina had been hand-rolled by Nanagadans in orbit; it was unfamiliar enough that the Teotl should have trouble. The Teotl, much to everyone's amazement, used the same protocols for mind-computer interfaces as the Gahe, and Maatan. It seemed as if a standard piece of technology got passed around. And only the humans were usually obstinate enough to try to reinvent the wheel.

"So you know we have a valuable resource of yours." John ignored the chills going up and down his spine, the tiny tremors.

"Yes. Does it remain alive?"

"Yes."

More waiting. "What is your price?"

"We want you to repair a ship of our own."

"It will be considered."

"Thank you." John folded his arms and stared straight ahead. The attempts to hack into his very mind finally stopped, frustrated by the nonstandard equipment in John's head.

The pilot labored itself into a semi-sitting postion. "You are accepted within us. Your role will be laid out in contract. That is your preferred form?"

"Yes."

The pilot shifted and the divan slowly raised itself on a single flowing leg that oozed out from under the rim and turned toward the flowing-teardrop-shaped shuttle.

"We make for orbit in one hour," the pilot boomed back at him. "Bring the translator to us with yourselves by then."

That soon?

"We'll all be ready," John said. The divan squeaked to a halt and the warrior Teotl shifted. John bit his lip and his fingers itched to dance across an imaginary control set to blast him the hell out of this situation.

"All?" the pilot repeated after several heaved breaths.

"My son and Pepper. They will come with the translator."

An explosion of random geometry flowed out of the divan's holographic display. The pilot almost disappeared under a hail of blue cubes, then the display shut down.

"That one called Pepper will not attend you. We forbid it. We have seen it attack, it is dangerous."

"You have your own protections. I need mine. If you do anything stupid, so will Pepper." John stood up in front of the advancing divan, daring the pilot to run him down. It was waiting for orders. Then the divan began to inch forward again.

"Yes. Yes, do so. Do bring the aggressive one."

The pilot moved the divan slowly up to the shuttle. John walked forward and closed his eyes as a warrior Teotl stepped out from underneath, obviously warning him to stop.

He did.

Somewhere deep in John's mind a single point of light blossomed, then unpacked itself further into a sliver of paper with a question mark on it.

John opened his eyes, the ghostly question mark fading from the air, and turned back around. Lithe Teotl closed in around him and herded him out of the gardens toward the street.

He walked on for several minutes.

Pepper hopped to his feet. "Well?"

"You were right." John fell into step behind him. They were free to go, but still being escorted out of range of the shuttle by Azteca. "Their interfaces are standard, I'm allowed access to them."

"Good." Pepper clenched a fist and smiled.

John could communicate with the shuttle. Still, it was a far cry from being able to fly it. Or even take it over. He hoped Pepper realized that.

But they were in and negotiating with the enemy.

Pepper led him randomly throughout the streets to lose anyone or anything following them.

"What do you think we're going to find up there?" John asked.

Pepper shrugged. "We're going to need something. Something other than a hostage to keep our edge."

John tapped the tiny flask in his coat. Pepper was the kind of man who wouldn't think twice about releasing something like that against his enemies, while John tried to forget he even had it as he let the dilemma simmer in the back of his mind.

Of course, the Loa could be manipulating him as well.

"I may have something," John said, and pulled it out.

But after he explained what it was, even Pepper turned it over carefully, then handed it back.

John refused. "You keep it."

"Why?"

"If we need to use it, you will be in a better position to trigger it."

Pepper kept turning it over in his hands. Then he looked up at the sky and pocketed it. "It shouldn't come to that."

John nodded. He hoped to hell not.

"You're slowing me down," Pepper said, "and we're still being followed. I'm going to go fetch Jerome and the Teotl. I'll met you back here in an hour."

Pepper disappeared off into an alley, and John kept walking, wondering what was following him.

CHAPTER THIRTY-NINE

Metztli hiccuped, and after the long stretches of silence, Jerome finally broke and asked, "Why you all running?"

"Ah, ah." Metztli scraped around and looked at Jerome in the dim green light. It coughed, a tiny hacking, and spit. "Our overlords have decided we are a threat for investigating advanced technologies. They destroy our nests, our ships, our supporters. It is genocide."

Genocide. That was something, Jerome thought, that Metztli and its ilk knew well.

"Old things," Metztli continued. "Very old. They control much: communications, and technologies. Very powerful, we are all their subjects." Metztli wrapped its tentacles around itself. "You are too, even in this place that your kind tried to hide itself in."

"Never heard of them."

"But they are out there, and coming for all of us. Coming here is our last chance for survival, we have been forced away elsewhere. We tried to take this world so long ago in anticipation of the coming wars, but we failed. Now we come again, with differing strategies."

"So you fighting them?"

"No. We run, now. Run and look to hide. We need your help."

"Help? Help you?" Jerome shook his head. "We know about the kind of help you bring, we don't want no part of it."

"Well," the Teotl said. "You really don't have a choice."

The door scraped open.

"We have no choice. Really?" Pepper slipped through. "People always have choices," he said.

"A wormhole never truly closes," Metztli said. "The expensive exotic matter is merely mostly removed, leaving a passageway impossibly small and therefore closed."

"Or you use really large nuclear weapons to blow the exotic matter out and destabilize the hole," Pepper said.

Metztli blinked and looked over. "Crude, and effective. But even after that with replacement matter, and enough energy, it can be forced back into shape."

"We saw." Pepper walked over to the Teotl and stood over it. "Detritus from the replacement matter and waste energy pouring out of it. An incredible project."

"The Spindle," Jerome said. "You talking about the Spindle, right?"

Pepper nodded. "Do you have the resources to open the next one, the one leading back towards our systems?"

"Barely. We exhausted much to reclose the wormhole."

"We don't have such tools at our disposal," Pepper said.

"We will teach you. We need to teach you."

"Because the bad guys are coming through after you, right?" Pepper smiled.

"Yes, yes," the Teotl hissed. "With your help, with resources we do not have now, we can keep the wormhole closed. Together."

"Toss me the remote," Pepper ordered Jerome. Jerome did so, and Pepper pocketed it. "How many ships and warriors do you have?"

"One ship. Fifteen warriors. Seventeen specialized units, five masters of the gene, seven masters of the metals and chemistries. Some shuttles. I do not know how many. Four hundred reproductive units. A thousand eggs incubating."

The thought of a thousand Teotl waiting to be born made Jerome shiver.

"We wish to bargain for any world, any world that no one wishes, and we will shape our eggs to thrive in it. We will sign any nonaggression pact. We will accept most terms. We will share any technology."

Jerome had imagined clouds of Teotl hanging over their world, ready to darken the skies. Instead, they had a desperate few dirty refugees, vulnerable and begging for their lives.

Pepper spread his arms. "Well, friend, you're well and truly up that creek, aren't you? And you are bringing down a great danger onto us. There are few reasons we should help you."

"What creek?" the Teotl asked, a concerned note in its voice.

"The same one humanity's been in for the last few hundred years. The same one you tried to send us up. Shit creek." Pepper snapped his fingers. "One ship, that's it?"

"That is it. We are the last of our kind. Many millions died after you shut the wormhole down that led to us. They died to protect us, to get us through and this far."

Millions.

"One ship to get me back out on the other side of the wormhole to civilization. One freaking ship," Pepper repeated. "I like those odds."

"They are not good odds," Metztli said.

Pepper smiled. "Not for you they aren't, no." He turned around and pushed the door open. "Time to leave." He pushed the Teotl into the wicker basket.

As Pepper dragged the alien out, Jerome waited until they passed, then picked up his pocketknife and followed them.

CHAPTER FORTY

The wind kicked at them, stirring Pepper's locks slightly as the odd trio waited before the Teotl shuttle. Pepper tasted salt, and a myriad of other things on the wind. He ignored it all and remained still as a pair of Teotl opened his coat.

One by one they removed items. The two shotguns first. Pepper kept the small flask John had given him in his hands, slightly obscured by the remote to the collar.

The irony of the creatures' own devices being used on them like this was Pepper's kind of irony.

"They're actually taking us up," John said. Pepper nodded. Jerome stood between them.

The disarming continued. Next came the brace of pistols by unbuckling a belt. The Teotl snorted as the smooth-handled hunting knife came out of its case, and the machete with the oak handle tugged out along with it. They found the two pistols by his ankles, stiletto strapped to his calf, and finally the handmade sword on his back.

Pepper stepped over the pile they'd made. "You're staring," he said to Jerome.

Jerome looked down at the ground. John grabbed his son's shoulder. "You sure you don't want to stay? You don't have to get involved in all this."

"I already in." Jerome shook free. "Far enough in it don't matter where I go now." Pepper agreed silently. The boy had as much a right to get off the planet as John or he.

They grouped up and stood at the shuttle's side. A split appeared in the shiny skin, a man-sized entrance growing to accept them. Pepper walked through.

Across the grass, from the edge of the city, Pepper heard a scream. The Teotl had what they wanted now. Someone was being sacrificed somewhere on the edge of the city.

John looked back at him. "You okay?"

"Keep moving, let's get this over with."

The shuttle's inhabitants swung from cocoons as it gained altitude, while the humans remained warily at the back, shuffled into a corner.

The Teotl were insane to let them into their lair. What new minds were controlling them? They'd lost a certain edge Pepper expected. Maybe the Teotl who had managed to land on Nanagada in the old days had been a particularly nasty sort.

He sighed to himself. Too much gray, not enough black and white for his taste.

They hadn't tried to kill him yet, though. That was a plus. He began to let the right hemisphere of his brain slip into sleep while he watched the bundles of Teotl inside the craft bounce around, dangling from the current top of the shuttle.

Then he noticed something, like the aftertaste of orange rind on the back of his tongue. Jerome and John leaned against each other, asleep. Peaceful. Out. Something in the air, targeted at them.

Pepper smiled. That was more like it. He closed his opened eye, slowed his breathing, and slipped into an apparent sleep.

CHAPTER FORTY-ONE

Pepper shook John awake. He looked around and gagged on the taste of orange rind.

"Jerome?" John staggered up and looked at Pepper. "What the hell happened? Where's Jerome?" They weren't aboard a shuttle.

"Easy, man, we're okay." Pepper steadied him. John swayed for a second, unfocused his eyes, and checked the time. It glowed fuzzily in his field of view, laid overtop everything he could see. He'd lost five hours. "Jerome is outside keeping an eye on our hostage."

"I've lost five hours?"

Pepper sighed. "I know." He wiped his hands off. "They gassed us on the way up and tried to separate us. Would have made for some nice negotiating on their part, having Jerome."

"What'd you do?"

"Grabbed the first warrior's arm when he came in to pick us up. I don't think they'll try again. Spooked them." Pepper's lips quirked, a grin, gone before John even realized it.

"Okay." John took a deep breath. A whole world trickled in through the edges of his vision. The walls, a polished gray rock of some sort, faded into swirls of bright, gaudy orange and blue. A clear patch glowed hot white, with squiggles of wavy lines through it.

Alien text.

John squinted, then held up a hand and cleared a section of his viewpoint, a window into the real. The drab wall returned. "The data overlays. They're the same that the Gahe and Maatan use. Standard." Everywhere John looked he could see and access data tied into the real physical location. It was a breath of fresh air. He hadn't been in an environment like this for a long time. It felt like coming home.

"Standard?" Pepper asked.

"Very."

Pepper nodded. "You start querying all this crap and learning it. I want you to be able to fly one of their shuttles."

"You think we'll be able to steal one?"

"The moment we get close enough to something we recognize we can run to, a ship, habitat, or a planet, yes."

Pepper walked out, and Jerome handed him the necklace remote for their hostage. John uncleared his vision and began looking around the room. Did it speak Anglic? It should, the Teotl had encountered them enough. He pinged it. The colors shifted and the wiggles turned into text.

Utility room B50. He could translate their text and access their public information. And why not? They were standard public data overlays, available to all.

Jerome walked in. "You okay?"

John nodded. "You?"

"Tired. Mouth tasting funny."

"Orange peels?" John asked.

Jerome frowned and looked at him. "Orange?"

Nanagada didn't have oranges. John had forgotten. He put a finger to his lips. He hadn't had an orange in so long he wondered if he even really remembered what oranges tasted like. "A fruit, can't find it on Nanagada."

Jerome shifted a bit, indecisive. "You scared, being here in the middle of the Teotl?"

"Of course." John summoned up a map of the Teotl starship from the public data overlay. It looked like giant, rocky potato. The thing was barely small enough to fit through a wormhole.

Right now it rotated for gravity.

John looked over and smiled. "I'd be insane not to be."

"I feel sorry for the Teotl, a little bit," Jerome said. "They ain't no more. They the last of they kind."

John looked at his son. As a boy he'd been told bogeyman tales of the Teotl descending from space in the great wars at the start of Nanagadan history. And told that some still stalked around Aztlan, causing trouble for Nanagadans. And particularly, little boys who didn't behave.

And yet he was still willing to try to wrap his mind around the various facets of the situation.

"You have sympathy for them?" John asked.

"No. But I think I coming to understand them," Jerome snapped. He looked directly at John, then grinned. "They running from something dangerous too. They scared. They ain't no gods, they just like all of we."

A pair of Teotl appeared at the door and pointed at John.

"Jerome . . ." John stopped at the doorjamb. Bit his lip. "Don't believe all that just yet. This wouldn't be the first time we played into their hands."

He turned around and Jerome shrugged.

"Listen . . ." Two Teotl flanked John.

"Need move," they grated at him in simplified Anglic. They smelled of rotting meat, and John grimaced when he noticed the glisten of pus on their joints.

"I want my son to come with us."

"Now. Move."

John looked back. "We'll talk later, Jerome."

The Teotl led him out into the corridor, and the door slid shut, sealing them off from each other.

They descended deeper into the ship, John's eyes getting accustomed to the faint dripping, the slippery floors, until they abruptly stepped out into a vast cavern.

Like standing on the inside of a giant world. But no grass or forests like a human habitat. Every available inch of the space dotted with glistening cocoons. Eggs. Teotl. Massive polyps sprung from a ground saturated with a nutrient web. John dug at this with a foot. Faint white wires that broke in a gush of fluid.

This was a colony ship festooned with the creatures waiting to molt into their various forms. An invasion force. John swallowed. Each of those things was capable of turning into a creature adapted for competing with humans for any environment they happened to be in. Or just shoving them aside.

The stump of Metztli's missing tentacle had been covered in an amoeba-like substance. Metztli inched toward John in a sedan festooned with spiny bones. The foot part of the sedan picked up speed, slipping down a smooth track toward them. Pepper followed close behind.

They both stopped in front of John.

The Teotl twisted and regarded John with lidded eyes. "We are the last of our kind, aboard this ship. We are in desperate need of your help. This is the truth. Can you convince your friend to take the collar off me?"

"You have lied before. I'd rather see it on," John said. "You talk as if reformed, but you let the Azteca take Capitol City, you rule it with fear."

"I know." The Teotl waved one of its healthy metal-tipped tentacles. "It was dirty, and quick, and uncivilized. But imagine that any moment now our devices holding the wormhole closed will be overcome. When our masters pour out from it to destroy us, they will destroy you too. It is in your interest to assist us."

John leaned toward the sedan and grabbed one of the spikes. He bent it under his hand. "You are designed to understand us and talk to us. I've met your type before. You're dangerous."

"We both are." It held up the stub of the tentacle John and Pepper had cut off. Then it tapped the collar. "As Pepper noted, if I try to remove this, I'll die. An effective device, we made. And on a bigger scale, no one won the mess we were orbiting. But despite all that hostility, even we are capable of learning from mistakes."

"Learning to put that behind us isn't easy."

"We did not pretend it to be. But we have a higher goal now. Survival. We do not want your world, it is yours to do with what you will. It's in too dangerous a position for us. We want to follow the other wormhole out to the human worlds. We want to find a place to hide there, and allies to help us keep the wormhole back where we came from closed. It will require a lot of energy." The Teotl's sedan began to ooze down the shallow trough, and John walked with it.

John looked around at the soft, wet corners of the world he walked inside. Suppose this was it for humanity and he had the remains of his entire race in this craft. What would he do with the weight of an entire species on his shoulders?

And what if this was just one big snow job?

"Where are we going now?" he asked.

"We will show you the reopening of the wormhole back to the human worlds. We are about to break orbit."

John paused. "Bring my son with us." He folded his arms and stared at the Teotl as it slowly slid past him. "I demand he stand with me. There is no reason to separate us."

"It will be done." The sedan lurched to a halt. The Teotl turned to John. "You are possessive."

"I want him to see this." Wanted him to see their return to the rest of the worlds, something John had dreamed of for far too many years. And he didn't want to be pulled apart. They'd been through enough. And if Pepper had something up his sleeve, better Jerome stayed close to John.

The sedan slithered its way along the track again.

"My son," John snapped.

"Will join us in the viewing, yes. You are very protective of your offspring. We go to join him." The Teotl wiggled a tentacle. "Come."

John unfolded his hands and followed the alien. Pepper leisurely strolled behind them both.

CHAPTER FORTY-TWO

Ahexotl had flown from Tenochtitlanome by one of the alien airships, and now his entire personal guard marched up the steps into the Minsterial Mansion. Xippilli watched them flow past his own warriors into the building.

He moved from the balcony, sat down at his desk, and waited.

Ahexotl walked in, his gold-threaded cape flowing behind him. He stood before the desk. The door shut behind him, and it was just the two of them.

Xippilli stared up at him.

"The gods are now leaving this world. They want another two hundred warriors to load into their machines, and then they leave."

Xippilli frowned. "We're no longer looking for the councilmen?" He had hunted down a handful of them for the Teotl, immortals like John and Pepper who founded Nanagada all those years ago.

"No, the Teotl are happy with the two we found them. They seem to be on a fast schedule." Ahexotl grinned. "Your work is done."

"I'm to step down?"

"Yes. The lenience disturbs the pipiltin back in Tenochtitlanome. And, Xippilli, I think it would be best for you to keep to the shadows for now. Your feelings are well-known, and your usefulness for finding immortals isn't needed."

"And you will take control of the city?" Xippilli said.

"Warriors are flowing over Mafolie Pass and into Brungstun, and from there they'll move along the coast towards this city. We are taking the whole land again. I am the new pipiltin of Nanagada."

Ahexotl's dreams of business had grown into desire for an empire. Xippilli wondered if the pipiltin back in Tenochtitlanome realized just how dangerous Ahexotl could be.

"What is to become of me?" Xippilli asked.

"A small, but well-paid, position as a clerk. You will be well looked after, my friend, despite your peculiar beliefs and love of this city." Ahexotl walked toward the window. "And as one land, trade will be ever so profitable. And don't worry, Xippilli, the blood will be spilled to our gods carefully. I am no more interested in giving the priests the power they once had than you are."

Xippilli looked at the new ruler of Nanagada and thought about his own future as a clerk, hiding and in fear of his life. He would see friends give their lives, no doubt, as sacrifices.

And then Xippilli listened to the sound of the warriors lining up to board the Teotl airship. The last one up.

He looked over at the pistol. Killing Ahexotl would bring another just like him and end Xippilli's life that much sooner. There was no way he could out-fight Ahexotl either, not by sword or by hand.

Xippilli looked out across the town and thought about the pens of Nana-gadans awaiting their fate.

"Ahexotl, I have a better idea," Xippilli said.

Ahexotl turned. "Yes?"

"Send me up to lead the warriors. Get rid of me and any trouble I might bring right now."

He'd caught Ahexotl off guard. "You really want to join them, in the sky?"

"Yes." Xippilli stepped forward and looked at the alien airship on the bright green grass lawn. "If I'm of no use down here, maybe I can make something of myself up there, with the gods."

He refused to look over. Let Ahexotl calculate for himself how convenient it would be to get rid of Xippilli, a well-known and loved leader here.

And up there maybe Xippilli could be of more help.

Ahexotl sat down in Xippilli's chair. "Okay. Go, go to the stars."

Ahexotl spun the chair around, pleased with himself. Xippilli turned to leave the room, trying to get out before Ahexotl changed his mind.

"Xippilli," Ahexotl said.

"Yes." Xippilli paused at the door.

"Up there, you won't be able to save your friends, or them you. The gods rule there, even if they aren't really gods."

"I know," Xippilli said, and walked out before Ahexotl could call him back.

CHAPTER FORTY-THREE

Two massive Teotl warriors flanked Jerome. They refused to speak to him. They looked straight ahead with silvered eyecaps glinting from the phosphorescent gleam in the walls.

He considered struggling. They were taking him into warrens, down tunnels, through what felt like miles of gloom. Jerome tried to keep track of the constant turns, but realized he couldn't.

They could kill him here in the gloom, easily enough. But that didn't make sense, he reassured himself. They could just as easily have done that in the room once his dad left.

A bright spot of light grew until it filled the corridor Jerome walked down. It bathed him in luminescence as a large gob of black fluid oozed down from the ceiling. Tendrils moved out to caress and sniff him. They withdrew as a large plug of rock rolled aside. The Teotl left.

John stood on the other side with his back to Jerome. What looked like a massive curtain of clear goo hung in the center of the rounded room. The wounded Teotl, Metztli, sat in its mobile chair next to John. It was still dirty, its dangerous necklace resting around its neck.

"Dad?"

John turned around. Metztli turned to look at Jerome as well. The chair with the large muscular leg underneath squirmed away from John, Metztli's tentacles dangling over the edge. "Are you okay, Jerome?"

"Yeah." Jerome walked forward, and the plug of rock shuddered back into place and sighed shut. "You?"

"They reopened the wormhole." John gestured at the translucent film hanging in the air.

Jerome stepped up to it and found himself looking into a vast abyss. He stepped back, heart pounding, and looked at the giant slimy curtain again.

"It's just an organic projection device," John said. "Come on, step forward again." He grabbed Jerome's elbow.

"Worm's holes," Jerome muttered. "Like the story about how we all got to Nanagada." He looked out into the black again. A faint glint at the center caught his attention.

"Waste energy," John said. "They're threading exotic matter back into the pinprick aperture of the original hole. It's like finding a small hole in a wall.

They're putting a piece of material through that's strong, and then spinning it, so fast, so that it expands, forcing the hole open."

Jerome looked at his dad and frowned. "And the hole leads to a place far away. To another star."

John smiled. "Yes."

"So how come they doing this one so quick?" It had taken hundreds of years for the other wormhole to open, as he'd understood it.

Metztli shuffled forward. "This takes enormous energies, and our home is set to provide those, but we are almost bankrupt from the effort. The other wormhole was even more damaged, tiny, and it had a throttling device installed on it that tried to rebuff our efforts. A present from our cousins, your Loa, who helped you to initially close it."

"And this wormhole is not throttled, just destabilized and its throat unsupported," John said.

"Correct."

"Amazing," John breathed. "We knew how to close them, but never knew how to reopen them." Humans had never had the resources to even try to make exotic matter on the scale needed, let alone use it for construction like this.

"But it means our killers will be coming after us soon. Despite our closing the wormhole behind us." Metztli spread its metal-tipped tentacles. Jerome noticed that they were tiny gold caps. He'd thought they served as protection when on the ground, but maybe they were a fashion accessory. "Time is of essence. We need a treaty as soon as we can and the help of your species."

"I understand." John looked over at Jerome, who looked down at the ground.

Something stirred in the ceiling. Jerome stepped backward and looked up, realizing that what he'd thought were fluted decorative arches fitted into the rock above their heads were actually legs.

The spiderlike creature above him lowered a globular head and hissed.

Jerome turned to the Teotl. "Do you fear us?"

The Teotl reached a golden tip up and scratched at Pepper's explosive collar. "I anticipate troubles," it hissed. "But I am not worried about my own life, just the perpetuation of my own species now."

That was interesting. These gods *were* worried about them, and yet dependent. Jerome liked that. "Just a few of us here, we ain't no threat."

"Your actions may affect our lives," Metztli said. "If we cannot keep the other wormhole closed, we will be exterminated."

Jerome shook his head. At the start of this he would have given anything to have a Teotl talk about its impending doom, and for Jerome to help destroy it. Or all of them.

He didn't feel as if he could now. How strange.

The massive stone door blocking them into the nerve center of the Teotl spaceship rolled aside. Xippilli walked in. Five Azteca warriors followed him.

Jerome stared at him, numb and angry. The man who had betrayed them all walked casually in, as if nothing were wrong.

"John, I need to talk to you." Xippilli walked quickly toward them.

Jerome looked around. He had no knife, he had nothing. And the murdering clot stood within his reach.

A steady rumble wormed up through Jerome's feet.

"We're moving," John said. "You were going to repair our ship." John walked forward. The Azteca raised their rifles and John stepped back.

Metztli cleared its throat. "The wormhole is ready now. We did not intend to open it and then return to orbit, we must achieve our goals first. We must be secure."

Jerome took a small step toward Xippilli, who watched John and Pepper, his hands near a pistol by his belt. The thundering increased, and Jerome could feel himself having to lean against it. He noticed Pepper standing behind them all, blending into shadows in a niche of the wall.

Was there a better time for revenge? It didn't come easily or announce itself. One had to grab it. Grab it before standing still and just hating burned him up from the inside.

Jerome threw a shoulder into Xippilli and knocked him to the smooth floor. "Murderer," he hissed.

"Jerome!" John shouted.

Xippilli fought back, but Jerome got his hands on the pistol. He jammed it up against Xippilli's ribs.

"I only tried to help." Their noses almost touched.

"Tell that to them that dead." Jerome pulled the trigger and watched Xipilli jerk as the pistol cracked. "Pepper would do the same. He was there, he saw what happened."

He could hear the snap of Pepper's coat, and as Jerome pulled his bloodied hands free with the pistol still clenched in them, he looked up to see one of the Azteca warriors slump to the ground as Pepper whipped toward Jerome.

Pepper grabbed him by the neck and yanked him up into the air. "What the hell are you thinking?"

Jerome choked, vision graying.

"Pepper! Drop him right now." John stepped forward with both hands tightened into fists.

Pepper threw Jerome against the wall. Jerome scrabbled to his feet, vision swimming in tears, and grabbed his bruised neck, taking deep breaths.

"He's endangering it all." Pepper turned his back to Jerome. "We should have left him on the ground."

Jerome fell back to the ground, dizzy.

"I'm on it." John dropped to his knees by Xippilli. "But you know what Xippilli did. He ran a big risk."

Pepper radiated barely contained fury. "He worked from the inside doing what he could. The boy's too full of misdirected anger."

"You're talking about misdirected rage?" John had stripped off Xippilli's shirt.

"He was running interference for us, taking on the evil to redirect." Just like that Pepper looked about, calm again. Metztli had backed away from all of them, its chair tilting.

"He's losing blood, gut shot," John said. He looked back at Jerome. Instead of fury, only a deep sadness masked his face.

Jerome swallowed and looked away. It felt as if cold water had trickled down his back.

"Get over there." Pepper turned around and grabbed him hard by the shoulder. He pushed him forward. "Get over there and help your father."

Pepper spun on Metztli. "You stay calm, this is a human matter."

Metztli's strange chair had moved him away from their circle. Jerome crawled past an Azteca warrior who lay with his head cocked at an odd angle. Pepper had broken his neck to stop him from killing Jerome.

Blood pooled in the floor around Xippilli, and the man hiccuped blood from his mouth, but couldn't speak. Jerome wanted to throw up. Instead John ripped his shirt from him with his free hand. "Bundle that up, hold it here."

John avoided looking at him. Jerome looked down at wet strips of cloth, then John grabbed his hands and pushed them onto Xippilli's stomach. "Keep the pressure."

Jerome's handiwork. Revenge. This is what it felt like. Wet and sticky, sickening. And a man lay in front of him slowly dying.

"You must wrap this up quickly," Metztli said.

"Shut the fuck up," John snapped. "Pepper, there are hundreds of Azteca on this ship and we just shot their leader."

Pepper looked over at the entryway to the control room. "Open the door, Metztli, and you will die."

"The door will remain closed," Metztli said.

A strange feeling flitted through Jerome as he watched. As if he were being turned inside out and then back again.

"Transit," John said to Pepper, as if were the most automatic and normal thing.

"I felt it." Pepper folded his arms.

"Please," Metztli said. "The man on the floor is of no consequence. We need your assistance."

"Why the hell are you still talking?" John snapped. "Unless you have a first-aid kit lying around, you're going to need to give us some time."

"There are no first-aid kits," Metztli said.

The entire room shivered, distant explosions getting everyone's attention. A keening sound from the walls threatened to deafen them.

"And that was?" Pepper looked around.

Metztli waved a tentacle. "There are a lot of vehicles out on the other side of this wormhole, human we assume. Someone fired a missile in front of us. We're broadcasting that we're no threat, humans are telling us to come in slowly and identify ourselves. We need your services, as I've been saying. We need them now."

"Who's out there?" John asked, looking up.

"We do not know," the Teotl said. "But there are ships, everywhere. Some of them match the ship names of ships that once defended your planet several centuries past, so we assume them to be hostile. Do you think they will fire on us next?"

"I don't know. Do you have any weapons?" Pepper asked. Blood seeped out over Jerome's fingers. He couldn't look down. But he could feel Xippilli's slow, ragged breathing under his hands.

The Teotl looked at them all. "No. The nest has no real weapons to speak of. We're slowing down as we have been asked." It leaned forward.

Pepper walked over to a length of screen goop. "Show me who's knocking and maybe we can start talking."

"Do you think the Ragamuffins are still waiting out there?" John asked Pepper.

Pepper shrugged. "Why not? We were still on Nanagada, weren't we?"

The rock under Jerome's knees shivered again, and Xippilli coughed up more blood and moaned.

PART THREE

Human Affairs

CHAPTER FORTY-FOUR

This was Ragamuffin home territory: a dim brown dwarf that gave off no life-giving light, a rocky world that the upstream and downstream wormhole orbited, and lots of random dirt and rock for ships to hide in past that.

A desolate area.

Etsudo had caught up to the *Shengfen Hao* and three more heavy ships as they moved through toward the Ragamuffins.

He'd scattered drones hundreds of miles out in all directions when he'd transited in. Enough scattered drones could put together a detailed image of whatever he wanted. Any one of them wouldn't have the ability to see the details he wanted, but the whole network could process the light hitting their optics to make a superarray.

The four Hongguo ships chased two smaller Ragamuffin ships, but had stared dumping speed as they'd come through the wormhole. The two wormholes orbited the rocky world in geosynchronous orbit, and now so did Etsudo and the Hongguo. A massive cloud of chaff and mines hung around the wormhole they'd just come through, enclosing it in a massive protective sphere.

The Ragamuffins were well defended against an attack, and Deng had barely stopped the *Shengfen Hao* from plowing into the mess.

Hongguo drones spread out from all the trapped ships, seeking to gain data about the situation.

Deng hailed him. "What are you doing here? We are not expecting you."

"I wish nothing more than to assist." Deng would have trouble believing it. But what could he do about it for right now? Etsudo would get away with it for a while, Deng would hardly have the time to care all that much or shoot him out of the sky unless he posed a threat.

"You have drones out?" Deng asked.

"Of course."

"Check the downstream wormhole, we don't have drones to spare. We're getting radiation readings from it. As if it were open."

Etsudo started turning his drones that way, opening up other tools to probe at the wormhole trailing almost a thousand miles behind them in orbit.

He waited as the scattered drones stitched together their impressions, losing a few to mines in brief, fiery explosions.

"Deng? There is something you should see." Etsudo passed along the images as they came. A very large cylinder of rock, like a scaled-down habitat, slowly moved away from the downstream wormhole. "The downstream wormhole is not only reopened, something really big came through from New Anegada."

Deng looked as if he'd been slapped. "We know roughly how many ships the Ragamuffins have. More ships are moving to flood the area. But this could change things. We'll need more ships, and need to get some drones down that thing. Hold."

Etsudo looked back out at the scene, closing his eyes to the cramped cockpit and the faces of the gamma crew staring back at him.

Behind the *Takara Bune* the *Wuxing Hao* and *Datang Hao* transited slowly into orbit with them.

"Our orders are changed."

"And?" Etsudo asked.

Jiang Deng rubbed his neck. "We'll first move to destroy that object. The Satrap recognized the design and function of that vehicle, it indicates it has the ability to reopen wormholes. Once destroyed, the *Gulong* will come to shut down the upstream wormhole. We will seal the Ragamuffins off."

"I don't have weapons, but my drones are clear of the mines and chaff, I can provide a good plot through."

"That won't be necessary," Deng said. And in Etsudo's lamina he could see representations of the three small ships like his moving out. The *Chen Yuan*, *Pao Ming*, and *Fei Ying*. He remembered meeting the captain of the *Pao Ming* once. A short, stodgy man who kept his hair long. Impractical on a ship.

The three ships fired their engines and dropped their orbit. They hit the first shield of mines.

"Are there people aboard?" Etsudo asked. "It's suicide." And then the thought struck him that he might be asked to follow them, and he wished he hadn't said anything.

"Everything is in a good state." Deng coughed. "It is for the greater stability, the Satrapy agrees."

Agreed or not, Etsudo stared as the burning hulks of the ships cleared a major hole downward and at an angle backward through the shield.

And even for Deng, the man was behaving strangely.

"Is everything okay, Deng?" Etsudo asked.

Deng didn't reply. "The *Wuxing Hao* and I are moving against that vehicle. You will follow and coordinate drone reconnaissance as we go."

And maybe be commanded to ram something.

The Hongguo had now become a military arm for the Satrapy, entirely, and this was nothing but a war, Etsudo thought.

"Imagine a world where any interdicted system could come back into the Benevolent Satrapy," Deng said. "Earth terrorists and Chimson fighters would all pour into our worlds and ignite a war to end all wars throughout the forty-eight worlds. It would be our end. We would be wiped out in response."

Etsudo rubbed his forehead as the *Shengfen Hao* moved its orbit lower and through the gap in the shield. As it slowed, the downstream wormhole would catch up to it. The *Wuxing Hao* followed, and Etsudo swept away visions of lamina to look at his crew.

Bahul and Brandon cocked their heads as the *Takara Bune*'s engines fired. They were patched into the navigation lamina, which gave them a crude simulation of the outside world. Enough to have seen the three-ship suicide run.

"We're following them down and out to the downstream wormhole, it's open again, and we're destroying whatever came through."

"We have no weapons," Fabiyan said.

"I *know* that," Etsudo snapped. "But you saw the other three, didn't you?"

"They can't ask us to kill ourselves to protect those ships," Bahul said.

"They haven't," Etsudo said. "Yet." They all paused to listen to the pattering of chaff and other debris against the *Takara Bune*'s hull.

"The Ragamuffins will attack us," Brandon said. "It's us or them."

Maybe. Hongguo called themselves the guardians of humanity. And the Ragamuffins on the run had kept trying to insinuate that the Satrapy had begun a pogrom against humans.

And what if it was true?

"Brandon, Michiko?" Etsudo opened his eyes. "Go to zeta and alpha crew, help them rig up their rooms as alternate cockpits. We're going to be on alert, no shifts."

"What are you doing?" Brandon asked.

"I am following orders," Etsudo said. Brandon's conditioning was weakening here. His desire to serve the Hongguo without question would begin to buckle as Etsudo looked more and more like a free agent.

There was no time to fix that.

And he was still keeping Nashara's secret to himself, not warning Deng about it. He had a gut feeling that if he revealed his small treason, he would be ordered aboard one of the ships. There his mind would be stripped free of its moorings and he would be remade into a subservient soldier.

Much as he suspected Jiang Deng's mind had been altered somehow by the Satraps. And all the other Jiang serving in the Hongguo.

CHAPTER FORTY-FIVE

Nashara watched the three Hongguo ships burst through the bottom of the Ragamuffin security cloud and tumble out with a cloud of debris.

"Do you think there were people aboard those?" Cascabel asked, appearing only to Nashara.

She suspected so.

Cascabel nodded. "I tried to hail them, to see if I could get into their ships and spread. You?"

"Destroyed before I could do anything." The desire to multiply out into fresh, virgin lamina made Nashara shudder. A sad waste.

"A waste," Cascabel whispered. "The other three ships, one of them is the *Takara Bune*. I'm trying for them."

Nashara knew. "He followed us here. Something doesn't add up with him."

"I know. I have this odd feeling. But I trust him." Cascabel shrugged and faded away from inside the cockpit.

The *Xamayca Pride* had dropped down and managed to get into a geosynchronous orbit several hundred miles above them. Holding the high ground and ready to power out of orbit and run for it if needed.

Nashara had pulled the *Toucan Too* through the shield and lay in front of and just above it, and both the *Starfunk Ayatollah* and Chistopher Malik's *Magadog* had followed a similar path. Neither could get back to the trailing wormhole anytime soon, only the *Xamayca Pride* could.

These ships were heavily armed Ragamuffins, weaponry bolted on from the days when New Anegada and Chimson faced constant alien threat. The Ragamuffins had retreated far into the unexplored areas of this wormhole stop, but all the old ships were still here.

No doubt all the higgler ships such as the *Queen Mohmbasa* had been bringing in the necessities, stuff they needed to survive all these hundreds of years holed up out here.

She'd forced them out of hiding.

"Kaalid, here." Monifa appeared to them all in the cockpit. "Got this damn time lag: everyone out there and all of we down here."

Ijjy twisted. "See those two big Hongguo ship?"

"Yeah, I can't take them with just the *Pride*, seen? Ain't go risk just my ship against them Hongguo. I can't talk to whatever coming through, the Hongguo jamming the area already."

Nashara cocked her head. "And if they're from New Anegada? We're leaving our friends standing alone in the middle of an attack."

"*Cudjo* and *Duppy Conqueror* coming down to back all of we up." There was a pause as Monifa tapped more people into the discussion. "Don Andery, Ras Malik, you there?"

"*Magadog* here." Christopher Malik appeared.

"*Starfunk Ayatollah.*" Andery frowned. "Why I seeing you double, Nashara?"

Nashara looked over at Cascabel, who'd joined the conversation. "Don't worry about that just yet."

Cascabel disappeared, but Nashara could feel her nearby, listening in.

"The Hongguo jamming me out something bad," Monifa said. "I can't talk to whatever just came through that hole back to New Anegada." She said the name fast enough that it sounded more like *Nanagada* to Nashara.

"But if we can talk to them, we have five ships to them three. It worth moving toward it?" Andery asked.

"If we raise them, yes," Monifa said. "I don't have no reply from the Dread Council, but I running this show and I say I want know for sure these people friendly before we rush in. That thing don't look like any ship I ever seen."

"I can stop the jamming, with a little help," Nashara said. "I need a string of communications drones, or buoys, whatever you have. The highest bandwidth you have."

"What you go do?" Christopher Malik asked.

Nashara paused for a moment. She was so used to keeping this deep within her. But this was why she'd been sent, and what she should be doing.

Cascabel appeared beside her with a smile. "You're not seeing double," she said. And Nashara explained what they were seeing.

"She ain't telling no lie," Ijjy said softly from behind her when she finished, and the captains of the other ships stared.

"Do I get drones?"

"Dropping them down now," Monifa said.

Nashara waved her hand. Now she stood on the hull of the *Toucan Too* with Cascabel and watched a shimmering line leap up toward the direction of the *Xamayca Pride.*

"Pretty nice visuals," Cascabel said with a smile, and clapped her hands. For a moment they both hung beside a large silver ball, then another, and a third, jumping along the chain of high bandwidth laser to the final destination.

It was a workable model for what they were doing, a metaphor Cascabel had whipped up as the process began. It was, Nashara thought, helpful. Or else the process would have been mysterious, scary, somewhat uncontrolled.

The final buoy played laser light across the hulls of the ships.

"I can't get into this *Shengfen Hao* at all," Cascabel muttered.

They flicked over to the other ship, *Wuxing Hao*. Nashara smiled, and shivered. She began to split down the middle, a ghostly image of herself moving down the laser light toward the moving ship.

And then it firmed up. "They don't know it yet," the newest Nashara said, "but I'm in."

"And?" Cascabel and Nashara asked.

"Call me Piper."

"Piper?"

"It works with the damn theme. What now?"

Cascabel shivered, shook, and split into two. The second one smiled. "Got the *Takara Bune*. Two out of three, not bad."

"Snag all the drones and let's talk," Piper said. "*Takara Bune*, what's your handle?"

"Please don't ever call me by the ship's name, it feels crass, don't you think?" the newest iteration of herself said.

"We're making this shit up as we go along," Nashara said, getting impatient with herself.

"Cayenne, call me Cayenne. Etsudo's ship seems to have the most drones, I'm getting it."

A moment later they had it. Everything but the *Shengfen Hao*.

Now Nashara could focus on the strange new craft. She found its signal a few seconds later.

A man's face appeared looping a message. A familiar face.

"It's Pepper," Nashara said, shocked. Cascabel, Piper, and Cayenne repeated the same thing with her.

Cascabel passed it on, and a window to Monifa appeared in the air between them. "It's Raga, they're Raga on that."

Monifa looked at the four copies. "You spreading?"

"Get down there," Nashara snapped.

"Of course." Monifa shook herself.

Nashara checked another window in her lamina to see the *Xamayca Pride* dropping down in orbit, several missiles already streaking their way toward the downstream wormhole.

"Piper, Cayenne, see what you can do about the *Shengfen Hao.*"

Far above them all, the *Cudjo* and *Duppy Conqueror* struggled to drop down fast enough. Pepper, the very founder of the Ragamuffins, was aboard that alien ship. It was no surprise, Nashara thought, that Raga made all possible haste to save him.

"Tell her to watch out for the *Wuxing Hao* and *Takara Bune* now," Nashara warned them.

"On it."

"Give them hell." Nashara smiled. She felt unleashed. And it was a good feeling.

CHAPTER FORTY-SIX

Etsudo felt it: the ghostlike presence of something else flitting throughout his ship's lamina. Something had smashed through their security and several of Etsudo's purposefully flimsy firewalls.

And then all the lamina fell away in shards, leaving Etsudo strapped in, blinking, and staring around at the gunmetal gray of the cockpit.

His world, usually carefully laid out to the patterns of feng shui, now looked like the inside of an industrial spaceship.

"Hello, Nashara," he said.

Bahul blinked and looked around, probably also confused about his lack of lamina.

"Etsudo? You figured out what I was very quickly. And you are no simple trader, you are Hongguo, aren't you?" Nashara appeared before him in the cockpit. Both Bahul and Fabiyan stared. Etsudo had not warned them in the least, they'd just been stuck wondering why he'd spent so much time in his quarters with so little sleep.

"Yes, I am Hongguo," Etsudo said. Nashara's projection wore military-gray slacks and had her hair shaved down the sides in streaks. She looked annoyed. "I was part of an arm that sought to control human activities through less violent methods."

"Looks like that's all falling apart," Nashara said.

"You're an emulated mind. This is remarkable," Etsudo said, changing the subject.

"And very illegal," Bahul said.

"Look, I know this is all new and interesting, but I'm taking over your ship," Nashara said. "Any attempts to mess with me and I turn you all into toothpaste. See where I'm coming from?"

"All the experiments we've seen, all the patents I've helped purchase and freeze, with all these the experiments in taking the human mind and digitizing it fail spectacularly. We are more than just brains locked away in mechanical bodies." Etsudo waved at the ship. "We are influenced by our environment, our reactions, our physicalities."

"Lamina," Nashara said.

"I'm sorry?"

"Lamina. If you can emulate a human body within lamina, it can pretend it is still a physical organism in the physical environment the lamina sits over-top and maps to. Don't get me wrong, it's fuzzy here, but just real enough I'm happy."

"Okay, Nashara." Etsudo bowed his head. "What now?"

"Well." The lamina Nashara closed her eyes. "We're going to bump your craft a little bit closer to this big, big thing that apparently reopens worm-holes. We have some friends on it that would like us not to bomb them. I'd also like to go home, Etsudo. It's been a long time since I've been home, when you bastards cut it off."

Etsudo nodded. "I apologize."

"The *Shengfen Hao* is attacking the alien craft my friends are aboard. The thing is spewing atmosphere, breaches all over the place. The hull looks like the far side of a moon, cratered everywhere. How long do you think they can keep that up?"

"What are you hoping to get from all this?" he asked.

"At first? Just wanted to get back to Chimson." Nashara sat down in an empty chair between him and Bahul as if it were real. "Now, the Satrapy is at-tempting to rub our race out, and I wonder if reopening Chimson is a good idea. I might be endangering them."

"The Satrapy is not trying to commit genocide," Etsudo said.

"Really?" Nashara tilted her head at him. "You that sure, Etsudo? Because there's starting to be quite a bit of evidence stacked against you. Lots of dead ships and dead habitats lying around lately."

"They have engaged in illegal activities."

Nashara leaned close. "Some of them. But all of them? There's a girl aboard the ship I flew in here that says her habitat's Satrap said it was over for the species, we're being exterminated."

Etsudo licked his lips. "That's a child speaking."

"Maybe. But then again, the Raga *are* being exterminated, and they're just a motley bunch of creaky old ships. They're harmless."

"Well-armed creaky old ships."

"But not engaged in vastly advanced technological research, my friend. They're only crime is arming themselves for defense. Why doesn't the Satrapy like that?"

"You can't arm yourself and say you are harmless at the same time," Et-sudo said.

"When it comes to genocide, the unarmed are always at a disadvantage,"

Nashara said. "I'll fight here and now rather than suffer a peaceful death later."

"You're a hostile individual."

"Yes." She smiled. "You know, I liked you Etsudo. Now . . . not so much. Sit tight, I'll be doing my best not to harm any of you."

"Nashara, please try to move the ship." Etsudo vibrated with excitement.

Nashara frowned. "Oh, shit." She was trapped in what felt like a bubble. A tiny artificial lamina deep in the ship. She'd been too fast, too cocky, too confident in her unique new form.

"You rage on as if it were a simple thing, Nashara. But who will pay for the fuel for my spaceship? Who will maintain it? If we toss out the Satrapy, it all collapses. For all your rhetoric, you can't just get rid of them. There is an entire civilization that revolves around them, and they around us." The Satrapy cracked antimatter in its habitats to support the entire ecosytem of ships and travel, at levels humans could not gain access to.

"The Satrapy has a monopoly on the technology. Give us time and we'll produce," Nashara said. "We managed on Chimson after you shut us out."

And even if it was true, the Satrapy was surely not going to destroy the Hongguo? No, this was targeted at anti-Satrapic elements. Dangerous humans. Angry humans. Troublesome humans.

The Hongguo and the habitats who worked with the Satrapy would continue on, as always . . .

He had won. He had a copy of her. Once he had a copy, he could work with it, maybe even to the point of getting it to help him against any other copies out there.

Backup lamina now surged into being.

"How the hell?" Nashara, audio only, sounded annoyed even through the fuzz of extremely low bandwidth connections. "Nothing but audio. You sealed me off."

Etsudo cut his crew out of the loop and subvocalized his reponse through the lamina at her so only she could hear. "It's illegal technology, yes. A gift from my father," Etsudo said. "A device that allows me to upload minds into a controlled environment, simulate and rewrite their activity, and write the changes back."

"Why does this seem familiar?" Nashara mused.

"You're dangerous, but now I know how to protect myself. I do abhor needless violence, but I can't have Deng rewrite my mind because he suspects I'm a traitor."

"Etsudo, I'm getting a déjà vu feeling about this." Then suddenly Nashara groaned. "You got into my head with this thing when I came aboard to interview, didn't you? What did you do?"

"Just a memory wipe. And a little trust. You needed a little trust. Because I'm going to need your help, need you here as crew." Another dangerous criminal to add to his motley collection.

Bahul and Fabiyan had remained silent for it all, just watching him.

"What now?"

Etsudo shut her off. Jiang Deng was screaming for his attention. When he tapped into the lamina, Deng appeared, his face cut and bruised, the screen filled with smoke.

"Get clear of the area," Jiang Deng said. Three men in plain gray uniforms stood behind him. "The *Wuxing Hao* mutinied or is under outside control, they're firing on us. We're moving on to attack the craft."

"I know about the takeovers," Etsudo said. "We managed to resist. Deng, you can't take this all on with one ship."

Deng stepped forward quickly and raised an arm toward Etsudo. "Help me, please."

The three men all stepped forward together at the same time and pulled Deng away. Deng screamed as he disappeared, then fell silent with a loud smack.

All three of the new feng turned to Etsudo and spoke together. "You are ordered to attack with us."

Etsudo checked the *Shengfen Hao*'s flight path. "You're crashing the *Shengfen Hao* into the craft?"

"You're going to pay for this," Nashara's voice broke in. "This environment you have me trapped in better be nailed the fuck down, because if it isn't, I'm going to worm through your security and *rip your mind apart.*"

"I'm serious and honest." Etsudo looked outside as they dropped closer. The *Shengfen Hao* flashed through the inky dark, missiles hitting its hull. "I'm not a monster like that."

"Etsudo . . ."

The *Shengfen Hao* hit the side of the alien craft and Etsudo flinched. His few remaining drones showed ripples spread out, along with a gout of flame and debris vomiting into space. All along the ragged gash white ribs held the rocky exterior on. The thing looked more grown than built, as if were some giant animal coaxed to grow into the form of a habitat-like spaceship.

Deng had gone to his death doing his duty. Would it be Etsudo's soon? Deng had not gone to his death willingly.

"She's broadcasting in Morse code with the ship's lights!" Fabiyan said. They cut her off, stored her, frozen, for later investigation.

Etsudo sighed. "She probably warned them, didn't she?" He'd had a good plan. Creating an anti-Nashara to negate any threat Nashara posed to the lamina of the forty-eight worlds.

"Here they come," Bahul muttered.

Yes. And now the question was, could Etsudo outrun them back to the upstream wormhole?

It took fifteen minutes to determine that the Ragamuffin ship coming after them was gaining. Slowly, very slowly. But gaining.

"This the *Magadog*," he was told. "Stand down to be boarded or get destroy. You choose."

If he could get back to the wormhole, through the Ragamuffin security screen of chaff and mines, then he would have safety.

Hongguo ships were broadcasting their IDs as they streamed out and readied themselves. Support had started to arrive, and not a moment too soon, Etsudo thought.

The more chaos, the more ships, the more likely he could dodge attention, keep his head low, and slip back out toward the rest of the worlds.

CHAPTER FORTY-SEVEN

Pepper stood in front of the clear curtain of goop as John helped Jerome slow Xippilli's bleeding. A waste. A waste. And Pepper could tell John was having troubling wrapping his mind around it.

"That last impact?" John asked. "That whole ship. How bad was it?" The control room, buried safely deep in the heart of the Teotl's nest ship, had vibrated and shaken for a full minute.

Metztli, still keeping well clear of the humans, said, "We lost many eggs, but not enough to damage our bloodlines. The nest is trying to repair itself, but our power source is failing. It is over. We need evacuation before the nest dies and kills us with it." Metztli waved at the curtain and it showed chaos. Ripped ship, a massive gaping hole. Thankfully the *Shengfen Hao* had not hit straight on, or the nest would have broken in half.

But it was still a mortal blow.

"They rammed us with a whole ship. Who are these people?" John asked.

Pepper sighed. He should have been excited that some of the original founding members of the Black Starliner Corporation still lived, still guided the Ragamuffins out there. He should have been standing with John talking to old friends, old faces, trying to figure out what to do next.

This transit should have been good, damnit.

Pepper looked back at the dying Xippilli.

Malik, one of the ringleaders of the whole BSC project, grayed out 'fro and all, looked back at him.

"Mr. goddamn Andery," Pepper said.

"*Don* Andery now, moving up. Pepper? You for real? I hardly believing my own eye here."

"Damn straight. It's good to see you." So many years, distant memories.

Some disturbing ones. Malik and Pepper had fought the Teotl in the first war fiercely.

Malik turned offscreen, then back to Pepper. His skin turned a shade browner as the bio-goop he was projected from rippled. "Wish I could say similar, but you return complicate things, man."

As if Pepper didn't have a few things he was juggling himself. "Who's attacking us? We need your protection."

"The Hongguo. They turning weird, man. Weird. But that ship that hit you were the last for now."

Pepper had no idea what the Hongguo were. But three hundred years meant a lot had changed. And now wasn't the time to catch up. Not yet.

Another dim boom rippled through. Metztli whimpered. "Another breach . . ."

There wouldn't be much left of the Teotl nest ship soon, Pepper realized. It was literally falling apart.

"Listen, Pepper, you evacuate in a suit, or pod, and we go pick you up, hear?" Malik said. "Just keep signaling."

Pepper leaned closer to the sheet. "Malik, we have to protect this craft."

"What you talking about?"

"This is advanced Teotl technology we have total access to own here." Pepper turned to Metztli. "We have to tell them what this ship can do to wormholes if you want their help."

Metztli held up a tentacle. "Wait." It closed its eyes. "Okay, it will be allowed."

Pepper face forward. "Malik, we can close and reopen wormholes with it, if you capture it. Malik, I don't know what numbers you have for an attack, but get every ship you can over here."

"Pepper . . ." Malik looked down. "Three century I ain't seen you. You asking me to walk into the heart of a Teotl megaship like this?"

"Yes." Pepper stared at him.

Malik shook his head. "You the big man. I go trust you on this. But only because it's you, you hear? And Monifa of the *Pride* go skin me."

"Get the ships over here," Pepper said. "Get the captains over here for a grounation and board us. There is a docking bay at the center of the forward axis we came in at." It was zero g, and they weren't accelerating.

"Anything else?"

"Bring me guns," Pepper said. "Lots of guns."

Malik spread his hands in an "of course" gesture.

"And watch out for the Azteca, they're probably going to be somewhat jumpy," Pepper said.

"Azteca?" Malik asked. "What the hell you talking about?"

"We'll explain when you get aboard," Pepper said.

Metztli watched the curtain of goop fade to translucence. "I live to see the end of my race."

"No." Pepper looked at the alien "I called a grounation. Our captains will be there, or at least near enough to talk and to discuss what happens next. We need your help with your technology, and you'll have a chance to speak your piece to them all. Take good advantage of it, but realize most of these ship captains will be somewhat antagonistic. Your cousins waged war on them, and there are many who will remember it."

"Thank you," Metztli said.

There was no favor being done. Pepper intended to own the Teotl craft now. The Teotl had nothing but their technology to stand on for bargaining.

"So now we should make our way out to the docking bays, meet the captains there," Pepper said.

"We need to get Xippilli on a stretcher of some sort," John said. "If we can get him aboard one of the ships, we can probably still save him."

Ah, Jerome, Pepper thought, letting himself shake his head. A man, and yet still not quite in control of the mess in his own head.

He couldn't stop thinking of Jerome as the young kid he'd first met at carnival and rescued from the Azteca so long ago.

CHAPTER FORTY-EIGHT

Jerome helped Pepper strap Xippilli onto a length of sturdy, weblike material that stiffened into a stretcher. Metztli had one of the dangerous spiked-skin Teotl deliver it, and with a smile Pepper kept his rifle trained on the Teotl until it left.

"Metztli." Pepper held up the button in his hand. "Your head if you play with me on this trip to the docking bays."

"No tricks. Our lives are in your hands."

Xippilli groaned as John and Jerome lifted him up, and Pepper walked ahead behind Metztli and his snaillike chair.

The odd procession left the control room for the corridors, taking tunnels known to be secure and airtight.

It took the better part of a slow hour to get to the elevators leading to the bays. They all piled in, and Jerome relaxed.

In the tunnels he'd been waiting for an attack. By Azteca under Teotl control, or by one of the dangerous Teotl.

Now it was just Metztli, still collared.

And the dying man. Jerome knelt and checked the cloth tied down across Xippilli's stomach.

What a horrible thing.

His stomach flip-flopped as he felt himself grow lighter. Jerome looked around the elevator, windowless and claustrophobic. "I feel funny," he said.

"We're getting to the center of the nest," Metztli explained. "Closer to the center, the spin doesn't create gravity. We float."

"Ah."

And as Metztli predicted, Jerome found himself bouncing off the floor and feeling dizzy.

Globules of blood broke free from Xippilli's bandages and floated in the air between them all.

"They actually go be able to help him?" Jerome asked again.

"Maybe," John said. "Maybe."

Metztli ripped his collar off so quicky Jerome didn't realize what had happened. Pepper spun and kicked off the roof, dodging Metztli's attempt to place the collar around Pepper's neck.

"Damn it." John pulled a pistol free from its holster, but in the close quarters Metztli had him beat, a free tentacle snapping out to grab the gun.

Jerome shrank back, pulling Xippilli's stretcher with him and trying not to bounce off the wall toward them as he did so.

Metztli filled the whole center of the elevator, tentacles writhing as Pepper tried to overpower it. "If you keep struggling, the gold tips contain neurotoxins deadly to humans, and I will use them," Metztli hissed. "Now that I finally have freedom, I can act to better serve my kind. Do not forget our desperation today."

Everyone froze. Metztli's gold-tipped tentacles hovered a hair's breadth away from all their necks.

"I always wondered why tentacles," Pepper said.

"Zero-gravity self-defense is more practical in this physical form," Metztli said.

"More to you than I suspected." Pepper looked somewhat bemused.

"Different forms for different purposes," Metztli whispered. "I need you all under my control, to bargain with. Your leaders might choose to save you and leave us for dead. I cannot watch my kind die. Your life seems valuable to these humans we've encountered."

"That's fair. I understand you." Pepper kept his hands out. The two stared at each other. Jerome tensed. This would be it.

The elevator shuddered to a stop.

"Get out," Metztli ordered. Jerome looked back and forth at the two, then started to try to move the stretcher out. Metztli twisted its torso and looked at Jerome. "No, leave him."

Jerome turned back. "We can't. He dying."

"He's useless and a waste of resources. We don't need it to control the Azteca, leave the body."

"No." Jerome wrapped his arms around the stretcher. He'd shot the man. That was a beef between humans. The aliens would not be doing any killing, they did not rule everyone as they thought.

Metztli snapped a tentacle in Xippilli's direction and Jerome flinched.

"Oh, shit," John said.

Jerome looked down. A small puncture in Xippilli's neck released a tiny pinprick of blood into the air.

"No, no." Jerome twisted around and stared at Metztli. "I don't understand."

"Jerome." Pepper shook his head. "Don't."

Jerome had thought he'd started to understand the Teotl somewhat. Understand what horror they'd faced fleeing through the wormhole. Sympathized.

But now Jerome felt anger bubble. He shoved the stretcher forward at Metztli, bracing his feet on the doorjambs. Creatures. Foul, disgusting creatures. Manipulative killers.

"There has to be a cure," Jerome shouted, as Metztli wrapped its tentacles around Xippilli and rotated in the air, throwing Xippilli and the stretcher against the wall and flying into Jerome while dragging Pepper along in the air like a puppet.

The impact knocked the air out of Jerome.

Metztli wrapped a tentacle around Jerome's neck while holding onto the doorjamb with another tentacle for leverage.

"Jerome, do not do anything," John said.

Jerome hung in the air with Pepper, breathing hard. They always looked out for him. His dad and Pepper. Even risking their lives for his mistakes.

Now Pepper was a hostage and at risk, and if the creature could kill Xippilli as casually as it had, it might well kill John for being not as valuable as Pepper.

It was time for Jerome to create an opportunity. Time to right things.

He screamed and twisted, snatching the collar out of the air and opening it. He managed to get around the raised tentacle and pushed the collar hard against Metztli's face. It cut deep into the Teotl's flesh and left eye, but as Metztli thrashed, the collar sliced into Jerome's hand. His thumb floated free with a burst of blood.

Jerome felt a quick, stabbing prick on the side of his neck.

Pepper hit the Teotl in the head, a crunching punch that Jerome could almost feel.

Fire ran down his chest and into his stomach. His eyes blurred from the immediate rush of pain.

"I'm sorry," Jerome told his dad. "I'm really sorry."

Metztli hung in the air, knocked out or hopefully dead, tentacles limp, as John grabbed Jerome.

Jerome tried to say something else, but already his jaw had locked, and he could only see his father's face as John leaned in.

John squeezed Jerome's hand as he convulsed, looking around in confusion. Tears welled up and drifted free of John's eyes.

"Pepper, kill that piece of shit." John looked over to his side. "Kill that thing *now*."

Jerome wanted to apologize, to hope they'd be okay.

And maybe it would be. People coming out of the wormholes had incredible skills. They might yet save both him and Xippilli, and Jerome would fall asleep and wake up somewhere nice and clean, well rested, fixed, several days from now.

Yes, that would be nice, he thought.

Very nice.

CHAPTER FORTY-NINE

Pepper watched Jerome's last spasm and bit his tongue until he tasted salty blood.

John looked at him, tears still leaking.

"Not yet," Pepper said, hating himself. "We need Metztli."

"Why? What the hell do we need that thing for?"

Being the calm one, eyes on the prize, really stank right now. "Because we need this ship, John."

"Fuck them."

"John . . ." Pepper didn't have words. He moved over, grabbed John's head, and touched his forehead to his old friend's. "We bring . . . the body . . . with us. We take care of things, like we always do. Right?"

John nodded slightly.

"Okay. We take care of things first."

John looked up. "I hate that calm you have."

Pepper tilted his head. "Okay. But just get your son, let's move on. There is time for grief later."

John pulled away with a sob and grabbed Jerome's body, which Pepper looked away from.

Grief.

There'd be a reckoning later. A full reckoning. Pepper pulled the Teotl closely.

These aliens, with their focus on adaptive personal engineering and sublimation of self to the greater good, were effective and dangerous. Ultimate survivors. They communicated and made you think of them as human. Words.

But they weren't human.

No.

Or at least, not human enough to realize that John and Pepper would not easily put this behind them.

Deep, slow breaths.

Then he yanked the collar out of the unconscious Teotl's face and pocketed that. Jerome had shown quick thinking, there. He'd done good. Stayed on his feet. Pepper admired that in a person. Jerome had been a young man with a mess for a past, but had pulled through and been dumped into a bizarre situation.

They should have left him on the planet, but even then, the chance was high Jerome would have been hunted down by some Azteca and sacrificed.

Pepper looked down at the Teotl.

When the time was right, being half-blind would be the least of this particular creature's troubles. That he vowed. That he would not forget, this moment, these feelings.

CHAPTER FIFTY

Nashara used drones and ships to create a detailed update to the world around them as she approached the crippled craft hanging a third of the way between the two wormholes.

"That one Hongguo ship is still just sitting still outside the upstream wormhole," Cascabel said.

"The *Datang Hao*." Nashara looked down at the scale model of their environment. The tiny tube hung nestled deep in the Ragamuffin shield. "Something important's on it."

"Something that could force a large, military ship like the *Shengfen Hao* to . . ." Cascabel waved and a ghostlike image of the gutted destruction appeared in the lamina before them. A long trail of debris hung out behind the alien craft, spewing out from large gashes in the hull. "Like it did the people aboard that habitat."

The image faded away. "There must be a Satrap there."

Piper joined them. Each version of herself was taking to wearing different clothes. And hairstyles as well: Cascabel had dreadlocks. Piper had kept a close-cropped military fade. "Most of my occupants are sealed within the bay docks, they're trying to negotiate with me now, rather than try to shut the *Wuxing Hao* down."

Nashara hadn't thought about that. Piper had been firing on the *Shengfen Hao* and also trying to fight the Hongguo from within.

"I'm worried about Cayenne on the *Takara Bune*," Piper said. They all were, but Piper had accelerated the *Wuxing Hao* up above them to try to catch up to the upstream wormhole since the engagement.

The acceleration had also served to pin her crew down until they'd agreed to cease their attempts to shut the lamina down and kill Piper in the process. Tidy.

Hell hath no fury like a Nashara, Nashara thought.

"The warning didn't say anything much," Piper said. "We're not sure if she's fighting with the crew, or dead, or captured. If captured, I'd hate to think of what is happening. I like Etsudo, but something about this is making me feel really uncomfortable."

"I agree." Cascabel nodded. "But *Magadog* is moving to help out with the *Duppy Conqueror* close behind, and we can use either ship's communications as a relay point to help Cayenne once they do their work. Joining in, that's a waste of a powerful ship."

Piper considered that for a second. There was one last thing left that Nashara wanted to try. Would her twinned self want to do it as well? "Then I want to try for the upstream wormhole. There are going to be a lot of Hongguo coming through, maybe more Satraps. If we get cut off, or destroyed, my being on the other side may help send warning to other humans. The girl did say this was a genocide, not just Raga-cide."

Nashara nodded. She'd come to the same conclusion. The word had to get out before Hongguo poured out of the wormhole. "Get everyone off your ship."

"I'm working on it," Piper said.

The *Wuxing Hao* began to speed up, moving into higher, faster orbit to overtake the upstream wormhole. An almost suicidal run, but if anyone could do it, she could.

Cascabel and Nashara turned back to each other as the *Toucan Too* slowly tapped the massive curve of hull before them.

Nashara popped her request for a mobile device with a high bandwidth communications array and lamina projection out to the Ragamuffins.

They replied that they would be able to set something up for her particular needs.

A large tender, the *Cornell West*, had made several stops at the large Ragamuffin ships patrolling the wormhole. There had been just a few terse messages back and forth with the ancient Ragamuffins aboard the alien craft. The cylindrical bulks of the *Starfunk Ayatollah* and *Xamayca Pride* already jutted from the docking bays.

A grounation would be held aboard the alien craft. And there would be enough Ragamuffin troops to solve any problems that might arise.

Nashara followed the *Cornell West* in and docked. She watched the outer cameras as muscular organic clams rose out of the walls to hold the ship in place.

Then waited for the bay to seal itself and pressurize.

Several Raga waited outside for her. They towed with them a large, silver, oblong sphere on oversize wheels for gravity and acceleration situations, tiny jets on the side for weightless areas.

They had large guns. Recoilless.

Nashara smiled and dumped a piece of lamina into the mobile unit. Several dishes and a whip antenna rose up as she began to test it. It puffed jets of air to move forward.

"Thank you," she said. Her physical body didn't have the raw signal power and bandwidth between the ship and itself once too far from the *Toucan Too*. With the mobile unit she could bridge that gap and use her body outside.

Without the mobile unit, her body would stop. Without careful adjustments, her heart rate would flutter wildly, until it died. And Nashara would remain in the ship, wondering what had happened.

"It's good," Nashara said. "I'm ready." At the center of the alien craft they all hung in the air. The two Ragamuffins turned and pushed their way off down a long shaft, and Nashara followed them. They moved along the center for several hundred yards, until finally they stopped. A massive plug or rock rolled aside, and Nashara stepped into a room of captains and strangers.

She recognized Don Andery floating above the table and shook his hand. Monifa Kaalid nodded. A handful of what looked like other highly placed Raga had come in with the *Cornell West*. Enough to make any decisions at this grounation stand for the all the Raga involved in this.

Twenty mongoose-men from Ragamuffin ships hung in a circle around the room, guarding exits and looking wary.

She moved in front of the other man she recognized. The gray eyes and the dreads. Yes. Nashara held out a hand. This was Pepper. It was like an electric shock, shaking his hand.

"And you are?"

"Nashara. Nashara Capsicum." She shook his hand, watching the frown at her name. "It's good to meet you finally, Grandpa."

In the pin-drop silence that followed, Nashara smiled and moved on, looking down at a man who crouched next to a body of a young man, maybe just over twenty.

A loss and a shame.

And next to him one of the alien Teotl floated. It had a slashed trunklike face and was missing a tentacle. "What's with this one?"

"He speaks for the Teotl," Pepper said. The grounation began to form a ball of people, all facing each other in the air. He moved closer to her, long dreadlocks floating above the collar of a cumbersome trench coat. "Are you really my granddaughter? Wouldn't I have to have had a daughter to have had a granddaughter?"

"I'm a second removed clone of you." Nashara twisted to look at him.

"Female though. When the Raga lost you behind the wormhole to New Anegada, they created several clones of you."

"Why?"

"You have something of a reputation," she told Pepper. "But mostly it was for your DNA. My superiors cloned me and several brothers and sisters. We were fitted with technology dangerous to the Satrapy and sent to get back to New Anegada and give it to you all for your use. Our DNA profile would be something the Raga here would know about and know that were truly what we claimed to be."

"The Satrapy?" Pepper seemed hung up on that. "The Gahe and Nesaru used that term to describe their alliance, but you all seem to use it differently now."

"You went and hid deep in the wormholes, well out of contact to create New Anegada. We know there was little communication, just a small bit of trade. The Satrapy hid deep behind the Gahe and Nesaru; even now it still tries to hide behind the Hongguo. But they were there. We are all just their puppets, except for Earth, New Anegada, and Chimson."

"Three hundred years." Pepper shrugged.

Nashara grabbed his arm. "Exactly. Look, the main reason I'm here now is because the Teotl know how to reopen wormholes. I want to go back home, to Chimson, and I'll do whatever I can to help if that's something we think can be done. It's been a long, long time since I've been back to my home."

"I can understand that." Pepper still stared at her with a bemused expression.

She turned to face the mass of people. It was time to start this thing. "I have a couple questions. For one, does this thing really reopen wormholes, and two, what do we do next?"

"Good questions," Pepper said. "Ask the Teotl about the first."

The alien twisted slowly. "Yes," it whispered. "But we need more power sources, more antimatter fuel, in order to achieve such results. It is a very expensive process, and we will not share it with you unless we have some guarantees about our safety first. Particularly since this nest is about to fall apart."

"Teotl," snorted an older, yellow-skinned captain who'd come in on the *Cornell West*. "We had fight you long enough back in the day, and now we got you. You go take what we give you, and it go be fair."

"Seen," a pair of Ragamuffins over in the corner said.

"Do not trust the Teotl," the man against the wall with the dead body growled. "Be very careful of their promises."

And so the grounation began as the Ragamuffin leaders deliberated what to do next.

Cascabel appeared, but only to Nashara. "Nashara, Piper wanted me to pass something on to you."

Nashara paused and peered into a new model of the area around the upstream wormhole. The *Datang Hao* had started to retreat back through the wormhole.

But other Hongguo ships were coming through.

The grounation would have to hurry up. The clock was ticking.

CHAPTER FIFTY-ONE

Pepper watched the grounation struggle toward a consensus.

"It insane," Ras Malik snapped. "After all the Teotl gone and done here, and they want protection?" Pepper was content to feel for people's positions. He racked his memory for faces, trying to remember the opinions and beliefs and experiences.

"We go need they technology," Don Andery pointed out.

"We take it," Ras Malik said.

They wanted to move the Ragamuffins into Nanagada. They wanted control of the Teotl technology. They weren't interested in helping the Teotl. But much of the Ragamuffin home base in this system relied on mines drilled into asteroids, a single cobbled-together habitat, and docks for the ships. Those couldn't be moved to Nanagada, and there was no guarantee that the Hongguo would shut down the upstream wormhole only. If they pushed the Ragamuffins back and shut down the downstream wormhole, everyone would be split again.

Pepper pointed out that still left them at risk. The New Anegada downstream wormhole had Teotl's former masters on the other side, masters that sounded awfully like the mind-controlling Satraps Nashara had described in an aside.

Pepper looked up as a far-off explosion echoed down through the ship.

"We die while you argue." Metztli shook a plain tentacle in frustration. Pepper had taken all the tips off. The Teotl insisted on being a part of the grounation, speaking for its people.

It wasn't out of nobility. Pepper suspected that Metztli was in bad shape and hanging on by a thread, and that Metztli was the only specialized type left that could speak for the whole nest. The others had probably died in the impact. Pepper felt an even deeper hint of desperation from the alien.

And the creature was right. Pepper looked over at John, quiet and huddled near the wall, still grieving.

"Well, we can't stand against all them Hongguo that coming down to that upstream wormhole," Dread Caine said. He'd arrived on the *Cornell West*, and his soft voice drew attention to him as effectively as raising his voice could. "So fighting to stay here ain't go work. I agree, we evacuate and let them push we back into New Anegada, and we take these Teotl on all the ship. With them technology, we might hold New Anegada against whatever go come through or maybe reopen this wormhole again."

Pepper twitched. He wasn't going to be trapped again for centuries more.

"Hey." One of the Raga pulled a machine gun up and flicked the safety.

Pepper pushed over, and in the doorway floated one of the Azteca warriors, next to a Teotl like Metztli, tentacles wrapped around the doorjamb.

A bipedal Teotl floated behind them.

"There are one hundred and fifty-seven Azteca with us, five of us," the new Teotl said.

"As I said," Metztli announced from behind Pepper. "We want assurances."

The Raga could take them. Recoilless rifles and more experience in zero gravity than the Azteca. Modern mongoose-men versus Azteca with rifles here in orbit.

But the Teotl might even that out. It would be bloody, Pepper decided.

Another dim explosion.

The alien craft was going to rip itself apart as they argued. Safeties clicked off all throughout the room.

CHAPTER FIFTY-TWO

The Azteca had stormed in and surrounded the conference room. The new Teotl shouted demands for written contracts and promises. The aliens' world was falling apart, and so had John's.

He'd been staying out of it, waiting to leave it all with his son's body. Ready to run and let Pepper do his thing, be in his element.

For Pepper, John would wait to kill Metztli. He owed him that much.

The woman, Nashara, stiffened. "Incoming! Everyone," she shouted, her voice amplified and booming from the mobile unit next to her. "Everyone grab something!"

The world exploded in debris around John. Thundering filled his whole world that screamed up and down his range of hearing until something popped and went silent. Hot white light filled the doorway and then faded away.

He drifted, watching silent screams until a large piece of rock smacked him in the head and he spun away from the wall, bleeding.

Nashara grabbed him using a mechanical claw on the mobile unit. It puffed its way through air to her dragging him with it.

"You okay?" Her lips didn't move. "Your eardrums are blown."

"I'm okay." John looked around, dazed. "How am I hearing you?"

"I'm talking to you through the lamina."

"Lamina?" John mouthed. "You mean data overlays?"

"Yes. I'm drilling straight in. I'll let you listen in through the mobile unit if you want."

He looked at her, impressed.

"Air's getting low." Nashara left him and grabbed Metztli from the middle of the air. "Can you fix the leaks?"

"Fix? Fix? The nest is falling apart," the Teotl screamed.

Jerome's body had floated free, eyes staring out at nothing. John gritted his teeth and turned. "Who the hell did this?"

Nashara looked over the mobile unit at him, face pulled into a grimace. Blood hung in the air in globules, leaking from scratches as people were flung into walls. "We've got Hongguo ships coming out of the upstream worm-hole, looks like one of them snuck a missile or two through at us."

John looked at the captains. "None of your ships caught that?"

"It won't happen again," one of them said. "We see how they jam it."

John looked at Nashara, some of the things she'd been explaining to the grounation coming back through the haze. "And you saw it because you're in the lamina, spreading out through other ships, wherever you can grab processing power, right?"

"I've taken over a Hongguo ship, the *Wuxing Hao*. That version of me picked up on the trick and passed back a warning."

They had a ship of the enemy's. "What are you doing with that ship?"

"Trying to run the Hongguo blockade. Warn the rest of humanity." Nashara shrugged. "They deserve a chance to fight back as well."

Fight back. Nashara looked frustrated sitting around waiting. They'd been talking about running for Nanagada. Cutting losses. Even Pepper had joined in, looking resigned to the idea but annoyed.

John looked around at bleeding Ragamuffins, still facing off against the Azteca despite the disruption.

Fuck running.

"Metztli tells us this 'nest' is unsalvageable." John faced the alien. "You can try and force us around with the Azteca here and we rip each other apart and you become extinct. Or you can work with us and live."

"You lie to us, you betray us," Metztli said. "How can we trust you?"

"It cuts both ways," Pepper said, before John could snap something else out. "You have to start somewhere. Besides, you and I both know you won't make it out alive if you fire the first shot, and I'm pretty sure I will walk out of here alive no matter what choice you make."

Metztli seemed to droop in the air. It waved a tentacle, and the other Teotl barked something out in Nahautl. The Azteca pointed their rifles away, many of them looking relieved.

"These Hongguo are coming through, but how are they going to close the wormhole?" John asked.

"A machine, the *Gulong*," Nashara told him.

"So we've lost the Teotl machine, we're threatened by the Hongguo, we need to take the offensive and capture the *Gulong* and hold it to keep the Hongguo away. Then we can negotiate. Until then we're going to be showing them our backs as we try to organize a fighting retreat? That is how people die, they'll hunt us down and scatter us. No. I'm not interested in that. How many of these ships do they have?"

"Just the one."

Pepper moved over to John and put a hand on his shoulder. "We go for the Hongguo? We hold that wormhole and that ship while Raga evacuate to Nanagada, and if we lose that position, we fall back to this wormhole."

"We take control of this," John said, looking at all the faces.

"A vote, now," said one of the captains. "We go lose people trying to board the *Gulong*, but if we can hold it . . ." Nods spread around the gathering of captains.

The grounation was done.

A vote was called, and Pepper shook John in midair as the captains weighed in. John grabbed his forearm and held on tight to it. "I'm okay, Pepper."

"We'll get . . . the body in a pod." Pepper looked to his side at it, then back to John. "Then we take control of this situation. And when it's done, then we'll grieve properly."

Nashara joined the impromptu huddle. "I'm sorry for your loss," she said to John.

"Thank you," John muttered.

Nashara looked out at the gathering. "It may not come to a physical boarding. I may be able to infiltrate the *Gulong*. If it has lamina, I would like to take that ship."

"Less casualties, and we have it as a weapon, I like that," John said.

The vote finished, captains were sending messages back to their ships to prepare them to hold Azteca warriors and Teotl, and for others to start preparing plans for the attack.

Already simulations would be tested out, heads put together.

"John, Pepper." Nashara grabbed both their arms. "You may want to stay on one of the larger ships, but you are welcome aboard the *Toucan Too*. We're not armed, but we're quick."

John nodded. "Away from the Teotl and off here, yes, I'll come. Pepper?"

"I think I'll split us up and get on the *Duppy Conqueror*. Old friends there, I know the layout. That ship's going to take on a bunch of the Teotl, and I want to keep an eye on them."

"That makes sense." John let go of Pepper's forearm. "Be safe."

"We'll see each other again soon enough." Pepper smiled.

"Soon."

"Let's move," Nashara said. "Air levels are falling and I want to be out and ready to move, we've turned into sitting ducks all docked here."

John floated away with Nashara.

CHAPTER FIFTY-THREE

Someone rapped on the hull of the *Toucan Too*. Kara looked around, wondering what to do. Nashara had left without saying anything; Ijjy lay sedated, eyes drooping.

The banging intensified.

Cascabel appeared in front of Kara. "Nashara didn't tell you what was going on, did she?"

"No." Kara was getting her head around the Cascabel/Nashara divide.

"There are friends at the air lock, they want to pick up you, your brother, and Ijjy and take them to get medical help."

"But what about the attacks?"

"The *Xamayca Pride* is going to act as a flagship, it won't directly join the fighting. From there they will also be able to transfer you out by tender to the other Ragamuffin hiding places in the system. It will be the safest place for you. There's no room for you in the ship that's going back right now, but there will be on a second trip, and you can join Ijjy and Jared there."

Ijjy looked up. "I ain't going. Let the girl go."

"Ijjy, you are no shape to stay on. She'll be fine here until the *Cornell West* returns for the second run, or we can drop her off ourselves when Nashara comes back from the grounation."

Kara nodded. "Ijjy, please, get yourself looked at." She could wait easily enough.

"You sure?" Ijjy looked at her.

"Very sure." She really, really wanted to go with Jared. But Ijjy had risked his life for her and been hurt as a result. She could not let him stay here.

"Okay then." Cascabel walked over to Ijjy. Since everything was weightless, it was odd to watch her stepping along the cockpit as if it had gravity. It just made the fact the Cascabel was a simulation hit home. "I'm going let the Raga in, okay?"

Kara nodded again, pleased to be included. Distant machinery whined, and the sound of boots clanked through the ship.

"Hello?" A heavily muscled man with silver eyes leaned into the cockpit. "I'm Dr. Aiken."

"Hi." Kara released her grip on the chair and floated over to Ijjy. "This is Ijjy, and my brother, Jared, is in another room. They both need to go with you."

"Okay." Two more men hung behind him, and a pair of women.

Ijjy coasted out toward them, and one of the men split off, towing Ijjy out toward the air lock.

The women both carried large machine guns, and they stared at Kara with silvered eyes that reflected and flashed light back at her.

Kara led them down to the room. "Is it safe to take him out of the pod?"

"No." Dr. Aiken drifted over, looking at the pod. "Too dangerous."

He nodded his head, and they moved to release the pod.

"Its battery life should keep everything going until we get back aboard the *Xamayca*. Fluids are low, almost out, but we can compensate."

Once they'd pulled it free, they held the pod between them, quickly shepherding it out toward the lock. Kara followed closely and at the lock put her hand on the surface, looking down at Jared.

She'd be back with him soon.

It would be okay, she silently promised him.

She snagged the edge of the air lock and stopped drifting with the group.

"We'll take good care of him," the doctor said, turning to face her as one of the Ragamuffins fired compressed air from a waistpack to speed them onward. They seemed in a hurry.

The air lock sealed shut, and Cascabel stood upside down on the roof behind Kara, startling Kara as she turned.

"We need to get back to the cockpit and strapped in."

"What's going on?"

"Incoming missiles." Cascabel saw the look on Kara's face. "Jared will be fine. The missiles will head for us, the *West* will be clear and headed for the *Xamayca* long before they are a problem."

Relief. Kara followed Cascabel back.

"How long do we have?"

"Minutes now. And the *Cornell West* is clear and accelerating." Cascabel cocked her head. "Okay, Monifa says we won't get any direct hits near docking, they're chaffing the area pretty hard to draw the missiles away."

Distant shivers and thuds made their way through the *Toucan Too*'s hull. "That was still bad, though," Kara said. "If we can feel it."

Cascabel moved to touch Kara's shoulder, then pulled her hand back as her fingertips slipped through, instead of resting on, Kara. "We're evacuating it all. And the captains here are calling for us to start attacking back."

The thuds continued.

"That was close," Kara said.

"Yeah."

"Nashara—wait, I'm sorry, Cascabel—be honest. Are you worried?"

"Flying through the remains of this thing when it falls apart will be messy. The attack will be messy. But I think it's our best chance."

Another near strike loosened some debris that softly struck the left side of the *Toucan Too*.

But Cascabel said she wasn't worried. And Kara was going to do her best not to as well.

CHAPTER FIFTY-FOUR

The *Wuxing Hao*, which Etsudo suspected of being taken over by Nashara, had passed well beneath them on a tighter, lower orbit. It didn't seem concerned with him at all.

He then watched it climb into a higher orbit, letting the upstream wormhole and its cloud of chaff and drones and Hongguo ships catch up to it. Now it was ducking and weaving its way toward the wormhole, explosions blossoming around it.

The Ragamuffin ship behind the *Wuxing Hao*, however, *was* concerned with him. The *Magadog* fired its first missile spread now that it had gotten within range. Once again, it called for Etsudo to slow down for it or be destroyed.

Etsudo drummed his fingers, checking simulations in the lamina, and realizing the cold truth. "I think I may have put us in a bad spot," he said.

His crew didn't say anything back. Bahul, Fabiyan, Michiko, and Brandon all looked at him as if not quite hearing what he was saying.

Etsudo continued, "I'm going to stop accelerating and let you all get out in pods. Fire your emergency beacons. I'll continue running. I know some of you might wait to light up your beacons until Ragamuffins rescue you, I understand that. I know Hongguo might try, but remember, most likely they'll wipe your minds. Just keep that thought before you light up."

He cut thrust and watched the missiles gain.

Bahul floated over and shook his hand. "Be safe, Captain. Be safe." Then he kicked off with Michiko and Fabiyan, who did not even look back.

Etsudo remained strapped in and shut his eyes. He watched the deadly points of light that represented a certain death get closer.

The Takara Bune shook as the pods left and streaked away.

Brandon came back and strapped in.

"You're staying?" Etsudo looked over, disappointed. Of all his crew, he did not need Brandon aboard.

"You think it so easy to betray the Hongguo." Brandon settled in. "You tried to get rid of those who would keep an eye of what you are about to do."

"Three minutes to impact," Etsudo said.

Brandon leaned his head back against the rest, which molded itself around his head. "You're going to hand her the ship?"

"Who else will call the Ragamuffins off?"

"And will you be able to regain control?" Brandon asked.

"No, she's too good." In a way it was a relief. Soon Brandon would know his secret, and Nashara would be able to spread it all over. "Bit-based SOS with our ship's lights, that was something else."

"Do you think they'll kill us?"

"I don't know." Etsudo looked at Brandon. He didn't have time to try to get him off the ship. Whatever happened next, happened. Brandon was bucking the changes Etsudo had made and would soon cause trouble.

He'd have to deal with that when it happened. "Nashara, in two and a half minutes missiles from your Ragamuffins will hit us. They're chasing us. We are in your hands, Nashara."

And Etsudo handed his ship over to her.

The ship jinked as Nashara took control. The acceleration shoved Etsudo to the brink of blackout, but then it stopped.

"First of all, call me Cayenne, not Nashara. It'll just be easier," she said, her voice echoing through the entire ship.

"Cayenne? Like the pepper?" Etsudo asked.

"Exactly. Okay. What other surprises do you have, Etsudo?"

"I'm out."

Nashara, no, Cayenne, appeared in front of him. "I doubt it, but let's put that aside for a moment."

"I apologize," Etsudo said. And meant it.

He couldn't see anything anymore, she had taken over all lamina, but inside he had counted the seconds to impact.

Time was up.

Nothing happened. Etsudo let out a long breath, glad to be alive.

"If you move," Cayenne said, "I'll accelerate so fast the blood will drain out of your head, and then I'll spin this ship until you literally fall apart."

"I expected no less," Etsudo said softly.

"Just so that we're on the same page."

Etsudo nodded. "I understand."

"I'm talking to the Raga. They're a bit jumpy and we have to keep our distance. But your timing is perfect, Etsudo. We're gearing up to attack the Hongguo. Apparently we want the *Gulong*." Cayenne grinned in front of them. It was clear she approved.

Brandon and Etsudo looked at each other. Brandon's lip curled. He did not like this, his strong loyalties were unbreakable, but at least he kept quiet.

Cayenne flickered for a moment, looking, Etsudo thought, slightly distraught. "Oh, shit, Piper . . . ," Cayenne said to herself, then flickered away, leaving the two men alone in the cockpit with nothing to look at but each other.

This was even more dangerous than Etsudo had suspected. Without the *Gulong*, the Hongguo were almost toothless. If they lost the *Gulong*, what would the Satrapy think?

And if they want far enough, and the news spread all throughout the Satrapy, what would become of the Satraps?

As others sensed weakness, order might be destroyed. Old injustices still rankled many, even among the Gahe and Nesaru living under the Satrapy.

It would mean worlds-wide chaos.

And maybe, Etsudo thought, freedom from the Satraps. A delicious and treasonous thought. Could the Ragamuffins actually pull that off?

CHAPTER FIFTY-FIVE

Pepper had acquired one of the nice recoilless machine guns the Ragamuffins carried. It was snub-nosed and easy to hang off a strap.

"This some ill stuff," Don Andery said. Several Azteca and Raga moved large, fibrous husks of cocoons through into the *Cornell West*. "Teotl on board Raga ships."

Metztli hung over the bay doors, directing.

Pepper nodded at the procession of unformed Teotl waiting to be hatched. "We split them up, different ships. Reduces concentrated strength."

"So they have we all infiltrate now. We all vulnerable."

"You're moving them to ships waiting out on the periphery," Pepper said. "The higgler ships."

"Dangerous. They still dangerous. What happen that you so soft on them?"

Pepper didn't bother replying to that. Soft. Right.

If Andery and his crew didn't see the potential to squeeze useful technology out of the Teotl, Pepper wasn't interested in baby-stepping Andery through it.

Just rehashing arguments anyway. As a founder of the Black Starliner Corporation, Pepper still had considerable power within a grounation. Besides, they'd all voted. It was time to get on with it.

"The Azteca go through first," Pepper said. "They're the more unreliable part of the equation." Warriors with a barely Copernican knowledge of the world fighting in zero g, who knew what went through their minds. Dragged from the ground to orbit and from ship to ship.

He was surprised how calmly they were taking it. Each Azteca had pinned a sick bag to his hip. The one thing they couldn't adjust to with a quick snap was space sickness.

"Attacking the *Gulong*." Don Andery stared off at the polished rock walls.

"At the least"—Pepper smiled—"we'll be remembered." He'd been hemmed in again. Destroying or capturing the *Gulong* might give him a way back out.

"We go be remember as bobo idiot them, not hero," Andery said. "The point of battle ain't to die for no glorious cause, but make you enemy to die for theirs. Some old friend had tell me that once."

Pepper folded his arms. "Old friend, you had hours to make a case in the grounation. It isn't my fault your imagination isn't up to the task of coming up with anything better."

Metztli, for all his wounds, moved from pillar to pillar and helped move Teotl eggs. Pepper noted every twitch and move of the Teotl. Every tentacle flip, filed away in the back of his head.

"Fuck you. No reason to be hackling me."

"Get a pod, or shuttle, and try and run for it somewhere, Don Andery. Just leave *Starfunk Ayatollah* for us to fight with."

"I ain't no yellow-belly," Andery protested.

"You're the one causing botheration about all this."

"Ain't no botheration," Andery groused. "Just talking."

"I'm done talking," Pepper said.

Metztli left to go deeper into the nest for more eggs.

"You want to come aboard the *Ayatollah* for the attack?"

"Getting aboard *Duppy Conqueror*," Pepper said. He moved closer to Andery. "Someone said Earth cut off, before it happen to us, we had heard rumors. The last ships the company sent came back empty."

Andery shook his head. "Was part of the Emancipation agreement. Freedom, but Earth was cut off, yeah."

"I see." That was like a sucker punch. Pepper blinked and looked around.

"Look. I got to go bunks, me rest now." Andery drifted away.

A good idea, catching a nap now while things still were spinning up for the assault.

And Earth was once more beyond his reach. Pepper looked down at his dirty boots and swore.

CHAPTER FIFTY-SIX

Nashara helped John add his son to the other bodies headed out with Teotl cocoons to the other ships.

He stood there until the dock alarms sounded.

"Come on," Nashara pulled him back through the chaos of the docks using the mobile unit, to the Toucan Too. Teotl cocoons festooned the floor, with the fifteen warrior Teotl still alive guarding several of the larger units.

Inside the *Toucan Too*, John collapsed, hanging limp in the air as Nashara guided him to one of the rooms.

John then grabbed the lip of the cockpit entrance. "Hello."

Kara, her feet hooked around a strap and floating in the air, twisted to face them. "Hello."

John moved in and held out his hand. "I'm John."

Shit, Nashara thought. She'd forgotten about the kid.

"I'm Kara." Kara solemnly shook John's hand.

John turned around. "She needs to get off the ship before we go after the *Gulong*."

"I know, yeah." Nashara entered the cockpit, squeezing past him. John smelled of sweat and moss, oddly.

Not a great combination.

She was back in the cockpit, her world. The mobile unit used grapples to secure itself inside the air lock, ready to accompany her on any outside trips.

John drifted away into one of the rooms. "I need to go rest a bit, before all this starts."

Cascabel appeared. "I'll start hunting down a seat for Kara."

"I don't want to go." Kara tilted her head and stared at the both of them.

"You're just a kid."

"I've seen more than many adults." Kara folded her arms.

"Look—"

"You have talked to me about the horrors of revenge. But if the Satrapy is going to kill us all, or take our minds, what can I think of myself if I did nothing? Could it be worse than Agathonosis?"

Nashara sighed, and so did Cascabel. They glanced at each other. It could be worse. She could certainly imagine worse herself.

"I'm sympathetic," Nashara said.

"But it's just not something we can allow," Cascabel finished.

"Do you think you are my parents?" Kara snapped. "No one here can tell me what to do."

"Okay." And Nashara saw a message pop up in her lamina. Cayenne was back.

Nashara could, of course, physically force Kara out onto one of the outgoing Ragamuffin shuttles.

Screw it. Cayenne was back and needed her, Nashara had more important things to care about.

"Okay," Nashara said. "Stay. It'll be dangerous. You'll help with wounded. We'll have Azteca and Raga aboard, and medical pods for the wounded. You're able to interface with lamina, so you'll be able to talk to the pods and authorize whatever medical treatment they want to give. Now I need a moment for an important conference."

Maybe seeing the chewed-up bodies that would come from all this would temper Kara's thirst for vengeance.

Nashara waved Kara out of the cockpit, and Cayenne and Cascabel appeared.

"Cayenne, what the hell happened on the *Takara Bune?*"

"Etsudo isn't all he seems," Cayenne muttered, then caught them up.

Nashara rocked back, as did Cascabel. "He what?"

"Altered our minds."

Cascabel looked at Nashara. "I don't feel it, I don't feel different, do you?"

Would they even know?

"Think about it," Cayenne said. "If this happened on Astragalai, would we even have stopped to consider whether his live was worth saving?"

"I would have flushed him out into the vacuum the moment I had the ship back then; right now, I'm not so outraged," Cascabel said, and Nashara nodded.

"I know," Cayenne said. "And I can't. That's a problem."

"Shit," Cascabel and Nashara said. "Can we still function?"

"I'm ready to face Hongguo. But we have to be careful with Etsudo, you know?"

Fair enough. That was done. There was Piper to deal with. She was getting the shit kicked out of her, the *Wuxing Hao* suffering enough damage it didn't look as if it would even get through the wormhole in one piece.

Cayenne was the closest, and she was able to get a tight beam through to Piper, who showed up in their midst looking wan.

"I know I'm virtual to you guys, a spin-off, but to me this is damn real. The ship is falling apart, and I'm losing processing power with it. I'm dying. For real. I'm not going to make it."

None of them knew what to say. Nashara reached a hand out.

Piper smiled. "Look, I'm going to try and get through one of the communications buoys, but it's a far shot, and I don't think I can. They're shut down, and I can't crack them."

Nashara, Cascabel, and Cayenne watched her fade out, all flinching as the connection died.

"We're gearing up for the attack on the Hongguo," Cascabel whispered. "I'll catch you up later, Cayenne."

And they all turned away from each other.

Nashara knocked on the bulkhead before rolling the door open. John blinked back at her as she drifted in.

The door shut.

"What's going on with the girl?"

"The girl wants to stay." Nashara kept drifting until she snagged a footloop under one of the bunk bed's rims. "I can't change her mind unless I drag her out myself."

John cleared his throat. "She's what, early teens? Good luck with that. Who is she?"

"Girl we found aboard a habitat, one of the last survivors. The Satrap had taken over, used them all as extensions of its mind."

"Plucky."

"Very."

"Reminds you of yourself, no doubt." John rubbed his eyes. He grabbed her hand and looked at her directly, pleading. "You are risking her life keeping her here."

Nashara looked down and pulled her hand away.

"Maybe. A little." Nashara rubbed her palms together. "I'm going to let her stay."

"If she means anything to you, you'll regret that."

"She is right, you know. I'm not her mother." Nor did she want to be. "And she's seen a lot. I think she should be allowed to make her choice."

John deflated. "I'm too tired to fight about something like this."

Nashara grabbed his collar and pulled him closer, oddly nervous.

He jerked back. "I've been through too much."

"I'm not trying to sleep with you." She let go. He'd just loaded his dead son into the cargo hold of the ship. "But do I make you uncomfortable, being Pepper's clone?"

She was keyed up, overfocused and overconfused.

"I just need to sleep right now."

"I've been running, and running for years, alone. And I just watched myself die, I think," Nashara said. "And I want to be next to a human being right now. Do you understand?"

"Yes," he whispered, and unsnapped enough for her to crawl in next to him.

They awkwardly lay there, until Nashara turned around and put one arm around his stomach.

He fell asleep within several minutes, and Nashara just lay there. She wasn't a monster, or a robot, just an very oddly configured human. This was what humans sought, and she still had it in her.

She could see what John couldn't: Cascabel right there in the lamina with her, unable to touch John but trying.

Azteca and Raga fighters came aboard, and Cascabel left to guide them into the ship and show them where to stow their equipment.

It only seemed like seconds later that Cascabel woke her up. "We think it's started, Hongguo communications traffic just leapt off the scale and they're moving."

Nashara carefully pulled herself away. "And?"

"Everyone is evacuated here, it's time to punch out and do this."

CHAPTER FIFTY-SEVEN

Etsudo looked up, surprised as Cayenne allowed a limited amount of access to the ship's lamina.

"We're not allowed in, we're going to hover in the periphery. Any movement and we'll be reclassified as enemy combatants," Cayenne told them. She sounded annoyed. "We get the privelege of watching this battle from a distance. Which means you two will be getting into a pod and leaving here, I can't take the risk of you trying to trap me again. And believe me, I'm being nice, I should have vented the air locks on you."

Leave and go where? Etsudo wondered. "You sound eager to get into the fray," he said.

"Piper just died." Cayenne looked around. "She took the *Wuxing Hao*, now it's just debris."

"One ship against the Hongguo, what were you thinking?" Etsudo asked.

"Trying to run the blockade," Cayenne said with a sad smile. "Trying to warn the humans out in the forty-eight worlds that the Satrapy was heading to exterminate us all."

Etsudo looked at her. "That's a big assumption."

"They're destroying the only armed human force they know of, they've completely taken over the Hongguo for their own needs. Look out there Etsudo, this isn't a normal Hongguo operation."

She was right. And in the lamina Etsudo watched the battle develop slowly.

Hongguo drones poured out through the security shield around the wormhole and madly accelerated out, hundreds of them destroyed as they smacked into new layers of chaff or mines the Ragamuffins had added to the shield.

Ragamuffin drones and mines whirled after their Hongguo counterparts. That dance went on for almost an hour.

Next up came a series of explosions beyond the upstream wormhole: a ring of low-yield nuclear bombs, blossoming flowers of fluorescing colors that expanded out in irregular balls of destruction and generating massive electromagnetic pulses. Communications and feeds dropped resolution, fuzzing out and consumed in static for several minutes before recovering. The next round a little farther out. The Hongguo were clearing the area.

A long, silver needle poked through the wormhole, crackling with massive bursts of static electricity that raced up and down the spire.

"The *Gulong*."

Small, flattened Hongguo fighters squeezed in past the needle of the Hongguo machine.

"To the races," Cayenne said.

Ragamuffin ships moved, seven or eight of them, engines adjusting their orbits to fall down toward the upstream wormhole from their higher orbits.

Another nuclear explosion blossomed in front of one of the Ragamuffin ships.

"They got the *Magadog* . . ." Cayenne was talking about the Ragamuffin ship that had overtaken the *Takara Bune*. The husk of the ship continued to drop toward the upstream wormhole, internal explosions ripping through it and bursting through its skin, debris raining off to form a cloud around it.

Another nuclear hit. Pieces scattered out into different trajectories.

Whatever happened, Etsudo was going to remain aboard his ship, and Cayenne was the ship now. He couldn't take it back.

"Cayenne." Etsudo licked his lips nervously. "I want to make a deal. If I can help you, can I remain aboard? Permanently?"

"I'm listening." And so was Brandon. He cocked his head and looked at Etsudo intently.

"You need to communicate out, and I can give you that. I can get you access to the communications buoys if you can get a drone through to the other side of the upstream wormhole."

Cayenne moved closer. "The communications buoys, really?"

"Yes." Etsudo nodded. "I can get you into them."

"No, you can't," Brandon said.

Etsudo looked over. Brandon had a gun out. "You are a traitor, Etsudo."

"I know," Etsudo said. "But to whom? Humanity, or the Hongguo?"

"The Hongguo serves humanity," Brandon said, and Etsudo gritted his teeth. He didn't believe that anymore, not really. Not after seeing Agathonosis ripped apart just to move a Satrap.

"You're the losing side," Brandon said to Cayenne. "And I don't think, Etsudo, that you are truly my fried. You both antagonize the Satrapy, demonstrate their worse suspicions about humankind: that we're unable to control ourselves, unable to coexist with them. This *woman* and her allies have caused a great deal of trouble because they're unable to work *with* something to better things, you feel obliged to completely oppose, even if it means complete destruction.

"You've not only made things worse for yourselves, but the greater part of the race as well."

"We're already lesser citizens, Brandon," Cayenne said. "Arguing how much lesser we're going to become, that's hardly an attractive way of arguing for your masters."

Brandon took a slow breath. "The Hongguo alone have kept humanity from being destroyed by the Satrapy for almost two centuries now."

"The Hongguo alone have kept humanity in their place for two centuries." Cayenne drifted in front of Brandon, who was still firmly strapped in so that she couldn't dislodge him by using the ship's acceleration. She usually walked as if there were gravity: this was new. Etsudo carefully flipped his straps off, but left them lying against him so that Brandon didn't notice. "You should have seen Chimson grow after we were cut off. We did great things."

And Etsudo believed her.

She floated between the two of them now. Etsudo launched himself at Brandon, passing through her. Brandon blinked for that critical second, and Etsudo smacked into his arm. The *Takara Bune* fired its engines at the same instant.

Etsudo grabbed hold of the gun and held on to it for all he was worth.

"Shoot it, shoot it," Cayenne yelled, floating over both of them. "Empty the chamber." Etsudo pulled the trigger and kept it down. A deafening stream of bullets struck the cockpit wall.

The moment Brandon wrapped his arms around Etsudo's neck and choked him, he knew this had been a stupid idea. Brandon was feng, Etsudo could not beat him physically.

Already Brandon began to break free as Etsudo gagged.

But the accelerating continued and the gun was empty. Etsudo felt three, four, seven times his weight pressing down on Brandon's arm.

"Give it up," Etsudo hissed.

Brandon did not reply, but sank his teeth into Etsudo's neck. Etsudo strained to pull free and rolled off Brandon, clutching the gun. The engines cut off the moment he fell. He struck another acceleration chair and still felt bones break. He groaned.

"Snap in," Cayenne murmured into his ear as Brandon burst free of his straps.

It hurt like hell, but Etsudo had never strapped in this quick. Brandon froze and had enough time to get one single strap back on before Cayenne smiled.

Etsudo had never pushed his ship as hard as Cayenne did for that second. The strap snapped, and Brandon fell farther than Etsudo had to a cockpit wall with a loud smack.

Then Cayenne decelerated, and Brandon flew across the cockpit to the other wall. And then she accelerated again, and blood splattered against the metal. He didn't scream, but Etsudo did. Cayenne kept doing it until Brandon hung limp, and quite dead, in the middle of the cockpit.

"Let's get those codes, Etsudo. We don't have a lot of time."

Etsudo painfully twisted to look at the ghostlike form. He wasn't sure which was scarier: Cayenne or the Hongguo ships out there.

CHAPTER FIFTY-EIGHT

Nashara ignored her cockpit. She sat in a model of the space between the two wormholes watching as the attack on the Hongguo proceeded. The five Ragamuffin ships dodged their way through their own security cloud and the Hongguo with only the *Gulong* in their sights. The Hongguo were running silent. It meant Nashara couldn't get into their lamina, but it also meant they were having trouble coordinating their defense.

The *Datang Hao*'s Satrap was a formidable enemy.

But within the next twenty minutes they'd transit and strike the *Gulong*, and then the real mess would begin.

Cayenne appeared. "I've got codes," she hissed.

"Codes?"

"The buoys. The Hongguo buoys."

Cascabel appeared, and all three of them nodded. "We send the message out."

"I'm on it," Cascabel said. The model shifted. Nashara and Cayenne watched Cascabel bounce information from the *Toucan Too* out through a chain of drones through to the *Duppy Conqueror*, which had just transited.

They could see visuals that Cascabel sent back to them of the Ragamuffin ship as it approached the *Gulong*. But Nashara didn't pay attention, she focused on the schematics as Cascabel cast her search out using the link through the *Duppy Conqueror* to boost the signal.

"Got it," Cascabel hissed.

And it lit up, a straight connection out, and with Hongguo overrides it was fast.

Cascabel shivered, blurred, and began to fade. "I've found lamina," she said.

And Nashara pulled back. Cascabel had been sucked clean out of the *Toucan Too*. Several minutes passed. "Cascabel?"

"I'm okay," a grainy Cascabel reported. "I'm spreading, multiplying. Happier hunting grounds here, and I've found something you'd like."

A laggy connection, timed out and slow due to the sheer distances involved, came in. A small video window.

"Nashara," Danielle of the *Daystar* said with a sly smile. She had to be just four or five transits upstream.

"You followed us?"

"You're the kind of person to keep tabs on. You know what I think about you. My superiors ordered me to follow you in. And then it looks like almost every Hongguo ship *ever* started moving in this direction. We're intrigued. We've never seen movement like this. It presents an opportunity. All through the League of Human Affairs we're opening our communications buoys, arguing about what to do next. Take advantage of this moment to launch our revolution, or just stay very close to watch and learn."

Danielle would be all about opportunity.

"The Satrapy is on the move to wipe us all out," Cascabel said. "The war has begun here. If they finish with us, they'll start on all humanity next. It's a now-or-never sort of thing."

The connection fuzzed out as an electromagnetic pulse washed over the drones Nashara was using to keep the link open. Danielle appeared again, her arms folded over her belly. "Tell you what, forty-two hours my force of five ships can get to you."

Nashara nodded. But there was going to be a catch.

Danielle continued, "Shortly after that, more will come. I'm going to make the first strike, and the rest of the League can come with me or not. It's beginning now. If you have the *Gulong*, we will fight with you. With the *Gulong* the League could fight back, we could turn the tables."

There it was.

With a smile Danielle leaned forward. "It'll be good to see you in person again, Nashara."

And then the connection winked out as several drones were slagged.

Nashara opened the eyes of her body and looked around the cockpit. "John, get the Ragamuffins and Azteca in the cockpit. We're going in at the *Gulong*."

Every little bit was going to help, and if the League was coming, she had a gut instinct they needed to have control of the *Gulong*.

Danielle would see that as another opportunity.

League help offered a solid chance at overwhelming the Hongguo. This was looking more and more likely, as long as they managed to hold on to the *Gulong* for forty-two hours.

"We're going in?" John asked.

"There might be some help on its way, and we need to keep the Hongguo from using the *Gulong* until then. I haven't been able to hack into that ship, and I'm thinking, as well, if we can get in there in person, maybe I can take over its lamina for us."

Nashara began adjusting the ship's course, getting ready to join the fray.

CHAPTER FIFTY-NINE

John swallowed as something clanged off the side of the ship and alarms indicated air pressure loss.

The cockpit remained secure.

Fifteen Azteca Jaguar scouts sat against the cockpit's inner wall. They carried their rifles and their clubs with metal studs hanging from their hips, still in full finery with feathers and cotton armor dirty and sweaty. Mongoosemen with machine guns sat on the other side.

Between those two parties sat two Teotl, bipedal with catlike faces and clear cartilage-like skin gleaming in the cockpit emergency lighting.

"They're randomly detonating nukes all over the fucking place," Nashara said. "Okay, here we are, hold on."

The cockpit whirred, acceleration pressed down from behind, then the side, then on top. Then it really rammed down on them, to the point that the Azteca screamed in fear as they slid around the walls.

Done. It lifted off his chest, his stomach feeling as if it were lifting up into his throat. Someone threw up.

Weightless now, except for a few jerks as Nashara thrust them closer.

A series of explosions, but not on them, and then the sound of scraping and shrieking of metal on metal, the sound of the *Toucan Too*'s engine thundering as it shoved them into something solid.

They were pushing the *Toucan Too*'s nose through the hull of the *Gulong*, into a large hole created by one of the Ragamuffin ships with a missile, somewhere around the two-mile mark from the *Gulong*'s tip. They were a bit late to the party, about twenty minutes behind the other Ragamuffin ships. But they were there.

"Seal it up!" Nashara shouted throughout the whole ship.

The Raga would be heading out, first run, and setting off hull-breach grenades full of emergency sealant.

John unstrapped and the cockpit door rolled open. The Teotl and Azteca followed him out along the corridor, dropping into the bay.

A Ragamuffin hung by the air lock, opening it. His silver eyes flashed back at them. "We ready?"

They nodded. He slapped the control, and the air lock rolled open.

John kicked out. Sealant dripped in long, goopy strings from the jagged tear in the outer hull wall, and he brushed it leaving the *Toucan Too*.

The *Gulong* was five miles long but incredibly narrow. It was also divided up by bulkheads with actual manual locks on them. Keys were required to open them. Wheels to spin the doors open.

"Explosives," John yelled.

Men moved over to the door and slapped five-inch disk along the door's rim.

"Fire in the hole." They scattered.

The door blew off. Small-arms fire started as Hongguo feng on the other side began defending their length of the ship.

Azteca warriors leapt through the breach as John moved away from the line of fire.

"Nashara, can you infect the lamina of this ship?" John asked. It would stop the fighting if she had control. At the least she could give directions.

"I can't find shit." She sounded annoyed. "As far as I can tell, there is no lamina. You're going to have to take the Gulong by force."

By force meant clubs and rifles versus machine guns. John bit his lip and slapped a signal repeater up on the lip of the rim so that he could keep in contact with the *Toucan Too*, then followed the Ragamuffins and the two Teotl over the lip into the mess.

They didn't know where the control center was, but presumably it was near the center of the ship. That meant a mile of bulkheads to fight through.

Other Ragamuffin ships in other sections of the Gulong were working their way toward the center as well.

It would be a long mile, John thought, peering through the smoke and chaos in the tight corridor.

CHAPTER SIXTY

Pepper threw a screaming feng back through a ripped hole in the bulkhead. He grabbed a dead one, pulling it around in front of his body as return fire ripped into it.

The *Gulong* rumbled.

"What was that?" Pepper shouted.

"The *Toucan Too*, other side of the ship," one of the mongoose-men shouted from behind him.

The last hundred feet behind Pepper was obscured with misty blood, pooled globules of viscera and awkwardly broken bodies hanging in the air. He'd moved ahead too quickly.

The mongoose-men floated up to him. "The *Cudjo* destroy," one of them reported. "Hongguo get through and hit it. *Duppy Conqueror* the only ship still in one piece out there." Another tossed a grenade through the open hole. Hongguo feng shouted and scattered.

The explosion scattered shrapnel back through, and the mongoose-men all curled up, holding small shields in front of them. Pepper felt the body in front of him jerk and thud.

"But you still have the backpack nuke?" Pepper asked.

"Several hundred feet back in a crate."

Pepper nodded. "Keep it back a bit, but I'd rather you get cut off from behind than lose that nuke."

He looked back into the hole and threw the body through and followed it to take the next section of corridor.

One by fucking one, each hundred-foot section, until they would make the control center. Pepper did what he did best and kept on moving, the mongoose-men struggling to keep up.

It was going to take five hours to reach the center if it kept taking five minutes to take each section. Pepper wanted to be there in two. Two was a blitzkrieg the Hongguo would have trouble recovering from. Pepper could keep up this pace for two.

More than that and he'd drop from exhaustion. More than that and they wouldn't have the time to take control and force the Hongguo back. They would get bogged down in the corridors fighting for the last minutes of their lives.

CHAPTER SIXTY-ONE

Three hours of hand-to-hand corridor fighting later, John and his two Teotl, three Azteca, and two mongoose-men blew the last bulkhead out. No return fire.

The eight of them ducked around the corner and out into a grand cavity deep in the center of the ship filled with hundreds of strangely quiet people who were shackled to desks on all the walls.

"Each of you take a door," John ordered. He tapped his earpiece. "Nashara, send the mobile unit, you stay in the ship."

She came back, slightly fuzzy. "I need more repeaters, they made it almost impossible to get a link in. I still can't detect any lamina in this ship, they're hiding it well."

John whistled at one of the Teotl. "You head back, bring her machine with you, and lay down more repeaters."

Now that he had a moment, John looked closer at the tired, vacant-looking people. Their heads had been shaved and they wore paper overalls.

None of them had even blinked. But someone at the far end of the chamber moaned, and the noise spread, until it filled the entire room.

The drone grew, modulating up and down. Then fingers all reached for beads on strings built into the desks in front of them. Clattering spread around the room, and the people moaned, noise spreading in patterns throughout the rows. And then the beads would clatter again.

Their eyes were constantly vacant. John shuddered.

"John, this is why I can't find any lamina," Nashara said. "This is how they run the ship. They're human calculators."

"You say the Satraps can control minds. The Teotl told me they were like parasites that attached to intelligent races. This . . . makes sense if you think about how a creature like that would think. Data overlays, or um, lamina, would be too unreliable, too hackable. This is a bulletproof way to protect an asset."

"Yes, but they also can control the ship somehow. Look for desks with controls. Something has to control the minds."

He wanted to keep the doors guarded, so John kicked out to the center of the room, spinning slowly and trying to find something like that.

There. A cluster of desks, like an eye in the orb of all the desks. An oval around a central seat.

John hit the other side of the room, then kicked off for it.

He landed in their midst and grabbed a desk. All men at these desks. All vacant-eyed.

Maybe.

They all pulled out guns. John licked his lips. "I wouldn't . . ."

But they hadn't even noticed him. They each turned their guns to the side to the person next to them to make a complete circle and then pulled the triggers.

The entire oval of controllers hung limp and dead, their brains blown out into the air.

John couldn't even find a response. He just stared.

In their center, a man in a blue uniform already lay dead, a shot through the bottom of his jaw up into his head.

John tapped his earpiece. "They just all killed themselves, Nashara." Too shaken even to be horrified, he just kicked away.

One of the doors blew in. Pepper and a horde of mongoose-men poured in.

"Pepper!" John shouted.

Pepper kicked off to join him. The man dripped blood in a trail behind him, and it dislodged from him as he hit the floor and grabbed a desk.

"What the hell is this?" Pepper looked around.

"A human guidance computer."

"No, I mean, this is the second one we encountered." Pepper pulled out a handkerchief and wiped his face off. "We have two-thirds the ship. The last third toward the front of the ship, the Hongguo still have that. Right before *Magadog* went out, they said there were Hongguo ships docking on the end to pour reinforcements through."

"That's true," Nashara's voice said. The silver ovoid of her mobile unit puffed through, then paused next to them.

"Can you control the *Gulong*?" Pepper asked.

"Give me time, yes," Nashara said. "I think I could. If we figure out where the manual controls are and substitue some our people, with me giving directions and running simulations here in the lamina. It's feasible. But it'll take time to figure out."

"Time we may not have," Pepper said. "We have no Ragamuffin ships left near the *Gulong*. It's just us on foot inside this ship and the *Toucan Too*. If we can't get the *Gulong* moving, then we have to ask more Ragamuffin ships to come down to this orbit and fight." Right now those Ragamuffin ships were watching a careful evacuation of Ragamuffin tenders and higgler ships out the downstream wormhole toward Nanagada.

"We need thirty-nine hours," Nashara said. "There are human ships coming to our aid. And most of the Ragamuffin ships should be done evacuating to New Anegada and can adjust this way."

"Thirty-nine hours?" Pepper waved one of the mongoose-men over, and he pulled a crate the size of a casket with him. "Maybe. It'll be dicey."

John helped a pair of mongoose-men crowbar the crate open. He peered inside at a missile with radioactive symbols painted on the tip. Someone had jury-rigged a control box on its top.

Pepper pointed at Nashara's mobile unit. "Is there visual on that?"

"Yes." A lens irised open.

"Let's broadcast a little something to the Hongguo."

"They are keeping shut down or I would have been able to take their ships," Nashara pointed out.

"Yeah, but I bet you they're doing some passive listening." Pepper tapped on the screen of the control box and pressed a bloody thumb on it.

The screen brightened, and Pepper tapped some more to bring a timer up on it. He set it to ten minutes, triggered the countdown, and faced the camera.

"Hongguo leaders. Hi, I'm Pepper, and I'm currently talking for the Ragamuffins. Behind me is a small nuclear device of several megatons. It's on a timer. Maybe your feng will push back into here, but I promise you, if they do"—Pepper made a popping sound with his mouth—"we will destroy the *Gulong.* If attempts to break up towards our section of the Gulong do not cease, we will destroy the *Gulong.*"

Pepper made a cutting motion with his hand. Then he turned around and stopped the countdown.

"And how long do you think that will hold them back?" John asked.

"I think that that should get us at least ten hours, don't you?" Pepper said.

"The Hongguo on the ship are stepping down," Nashara reported. "It's a cease-fire for now."

"Breathing room." Pepper smiled.

"But the Hongguo ships have us surrounded," Nashara said.

"And you can't infect them?" Pepper asked.

"They've figured something is infecting ships using high-bandwidth communications. They'll listen to voice, but they're isolating and firewalling it,

I'm not getting through. It's all about time, now. And, Pepper, Cayenne from the *Takara Bune* says there's a second chamber of human computers."

Pepper nodded. "I saw it coming in. They're all dead, someone shut the air off to them before we got there."

They all stood a second, quiet.

"And the cavalry you've called in?" John spoke up. "Who are these people?"

"The League of Human Affairs, an assortment of freedom fighters, or terrorists, depends on how you look at them," Nashara said through the speakers of the ovoid.

"They just want to help us out of the goodness of their hearts?" Pepper asked with a grin.

"They want the *Gulong*," Nashara said. "They'll join the fray if we still have the *Gulong*."

"Well, then we better hold it until they get here," Pepper said.

CHAPTER SIXTY-TWO

John strapped himself into the room and scrubbed his face clean with a wet-cloth, ready to collapse and sleep, but knowing he couldn't afford to. Thirty hours to go. The Hongguo had remained quiet, a tense détente, presumably listening on a few radio channels. Their ships clustered around the *Gulong* near the upstream wormhole. A few Raga ships had tried attacks, breaching the security cloud to get to the *Gulong*, and paid in hull damage and lives for the attempt.

"They're moving." Nashara appeared by his side. John jumped and shoved his hand through her, hitting the bulkhead and splitting his knuckles.

"I'm so sorry," she said. "I didn't want to take the time to walk my body down there."

"Who's moving?" John rubbed his knuckles over the wetcloth, leaving a streak of blood.

"Five Hongguo ships are trying for the downstream wormhole, three of them stopped by flack and mines; the other two are being chased. They're headed for New Anegada, John."

A smart move. Take something they valued and they were going to do the same. Two spaceships could do a lot of damage with missiles and nukes to Nanagada.

"We got to help them." John spun around and grabbed the door. "How fast can we get the ship ready?"

"We can't run that Hongguo gauntlet, John. You know that, you're a pilot."

"We have to do something. They're going to hammer the planet," John replied, but with less authority.

"They can only do so much damage, just two ships."

"Damnit, these aren't odds, these are people down there!"

"John, there's nothing, I mean nothing, for them that you or I can do. The best thing is to hold the *Gulong*."

John pushed his head against the mirror. "Thirty hours."

"Thirty hours," Nashara said. "It'll take the Hongguo ten to fifteen to reach New Anegada at their speeds. The Ragamuffin ships there might be able to get to them. They won't have much time above the planet. They're using this to force us to talk."

"I know," John said. "I know."

It didn't make it easier, imagining Hongguo ships appearing far over Nanagada.

Thirty hours.

CHAPTER SIXTY-THREE

Kara sat in front of the three medical pods, watching the men inside lie asleep. The readouts all glowed green, and when she queried them, although she didn't understand the medical terms quickly enough, they reassured her that all was well.

So many others had died. She was almost getting used to it, as if it were part of life to see tortured bodies, from Agathonosis to this ship. A long trail of bodies.

Outside, however, someone was punching the wall and shouting in anger. She kicked out and found John, their newest passenger, huddled up against a wall.

"Are you okay?" She put a hand on his shoulder and he flinched.

"Been better." He smiled at her. "A lot of people are going to die down on New Anegada."

"A lot of people have died already," Kara said. "I don't think it's going to stop anytime soon."

He cocked his head and looked at her. "That's truly dark."

"It's what I've seen."

"I'm sorry. No child should see death and war." He cleared his throat.

"These people, they only have one machine like this, right?" Kara asked. "Yes."

"So they're trying to trade with you. This machine for your planet."

"I know." John sighed. "But that doesn't make it any easier, because they're going to do something to show they're serious."

"We must hope it is a small demonstration," Kara said.

"Yes, but we must also prepare for the worst."

"Why is that?"

"Because, we aren't dealing with humans," John said. "This thing, the Satrap, commands the Hongguo moving to Nanagada."

Kara nodded. "You're right. The Satrap doesn't think like you or me, it's something else. And destroying a planet might be something it thinks would cow us. Or maybe divide our forces."

John jerked back and stared at her. "How do you know that?"

"I've faced them before," Kara said. "It's pretty hopeless, but I've made it this far and I don't want to give up just yet." Jared was safe out there, being looked at.

"People live under these things, out there now?"

"Our histories say they used to only live among the Gahe and Nesaru," Kara said. "And I think now that they came out among the forty-eight worlds and built habitats for themselves and some humans to live in so they could study us. Study how to control or destroy us."

John shook his head. "I'm getting tired of aliens pushing us around."

"Well, we're pushing back. That's hard work."

And the man suddenly laughed. "Yes, it is. Thank you."

Kara watched him coast his way down the corridor.

CHAPTER SIXTY-FOUR

Pepper almost shot Metztli as the Teotl burst through one of the broken bulkheads, tentacles akimbo as it flew through the air. Pepper reholstered his gun.

Two mongoose-men floated near the sealant goop around the breach in the *Gulong*'s hull, trying to see if they needed to add more to stop air loss.

"The chamber is under attack," Metztli said.

"More Hongguo?" Pepper asked. "Nashara, I don't like surprises, can you see anything?"

"They found a damn blind spot, I'm moving drones to look. Hold on." There was an annoyed sigh.

"The Hongguo landed a ship on the hull, they cut their way through. My warriors are holding them," Metztli said. "I don't know how long they can last."

"The Hongguo in the first third of the ship are moving again as well," Nashara reported. "They're fighting their way toward us."

Damnit. Nineteen hours to go. Pepper moved toward the *Toucan Too*. "Come on, kid," he yelled at Kara, who'd been out of the ship, inspecting the tip for any damage and patching it.

She started fingertipping her way up the hull toward the air lock.

Three suited bodies, Hongguo feng, burst through the sealant. They fired. The two mongoose-men taken by surprise died. Their guns spun off, clanking down the *Toucan Too*'s hull.

Pepper bounced into the air lock, pulling his guns free and leaping back out.

Metztli flew past him and struck the nearest feng, ripping an arm free with a tentacle. Pepper shot the other point-blank, but not before getting hit in the shoulder and thigh.

He swore several times.

The third feng flew down along the hull toward Kara before either Metztli or Pepper had time to hit him.

She'd sprung free of the hull, grabbing one of the Raga machine guns, just as the feng smacked into her and swung around, trying to use her body as a shield, or her as a hostage.

The girl jammed the point of the gun under her armpit and pulled the trigger with her thumb.

She kept firing long after the feng died, leaving a long stream of blood as he flew on and hit the deck, bounced, and spun away.

Nashara's voice bellowed out from the ship, "There are more of them coming up the hull towards us, they're using nonreflective cool suits, hard to spot."

Pepper looked at the girl. Her hands were shaking. He coasted out and grabbed her.

"You're hurt," she said, looking at his shoulder.

"I know. You?"

"I think I'm okay." Her voice wavered.

Pepper pulled her with him into the lock. Nashara appeared and looked over Kara. "The chamber is close to being overrun. I'm losing repeaters all throughout the *Gulong*. If we stay much longer, we'll be overrun too."

"And you don't know how to control the *Gulong*?" Pepper asked.

"Not yet," Nashara snapped. "It isn't happening."

"Then we hang on as long as we can. We have no other choice." Pepper leaned back in. "Someone get this girl a gun."

John flew in with a machine gun in hand. "Let's get Kara into a room," he said. "She does not need to be out there."

"We need every hand," Pepper said. "Every. Hand. We have nineteen hours left."

"We're not making nineteen hours," John said.

"Speak for yourself," Pepper spat, and kicked off down the corridor looking for more weapons. He'd give the Hongguo nineteen hours. It would be nineteen hours they'd never forget.

CHAPTER SIXTY-FIVE

Cayenne appeared in Nashara's vision. "I see a lot of movement around the *Gulong*, what's going on?" The feed hissed and sputtered, pushing through Hongguo jamming and hopping several drones to reach her.

"We're not going to make it down here," Nashara said.

"That bad?"

"That bad." The moment of silence stretched, neither sure what to say. Then Nashara shook her head. "She lied."

"What?"

Nashara showed Cayenne the cloud of flack approaching the *Gulong* that Cayenne couldn't see from her side of the wormhole. "The League has arrived. Danielle was giving herself a margin."

The first wave of drone nukes shot through, hitting the Hongguo ships and splitting them apart. Then the smart chaff, thousands of cylinders flung through to burst out and confuse the scene.

Nashara smiled as Danielle hailed her. "You lied," Nashara said.

"We lost lives getting here this quick," Danielle said. She looked grim, serious. "For the cause."

The five League ships used their nuclear drones to quick effect, using surprise to roll over the Hongguo at first.

"We can escort you to safety," Danielle said. "You're going to have start moving."

Nashara shook her head. "We're dead in the water. We can't move."

Danielle swore. Nashara watched as the seven remaining Hongguo ships reformed into a starlike pattern.

Cayenne appeared. "Is that a pattern?"

The starlike group of ships swirled out and fired a concentrated burst of missiles at the League ships. Danielle scattered, focused on dodging them, and the Hongguo had the offensive.

Nashara was already on it, burrowing the space around the *Gulong* for transmissions coordinating the Hongguo attack. "Got it."

Danielle appeared, grunting against the massive acceleration. "Where are your other ships? Five against seven isn't going to be pretty."

Raw lamina yielded to Nashara. She shivered and split, three times, and then she was in three of the ships. The star pattern fell apart. Three new copies of herself appeared with three smiles. "Keep going," they said.

And Nashara laughed as she followed the source back toward the *Datang Hao*, where the Satrap was risking high-bandwidth communications to control the Hongguo ships.

A window in the lamina appeared before a great wall of defenses, and Cayenne saw her enemy for the first time. A balding, saturnine woman; a heavy child; a dour-faced man. "Who are you?" they asked, all their mouths moving in unison.

Behnd the trio a tank of pink liquid stirred. The dark shadow in it, that was the actual Satrap. That would be the creature Nashara and her sisters would dump into the vacuum and watch boil its insides out.

"I'm Nashara."

"I'm Cayenne."

And then they both shattered the window and began to rip into the wall of defenses the Satrap had. Firewalls, yes, but it had opened them up to control its small fleet. It would die for the mistake.

The three ships she'd taken turned on the other four. There was no time for names, just fast destruction. And the League ships unloaded more nuclear drones into the ball of fighting.

Nashara winced as two of the ships hosting copies of her mind split open and died, and then the third hailed Nashara.

"Call me Ada," she said quickly. "Get Danielle off my ass, and then we need to help Cayenne get the Satrap."

"Fellow freedom seekers," Danielle's broadcast rippled out from the *Daystar*, "who are rising up against our vicious alien masters, news of your valiant struggle has spread throughout all human communities thanks to our newly launched communications network. You have friends, true human friends. We believe in your cause, and we are here to help."

"Don't pay attention to the propoganda, let's move," Nashara said. She followed Ada across a string of buoys, and then Cayenne stopped them.

"I got it," Cayenne shouted, and showed them a representation of a giant wall with a tunnel bored through it. Nashara could see on her navigation windows that the *Datang Hao* had changed course and now wobbled toward the wormhole's edges. "I got in and boosted it, locked the controls."

The Satrap's trio appeared, mouths in perfect sync for the Satrap. "You are not so different from me."

"You are nothing more than a parasite," Nashara said.

Danielle continued, "The League of Human Affairs lends our hands to yours. Our warships stand ready. Human destiny is at hand. We can lift off the chains of our oppressors and strike them down and take our rightful place among the stars. Even now we are rising up against Satraps on worlds all throughout the Satrapy."

The *Datang Hao* struck the wormhole at an angle, breaking itself open against the incredible tidal stresses. One-half continued past the wormhole leaking debris. The other half transited, appearing within sight of the *Toucan Too*.

"We are proud," Danielle said, "that you have chosen to rise with us."

Ada looked over at Danielle's obviously prerecorded message. "They're going to take the *Gulong* from us, aren't they?"

"Yes. But I imagine," Nashara said, "that Pepper, John, and the Ragamuffins won't hand over New Anegada."

CHAPTER SIXTY-SIX

Pepper sat in the chamber with Raga mongoose-men and a handful of Azteca with the large crate that had once housed the nuke in front of him.

A day ago he'd been getting ready to fight for his life and was not sure he'd make nineteen hours.

The doors clunked open and men in deep blue armor walked in. Mirrored visors on protective helmets looked around.

They had red fists as an emblem over their chests.

One of the suits of armor puffed over, and the mirrored helmet slid open. A Slavic woman with short hair tapped her chest with three fingers in front of Pepper.

"On behalf of the League of Human Affairs I salute you," she said. "Your incredible work has inspired many to throw off their shackles and rise up against their oppressors."

Pepper stared at her. John had left with Nashara and the *Toucan Too* to return to Nanagada. He wanted to see what damage had been done, and what would be needed down on the surface.

She looked slightly discomfited by Pepper's stare, but continued, "We are proud to offer you a medallion commemorating this historic event."

Many high-ranking Ragamuffins had died, along with their ships. The remaining Ragamuffins that could fight clustered around the wormhole, checking traffic and stopping any but Ragamuffin ships from going to Nanagada. That irked the League.

But not enough for them to try to cross into Nanagada. Pepper had told Danielle in a brief meeting that New Anegada, or Nanagada, whichever one preferred, was Ragamuffin. It would not be joining the League of Human Affairs.

Though they would work with them. The League's uprising had just begun, there was a long war for human independence in front of them.

Pepper took the medallion and pocketed it. "I need a ride to Nanagada."

"There is a ship docked here for you, a *Takara Bune*."

"Thank you." Pepper grabbed the crate and moved.

"What's in the crate?" the woman asked.

"None of your business." Pepper floated out of the cavern with one last look around.

"Sir?"

Pepper wearily turned. The woman clenched her fist and held it up. "Humans first!"

Pepper licked his lips. Then held up a fist. "Sure."

The human calculators had sat throughout the entire thing, staring at the abaci in front of them and waiting for their next instructions.

The Ragamuffins had won this battle, but somehow the League had come in and taken the clear victory away. It felt like a loss, Pepper felt, to hand this all over and walk down the corridor.

He didn't like that at all.

Several League soldiers bundled him and the crate up in a vacuumproof baggie and tossed him out across a line to the *Takara Bune*.

Inside the lock, Pepper ripped his way out to find a small man waiting for him.

"I'm Etsudo."

Pepper shook his hand. "Thank you for the ride."

Etsudo cocked his head and looked at the strap of the medallion floating out of Pepper's pocket. "You got a medal too?"

"Yes." Pepper took it out. He clenched it in his fist and squeezed until it folded in half, then he tossed it into the grating. Let it blow out the next time the air lock opened to the vacuum.

"We're tossing the line now and heading for New Anegada," Etsudo said, and the ship rumbled as it accelerated.

Pepper touched down to the floor. Nashara appeared, projecting herself in front of them both. "Grandpa!"

"You seem to be everywhere these days." Pepper walked up the ship's center core.

He decided to skip going to the cockpit as he found the small galley. He rooted around the freezer locker and grabbed a dish. He pulled the top off and watched it heat as he squeezed into a seat.

Pepper wiggled his hands and pointed at the locked drawers. "Fork?"

"Yeah." Etsudo fished one out.

"The League is asking everyone to rise against the Satrapy. With the *Gulong* they can close down wormholes to strong Satrapic areas. Already aliens are being deported from some heavily human habitats for those areas. They're calling it 'firewalling.' They want to create a human government, and human worlds." Pepper looked down at the potatoes and gravy and wrinkled his nose. "What do you think the problem with that is?"

Etsudo leaned forward. "We can shut these artificial borders, but even at sublight speeds, sooner or later, we will deal with other species, and creatures stronger and more powerful than ourselves. If we don't have models for dealing with this that don't involve all-or-nothing antagonism, we will, not now, but one day, become extinct as a species."

"Exactly." Pepper stabbed the air with his fork. "Exactly."

He looked around the *Takara Bune*.

Nice ship.

CHAPTER SIXTY-SEVEN

Nine days had passed since Jerome's death.

John stood in the garden, the Wicked High Mountains just peeking over the trees, the distant boom of seawater hitting the rocks by the road regular and almost reassuring.

He looked back at the sea of faces. Friends of Jerome's, such as Daseki and Swagga, shook his hand and walked on. Friends of the family came from all over Brungstun, the small town, dressed in their best.

Nashara stood beside him, with the dinged-up mobile unit using wheels to follow her up to the graveyard.

The priestess, dressed in her robes and colorful earrings, handed John the jar that she had declared held Jerome's spirit.

Everyone followed John down the road, to the point where it crossed with the path leading down to the beach, and John threw the jar in the crossroads where it broke.

The crowd sighed.

Kara stood there after the crowd dispersed, looking tired. The first day on the surface she'd stumbled around a lot, staring up at the sky, falling to the ground as she adjusted to the perspective of standing on the surface of an entire world. They'd given her drugs for mild bouts of agoraphobia that left her huddled inside rooms at times. "Why did you throw the jar?"

"Here they believe his soul was in it," John said. "When we smashed it by the crossroads, we released his spirit to the land of the dead, where it belongs. It's old Vodun, strong in these parts of Nanagada."

"And you believe this?" Kara cocked her head.

"It doesn't matter what I believe." John smiled. "It's a ritual. It's . . . somewhat therapeutic. It's important to many that came here today."

"John?" Kara's voice trembled. "Jared still isn't here yet."

John looked at her. "He's on his way."

"If he's dead, I'd like for you to tell me. Don't treat me like a child. I'm not a child." She looked straight at him, like a small soldier.

Nashara walked over just as John reached out and put a hand on Kara's shoulder. "I swear he's alive, Kara. We're going to go see him as soon as he arrives." He looked up at the sky. "The League is doing a good job. They've stopped the fighting out here, and Jared will be able to come to you soon."

She stepped back. "Okay."

But she didn't look convinced. She turned and walked back up the road toward John's Brungstun house.

He hadn't been there in years, but had cleaned it out and given Nashara and Kara rooms.

"She doesn't believe you," Nashara said. "She assumes the worst."

"She's seen the worst," John said. "When are you going to be leaving?"

"I'm loving being here, for now. I'd like to stay a little while and relax, unpack everything, you know?"

"The room is there for you as long as you want it."

This time Nashara grabbed his shoulder. "Hey, things are going to be okay."

John smiled. "I keep telling myself that."

And soon enough, he might even start believing it. He turned to go walk back up to his house, leaving Nashara near the shards of glass.

CHAPTER SIXTY-EIGHT

Planets were beautiful, Nashara decided. She spent every day of the next week luxuriating in just trundling around with the mobile unit: walking off into the bush, smelling the mango scent on the wind from John's backyard trees, and even going down into town to the market despite the stares she got.

And after a week, John started coming out of his shell.

And several days after that, he found her on one of the piers watching the boats bob at anchor in the harbor.

"You ever been sailing?" he asked.

"No."

So John helped her into small boat that shook alarmingly and creaked. Water sloshed around the bottom.

The wind was brisk, but it didn't seem to bother John when the whole boat tilted over as they sailed out. Nashara swore and grabbed the mobile unit, in case they got dunked, but he laughed and let one of the ropes out, and the boat leaned back to normal.

They sailed far out past several reefs, to a private sandy beach, where John shouted in surprise as Nashara let herself fall backward and hit the cold, turquoise-clear water.

The *Toucan Too* was parked several miles away, near a massive clearing outside this small town that perched on the rocks near a natural harbor. Her brain sat inside it, she knew that. It broadcast itself through the mobile unit, and her sensations were sent back to the ship's lamina by her body, with its Chimson-manufactured implants. It was all an illusion.

And yet, unless she actually chose to sever it, it felt real enough to hold her breath and fall away from the mirrorlike surface of the water until her back hit the sand.

Yes, this felt good, she thought. Felt right.

She was going to stay on Nanagada. Stop moving.

This was home.

CHAPTER SIXTY-NINE

Someone shook Kara awake. A large man, with a top hat, and dreadlocks, and a coat that seemed to swirl on its own.

She blinked. "Pepper?"

"Come on," he said. "I have someone for you to meet."

Kara followed him out of the medieval-feeling stone house, but before she got to the front door, Pepper grabbed her shoulder. "Do you like it here?"

"What do you mean?" she asked.

"John, and Nashara, they're going to let you stay. Do you want to stay?"

She looked around. "I just want to find out whether Jared is alive. I don't have anywhere else to stay, so it's a stupid question."

"Okay."

Pepper opened the door, and Jared stood there with his stupid, dirty Raggedy Andy doll.

She almost knocked him over with her hug. "Thank you, Pepper, thank you. Are you okay, Jared?"

Her brother nodded. "I was scared you were gone too."

"I know. Me too."

"Where's John?" Pepper asked her. "I need to talk to him."

CHAPTER SEVENTY

Pepper stood on the pier, waiting as they pulled in. His coat flapped in the wind.

"The *Lucita*," he said, nodding at John's boat.

"Where were you for his funeral?" John asked.

"Not here. And that's all we'll say about that." Pepper leaned over and helped Nashara push the mobile unit out, then gave her a hand.

He lifted her up completely, then deposited her gently on the pier.

John tied the boat up, then jumped up himself. "I hoped you'd be there." They'd seen so much together, and Jerome had looked up to Pepper like an uncle.

Pepper ignored it. He walked ahead. "I have something for you, John. A present."

He led them to a small warehouse at the edge of town. Rows of doors ran along the palm-tree shade.

"Stay outside, Nashara." With a boot he nudged the door open and walked in.

John followed him into the murk as the door closed behind them. Pepper clicked on a gaslight in the corner of the room.

A large crate sat on a bed of straw in the corner.

Pepper grabbed a corner and ripped it off with his bare hands and a grunt, then grabbed the top and tore it off, tossing it aside.

The crate fell apart, revealing the Teotl Metztli, sitting in its own filth and blinking at them. It mewled and scuffled back, pushing itself until it was up against the corner of the wall.

A fetid, rotten smell hit John.

Pepper slapped a gun in John's hand. "I told you there would be a reckoning later. You insinuated just now that I didn't care for Jerome, but don't you ever make that mistake." He gripped his hands over John's on the gun and squeezed. "I forget nothing. This is my gift."

John squeezed back, fighting back tears again. "You loved him too?"

Pepper brushed the arm away and looked away. "Wouldn't go that warm and mushy, John."

"You felt *something*."

"I protected him. I protected him for you when I first met him. Kept an eye on him later. And here I failed. I don't like to fail. We should have left him in the bush outside Capitol City."

"I know." But then there he might have died too, attacked by Azteca, or by an accident, or by something else. There were no guarantees.

"Then there it is. That's done. You have this, and I've done this for you."

John shook his head, not sure what to say.

"There's something else." Pepper pressed something into John's other palm. A broken vial.

John looked up. "Pepper. That's genocide."

"Maybe." There was an expression on Pepper's face. Anger? Or hurt. "You and I disagree about the League. So I'll give you a question with that piece of glass. Do we choose to try and live with these aliens, or any aliens? Do we learn to adapt and grow with them, because more powerful creatures will come to us one day? Or do we go it alone, fighting to the brink and never pulling back? The Ragamuffin ships are creating a cordon near Chilo that they're not allowing the League to pass through, because the League wants all the Teotl and their technology as well as whatever remains of the nest. They already have the *Gulong*, Raga won't be giving them anything more. But that's a big issue we need to solve."

"Pepper . . . the vial." John was more worried about that.

"Some of them will figure it out and quarantine themselves from other Teotl. It'll just be a lonely existence for them."

"I can't . . ."

"Anyway." Pepper walked to the door. "I did what I did. If you feel merciful, let the Teotl all know what I released, it'll take a few weeks to make its way across the various ships and population centers, and if you tell them now, they can prevent the spread and live. But you can think about that later. First . . ."

He tossed a hacksaw and set of pliers on the ground in front of John.

"Good-bye."

They shook hands firmly, then Pepper shut the door on John.

In the corner of the room Metztli shivered, looking with its one good eye at John.

"I saved your lives," it mewled again.

"Yes." John nodded. "But you didn't save *his*, did you?"

He squatted in front of the alien, gun in his left hand.

CHAPTER SEVENTY-ONE

Pepper walked out and smiled at Nashara. She cocked her head.

"You look comfortable here," Pepper said with a smile.

"I don't think so," Nashara said. "But, yes, I'm staying."

"I should be unnerved that my cloned self wants to sell its feminist militant side out and try and have babies."

"Fuck you. I have no womb." She considered sucker punching him, but it was Pepper. It would have as much effect on him as it would on her. "I'm not settling down. This is just going to be my home. John is going to be my friend. This place needs protecting, it needs people like me and you. You know that."

"Yes, but you should tell him you like him."

"He'll find out soon enough."

"He's broken goods, he might take some gentle hints." Pepper folded his arms and regarded her.

"I know."

"You're going to settle down, help with the kids, hang out around town?" He smirked. "Cook dinners?"

"Not my style, Grandpops. There are governments to reform, military strength to create if we don't want the League running us over. And then, I want the Teotl to help us figure out how to get Chimson back into the fold. My real home."

Her stance was just as aggressive.

Pepper nodded, he'd just been pushing her a bit. "There are wolves out there, like the League. Even humans can be dangerous to humanity, right? The League is near xenophobic, we can't have that built in, the backlash will be too great. I'm planning on heading out with a couple of your virtual selves and Etsudo to scout out what is really going on among the forty-eight planets. See, these people, they need protection from the wolves. They need domesticated wolves, like you and me, right, Granddaughter?"

"Sheepdogs."

Pepper nodded and smiled. "Sheepdogs, exactly."

"What are you off to do then?" Nashara asked.

"Going to join *Takara Bune*, you, and Etsudo. I want the *Gulong* back, or at least the technology, just in case the Teotl here are . . . unable to rebuild the technology they had in their nest. And . . . a few other things I need to check up on way out there. I think we'll be a good team. We'll curb the League as best we can."

"I'm good people," Nashara said with a smile. "I won't let you down."

"I know." The crack of a pistol shot jerked Nashara into the air.

She spun back toward the door, but Pepper grabbed her arm.

"He's okay. It's just sheepdog shit, you don't want to know," he said. "Just, do me a favor? Don't ask about it."

"Okay." Nashara stared at the door, and John slowly walked through.

She grabbed his arm as he wobbled a bit. He was crying. Pepper grabbed her before she could go over and rested his forehead against hers. "Treat him well," he said. "I'll clean this up. Take him home."

"Okay." Nashara pulled away and walked over to John. "Come on, John, let's go."

She helped him along the road. After several minutes he pulled himself together.

"Thanks."

"It's no problem."

He stopped walking. "I need you to do something for me."

"What?"

"I need you to use your connection to contact all the ships that have Teotl aboard them. There's something we need to warn them about."

He looked back down the road, and Nashara followed his gaze.

But Pepper was already gone.

EPILOGUE

Cayenne was three days and too many transits upstream from Chilo, where the Ragamuffin ships patrolled with a watchful eye at the League of Human Affairs. Only Ragamuffin ships were allowed past Chilo.

The Raga high council had decided to keep calling the planet New Anegada, but call the countries of the prime continent Nanagada and Aztlan. It was where captains argued how to integrate the new Teotl and their technologies. It was the return of a whole livable planet to the human race for the first time in as long as most could remember.

It was home.

But this was Astragalai Cayenne orbited right now.

Copies of Cayenne dwelled within navigational buoys and corrupted the lamina of Gahe habitats. In the confusion her selves provided, Ragamuffin and League ships transited in through the wormhole. Now men and women prepared to drop to the ground and engage Gahe hunt packs.

Pepper belted up for battle in the holds of the *Takara Bune*. Etsudo bounced from wall to wall in his cockpit. Mongoose-men from New Anegada and mongoose-men from Ragamuffin ships prepared to hit the ground.

Cayenne smiled and accepted an incoming message from the *Daystar*.

"Hello, Danielle."

Danielle smiled. "Cayenne. It's so odd to be calling you that. But then, one of your . . . selves that dwells in the Villach lamina calls itself Velvet. I think you ran out of Pepper-related names?"

"The joke got old." Cayenne watched the first wave of shuttles depart for the fringes of the upper atmosphere.

"I wanted to warn you that after this, the League thinks it is powerful enough it doesn't need your help to continue the revolution." Danielle wore a blue uniform with star-shaped medals, shoulder pads, and double rows of brass buttons. "You're to return to New Anegada. I warn you now because some of my colleagues agitate to find countermeasures to your trick, and others to destroy your ship and turn off Satrapic lamina everywhere."

They were out here to see what the League was doing and to help free humans where they could. The League's methods had veered into the extreme, whole purges of anything nonhuman in systems they held. And the Ragamuffin council wanted them to keep a close eye on developments in the forty-eight worlds as they fell into war. The *Takara Bune* would be skulking around a while longer.

But no need to tell Danielle that.

"Thanks for the heads-up."

Danielle laughed. No doubt she suspected what Cayenne and her friends would be up to. "Pitt's Cross, that landing will be personal for you."

"Of course."

"What will you tell them, when you land?" Danielle asked.

Cayenne had been thinking about that.

"We come to free you from your walls," she whispered to Danielle. "You can take arms with the League and turn your anger on the Gahe, or you can leave the planet and find yourself welcome among any number of free human communities. These decisions are yours to make. And the consequences will be yours to receive as well. This will be a real emancipation." And it would be the first time in centuries that so many would take that heady freedom for themselves.

Cayenne cleared the information around her away and cut the connection to the *Daystar*. She watched the pinpoint flares of hundreds of nuclear explosions blossoming all over the surface of Astragalai as she descended toward Pitt's Cross for the second time in her life.

ACKNOWLEDGMENTS

I have an inordinate number of thanks to people who cheerled and critiqued me through the whole process of that often stubborn beast known as the sophomore novel. So, big thanks to the following:

Nancy Proctor and Ben Rosenbaum at Blue Heaven 2004 for heavily critiquing an early start to this novel, as well as to the rest of the 2004 crew: Chris Barzak, Lisa Deguchi, Roger Eichorn, Charlie Coleman Finlay, Karin Lowachee, Paul Melko, Catherine M. Morrison, Amber Van Dyk, and Lori Ann White.

The 2006 Blue Heaven workshop: Charlie Finlay, Paul Melko, Tim Pratt, Greg van Eekhout, Bill Shunn, Catherine M. Morrison, Sarah Prineas, and Brenda Cooper for their insight, with special shout outs to Sandra McDonald and Mary Turzillo for the in-depth reads.

Lovely high altitude thanks to the folks at Rio Hondo for looking at a segment of the novel while in progress as well: Howard Waldrop, Carrie Vaughn, Nina Kiriki Hoffman, Kelly Link, Michael Bateman, Walter Jon Williams, Maureen McHugh, Daniel Abraham, Mary Turzillo, Gavin Grant, Jerry Oltion, and Geoffrey Landis.

Wow, I'm truly honored to have such amazing friends and acquaintances who put up with me.

More thanks to:

My agent, Joshua Bilmes, for all his work selling rights and talking me off the ledge during various stressful points throughout writing this book. To my editor, Paul Stevens, whose patience, friendship, and edits always guide me out of the desert. Irene Gallo and Tor's excellent art department for making such an awesome package for these books. My copyeditor of two books now, Steve Boldt, who rocks, and the rest of the Tor book production team.

Super big thanks to my wife, Emily, for putting up with many all-nighters, and who has learned that finding me out on the couch upside down with a pillow over my head means I'm working out a difficult issue with the novel and not trying to smother myself out of frustration (they can look similar).

And lastly, thank you. Thank you for continuing to support me and my writing by reading my books. Thank you everyone who visits the blog at TobiasBuckell.com, and thanks to all of you who write letters and e-mails. Without you none of this is possible.